RAIN

RAIN

ADAM C. KELLEY

Quailsong Press

Contents

To those who value a storm

With gratitude to family and friends who spent hours editing and suggesting changes, especially Alta, Johanna and my tribe of monkeys.

56 days hath September
April, June, and November
All the rest have 57,
except for February which hath
56 on evens
57 on odds
and 58 on oughts.

*One Martian year = 1.88 Earth Years

Scarlet streaks silent 'cross the sky
Windswept desert lets time go by
Watching with impassive face
Heart beating full and slow
It holds us a moment
and lets us go

One

Jake fixed his eye on the horizon and took a ragged breath. It was too early for walking. He should wait another hour for the frost to melt and soften the air, but the journey would be slow with the old man.

Jake went to him, helped him dress, fed him what he would eat, and placed his oxygen mask. He shook the frost off the tent, stowed it, and looked at him. The old man nodded and they walked toward the sun and away from their long shadows.

Dawn was short and too crisp over the northern badlands. Pink and orange light played over the undulating landscape of rock and deeply carved canyons stretching out from dusty dry flood plains in the north to the peaks of jagged little-worn mountains in the south. Too quickly it gave way to the stark light of post dawn, washing out the shadows that gave the bleak landscape its brilliance.

Talking was difficult in the morning hours, so they glided silently through the terrain until the old man nudged him, pointed at a lizard, and smiled.

Jake smiled back.

The old man pulled his mask down and said, "Do you remember how angry your mother was when they got into the garden?" Then he started to laugh, but after the first sharp intake of air thought better of it and chuckled instead.

Jake remembered. Once the sage and the first generation of insects had taken hold, his father had taken a leap and brought in the lizards. Jake had noticed he started them near the house so he could watch and see how they would do. That meant he wasn't as sure as he made out to be when the others just shook their heads at him and waved their hands as if to shoo away so many gnats whenever he spoke of it.

"The badlands won't be able to support something so large for at least another fifteen *years," they said. But it was his father's call, his stewardship, and if he wanted to blow a half year's budget on dead sagebrush lizards it was no concern of theirs.

Ahead, the sun was lighting the peak of the mountain, with the bottom still in darkness, so it appeared to hang in the air waiting for them to fly up to it. They were making better time than Jake had expected. The old man was old, but not as frail as he looked. Jake wondered if it was really time to make this trip, but that too was the old man's call to make.

By the time they reached the foot of the mountain the light had slid down to the ground and begun raising a fog. Looking up they could no longer see the top. As they climbed, the old man's strength returned. Half way up Jake stopped and put on his own mask; the air was still thin at altitude. At night on this mountain the stars still shone without any twinkling, not like in the canyon cities, where even when you got away from the lights, the stars winked and blurred. At least, that's how he remembered it. He hadn't been up that mountain in five *years, or even in the badlands for over two *years. How much had the air thickened in that time?

When they reached a plateau, they found a warm spot in the sun, leaned against a rock and rested. "I'm glad you're here," the old man said.

Jake gathered his thoughts and said, "I didn't mean to be gone so long... or really, I didn't think you would get old so fast."

The old man smirked and said, "Neither did I." After a pause he said, "Don't fret about it. You did the right thing."

Jake remembered the day they both knew it would be this way. He was fifteen half-*years old and full of books and ideas. The old man (had he been old then?) came into the kitchen out of a dust storm and said he could use some help in the morning, on the backside of the mountain.

"I don't have time to nurse a patch of dusty sagebrush," Jake had said.

The old man started to open his mouth, closed it then responded, "I guess they are dusty at that," and left the room. After that he talked about his work less.

"Come on," the old man said. "If we sit here too long, you may have to carry me the rest of the way." They stood up, adjusted their gear, and started the final ascent.

They reached the top just as the fog was clearing from the plain below. The sun was coming in at an angle that lit up the tiny reddish-greenish ponds the old man had built every few kilometers wherever he could find a promising place to dam. To Jake they looked like glitter scattered across the desert. By the middle of summer they all dried up, but the little plants and dune grasses around them still managed to find the water underground.

The old man followed his eye, and ventured, "I've been wanting to try cottonwood trees around some of the larger ones, but it's probably still too soon. I've got some seeds stashed in the barn by the rover. Would you take some of them before you go and sneak up here in a few *years and give it a try?"

Jake nodded, "I'll sprout them and get them to the sapling stage first. I'll do a few each year until I see them start to catch, then more."

"That's right," the old man said and patted his arm. "Those college kids the Department sends up here now are good at measuring things, but they don't have your touch. Don't let them catch you though. Let them wonder how they got there. They'll probably write a paper about it." He chuckled to himself about it for a while and then lay down with his head on Jake's lap and drifted off to sleep.

Jake stroked his thin faded hair and looked over the desert. In the spring and fall it was often pretty. The light filtered through enough atmosphere to take the hard edge off of it and the plants were either young or flowering, or covered in whatever seed or fruit they produced.

The winter was desolate, cold and harsh, and the summer was harsh in a different way, full of thorns, business, sharp shadows and bright light.

The unpleasantness of summer had made it easier to leave. The draw of knowledge to gain, other young people to meet, and a life to begin had been enough to make his decision certain, but seeing that gray landscape at its ugliest as the old man drove him into town had made it easier. Easier, at least until the shuttle lifted off and the old man had grown smaller than he had ever seen him, standing alone on the platform looking up at him.

Jake startled slightly when the old man sat up. That seemed to amuse him, but he didn't say anything. He just got up and started collecting stones and arranging them in a U shape against an outcropping. The spot afforded protection from the prevailing wind, but still allowed a good view while sitting inside it.

Jake did not join him. The old man continued piling up stones until he had built the walls a little over a meter high on each side and then he plopped back down next to Jake and rested. They sat there in silence until the old man caught his breath. Then he slapped Jake on the leg and they both got up and finished the structure. Jake found a large flat rock for the roof and wrestled it into place. When they were done it looked pretty strong. "Don't close in the front until the trees are grown. I'll want to see that and there's nothing big enough in this desert to disturb me yet. Probably won't be for thirty *years," he said. Jake nodded.

The old man gave him a long hug, and said, "I'm proud of the man you've become. Do good things. I'll see you when it's all over." He let go, crawled into the shelter, sat with his back against the cold stones, and took his mask off.

Jake took off his inner jacket, folded it and put it behind the old man's back to soften the stones, then lay down in front of the shelter and put his head on his lap. The old man stroked his hair and then began singing pieces of some old song Jake couldn't remember, but still knew somehow.

He closed his eyes and tried to listen to the words, but sleep blurred his mind and made it impossible for him to resolve their meaning, and it didn't matter. At some more ancient level Jake already knew they meant he was safe and could sleep deeply because the old man would keep him safe, and that it was the last time it would be that way for a long time. So he drank it in and slept.

Two

Jake's eyes opened in the eerie silence that comes with altitude. The hand on his head was cold. He closed his eyes and tried to go back an hour, but it was past. The silence was broken by a thin rumble of thunder rolling up from the valley below, distant but with undeniable power. The clouds stretched out below him to the horizon and beyond that, to the sea he imagined, and they were growing closer.

Jake arose and looked at his father. He wasn't there anymore; just a wax likeness, head bowed. He shivered as a cold breeze cut through his jacket.

He walked to the edge of the cliff and the path down, kicked a rock and watched it bounce, wishing he could stay on the mountain, out of the rain until the storm passed.

He wished he could stay still longer and watch the stars come out. But this mountain would be no place for a living human when those clouds finally hit and rolled up over it, drained of rain and sparkling with electricity. He tightened his gear and began to descend.

When he dropped below the level of the clouds his motions slowed. He stopped and scanned the plain below him, eyes pausing on the high sheltered points where he could hunker down and wait for the rain to pass. His eye landed on another spot, temporarily lit by light breaking through the ragged edge of a cloud. A brilliant spectral reflection flickered back at him. He pulled out binoculars and saw a lone rock crawler sitting in the middle of a wadi. Jake checked the orbital view they had pulled yesterday. No truck. This was new. Jake checked his watch. No lock, he was too close to the mountain, or maybe there wasn't a satellite overhead at the moment. He took the bearing and distance to the rock crawler and his own current position, then noted the crawler location. He took one last look through the binoculars. There was a hint of motion. He startled, paused, then broke into a run.

As he hit the foothills he lost site of the truck, but his watch clicked a lock notification. He set transmit to "local broadcast-eight kilometers," and called out, "Truck operator: get to high ground immediately." Rain began to splatter his face, but there was no response. He started running again, transmitting: "Get to high ground now," over and over as he ran. The rain intensified and Jake had to slow to avoid falling. His watch clicked "Loss of Sync," and he fell silent, but the words still pulsed through him. He came up over the last hill and saw a river where the wadi had been.

He checked his location against the map, and looked around futilely. "Downstream," he thought and raced along the ridge parallel to the wadi. At a high point he paused and scanned the wadi as far as he could see, imagining a dozen shapes in the swirling water, but nothing substantial appeared. He climbed on top of a boulder and continued searching, but saw nothing. He turned to climb down when something cold grabbed his ankle. He reflexively jerked it free and jumped clear of the boulder, then stood ready and watched. Nothing happened. He became aware of the rain again. He walked around the boulder until he could see the other side and saw a human form huddled against the rock.

He touched the shoulder. It was ice cold. The form turned and looked at him with silent uncomprehending interest. It was a woman, soaked through with cold rain and no longer shivering. The rain picked up strength. He looked for a flattish, sheltered spot, opened the tent, and took her arm. She followed, eyes unseeing, and went into the tent.

He set up the stove and it hissed to life, heating water. He turned to her, put his hand on her cold shoulder and said, "We've got to get these wet things off you." She struggled with her soaked sweater for a second and then held her arms up, and then she was five half-*years old sitting on her bed, and it was late at night after a long trip, and she could smell her father's shampoo on rain wet hair as he helped her with her pajamas, and she could hear her mother in the kitchen humming and making something warm, and the room was warm, and her bed was soft, and the storm was safely outside. When all her wet clothes were off, Jake covered her with his coat and a knit hat.

"Chocolate," he said and there was a glimmer of recognition in her eyes. He put her hands together, and pressed a metal cup into them. She sipped, and grimaced. He put his hands up to steady the cup and said, "It's not hot. You're cold. Drink it." She sipped it again, then a little more, and finally she drank it. He took the cup from her hands, refilled it and drank himself. She began to shiver, and then slump. He pushed her into a sleeping bag, and zipped it up. She continued shivering. He stripped down to his boxer shorts and climbed into the bag with her. He held her from behind with his hands around her waist. She was shockingly cold to the touch and the first thirty seconds were an act of will to maintain contact, but gradually her skin warmed and it became easier. After half an hour her shivering stopped and was replaced by a soft weeping, which subsided into the even regular breathing of normal sleep. As he listened to her breathing, his own eyes filled. The ability to categorize his emotions collapsed and he drifted on a mix of sensations into the dreamless sleep of the old.

Three

When he opened his eyes, he didn't know where he was. He had no name, no history. He was a part of no narrative. He simply was. This did not immediately concern him. He observed the room he was in. It was made of fabric, a tent, strewn with carelessly placed objects. The air in the tent smelled of warm fabric, mud, and body odor. The sun was high on the tent wall so it was late in the morning. There was a woman in his arms and her smooth belly under his hands felt both familiar and new, but he didn't know which was right. He considered the possibilities.

A wife? No.

A friend? No.

A sister? No, clearly not that.

And then the details of the previous day began to trickle back into his mind until he was back in the flow of the life he had been leading.

He became aware that he liked the feeling of this woman pressed against him, and began to be aware that feeling was a hazard to both of them. He eased himself out of the bag, being careful not to jostle her more than necessary, and dressed.

Her clothes were still too wet to be useful. Even if they had dried, the mud would have turned into the irritating ever-present dust of the frontier and made them more painful than useful as clothing. He dug around in the pack and pulled out his father's change of clothes. They would be a little big on her, but a closer fit than his change of clothes would be. He left them next to the sleeping bag, gathered everything else and dragged it into the sun light outside.

The desert was in one of its kinder moods. The sun was warm, but the air cool. The rain had wet down the dust and left the air impossibly clean and the sky an impossible blue. The sun was still low enough in the sky that it lent the land features by casting shadows. It was the kind of morning that breeds adventure.

He set the pack in order, set up the kitchen properly, inventoried their food, and spread wet clothing out to dry. While he did, he noted her gear. She had a basically useless sweater, a light shirt, some pants, socks, unmentionables, and an excellent pair of boots. Her watch was still working, but it didn't see her jewel, or her uplink. He felt around the waistband of her pants and found the small pocket in back were the transmitter was hidden. It was shattered, broken in pieces. "So much for that," he said. He carried the watch closer to the tent and it linked to her jewel, which was probably still attached to her earlobe.

He grabbed a printed map and went back to the top of the hill to take his bearings. If they pushed hard they could make it home by about 2:00 a.m., if it didn't rain, and if she had excellent night vision. His finger found Wilderness Hut #3 on the map. It would add about three hours of hiking to the total trip, but they could reach it by night fall, even with a late start, and there would be an emergency stash of food there (even if it was old jam and canned meat and everything else people didn't like well enough to carry all the way on other trips) so they could eat full rations and that might be valuable considering their depleted condition. He looked at the sky. He could call in an air evacuation. That might be the wisest thing, even though it was expensive and would bring attention he would rather avoid for a few days. He walked back to the tent and found her sitting against a rock watching him. She had on his father's clothes, plus the knit cap and her boots and watch.

He tried to remember how long he had been out of camp. Ten minutes?... at most, and wondered how long she had been awake.

He slowed his approach and stopped at twice the usual personal distance. "I was about to make breakfast, would you like some?"

She nodded, cleared her throat, said "Yes please," and softened her expression a little but she didn't take her eyes off of him.

He grabbed a container with a slice of cake in it and tossed it to her. "It'll take me a few minutes to get the rest of this stuff edible. You can start with that."

She caught the container.

"It's the last real food we have, the rest is all dry stuff," Jake said.

She fingered the container open and began eating, but she kept her eyes on him. He turned away and got down to cooking.

"It's chocolate - you like..." he started to say and then dropped it and turned away, his ears turning redder than normal.

She started laughing.

He turned to face her. "What?" he said.

"Nothing! Nothing, I just..." she said and then burst into a new round of laughter when she saw his face redden. She finally ended with a sudden, "I have to pee," and ran around the side of the hill. He shook his head, and went back to cooking.

When she got back the food was nearly ready. He had cooked basically everything they had left, rehydrated meat, mashed potatoes, powdered eggs, and some pudding. They might go hungry later but he decided it was important that they not be hungry now. He had squirreled away some sugared yams for their lunch.

They gave thanks, ate it, and leaned back against a rock. She was sitting closer than before but she kept an eye on him. "Have you decided I'm not a rapist?" he asked.

"Almost," she said smiling, but she kept watching him carefully.

"I'm Jacob Wyatt Billings the second," he said and extended a hand. "Call me Jake."

She took his hand, shook it. "I'm Elisa P. Waddell the first," she said, stopped awkwardly and smiled thinly.

He nodded, and turned to cleaning pots and stowing gear. When he had finished he said, "Waddell, is there anyone you'd like to call and let know you're all right?"

"Yes, but my uplink is broken. Could I …" He nodded and worked his uplink out of its pocket.

"The code is on a piece of tape on the back," he said, and handed it to her.

"Secure!" she said.

"I'll need that back," he said.

She smirked at him.

"I'm going to get some water from the wadi," he said and let the unintentional rhyme fade before adding, "I'll be gone at least thirty minutes." He turned again, then turned back and said, "Oh yeah, here are my sunglasses and my wallet. I wouldn't want to accidentally drop them in the water, so will you take care of them for me?" he said nodding his head. She nodded back with mock seriousness, tinged with something real, and he went down the hill.

When he came back 45 minutes later she was lounging on a rock with her eyes closed, her face to the sun, his sunglasses on her head and his wallet next to her lying open.

He paused. It was the first time he had seen her at ease and he didn't want to break that moment. He was about to turn away when she looked at him. For a moment her face was still calm and confident, but then it clouded over in doubt.

"Were you able to get a hold of anyone?" he asked.

"Yes, my parents. It turns out they know your father, and he must talk about you a lot, because they aren't too worried," she said, but there was almost disappointment in her voice.

"Did you look me up?"

"Of course," she said sounding almost offended, but then her face darkened again.

"But…" he prompted.

"But I can't decide who you are, and I don't know whether I should be grateful to you or hiding from you and calling for an evacuation."

Jake looked down. When he looked back he said,

"I can see where you're coming from and if you need to call for evacuation you won't need to hide. You can stay right here with all the gear and I'll sit on that rise over there where you can see me and I can keep an eye on you until help comes. I only ask that you leave my uplink and essential gear when you go because I want to get home safe too, and I won't be taking the Evac." He stopped talking and stood looking at her.

"But..." she prompted.

"But you really are mostly safe... and I am curious about how you ended up here... and for some reason I want you to like me."

They looked at each other for about five seconds, and she finally said,

"OK. I guess if I'm wrong about you at least they'll know who to question and where to look for the body, but I need some answers."

"OK," he said, and sat down next to her.

"I know all about hypothermia rescue, and I remember just enough to realize that you probably did the right thing, but... did you look?"

He looked at her for a couple of seconds, finally understood what she meant, and then started laughing. She smiled and then punched him in the shoulder. He put his hands up and said, "It wasn't like that. You were muddy and cold to the touch, and I was afraid you might die on me. I couldn't avoid seeing a fair amount, but that's not where my thoughts were. It was all pretty clinical."

She relaxed a little and said, "So, it didn't even cross your mind?"

"No. I mean not immediately... I intended to get in my own bag once I was sure you were warm enough because I didn't want either of us to be embarrassed, but I fell asleep."

She didn't say anything for a while, and then when he was about to turn away she said, "I'm grateful. Thank you."

"I'm glad I saw your crawler. If the situation had been reversed you would have done the same."

She thought about it and nodded.

"I don't remember much. I just remember being cold a long time and then suddenly I wasn't cold at all and that vaguely worried me, but I couldn't see what to do about it, and then you were offering me hot chocolate." She was quiet for a few seconds and then added, "The sun feels really good, would you mind if I took a little nap before we get going?"

"Go ahead," he said. She leaned against the warm rock and was asleep in seconds. He replayed the conversation in his mind and then she turned and her head was on his shoulder, and it felt right to him, and although he was tired he stayed awake, feeling her there, and looking out at the range around them, and feeling the breeze swirl around them whispering the secrets of small creatures, and feeling like they were the only people left and that the whole world belonged to them.

When his shoulder got stiff and it was clear she would sleep a while, he laid her down, rolled up a shirt for a pillow and put it under her head. She stirred a little and he lay down beside her and she held his arm.

About noon he decided it was getting late and quietly got up, struck camp, and got everything ready. Then he scouted a little, mostly to think. When he came back she was lounging on a rock eating one of the sugared yams he thought he had hidden, with his sunglasses pushed up on her head.

"Feeling better?" he accused.

"Yes," she said looking straight at him. "Although I'm not sure I should. You're not quite the safe hick I was starting to hope you were."

"You're only saying that because you haven't known as many hicks as I have..."

"I tried calling your father, but he didn't answer. I wouldn't have taken his word for you anyway... unless he said something bad... but apparently the last girl you went out with thinks you're a good guy too. According to her last post she thinks you might be gay."

"I'm not gay!"

"I know!" she said and hopped down from the rock.

"Is there anything else?"

"Yes, you have no criminal record, so apparently I'll be your first victim."

"Or maybe just my first conviction."

"You graduated 3rd in your class, but in of all things Xenobotany. Why Xenobotany? It's not like it's the top paying job anymore."

"I grew up with botany and I like it. I'm not so fond of desert life, but that's different. Why, what did you major in?"

"Xenobotany."

"You're E.P. Waddell? I thought you were an old fat white guy."

"Well now you know better."

"Yes - I do!" he said, and she couldn't find a response for a second.

"Did you happen to look up the weather while you were on there?" he asked.

She sat down on the rock, pulled down the sunglasses, paused and said, "Sunny with day time highs of sixteen degrees Celsius, lows of o and a chance of frost through... tomorrow night," she pushed back the sunglasses and smiled at him in triumph swinging her legs against the rock.

"Give me back my uplink and glasses!"

"Why? Are you going to look me up?"

"No, because you already broke yours and we may need them," he said.

She handed him the uplink, but kept the sunglasses.

"Besides, the fact you looked me up is enough for now, Miss Waddell."

"Call me Ellie."

Four

When they finally left camp, they walked down into the wadi and followed it more or less north hoping to catch sight of the rock crawler before they had to turn east towards the wilderness hut.

The water had entirely disappeared beneath the sand except for the occasional pool, which usually got a minor looking over by one or both of them.

The day's conversation had given over to a silence that was neither awkward nor unwelcome. As they walked they maintained a constant proximity to each other, even though they seemed to be watching the trail or observing various things along the way.

After about a mile they found the twisted remains of the rock crawler pinned under a bank in a turn of the wadi. It still sported its cheerful yellow paint, but the carbon shell had burst at several points and flattened out. The steel frame was twisted so that the rear wheels were at nearly a ninety degree angle from the front wheels, and the doors and hatches were completely missing.

"I hope you bought the insurance," Jake said.

They poked around the shell, but didn't find any of her belongings. In the trunk they did find the emergency kit smashed up against the frame. Ellie opened it and water flooded out of it along with empty wrappers from high energy biscuits, a soggy first aid kit, a Mylar blanket too small to cover any particular body part, and a sealed packet with a cheap uplink, watch and headset inside.

Jake nudged the wrappers. "I guess someone I know got hungry when he was cleaning out the trunk."

Ellie picked up one of the wrappers and looked at the expiration date. "Looks like he did me a favor by eating them," she said.

She picked up the sealed package and ripped it open. The uplink wouldn't light. "Cell's dead," she said and flipped it over photovoltaic side up and slid it into her uplink pocket.

"Better get some pictures," Jake said.

Ellie lowered his glasses over her eyes and walked around the vehicle. Then she checked her watch and nodded.

They continued downstream for another quarter mile. Along the way they found part of her pack, but the contents were all gone. They turned out of the wadi and onto the broad plain and as soon as they were clear, Jake's watch clicked sync. Hal's name flashed across it.

"You're going to want to hear this!" Jake said, but put his finger to his lips. She nodded and they both answered the call.

"Hey Jake buddy, when did you get back?"

"About a week ago. How've you been?"

"All right, I've got a couple of new ventures going that I think are going to work out. How's it with you?"

"Fine, I'm just trying to figure out what to do with myself now that I'm done with school."

"You could always be your old man's assistant," Hal offered and then laughed at his own joke.

When Jake didn't join him, he moved on. "Hey listen Jake, I hate to bother you while you're out communing with nature and pondering and all, but I lost contact with one of my rock crawlers yesterday a couple of kilometers southwest of you. Since you're so close, would you mind running up there and checking on it for me?"

"I don't know Hal. If that old rock crawler of yours quit on some short tempered geologist and he's looking for a fight, I think you should explain things to him."

"It's not a big old geologist this time. It's just a little 45 kilo canyon girl. She'll probably fall all over you for rescuing her. I'd go up there myself, but I figure you'd know how to handle canyon girls better than I would."

"Hold on Hal. You left a 45 Kilo canyon girl stuck out on the frontier with no transportation since yesterday in the middle of a storm?"

"It's not like that. I always make sure they've got emergency supplies, and you know I don't go out there in storms. We can't all be desert rats like you. It's probably just the transponder went out or she'd have called or something. You just look around for me. I'll bring you some of those tomatoes your father likes the next time I come by."

"You're a real prince Hal. Send me the last known location and time of contact, and I'll see what I can do, but I'm not hauling out any bodies. You got that?"

"Got it. Thanks Jake. I'm sending it now."

"Hal, did you plot these coordinates on a map?"

"No."

"Do it."

"Ah man... it's right in the wash isn't it. Maybe the transponder just shook loose. It could be OK," he said, but didn't sound too reassured.

"I'll call you back."

They disconnected.

"Well, there's your harmless hick for you."

"Wow!"

"Actually he is mostly harmless, but sometimes..."

"Why didn't you tell him you found me?"

"It gives him time to think about it."

"Nice."

They walked on. About 3:30 they stopped at one of the ponds. It had a thick mat of algae and its dusty bare shores were uninviting. It was rarely warm enough to want to swim anyway. Below the main pond there was a series of smaller ponds where the water was clearer, the soil having settled out in the upper ponds. Ellie pulled her hat off, and set to scrubbing her hair. Jake stuck his whole head into the pond then shook it out. While Ellie combed her hair he sent the rock crawler pictures to Hal. He figured the time stamps would give him a clue. But when Hal called he wanted him to go back and get some pictures without the time stamps because these would get him in trouble with the insurance company. Jake told him to get his own unstamped pictures, and then Hal finally asked kind of sheepishly, "Any sign of the girl?"

Jake hesitated and said, "Yeah, she's right here with me. She's fine," then disconnected.

As they got going, Jake pulled out his candied yam and was about to bite into it when he noticed Ellie watching. He looked at her. She pretended to be looking beyond him. He handed her the yam. She broke off a piece and handed the rest back. He did the same and handed it back to her. It went on like that for the better part of two kilometers, until the pieces became so ridiculously small that it became a game to see who would have to eat the last piece. Jake finally won by smearing the last bit of yam powder straight onto her clenched lips.

After that they walked in silence enjoying the exaggerated northern afternoon light. Then Jake asked, "How did you end up down in that wadi?"

"I was scouting along the edge trying to find the best way across, when suddenly the right side started dragging. I tried to correct by pulling back on the left side and pushing forward on the right but it lurched which threw me backward, and that made it buck. It kept getting worse until I wound up in the wadi. Then it wouldn't move at all. When I got out and looked, there was hydraulic fluid everywhere. I tried to call Hal and got nothing. When I reached back I could feel the uplink was broken. After that I figured I'd better just stick with the crawler since it's big, yellow, probably has a transponder, and would keep me out of the rain and wind. Looking back, I should have just let go of the controls, but I was close to the edge and it made me nervous."

"When did you realize you had to get out of the wadi?"

She looked at him for a minute trying to decide something, then said, "Something told me I had to get out. I fought the idea, but when I saw the rain coming I understood. My gear was all in the trunk and it was jammed shut. By the time I made up my mind, there was no time to fool with it, so I climbed out of the wadi and waited. After five minutes, I couldn't see the crawler anymore."

They reached the hut after sunset. Jake checked the cells: 80% power. He checked the methane tanks: 98% full. He checked the water supply: 100%. He'd check the rest in the morning. The boiler lit on the first try so he went back to the hut and announced there would be hot showers. Ellie had been busy concocting a surprisingly edible hot meal from the odds and ends available, so they gave thanks and attacked it.

When they'd finished the dishes, he said, "I'm not sure you ever actually got warm today. Why don't you take the first round? The water should be hot by now." Her face lit up at the thought. He threw her his shampoo and soap. "Sorry, no conditioner."

"I don't care!" she said smiling and went out to the shower.

Jake lit the gas heater at the back of the hut. Then he got out a change of clothes for both of them and started washing them in the sink. He had to triple wash them to get the last of the sand and salts out of them. Then he ran them through an old wringer someone had cobbled together from rolling pins and clamps and hung them up in front of the heater. They would dry fast in this climate and they might even be glad for the little bit of moisture they would add to the hut's air.

When he got done she was still in the shower. He poked his head out of the door and heard her singing to herself. She was OK. The hut was small and close. He decided to take a walk. As he walked he remembered the afternoon and smiled. But then his mind switched to a mountain behind him and his smile faded.

Ellie watched the steam rising up out of the open stall and felt the warm water cut through the stinging dust she was encased in. The stars above were brilliant and a little fierce, but beautiful. As she cleaned her arms and legs she could feel the soreness in them. She was young and already recovering, but she was aware she wouldn't always be. The warmth from the shower clung to her as she sprinted for the hut, trying to keep the filthy clothes from touching her clean body as much as possible. When she got to the hut he was gone. The hut was warm and had the lingering smell of their meal, and there were clean clothes hanging in the back. She quickly changed into them and brushed out her hair. "It's good to be human again," she thought.

After his walk, Jake showered and changed and went back to the hut. They stayed up eating jam with a spoon from a shared jar for desert and trading stories about school, and awful part time jobs, and various roommates, and problems with professors and boards.

"You know, I've read your thesis," Jake said.

"Including my review board, parents, and myself, that brings it up to seven people."

"It's not bad. My father sent it to me. He asked if I thought some of the exotic mosses you described might help solve our little organic matter problem with the soil."

"Just guessing by the way that soil burns, your alkali problem might complicate using the moss, but we might be able to find a way around that," she said, lighting up a little.

"We probably could," he said musing. "I was actually thinking that if we started it on the uphill slopes above the ponds, it might get going."

"We could take a look at some sites on the way home tomorrow and we could pick out some varieties to try. I'll send you the spores as long as you promise to let me come visit my babies."

"Deal," he said a little too quickly.

After a moment he ventured, "So what did your parents really say when you told them you were wandering the desert with a potential rapist?"

"Well, first I told them I'd crashed but was OK and they were a little concerned. Then when I told them some strange guy was giving me shelter but I didn't know if it was safe or not, they got more concerned. So they asked what your name was and when I told them they both started laughing, but then my dad suddenly got serious and asked if I was sure that was your name. When I told him I had your wallet, they started laughing again and told me it wasn't the first time I'd been camping with you and to be good, like I was on a date. Apparently, they came here on a survey trip with your parents when we were toddlers and brought us along. They've been corresponding ever since."

Jake covered his eyes and asked. "How did you decide to come here?"

"I just needed a break," she said.

"Yeah, but how did you pick this location," he said.

Ellie thought for a moment, then her expression changed and she tersely spat out, "My parents suggested it," and closed her mouth, then added "My parents would absolutely do something like this if they thought of it, but what about your Dad?"

Jake raised his hands and shoulders and said "Probably not..." and let them drop.

"We should watch his reaction when we get back to your place," she said conspiratorially.

Jake's expression changed. He started shaping a word then stopped, grew distant, and got lost in other thoughts.

"I'm tired," he said, and forced a smile when she asked if he was OK. They knelt together, then crawled into their respective bunks and everything grew quiet.

When Ellie woke up in the middle of the night, she knew he was gone.

Five

She had known he was gone even before she noticed the silence or the subtle difference in temperature of a hut with only one person in it.

She calmly considered the route she could take in the morning to get to civilization. If the maps were to be believed it was less than a day's journey and easier terrain than they had already been on, but these thoughts were mere mental gymnastics. She knew he was not far off and that when she woke up in the morning he would be in the bunk below her as if he had been there all along. Her mind wandered onto the awkward ending to the evening, then to the pile of clothes folded neatly at the foot of her bed that were too large for her, but too small for him, and then to the duplicate sets sleeping bags, and eating utensils, and then she understood.

She heard something in the wind outside, distant, and wondered if he was OK; if she should give him privacy; or if she should go find him? As she wondered, she could see him in her mind sitting alone in the rocky field above the hut, huddled in his coat against the night wind and she could feel his solitude. She dressed quietly, even though there was no one to hear her, and stepped into the night. He did not hear her coming and looked surprised when she sat down next to him. She took his hand and leaned into him and the wind lost some of its punch. They sat that way for an unmeasured time, then he slowly got to his feet and stared at the mountains behind them trying to see something in the dark shadow that loomed against the fierce stars. Then after a while he looked at the ground. Ellie stood and put a stone at the spot on the ground he was staring at, then another. Jake looked at her, and she put down another one forming a circle of stones. She laid more stones on top of those and then Jake, as if without deciding to, picked up a stone and added to it. They continued moving every loose stone they could find into the pile for a long time, and when the wind finally blew in the clouds and wet snow that chased them inside, the pile stood nearly two meters wide and tall. Inside Jake hugged her, because he could not say thank you and as dawn began to light up the snow, they both sank into a quiet sleep, and Jake dreamed.

In the dream he was on the mountain and his father was standing beside him and as they looked across the plain below, his father pushed him from behind and he flew, soaring over wadis and ridges and ponds and vast fields of sagebrush and young junipers. As he soared higher and higher, he saw the junipers grow tall breaking the wind and a grey-green wave of life begin to creep over the land from the ponds outward, and behind the grey-green a wave of gold-green grass spreading out in all directions, and when he had flown almost to the top of the sky and stars began to appear in broad daylight he found he was looking down not on a sage desert, but a savannah. And as he looked he began to fall and he was giddy with the speed of it, until he remembered he was falling and pulled up to coast over the land speeding below him and he began to see animals grazing in the grass and looking up passively at the strange bird flying over them, and then spruces and alders shot up out of the ground seventy meters tall blocking his path and causing him to swerve left and upward arcing around the sprouting boreal forest and back towards the mountain where he could see the old man pointing at something glinting in the plain below. As he turned to follow his gaze, he saw a woman standing in the middle of a vast meadow and as he came closer gliding past a large white moon known only in nursery tales, a small child stepped out from behind the woman and stood watching him approach, and as he got closer another child stepped out from behind the first, and then another and another until the line of children stretched beyond the horizon, and when he finally touched the earth standing directly in front of the woman he looked into her face and recognized her. "Ellie!" he said.

He was surprised to hear her voice come back to him from a different direction and a greater distance than it should be. As he puzzled over it, the image dissolved and a gray light replaced it, seeping across the room. It was raining outside. Ellie was standing by the hot plate with a spatula in her hand trying to turn canned meat and powdered eggs into a breakfast. She looked at him, but then decided he was sleeping and turned back to her cooking.

He watched her cooking for a while then closed his eyes listening to the clatter of kitchen utensils and absorbing the moment. When he opened his eyes again food was on the table and Ellie was setting the places. He moved and she looked up, smiled at him, then realizing his predicament went to the window and looked out into the rain while he dressed.

At breakfast there was little conversation. Jake alternated between staring at her and looking out the window over her shoulder. Ellie at times busied herself with her food and at other moments met his gaze and held it. When they were finished eating, he reached across the table and held her hand. It was relatively small and white, with ragged short fingernails and dirt under them, and surprisingly smooth given the work they must be used to. He looked at her eyes and found she was already looking at him with her head to one side, and a calm, moderately puzzled look on her face. "Thank you," he said, but it sounded out of proportion to the situation. He let go of her hand and looked away, but she did not let go and when he looked back she said, "Anytime."

After they cleaned up the meal, Jake began patrolling the small hut looking for something to hang his energy on. There wasn't much. He rechecked the heating system, inventoried the supplies and made notes about what he ought to bring the next time he came this way. He eyed the ancient ceiling for any sign of leaking.

When he appeared to be running out of things to do, Ellie picked up a paper book displayed prominently on the table beneath a shelf of canned goods, and asked, "What is this?"

Jake responded, "It's the hut log."

Ellie started thumbing through it. The earliest entries were fifteen *years old now. "Is this the original log for the hut?" she asked.

"No. That's the fourth log. The first one is at the Smithsonian. There's a copy of it in the library. We've been trying to get the original back for *years, but we just get the run around. The second and third are in the archives at Paititi... with copies in the library."

"Who would send the original to Earth?" "

No one sent it. The astronauts took it back with them."

Ellie looked at the hut again, and she could see there had been an inner door originally, and that the window was far newer than the rest of the structure.

"So this wasn't originally a wilderness hut, was it?"

"No. Welcome to Arabia Terra base 3. We don't let much go to waste around here."

Ellie was thoughtful. For a moment she felt a pang that it hadn't been preserved in its original form, and yet it had never been a museum piece. Its current use was not far different from its original one. Maybe it was even more fitting this way.

She resumed thumbing through the pages. Each entry started with the date, the names of those present, and the weather. On some entries that was all. But many also had writing after that.

Some were oddly personal.

"Ate peaches and beans for dinner – Yum!"

"I miss my wife."

"I stole $20 from my brother's wallet and he still doesn't know."

"OK. Who took the label off of the can of soy cheese."

"I am going into the wilderness and I do not intend to return."

"I should'a brung toilet paper!"

Some were philosophical.

"You cannot understand the sea, until you go to the desert."

"The rain has washed away my crimes."

One contained detailed drawings of lichens, sage flowers, and tiny bees.

There were dozens of entries by Jake's father. Mostly the shorter kinds of entries, but also one which said, "Since Nora passed the boy spends every waking hour roaming these hills, and the walls don't talk, so I am alone."

Near the front of the book was an entry that read, "May 16, 0065 - Nora, Jacob I & Jacob II Billings with Chris, Lillie, & Elisa Waddell. Clear skies all day, cool, windy in the evening with lots of dust. Just returning from our first annual survey of the lower elevations. We have big plans!"

She ran her fingers over the entry lightly, trying to pull more from it, but then closed the book.

"Don't close it," Jake said. "We still have to make our entry."

Ellie looked a little horrified at the thought.

Jake rolled his eyes. "You go first, I'll add on at the end and I won't even read what you write."

It stopped raining and Jake took the opportunity to escape outside and check the big equipment.

Ellie reopened the book to the first blank page, and wrote:

- *"March 43, 0076 – Elisa P. Waddell and Jacob W. Billings II - Sunny & cool on the 42nd, followed by wind and snow in the early hours of the 43rd, and heavy rain during the day.*
- *Ellie – I came to the badlands of Arabia Terra soul searching and looking for my future. Instead of finding it, I crashed my rock crawler in a wadi and found a wild man raving in the wilderness."*

As she finished, she smirked at how his face would look when he pretended he hadn't read it. But then it seemed to ring hollow to her, or rather, not hollow, but wrong. She paused, lifted her pen over "Instead of," but stopped herself and closed the book.

Outside Jake was puzzling over why the methane tanks weren't re-filling. All the valves were in the correct position. It was cloudy out, and they were using a little electricity in the hut, but there should still be enough power to run the system. Jake walked over to the methane unit, wiped the caked on dust off the "Insitu-Propellant Manufacturing Unit" label with his hand, and inspected it.

It looked dead; no compressors running, no heat coming off of it, nothing. He checked the panels and the nearly worthless cells. The cells were at full charge for what it was worth, so they were clearly getting power. The breaker on the cell side was closed, and the switches were in the correct positions. He went and got a big wrench out of the storage closet and marched back to the Insitu. The wrench wouldn't help, but getting it gave him time to think, and it felt good resting on his shoulder.

He set the wrench down and opened up one of the panels. Despite its age this was easy because it had been designed to be maintained by people wearing thick gloves. He looked around and found that the Insitu had its own internal breaker. He rocked it back into the on position and it promptly flicked off again. Finally he opened up the bottom panel and water came flooding out. He looked at the lips of the panel and there was a groove with an ill-fitting dried out gasket sadly wedged into it. On the inside of the panel "3 mm" was written in pencil and then crossed out and rewritten "2 mm." Jake shook his head slightly. He left the panel open to let things dry out and went back to the hut.

As he approached, Ellie was coming out fumbling with her sweater. He had now seen her weary, exhausted, and even unconscious, but this was the first time he'd seen her plain tired. He gave her his jacket. She smiled and put it on. It was a bit late in the day to start for home so that left them with awkward unscheduled time. Jake took her to one of the test plots. It had square metal frames laid in it to make accurate plant density counting possible, and they both automatically took to counting in different frames. It didn't look much different than the last time Jake had been there before he left for school except that the frames were getting rusty. There seemed to be a lot of rust these days. He remembered being surprised as a boy when he found rust here or there, but it seemed more common now. Ellie stood up, dusted off and came to where he was standing. They entered the new numbers into the data base and ran a quick graph.

"It's flat," Jake said.

"It's worse than flat. It's declining slightly," Ellie said.

Jake took another look at the numbers. "It is a little lower each year, but it's not statistically significant."

"No, it's not, but look at the plants. There are no young plants here. It doesn't look like a new plant has taken root in *years," said Ellie.

Jake flipped through the results for other plots. There hadn't been many surveys done in the last few *years, but what there was mostly followed the same trend.

They checked some grids a few kilometers on the other side of the hut and found the same thing. They checked the leaves and roots to see if there were disease or some uncatalogued pest, but it all looked clean. They gathered samples to bring back. When they were done, the sun was setting and they leaned back and watched the stars come out. It was cold so they sat close to each other with their backs against a still warm rock. "Have you ever seen the meteorites come in?" Jake asked.

"No. I've always meant to, though."

"Well, watch over there and any minute now you should see a batch or two."

They watched in silence, huddled together, until various arms and legs and butts went numb. Ellie was just starting to accuse Jake of being a liar when he pointed and the northern sky lit up in streaks of blue, green and white light sparkling and sizzling till they disappeared over the horizon. The show lasted for ten minutes before it trailed off. When it was over they noticed that dew had started to form and they were getting wet. They got up and moved toward the hut.

On the way, Ellie told him about once when asteroid slices hadn't separated completely and they had to evacuate the canyon. "My parents drug me all the way up to the temple grounds and we sat waiting for the tsunami to come. After half an hour this little one meter wave came in and knocked over some of the garbage cans on the beach," she said.

"A tragedy," said Jake.

"It was! In all the excitement I lost my favorite pair of sandals."

When they got back to the hut they ate a cold dinner of whatever caught their attention on the shelf and then knelt together. Somewhere in the middle of prayers, they both fell asleep. Jake woke up about an hour later drooling on his hand. He wiped it off on his numb legs and looked at Ellie sprawled awkwardly over his bunk. He rolled her up into it, pulled off her shoes, and tucked her in. Then he climbed up into her empty bunk, settled in, and fell asleep to the smell of her hair on the pillow.

Six

Jake was up first. He wrote a long entry in the log underneath Ellie's entry. It spoke of his father's death, and of finding Ellie, and said, "I came back to this place to say goodbye, to close a chapter of my life, and turn my back on it forever. But as the miles unwind this place calls me home, and chapters I had not anticipated open." After looking at the entry for a moment, he looked at Ellie. She was watching him. He put the pen down and closed the book.

Ellie had been watching for some reaction that would show he had read her entry, but saw none.

By 7:00 o'clock they were dressed, packed, and sitting next to each other on the same side of the table so they could both look out the window. They were sipping hot chocolate and watching as the sun began blasting away at the morning frost on the ground outside. They chatted lightly about books and music and always eventually about plants of one kind or another. As they talked they mostly kept looking out the window with only occasional glances at each other. The quick fog rising up from where the frost had been was hypnotic as it twisted in shafts of sunlight. She did not seem to be aware that moving close to talk had lined her leg up close alongside his leg. He was acutely aware of it and the warmth seeping through layers of fabric, but he didn't move.

When they judged that the air was warm enough, they strapped on their gear, shut down the hut and went outside. Jake double checked the Insitu hatch, which he had taped shut, then he made sure the tanks were full. He vented a little methane just to hear it kick in and start making more.

He faced the way they would be walking, patted his own pockets and thought for a second. Then he said, "Just a second," and went back into the hut. Through the window Ellie saw him pick up the pen and add a quick line at the end of his entry. Then they walked.

During the first half hour they were accompanied by wisps of brilliant fog and it seemed somehow irreverent to talk. Once when the fog swirls were particularly beautiful he reached for her hand, and she didn't pull away. It was good to see this together. The fog eventually disappeared altogether and with it the need for silence.

They began discussing ideas for how to accelerate plant growth, which led to a discussion about land management plans, which led to a discussion of politics, which led to a discussion of philosophy, which led to a semi serious discussion of the nature of mankind, which led to some tongue in cheek accusations about the nature of man, which led to good natured banter. And then it was time for lunch.

They found a good spot on a rise and bathed their faces on a fresh breeze and let the warmth of the spring sun tenuously work on their backs, as they ate. Ellie was lost in thoughts of some other place or time. He let her be. When she came back to him, she looked at him funny as if trying to decide whether or not to say something. Finally she said, "Can you explain something to me?" Jake shrugged slightly. "When I was in that rock crawler in the wadi, I knew I had to get out because a voice told me to get out. Not my voice, or some imaginary voice in my head, but a real sitting-in-the-cab-next-to-me voice, your voice. Is that supposed to mean something?"

Jake finished chewing his food, thinking, and looking out across the landscape. Then finally he looked at her and said, "I was telling you to get out of that wadi. And I think it means that God has better technology than we do," he paused and looked away again, trying to decide something, but said nothing more. When he looked back, Ellie was looking back at him expectantly. "That's all I know for sure," he said. She waited. "My next thought was 'and I know God works through family whenever he can', but we're not family so it's not relevant," and he looked away like he had said too much.

Ellie took his hand and looked him in the eyes, "I don't know in exactly what way, but I think that we are family." The moment held, and some fact became established between them without concern for its implications, and then it was gone. Lunch was done. It was time to go. They both stood, and as they began to walk again he draped his arm over her shoulder and said, "I know one thing. You're not my sister." She looked up at him, flicked his arm off her shoulder, and said, "No, I'm not." Then she picked up speed, but he matched her pace.

After a couple of hours more walking they came to a larger pond than Ellie had seen before in the area. The land was getting flatter, so it was possible to flood a larger area with a small dam. This pond was also different because its shores were not as barren as some of the others. In fact its shores were not at all natural looking. To begin with, there were counting frames scattered in various sections around the shore, and there were different varieties of grasses growing with different success in each section. Ellie's eyes lit on a section with some moss growing in it, and started moving in that direction with Jake in tow. When they reached it, she dropped down on the ground at eye level with the moss and examined it. There were three different varieties but one had died out completely and the third was struggling. Ellie stuck a finger into the soil and tasted it. Then gesturing to the first two patches she said, "These two don't mind the alkali so much but they can't handle the cold at night. This one doesn't like the alkali, but it can take the cold." She got up and dusted off, humming to herself.

"It doesn't look that healthy to me." Jake said.

"It's not happy and it won't grow very fast."

"OK," Jake said confused.

"These are standard varieties. I've got better adapted varieties than those growing on my gym shoes... assuming they haven't cleaned out my locker. The fact that their growing at all means we are in business. See!? Your father was growing moss, not trying to set us up," she said and raised an eyebrow at him.

They poked around some of the other sections. Jake noticed a few carp in the pond, but it was getting late, so they moved on toward the nearby ridge. When they passed over it Ellie could see a small house about two kilometers away with gardens on two sides and what could pass for a municipal yard in the back. There was a barn that was three times the size of the house, several green houses, and the largest Juniper trees she had ever seen. As they got closer she could see that the house was an old, low slung adobe. When they arrived, she saw the house was larger than it looked from a distance. Inside Jake turned on the lights, and turned up the heat. He lit the fireplace and gestured for Ellie to sit close to it, while the house warmed. The living room was tastefully decorated ...for eight *years ago, but it was more welcoming than she had expected when she first saw the house. The house was very quiet. Jake didn't seem to notice the quiet. He was in the kitchen putting together a quick dinner. He set some hot chocolate to warm while he inventoried and then got dinner cooking. He brought her some chocolate when it was warm enough and returned to the kitchen.

After dinner they sat by the fire and talked for a while. Jake told some stories from when he was a child and Ellie told a few of her own, but the warmth and the food were taking a toll, so after the second time one or the other had nodded off, Jake rose, made sure the guest room was made up properly for Ellie, and got her settled. Once Ellie had shut the door he stood in the hall momentarily perplexed. He hazily wondered if he was supposed to go to his father's room or to his childhood room. He finally chose the latter and crashed on the bed.

When morning came and each had showered and the breakfast dishes were done, they sat across the breakfast table from each other silently looking at each other. Each afraid to say something that would fracture the moment.

Finally Jake asked, "When do you need to get back?"

"My ticket was for today, and I left a lot undone back home. I guess it should be today," she said.

"I have some things to do as well," he said. "Would you mind if I came to see you when I'm in town?"

She looked at him, shook her head slightly and then wrote her parents address on a piece of paper and slid it over to him. "I'll be staying with my folks for a while, until I get my assignment, even after that they'll always know where I am."

When they got to town Ellie went to settle up with Hal. He was about to start into his usual "Surcharge and Cleaning Fee" routine, but then he saw Jake looking at Ellie; he lost focus and forgot the whole thing. They had some time to kill so they went window shopping, which didn't take long. Jake looked at some boots. They had soup at a little place by the air terminal and then waited outside. Ellie looked at the town around her as if trying to decide something, but came to no conclusion. She looked up at Jake and smiled at him. When the transport landed and it was time to go she put her hand on Jake's cheek, looked at him until they both smiled, and then got on board.

Jake watched the transport lift off slowly, turn, and then accelerate until it disappeared over the horizon. Then he became aware of his surroundings again, and Hal peaking at him from his doorway. Jake waved at him and he turned back to his business.

On the drive home Jake relaxed. He hadn't been fully aware that he had been tense until he felt himself relax. There was a certain peace, or at least simplicity, to being alone again. He put the pedal down, and disappeared into a cloud of dust, shouting.

Thinking of that moment
later...
She'd think that a moment later
She'd drifted from a pastel dream
to let reality bleed back

Seven

Ellie watched Jake grow smaller and smaller below her and then leaned back in her seat and exhaled as the transport picked up speed. She looked at the cabin around her, all clean and orderly. Her clothes and hair were clean and the dirt was scrubbed from under her fingernails. The air was warm, and the engines droned contentedly at quarter power.

The desert itself receded from the windows. She closed her eyes and felt the slightly worn arm rests under her hands; heard the low murmur of voices and the rattle of plastic vibrating with each small shudder of the transport. She felt the pieces of her soul knitting back together and was surprised there had been a split.

An attendant brought her a snack and something to drink and as she thanked her she realized they were about the same age. The attendant wore a ring on her finger and Ellie wondered where she lived, what her husband was like, and whether or not she liked her job. She moved on. Ellie's mind shifted to the possibilities awaiting her. She sat up straight and began hurriedly making notes of things she needed to do when she got back. She noticed how quickly her hands moved across the paper and how easy it was to make decisions and smiled at the nimbleness of being whole again. The desert had done its job, made her grateful for her life, made a vivid contrast to real life. It had created a memory that was real but unattached. There was simply no hook to connect it to her life.

She put the pen away satisfied, leaned back in her chair, closed her eyes, and smelled damp sagebrush.

She opened her eyes.

She could see Mount Olympus rising through the cloud cover in the distance, solid and moody, then the transport changed direction and she saw the valley where she had spent most of her life growing larger in the window. She couldn't make out anything through the clouds, but she knew the bay, the city, and the farmland beyond without seeing them, and above them all on a bench below the rim of the canyon would be the temple complex with its libraries and hospitals crowded back against the canyon wall to let the temple stand out in front of them alone.

The engines throttled up and soon they were sitting at the air terminal. A light drizzle wet the hand rails as the crowd descended from the transport and ran for the cover of a walk way. She had no baggage, and no one was expecting her. The afternoon was hers to do with as she pleased.

On the street, store lights lit up the raindrops on their windows. She stopped at a little clothing shop she knew and bought a new jacket that shimmered like a rainbow trout when it adjusted to the weather outside. She walked past her old apartment and the campus where she had spent the last three *years of her life.

The buildings seemed smaller and more tired than they had a few weeks ago. She didn't stop. What few things she had left to clean out she could get later.

On the far side of campus she stopped at a cocoa shop, ordered food, found a book on the rack, and settled into a booth by the window looking out. There were no deadlines, no expectations. She sat as long as she wanted and then left. Outside she stood looking at the campus for a few minutes, then turned and signaled a taxi.

When she got to her family's house, no one was home. It was quiet and orderly. She wandered from room to room trying to catch glimpses of memories. She finally settled in her old room and listened to the grandfather clock ticking loudly down the hall. She began to drift into sleep and slid under the covers of her bed. As quiet seeped into her mind she thought she heard her father's voice in the front room, felt her mother peering in at her, but as she fell further it changed and it was Jake's voice and he had come in and was lying next to her, and she didn't mind at all.

Eight

When Jake met with the district recorder, the old man didn't seem surprised by the story he told him. He mechanically took down the details, took a cursory look at the medical records and the note his father had written before they left, took images of them, and filed his report.

"We'll scan the body from a respectful distance... just to make sure, but that should be it. I'll send you a notice when your certificate is ready," he said and ambled out of the house.

The well-wishers were harder. Word leaked out within hours of the recorder's visit, and by the time the official notice appeared pretty much everyone in town already knew. Jake took the first few calls, but let the rest go to mail. Casseroles appeared with old women he remembered being much younger. He received them with as much courtesy as he could muster, but the events of the previous week had already done what could be done.

"A strong boy," he heard one of the older gentlemen say to his wife when he was leaving, but he was sure there were at least a few who thought "cold" was more accurate.

The official memorial service was Saturday. The bishop welcomed everyone. Jake's old Youth advisor recounted the cycle of pre-mortal, mortal, and post-mortal life, and the role of the atonement and resurrection, and though Jake noticed some of the older folks sneaking a glance at him during the talk, it didn't matter. The words felt new again. That was followed by a hymn Jake could not remember, but which the older people sang with their eyes closed. Someone Jake recognized but didn't know very well got up and tried to describe his father's life. He recounted the facts, figures, and public record awards he had received. He told some stories about how hard it was to catch him at home. Then he spent several minutes talking about how wonderful Jake's mom had been and then just sort of ran out of things to say and sat down. Jake didn't blame him. His father had not been particularly active at church since his mother died. He made it to church most Sundays, but even when he was there his mind was often ranging over some distant hill.

Jake stayed until the chairs had all been put away and then stood talking with the others who had stayed. His old Advisor was asking him what his plans were and Jake didn't mind telling him. He was one of those who remembered Jake actually had been active at church before he went off to school. Maybe it was because he hadn't had much to say in those days, or because his father had been distant for so long, or because he left for school the first chance he got, or because he'd gone to school in rough necked Olympia instead of Paititi; but he knew by the tentative approaches, the fellowshipping efforts, and the little glances that half the ward remembered him as inactive. It didn't really matter, but as he looked around the circle of those that stayed to put away the chairs, he was pleased to notice almost all were people who remembered him correctly.

As Jake left the building he saw Hal in a corner of the parking lot, looking at him. He got up and started moving toward him with something in his hands.

"Sorry about your dad," Hal said and handed him a box. Jake started fumbling with the box and Hal stopped him and said, "They're tomato plants. Your dad was always after me to give him some, because he said they taste better, but don't open them here. They're unaltered... original stock. You'd best get them into the green house as quick as you can."

Jake gave him a one armed hug and Hal waved him off embarrassed.

On the way home, Jake began to relax a little. "At least that's over," he said to no one. Even as the words came out, he knew it wasn't quite true. The official memorial was over, but there would be another one.

He didn't know when they'd come. That was the trouble. They'd come though, and all about the same time. He didn't really know how they all knew when to come. Maybe they called each other, but that was hard to picture. More likely it was like a flock of birds all turning at once because they all knew the terrain so well that they knew when the leader was turning before he turned. However they did it, he knew he'd better check the supplies.

Nine

When Ellie emerged from her room it was after 9:00. Her mother called
out, "The dead have arisen," her father looked at her and said, "You
don't look much worse for wear." Her mother brought a plate covered
in fruits Ellie hadn't seen for weeks before retreating to the kitchen to
get started on something hot.

"Since when does mom cook?" Ellie asked.

"She started picking it up again a little after you left for school."

"Hmm, figures," she said, picking through the fruit.

"The girls were disappointed they didn't get to see you before school.
I think they were expecting an adventure story from you," he said.

"Well I guess it was sort of an adventure, but I don't know how good
a story it makes," she was interrupted by her mother rushing back into
the room with a steaming plate of fried eggs and potatoes saying, "Hold
on, I want to hear this too."

She began telling the story, but when she opened her mouth what
came out was not the narrative she'd half planned but a painting of pale
pink desert mornings, and golden afternoons when sunlight bounces off
canyon walls, and of swirling mists after rain storms and the intimate
sound of water falling into pools in the dark parts of narrow gullies.
As she told it she saw her parents glance at each other and as if they
knew a joke she couldn't possibly understand. When she stopped mid-
sentence and stared at them, they laughed and urged her on. Then she
got to the events, leaving out the more embarrassing parts. A couple of
times she saw her parents look at each other. Only when she told them

Jacob was dead did she see concern on their faces. Even that was more wistfulness than worry. Her father glanced at his calendar.

She finished saying, "Even with the drama, it was a good trip. It cleared my head and I'm ready to get on with life."

When no one said anything she added, "It will always be one of my favorite memories."

Her Father nodded seriously until Ellie threw up her hands.

Her mother changed the subject, "When do you expect to hear from the Department?"

"They should have sent something already," Ellie said.

"They may have tried. I got a failed delivery notice yesterday, while I was out," her father said. "They're going to try again this morning."

"Why don't they just tell me my assignment!" she said in frustration. "I don't know why we have to wait for an ancient letter to arrive. It's slow, and stupidly expensive. What do they think I'm going to do, frame it and hang it in my office?" she said.

"Some people do," her father said and she blushed remembering her father's first assignment letter was on the wall not eight meters from where they were sitting. Her father laughed and breakfast was over.

A few hours later, when the letter was actually in her hands she sat down in the front room with it and gestured with her head for her parents to sit down across from her. The front room was not normally where they gathered. It was for guests, but somehow it seemed right. "Shouldn't we wait for the girls?" her mother asked.

"We can open it again later. Why don't you go ahead and see what it says," her father said.

Her hands shook a little as she opened it. She was assigned to the upper farmlands at the southern end of the Canyon. The effort was partially self-funded out of farming proceeds so there was no need to go begging for budget and there were good roads and frequent trains so it would be possible to visit home on weekends. The assignment had a future in it too; everything she learned would be directly applicable to the commercial side, and everyone knew budgets would only get tighter on the public side. This was everything she had hoped for.

She looked at her parents. "Did you have anything to do with this?" she asked.

They shook their heads, "We've always said we'd stay out of it and we did."

She showed them the letter.

They looked at it and said, "This is a good assignment."

She smiled, but it faded. She smiled again.

"I can't believe this," she said. They hugged her and let her slip away.

In her room, she stared at the letter. She would have to respond soon. She would accept, of course. To do anything else was unthinkable. She brought up a keyboard, typed out a brief message accepting the appointment, and let her finger linger over the send button. She closed her eyes to push the button and saw the desert stretching out before her. She pulled her hand away from the button, closed her eyes again, and listened. She opened her eyes and stared at the words she had written. This was what she should do. She should accept the assignment. She pressed send and felt a loss, but it was a clean loss. The future she had imagined and sought was beginning to happen, but it was no longer clear. She could no longer envision it the way she had, and surprisingly, that was OK. She would go. Some doors would open and some would close and that was OK too. She dismissed the keyboard. Closed her room and went out to tell her parents.

Ten

The whole family saw Ellie off at the train station, her oldest little sister pouting, more because she wasn't allowed to accompany her than because Ellie was going.

The train pulled out from the station smooth as glass. In town, it didn't go much faster than a car, but it picked up speed out of town. Ellie was amazed to see the acres and acres of orchards flying by her window so fast she could not focus on any single tree, or even row. The orchards continued with only short breaks for two hours; apples, pears, nectarines, cherries, persimmons, almonds, apricots, plums, and peaches. She had, of course, known they were there. Known roughly the production numbers, acreage under cultivation, the varieties, and even the subtle manipulations that made them thrive in poor soil, thin atmosphere, and cold nights. Seeing it was another matter. Soon the orchards began to be interspersed with fields of newly sprouted sun-flowers and grain crops, and she knew that a few hours beyond her stop these would take over completely.

At her stop she gathered her luggage and sat on a bench waiting for her ride. A woman from the university extension was supposed to pick her up but after half an hour of waiting what finally appeared was a truck newer and cleaner than anything the extension should have. It idled up slowly, the driver looking for someone on the platform, and then finally stopped in front of her. The passenger window opened and a man's voice called out, "Are you Ms. Waddell?" Ellie nodded and the man hopped out of the truck and approached her. He was a young man, a few half-*years older than Ellie wearing blue denims, a checked flannel shirt rolled up on his forearms, and immaculate boots that appeared to be real leather. His forearms showed he had done some work, but when he shook her hand his hand was firm but smooth.

"Sorry about the delay. Cava was supposed to pick you up, but she got stuck out at an upland ranch. I'm Titu. I'll take you up to your station."

"It's alright, it's a beautiful day," she said.

He grabbed her bags and put them into the back of the truck and Ellie climbed in. The town they drove through was busy. They drove past banks, equipment stores, grocery stores, grain elevators, and a couple of new packing plants. Kids were everywhere, most waiting outside shops, some dangling their legs over the edges of loading docks, and some surprisingly young ones were loading up trucks and driving them too.

"School's out already?" Ellie asked.

"Yes," said Titu and after looking around added, "But don't worry, they'll settle down once the serious work gets started."

"It's not that," she said. "It's just that the lower schools don't let out for another week in Paititi." He nodded. Ellie looked at the kids and imagined growing up here. If her parents had stayed on her great grand-parent's homestead (or really station, it was before homesteading), she might have.

The station was about as she expected it, large and old. It was probably one of the oldest buildings in town. But there was a newish truck parked in the yard and she dared to hope. Titu put her things on the porch and said, "Go on in. It's open. If you need anything, give me a call." He waited until she was inside and then drove off.

Inside, the station was musty, with small personal quarters, large work areas, and plenty of guest rooms.

She unpacked her things, which didn't take long, and then went into the yard among the young trees and felt their bark and looked up at the sunlight coming through the leaves. She could almost feel them breathing, producing not just fruit, but oxygen, and drawing moisture out of the ground into the air. She could feel them all around her and it seemed like they were happy in their simple way; happy to taste sunlight, happy to sip water, happy to breathe air, happy to feel warm dirt between their roots, and happy to hum in time with Ellie. In the middle of the yard there was a red rock too large for the early settlers to clear easily, a mini mesa. She climbed it and looked over her trees and fields. Closing her eyes, she leaned against a breeze and felt the sun on her face and then had the unnerving thought that she might be visible from the surrounding homesteads.

She opened her eyes, and found herself alone with her trees- or really the people's trees. A station was a stewardship; like a homestead, but with a different flavor. There were monthly reports to superiors instead of just annual stewardship interviews. The work you did was always to improve the productivity of other people's stewardships, or to improve new lands that would eventually be other people's stewardships, or to maintain wilderness. She closed her eyes again and let those thoughts slip away and listened to the trees whisper softly.

After lunch, Cava stopped by and apologized for not picking her up. She was a good five *years older than Ellie, and short, but not heavy, with dark hair, a cowboy hat pushed back, and the hint of joke always in her eyes and around her mouth.

"So, what did you think of Titu?" she asked.

Ellie shrugged her shoulders, "I doubt we exchanged three complete sentences." Cava nodded and moved onto safer ground.

"So, what do you need to know?"

"Well, first off, where is the previous station steward?"

"Oh, he jumped ship and signed up with Empaqueme about a month ago. Guess they had some work to be done they didn't want winding up in the public domain. He left his address on the bulletin board, but he'll never return your calls."

"OK. I assume there's been some work piling up for the last month, so I guess I'd better check the assigned work queue and start clicking down the high priority items."

Cava just chuckled at her. "Listen, before you do that you better check with Titu's papa. He's the unofficial leader of the growers around here and they always have some high priority items that don't quite make it to the work queues, and believe me, the ones that don't have requisition numbers are the ones that matter."

"Why?"

"You'll figure it out. Now, let's go into town and I'll show you where not to go shopping."

They climbed into Cava's beat up truck and drove under the tracks to the far side of town. On the way they passed a dingy looking super-market- "Definitely not!" pronounced Cava, "especially not the produce. They pick it here in the canyon a little green so it will ship well, ship it all the way down to the distribution warehouse in Olympia, and then ship it back up here, where no one will buy it." They passed an even dingier small hardware store, "That's Stan's. It's been here forever. Any odd hardware you think you need to order on-net, check at Stan's, they've got it. George runs the place, he's a nice guy."

"I thought it was Stan's," Ellie interrupted.

"It is. Stan has been dead for ten *years, but it'll always be Stan's." They passed several newer larger stores and Cava pointed out which ones had free delivery of heavy items and which had the best prices, and then they pulled into a parking spot a few blocks from where the street was blocked off for the market.

The streets hummed with the sound of good natured haggling, and less good natured gossip. To Cava's amusement Ellie stopped at every stall for the first block looking at the spring vegetables and newly thawed frozen fruits from last fall, asking each grower where his farm was and how old their trees or fields were and which revision of each kind of fruit tree they were growing. After the first block, Ellie noticed Cava smirking at her.

"What?" she said.

"Nothing. You're getting it. You want to know what's really going on; don't read the reports, go shopping."

They slowed down a little after that. Ellie bought some food, some fresh curtains to replace the horrible stained ones that had been there since before there was air and a hammock so she could nap out among her trees on fall afternoons. Then Cava took her home.

Eleven

Chris glanced up from his desktop when someone came through the door. It was Ed, his boss. He came in and casually sat on the corner of his desk, the documents in that corner skittering and scattering to avoid being obscured. Chris winced slightly as he thought about rounding them up, but Ed kept beaming his beatific smile at him.

"So Chris, I hear your daughter got a plumb assignment," he said.

"Yes, she's very pleased with it."

"Good, good, that's the way things ought to be. She'll be a breath of fresh air up there. You should have seen some of the applications we turned down for that post."

"I deliberately didn't see them."

"I know Chris, I know. No one's questioning your integrity here. I'm just saying that it'll be good to have one of our people up there, someone we can count on."

Chris decided not to bite. "Thank you," he said, and waited.

"You're welcome," Ed said smiling conspiratorially. Then he tapped Chris's desk with his stylus several times until the right document appeared. It was a list of names. "I'd like you to go through the reports for these people going back five *years and find all the errors and mistakes in them. Give me a report detailing what you find."

"Are you looking for something specific?"

"No, I just want to know if the reports are accurate."

"We really have no way of knowing if they are accurate or not without going into the field and doing audits. I can compare the reports with satellite images, but half the time they are using satellite images while they are generating the reports, so that rarely yields anything," said Chris.

"I've talked to the Audit Department already, but you know they aren't especially cooperative. Just go through the reports and find everything that's out of place or sloppy. Find all the math and spelling errors, even logical errors if you notice any. It shouldn't be too hard with this particular bunch of clod hoppers."

For a second Chris considered his options.

"Why isn't your nephew Alex doing this?" he asked.

The smile on Ed's face flickered out for a fraction of a second, and then came back full force. "Because, I need a senior person on this. It's very important."

Chris nodded, but said nothing.

Ed said, "Thanks buddy, I'll need it by Friday," slapped him on the shoulder, and left.

Chris clicked a small icon near his left hand, and looked over the list of names. He knew most of them personally. They were the old timers. He would find plenty of errors in their reports, because they didn't take the reports seriously.

In a way, they were right. Those reports were rolled up into summary reports that predicted oxygen levels, surface albedo, atmospheric H2O, soil conversion and retention, and such for the next six months, but all those things were directly measurable, and automatically calculated based on continuous satellite monitoring, so the estimates were useless and nobody really read them. There hadn't even been any monthly reports until about ten *years ago when somebody suggested it would be a way to prod the stewards to review their own work more often. He leaned back, looked at the ceiling for a while, then smiled and got to work.

When he sent the report that Friday it read:

> • "Per your request I have reviewed the reports of the fifteen individuals listed at the end of this document going back five *years for accuracy. I

found 327 spelling errors, 43 mathematical errors, and ten logical errors; however, all were minor and would not have changed the conclusions of each report. Also, available data indicates that predictions based on the reports compared with actual measured results were within the normally expected statistical deviation. Therefore I conclude that the reports issued were accurate."

About three minutes after he sent the report he heard Ed's chair bump into his office wall a little harder than normal. Thirty seconds later he was standing in his doorway with a forced smile on his face.

"I got your report. I was hoping for a bit more... detail. Maybe you could break it up into sections for each individual steward."

"I'm sorry. I'll get right on that."

Ed left. Chris pressed the little icon, cleared his desk and began assembling a massive sixty page document filled with satellite imagery, statistical analysis, snippets from past audits, maps, quotes from reference works, and ending with the same conclusion as before.

After he sent that one he heard Ed's chair hit the wall, then silence. Finally Ed just sent an email thanking him and walked down to his nephew's office.

Chris backed up his archives off site, tidied up his desktop, and went home the long way, enjoying the ride.

Twelve

On the second day Ellie woke up to the sound of vehicles bumping around on the roads around the station. She wrinkled her brow a little. When had the sound of trucks come to seem out of place to her? She had always lived in the city. At school she had lived on some fairly busy streets and had never really noticed the noise. But here on the edge of her orchard it seemed out of place.

Then her mind fully engaged. She got busy. There was no set schedule to follow, and it was exciting to choose what order to do things in and which tasks to do today or tomorrow. She had to be able to show that she had fulfilled her role, but it was up to her to determine how she would do it. That made the day an adventure to be planned.

She got up, prepared, and checked her mail. There were some auto generated greetings from the Department and that was about it.

She checked the requests queue, and found requests for information about which varieties would be best suited to this situation or that, which she answered briefly and then passed on to Cava. There was an old request for a variety of barley that could better tolerate the more alkaline soils of the extreme uplands. She had to smile at that one. If they had spoken to Cava about it she would have told them to plant wheat or dune grass that was already adapted for those soils, but the barley had been paying a lot more the last few *years. She admired the pluck of what must be a young farmer trying to get ahead a little faster. She sent off a note to see if they were still interested and moved on.

There was a request for a "blight resistant" potato, which puzzled her because all the varieties already had a basic blight resistance, and there simply was no blight on this world. To make sure there never was any, they had never imported live plants, only seeds and spores, which were grown and manipulated in sealed environments. She looked at the address of the sender. It was in a very old format, so this was probably an old farmer living on some clay soil that was having a rot problem. She forwarded it off to Cava suggesting he might need some help with soil preparation.

There was also a request for a rot resistant peach, which made no sense given the crystal dry air throughout the whole canyon. The usual problem for *years had been to build in a tolerance for the dry air, smaller pores for the leaves, a waxy bark, and a thicker skin on the fruit. The fruit would shrivel into fruit leather before it would rot. She forwarded it to Cava suggesting they might need some help with their irrigation.

She also noticed that there were no notes at all on any of the requests, and except for the information requests, there hadn't been any new ones in over six months.

She sat and thought about what she had heard from the farmers at the market. There had been a near consensus that yields were down year over year, and of the fruit being smaller, tougher. She checked the yield figures for the area and they were down. She expanded the graph to include the last five *years for the area, and for the last three *years they had been trending down mostly, but it was slight. This year was the only significant decline, but even that was small. Maybe there had been a slowdown in planting or a shift in market preferences, or maybe just over planting of orchards in previous *years had caused prices to drop and farmers not to spend as much on fertilizer, or not bother to harvest everything. Except when she checked commodity prices for the crops grown in the area, they were mostly up slightly.

She was still puzzling over it when Cava called.

"So, I see how it is," said Cava.

"What?"

"You're going to clear out your queue every day by tossing all your requests over the wall to me are you?"

"Yeah, both of them," Ellie said.

"I wouldn't think there was much more than that in there," said Cava.

"Gee thanks."

"Don't mention it."

"Seriously, there must just be some irrigation or drainage problems and what I know about that comes straight out of a book."

"You're probably right. I'll check it out."

"Thanks."

She was just trying to remember where she left off when a new message came in from the upland farmer. Yes, he was still interested. Yes he was available to discuss it, "Why not today?"

"Why not?" she responded.

It was a chance to try out her new enough truck. She grabbed a soil kit and jumped into it.

As the orchards thinned out into sunflower and then wheat and other grain crops she saw the canyon walls again, and felt more oriented. It was good to drive. She tensed up a bit when the road skirted a cliff, then made herself relax. It was a new farm on the edge of the new soil. The soil was barely out of dune grass and could barely support anything. The farm house and barns were the small prefabricated kind that everyone started out with, and they weren't in the best spot for them either. There was a little knoll that looked over the whole property not far away that would be better. As she got closer she could see it already had a road cut into it and that there actually was a foundation there, probably put in on some of the slower days during the winter.

She stepped out of the truck. The wind whipped her. She shivered and looked for the coat she hadn't brought. The little hollow where the house was had the advantage of being out of the direct wind, so maybe it wasn't such a bad spot after all. The farmer's wife and two young children were in the vegetable garden picking sugar peas together. Ellie watched them for a minute before approaching. The wife was young, she thought before it occurred to her that they were about the same age. The kids were perhaps three and five half-*years old and they weren't particularly good at picking peas, but it made a pretty picture, the three of them in the green plants with the plains stretching out beyond them. They looked up when they heard her coming and came out to greet her.

"Go get your dad," the mom said to her older boy who immediately ran off in the direction of the barn. Then straitening and extending a hand she said, "You must be from the Department."

Ellie took her hand, and said, "I'm Ellie. Pleased to meet you."

"Julie," the mom said, "and the pleasure is mine."

The younger girl was hiding behind her mother's legs and holding on.

"And who's this?" Ellie said squatting down to eye level.

"Tanya," said Julie, "Say hi, Tanya."

Tanya pulled her face back behind mom's legs.

When her husband appeared, he was not especially handsome, but he walked with a confidence that tended to make people forget about that. He greeted her warmly and they all went inside.

When they were seated, Ellie said, "So, you want to try barley?"

"It's Julie's idea really. I've tried to tell her it's too soon for it here, but we've tried a few test plots and although the yield is actually negative, some of it does survive."

Julie started making her case. "If we could get it to produce, it would be just as good at building soil as the wheat, but with a better return. Plus it can't be healthy having all this acreage in just a few different clones of wheat. We're just asking to get wiped out one of these *years." Ellie hadn't thought of the monoculture angle. She had a point. It was something they had debated in school, and there were policies in place to try to use the station stewards to create more varieties, but in the end yield and healthy plants tended to trump diversity.

"Well, I can't promise I can get it done quickly, or that it will work at all, but I'm willing to give it a shot."

Julie shouted and gave her husband an affectionate shove. "See!" she said.

"I only said I'd try..." Ellie said, but no one was listening.

"Were you able to do any traditional selective breeding with your test plots?"

"Yes, but we're only on the second generation, so there's not much to show for it yet."

"It's a start."

They all went out to the test plots and looked at the sorry little plants. Ellie tested the soil. It was better than she thought, but still, "I'm surprised these are still alive."

"They're tough like us," Julie said.

Ellie dug up five or six of the best plants and put them in a box to take back to the station. Then Julie took the kids, who were fussing, back to the house and John took Ellie around the farm testing soil in different places and discussing average moisture and the availability of irrigation until Ellie had a feel for what characteristics the barley would need to be successful. They went back to the house, Ellie said her good-byes, and as she drove away she looked back at them. John had his arm over Julie's shoulders and they were turning to go inside the house. The kids were clamoring for their attention like so many baby birds, and then they closed the door.

On the way back her mind was already going through the gene library trying to remember what traits were available and compatible with barley. She could see possibilities, though she knew as well as any-one that living systems could always surprise you. You could always do things to them, but you could never be completely certain what they would do in response. She cradled the container of young barley plants close against her leg whenever they went around a corner and managed to get them home intact.

She hadn't been home ten minutes when she heard a knock at the door. It was Titu. His hair was perfect. His clothing was impeccable (probably tailored), and his boots immaculate with a soft warm shine that was hard to imagine in a rural area.

She paused a little too long and he laughed softly.

"Didn't recognize me, did you. I'm sorry. I was just on my way home from an appointment."

She smiled, resisted the urge to wipe the dirt off her nose and invited him into her office, but he shook his head and said,

"It's getting a little late," then added with a grin, "and this is a small town."

"OK," she said, "what can I do for you?"

"I'm just here as my father's errand boy. He'd like to invite you to dinner at our house next Friday to welcome you to the community and introduce you to some of the neighbors."

"That would be great," she said, "What time?"

"Seven."

"I'll be there. Thank you."

"Good night," he said and turned to get back in his truck.

She closed the door and realized that her shirt had pulled out and was hanging loose on one side through the whole conversation.

Thirteen

The next morning when Ellie got up, she knew exactly what she was doing all day and there was a sort of exhilaration to having a single focus. She went straight to the lab and upon studying the equipment more closely, was surprised to find it was top notch. In fact, it was better than the equipment she'd had at school. It was only two *years old at most. This equipment wasn't cheap. A few of the more intricate components still had to be imported. She fired up the synthesizer, built a test sequence and blinked when it completed in half the time she had expected and without any of the customary rattling that usually signaled the beginning and end of a run. She pulled up the specifications and found it could produce sequences more than twice as long as she was used to, which put it over the size of most useful sequences and meant no more laboriously pasting them together. She didn't have to put the sequence under the scanning scope to know it would be perfect. How had her predecessor managed to get this? "I take back everything bad I thought about him," she announced. At first she just kind of stared at the gear, afraid to touch it much, but as she began to think about what she could do with it her hands got busy.

First she carefully pulled apart one of the more hardy barley plants until she found the fast growing tissue and placed some of it in the scanner. The scanner was also top notch and had the full sequence in under an hour. While it ran she pulled up the full sequence for upland barley version M2208, currently the most popular, the original Martian barley, two hardy unaltered Ukrainian and American barleys, and a wild barley, and set the display to color code the differences between them. Next she pulled up the standard trait library, filtered it for barley compatibility, and then searched for alkaline tolerance traits, drought resistance traits, and salt tolerance traits. Finally in a separate display she brought up the organism emulator, stuck the energy budget meter up in the left hand corner of the display where she liked it, and the unfavorable interaction warning up high on the display where the other fields wouldn't cover it. When the new barley plant came up she added it to the comparison.

Then she used a favorite short cut of hers and simply imported everything that all versions had in common into the emulator and dismissed it from the other displays. The emulator status widget showed a grey frowny face with x-s for eyes and its tongue hanging out. "Yup, that would be one sick plant," she said to herself.

Next she started comparing the areas of difference. As she compared them she couldn't help but admire the wild barley. It was a marvel of efficiency, not so much in its coding, but in its energy management and survival strategies. It had a beautiful complexity with a singleness of purpose to it. The wild barley wouldn't give you much to eat, but it could survive and even reproduce in a wide variety of situations. Its progeny would be more diverse as well, making sure at least some of them could survive whatever unpredicted changes came in the next season. It was a richer pallet of traits, with few of them completely pointless. There were even hints of mechanisms that might allow the barley to select the expression of genes in some of its progeny based on current conditions, though these were poorly understood. By comparison, most of the tricks of nature, early farmers, and modern botanists consisted of selectively breaking things, like mutilating the feedback loop that prevented the plant from storing too much energy in seeds. Others were just as startling, like finding a complete sequence from arctic fish used for frost resistance plopped unceremoniously between two completely unrelated metabolic functions. She made a face like she had tasted something nasty when she saw it, but then stopped herself. These changes had been about survival, not art, and they had been made slowly, with crude tools, largely by people who didn't really have the time to be doing it all, but did it anyway, and it had worked. These changes had fed more people than anything she was ever likely to produce.

She selected all the obvious traits, moved them over to the emulator, and dismissed them from the other displays. Then she started mixing and matching traits for the remaining differences using hunches and educated guesses, saving different versions as she went along. When she got done, she had five rough designs that appeared healthy in the emulator, didn't exceed the plants expected energy budget, and didn't have conflicting traits breaking each other's machinery. She also had two other intriguing designs that flat killed the poor emulator plant, but were so interesting she couldn't bring herself to delete them. She checked the emulator for expected expressed traits of the plants, and as she expected none of them stood out as clearly better adapted to the conditions on John and Julie's farm than M2208, but Ellie thought these versions were overall healthier.

Ellie remembered one of her lab instructors taking her to task in her undergraduate days for spending extra time "reinventing the wheel" on each plant. The instructor was irritated that others had to wait to use the equipment. It had actually become a pet peeve of his that semester and had continued to be a point of criticism until one of the older professors nearing retirement heard his comments and said, "Let that girl be. She's having fun, and she's learning more on her own than you ever taught her." After he shuffled off the lab assistant had muttered about the ossified old fart minding his own business, but he stopped bothering her about it.

Next she started replacing sequences, and adding sequences from the library to each of the five versions until she had thirty different versions. When she discarded the versions that couldn't live it brought them down to fifteen, and when she discarded the versions with conflicting traits, she had ten. She looked at the expected characteristics and there were three that met all the criteria. She stepped back a little from the displays and tried to get a high level view of each. There were two that seemed to have the balance and art of something that could actually live in the real world, but even the third didn't seem fatally flawed. She had plenty of room left in the plants' energy budgets on all three versions, so she decided to sign them, by putting in a small trait from the wild barley. She chose one of the older sequences that used very little energy and shared no significant machinery with other traits. She looked at the notes about the sequence and saw there hadn't been much work done on it, but it was thought to be a leftover from an old method of repelling insects, an orphan sequence with no real function. "Perfect," she said out loud and put it into each version. They each still had healthy budgets, no bad interactions, good expressed traits and adaptation, and a nice green smiley face with yellow petals around it in the status icon. She saved everything, and shut down the systems. The room grew quiet... and dark. She looked at her watch in surprise and found it was after 10:00 p.m. She also realized she was famishingly hungry.

By the time she was finished in the kitchen, there was no produce and several other things had run out. Fortunately, she knew all the right places to restock.

Fourteen

When morning came, Ellie hurried through her mail, intent on getting her new barley code into living tissues. But as she gulped down her last remaining food, there was a knock at the door. When she answered it a girl of about fourteen half-*years was standing awkwardly waiting on the porch, absently spinning a small leaf between her left thumb and forefinger.

"Can I help you?"

The girl glanced up, "My Mom sent me to bring you these eggs." She lifted a basket she held in her right hand, "and to ask if you could come by some time and take a look at her orange tree that's not doing well."

"Thank you, I was all out of eggs, and yes I'd love to see your mother's orange tree."

The girl looked up at her, said, "Thanks, I'll tell her," and spun on her heels to make her escape. The motion was so fast that she was gone before Ellie could call her back to find out where she lived, but it didn't matter because she could see her disappearing through the trees of the house on the other side of the street.

Ellie went inside, stowed her eggs, and paused. She finally concluded it would be better to go over and check on the orange tree before getting started on the barley. That way she could work without interruption.

She went out into the morning light and crossed the street. The trees were starting to put on little fruit buds, but it would be a while before the first real fruit of the season. Still, the trees were in full leaf, the power of summer just under the bark. The girl's house was nearly as old as the station and the living room she was shown into had the aged smell of a hundred past meals. The woman who came to greet her had a worn dress and smelled of peppermint, soap, and cooking oil smoke. Ellie worried a little that she had come too early, but the dishes in the dryer by the sink were dry and the feeling of morning had already abandoned the room. The woman wiped her hands and shook Ellie's.

"Matilda," she said. "Thanks for coming so quickly," and motioned for Ellie to follow.

Ellie caught a glimpse of motion out of the corner of her eye and saw that the egg girl was following as well. They went through the back door into the barn yard to a small greenhouse on the far end of the yard. The barn and outbuildings were newer than the house but still quite old and in need of repair. The yard was orderly, with everything in its place, and yet some things clearly hadn't moved in a long time. The vegetable garden had a hand constructed stone wall around it that was more than was really necessary, but the trellises within were broken and faded.

The greenhouse was like the rest. It had been a beautiful structure when it was first installed, with real glass and wrought iron. The glass was still kept clean, but some of the panels had been replaced with thin plastic sheets and others had cracks in them that had been taped over from the inside.

"This is a lovely greenhouse," Ellie said. Matilda looked up at her with a half-smile and said, "It was a wedding present from my husband." Inside the green house was a single large orange tree that still had some fruit on it. The leaves were looking a bit yellow. The woman patted it affectionately and said, "I know it's a bit extravagant but I told Henry, my husband, when he asked me to marry him that I would only follow him up into this canyon if he bought me an orange tree. And he did. So, do you think you can save it?"

"Let's take a look." She examined the leaves and bark and saw nothing unusual but the color. The ground around it had been tilled up recently and was the right level of moist. She noticed the girl watching her from the door of the greenhouse.

"It looks like it's just missing some nutrients."

"Well I gave it its nitrogen, and its acid just like I always do."

Ellie felt the soil again and pulled out a portable analyzer to check it.

"Iron," Ellie said. "It needs iron," and she wrote out a concentration to apply.

"Who would've thought there'd ever be a need to add iron to the red planet?" Matilda said and laughed at her own joke. Ellie smiled along.

As they walked back toward the house, Matilda started chatting about town gossip, the crop prices they were expecting, and how expensive everything had become. Ellie didn't know what to say about any of it, so she just nodded along, and that seemed to satisfy Matilda.

When they were almost back to the house, Ellie spotted an older man coming out of the barn.

"Is that Henry?" she asked.

Matilda looked up and hesitated before saying "Yes," and then waving him over. He came forward a bit unsteadily and stood a little too close to Ellie, grasping her hand a little too long. His wife introduced Ellie.

"It's a pleasure to meet you," he finally said after staring a little too long. Apparently he had found a use for last year's over ripe fruit, because the smell of alcohol was overpowering, and he was breathing a little more loudly than seemed necessary.

"She's here to fix up the orange tree," Matilda said also a bit louder than normal.

He blinked comprehension and then finally said, "Well, better than that damned Peruvian woman," and went back into the house. Matilda flushed a little. "Sorry about that," she said, "It's been a tough year. I better go see to him." Then she followed him into the house and the girl stepped forward to walk her home.

When they got back to the station the girl looked up at her and said, "Thanks for helping with mom's orange tree. It means a lot to her." She looked back down, but as Ellie opened the door wider she noticed the girl looking past her into the station.

"I never got your name," Ellie said.

"Anabelle," she said.

"Anabelle, would you like me to show you around the station?"

Anabelle looked up. Ellie opened the door and gestured.

Ellie took her to the lab and showed her the equipment and what it did. She took a swab of Anabelle's cheek and ran it through the analyzer while they played around with the rest of the gear. It was still chugging along when Anabelle started to look uncomfortable, so Ellie stopped the analysis and looked at the partial results with her. "Well, you're definitely a primate of some sort," Ellie said and Anabelle laughed because humans are the only primates. Ellie led her into the kitchen and said, "This is the kitchen. It's for cooking food." Anabelle rolled her eyes, but at least she was looking at her.

When Ellie opened the kitchen door to let her out, Annabelle said, "Thanks for showing me around. I've always wondered what was in here." As she turned to go she paused and said, "He isn't always like that you know."

It took Ellie a second to figure out who she was talking about, but then she nodded and said, "I didn't think he was." Anabelle looked at her out of the corner of her eye, but seemed pleased, and was gone.

"Now to the barley!" she said, but the momentum of the morning was gone. She began to gather files for the build, but then stopped and looked out the window. She checked her messages and found nothing interesting. She went into the orchard, climbed up on her rock and listened to the leaves rustling and the sounds of the town around them. After a while, she hopped down and went back into the lab. She finished gathering the files, arranged them in order and fed them into the utility that turns them into build files the sequencer can understand. Then she stopped and wandered into the kitchen.

She was out of everything but eggs. She got out a mixing bowl and a frying pan and was about to crack the first egg when there was a knock at the door. She put the egg down.

Titu was at the door, dressed in work clothes.

"Hi Titu," Ellie said when she opened the door; "does your dad have another message for me?"

He smiled faintly, and said, "No, this is business. Your predecessor was helping one of our neighbors with some new sugar beets, but they're not working like they're supposed to. I was wondering if you could take a look and see what's going on."

"Yeah, I could take look. Come in; let me see if I can find his notes on them. You wouldn't happen to know the work order number he was using?"

"No." Titu said, and shifted his weight onto his heels.

Ellie eyed him for a second and said, "I'll just poke around for a minute and see if I can find it." After a minute of searching, she said, "I can't find it. I don't think it's in the system."

"Yeah, it might not be. It didn't seem like he liked paper work much."

"Well, let me see if he left any informal notes, or if some of the files are still on the equipment."

"No need. I've got everything right here," he said and held out a memory pearl.

She raised an eyebrow, took the pearl and still looking at him dropped it into the slot on her watch. She took a quick look with her glasses and then said, "Let's go."

Titu glanced at the bowl, frying pan and eggs laying out and said, "We'll get something to eat on the way back."

Ellie shrugged and they left.

Fifteen

Apparently the word "neighbor" was relative. The property was no-where near Titu's family property. It was up against the west wall of the canyon and the site of green crops growing beneath the red rock walls was startling. "The marvels of irrigation...," she said out loud. Titu seemed to take it as a compliment, rather than an expression of surprise, and though she couldn't see what he thought he had to do with the whole thing, she let it stand.

The farmer was a tough short man in his fifties who didn't have a lot to say, but looked like he had a lot on his mind. He took them into an old rock barn and showed them a pile of beets. They were a pulpy mess.

"How long ago were these harvested?" Ellie asked.

"This morning," the farmer said, "Most of them are like that before you even harvest them. Come on, I'll show you."

They went out into the test plot and fully half the unripe beets were falling apart. Not rotting exactly, just flaking apart... and then starting to rot.

Ellie said, "Let me get some samples and then do you mind if I work in your barn for a little while?"

"It don't bother me any," he said, "If you need anything just call."

Ellie and Titu lugged the equipment into the barn, then Ellie pulled her glasses down and got to reading. After a few minutes she said, "This is no great mystery. They're doing what they were designed to do. He engineered them to fall apart. The question is, why would he design them to do that?"

"No mystery there." Titu said. "That's what we asked him to do. The current process for making sugar involves slicing up the beats, passing them through two different chemical vats, pressing them, and only then starting to refine the sugar. We wanted a way to use our apple juice presses in the off season without having to modify the facility much. Only the beats aren't supposed to fall apart until after they are harvested."

"So, why are they doing it now?" Ellie said.

She went silent again, staring into her glasses. After a while, Titu waived a hand in front of her glasses. "Reading or snoozing?" he asked.

She jumped a little and said, "Sorry, I was just trying to visualize how they express the gene that creates the enzymes responsible for this. I think I've got it now."

She pulled up her glasses and moved to the equipment set up by the pile of beets. She put some samples in. "Just doing a chemical analysis to confirm high levels of the enzymes," she said. "Yep," she said then repeated the analysis with beats at different stages and started graphing the results. "It's like I was saying. They're doing what they are supposed to do. They're just doing it at the wrong time." Next she sampled air, water, soil, everything she could think of that would come into contact with the beets and building profiles and organism inventories for each, but before she could finish her stomach started rumbling. Titu tactfully ignored it, but after a third particularly loud and artful rumble, neither could keep a smirk off their faces.

"Maybe we should take a break," Titu said.

"Maybe we should." Ellie agreed, "I can finish this up back in the lab any way."

Titu nodded and disappeared, leaving her to break down the equipment and haul it back to the truck. When she got to the truck with the last of her stuff, Titu was coming from the direction of the farm house with a basket in one hand.

"I said our goodbyes for us and told them you'd give them a call later to discuss your findings. They fixed us a lunch," he said hefting the basket.

They climbed into the truck and Titu drove in a direction Ellie had never been along the canyon wall. As they drove, the canyon walls got shorter until the road angled up into a side canyon. Then they turned back and drove along the top of the canyon wall until they came to a large reservoir. They got out and walked along the shore with the basket to a hill covered in dune grass overlooking the lake and the canyon below. The wind coming off the canyon rippled the grass as they spread a blanket and began eating. Ellie half-heartedly wished for a kite and some string, but just being there was enough.

The wind tugged at Ellie's hair and she felt herself giving in to it, leaning back and letting it play across her face. She watched Titu hunting up food for her in the basket and handing it to her. There was an easiness in his manner. It was as if he already knew the outcome of everything and only needed to confidently play his part. He looked at her and realized she was watching him, but instead of being embarrassed he smiled back at her. The food was good, simple homey things.

"Thank you for helping my neighbors," said Titu.

"It's my job."

"Yes, but you didn't get all bureaucratic on me."

"You're welcome and thank you for lunch," she said.

Titu nodded and looked out over the valley.

"You like helping your neighbors," Ellie said.

"Yes," he said, holding his gaze on something over the horizon for a second before turning to look at her. "I help them, and they help me. That's the way it works." He returned his gaze to the horizon and she could see faint creases in the corners of his eyes when he squinted.

"What did you want to be when you grew up?" she asked.

He thought about that for a few seconds and said, "I think when I was very little I wanted to be my father...," he turned to face her, "but now I think I'd like to be a musician."

"What do you play?"

"Nothing, that's the problem," he said straight faced.

She shoved him and said, "No, seriously."

"I am being serious," he said, smiling at her. "I wish I could play an instrument. Don't get me wrong. I like agribusiness. I'm good at it, and I'll be doing it the rest of my life, but I think it would be fun if I could play in an ensemble with my friends on weekends and evenings."

"Why don't you?"

"It gets complicated," he said, looking over the horizon again. Glancing back he added, "What about you? Did you always want to be a botanist?"

"For a while I wanted to be an astronaut, but it was more the romantic ideal of the old explorers than the asteroid wranglers and long distance cargo haulers of today. Other than that I didn't give it that much thought until I got to college. Even then, I had just always been with plants and getting into my parents lab equipment, so it made sense."

"Do you like it?"

"I like the art of it. I like helping people. I like plants. I'll let you know in a few months if I like the rest."

After that they fell into a comfortable silence.

The shadows started to grow, but neither wanted to move. Finally Titu stood, and began putting things back into the basket. Ellie helped him fold the blanket, and they walked back towards the truck with no hurry. They walked side by side shoulders almost touching. When they got to the truck she got in while he stowed the gear. It was warm inside the truck, and there was the smell of dirt, leather, and Titu's shampoo.

There was little to say. Titu's strong hands casually guided the truck through the twists and winds of the road until they were on the canyon floor and fully in the shadows of the nearest wall. There was something comforting in being sheltered by that massive block of continental crust, and in the warmth of the truck, and the coming darkness. She fell asleep.

She surfaced when the hum of the motor changed. She was slumped against the window and there was drool on it. She quickly but casually wiped it up with her sleeve. Out of the corner of her eye she saw that he hadn't missed it, but he said nothing and she looked around and saw they were close to her station.

He helped her get her things inside, said goodnight, and drove off in the direction of home.

Ellie closed the door and the station was quiet and empty.

Sixteen

In the morning Ellie decided not to check her mail first thing. She had plenty of work backing up and, more importantly, except for eggs she was out of food. She got dressed, hopped into the truck and made a run for the market.

When she got there, the vendors were still setting up their colorful sunshades and unloading trucks. There was the good natured banter of long associates in a shared industry and the upbeat rhythm of voices that expected good things from the day. Even the sleepier folks that had driven the farthest and put on the groggiest personas still had hope for a good market day in their half-lidded eyes. She kept her ears open for little bits of news as she went from stand to stand. The negotiating was tougher this early, but she didn't mind. She mainly negotiated for sport and to maintain respect, so the final price didn't matter much. She heard nothing of particular interest and soon found herself back in the truck.

Despite the samples she had tried she was still famished and resolved to eat breakfast right there in the truck. By the time she got the groceries back to her house, she had eaten half of what she had bought to last a week and was still faintly hungry. She fried up some eggs, and sat down to eat them. Then she began scribbling a "to do" list on a napkin. Barley, sugar beets, reports. It was enough to keep her busy for several days. She decided to stand up, but her fingers twitched to check mail. She resisted for a minute and then finally gave in and called it up. She skimmed through finding mostly things she could safely postpone or ignore, but then her eyes caught on the word "Billings." She opened it.

"Dear Ellie: Congratulations on your assignment. I've heard it's an excellent one and not one usually given to recent graduates. Do you like it? You'll have to tell me all about it.

I'm still unemployed, but I don't think I will be for long. I'll let you know what I'm up to when things are more definite. In the mean time I've about got things under control here. My father's affairs are finally in order and I've been organizing his things. I hadn't noticed before but he doesn't really have that many things. He just never put them away so it looked like more. He did put my mother's things away though, in boxes underneath his bed. Maybe when I've decided what to do with his things, I can decide what ought to be done with hers. Until then I'll just put his boxes under there with hers.

I walk in the mornings, just before sun up so I can look at the bright stars and then the sunrise and often you are here with me. At least it seems that way.

I'd like to come see you when things are settled here. Would you mind much?

-Jake

P.S. Hal says hi. He has a shiny new Rock Crawler in his yard. He says he'll give you 10% off on your next rental.
P.P.S Where are the moss spores you promised me?!"

Ellie closed the message, and stared at the refrigerator. That strange boy and the desert were suddenly luminous and present. She shook her head to get it out, opened the message again and tried to decide what to say. Then wrote,

"Thanks.

I like my new job and am meeting lots of interesting new people. I don't have any spores ready, but I'll get some put together for you and send them in a little while. Sure, you can stop by whenever you are in town. Let me know when you're coming and I'll arrange things so we can show you around. I hope your plans work out.

-Ellie."

She looked at it for a minute, closed her eyes, and added,
"P.S. Tell Hal thanks for the offer, but I'll pass."
She hesitated, and added,
" P.P.S. I never thanked you for what you did for me. It had to be as awkward for you as it was for me, but I owe you my life, and I am grateful."

She hit send before she could think about it anymore. Closed the mail and stood up, paused, added "moss" to the bottom of her "to do" list, and went into the lab.

She wanted to work on the barley, but the sugar beets seemed more urgent. She pulled up the "breakdown" segment she had been looking at. "Self-destruct" might be a better description.

The segment was a combination of standard bacterial cellulase and fungal lignin peroxidase sequences, but with a novel trigger: a potato nitrate detector normally used to slow shoot growth in low nitrate soil.

"So, when nitrate levels get low, it destroys its own cell walls...," she said to herself, "and nitrate levels would definitely get low when you yank the plant out of the soil."

She frowned. It was clever, but not elegant. The plant would have to use its stored sugars to run the process, and not all beets would decay at the same rate leading to processing problems. Still the savings in processing and the reuse of equipment might make it worth the other losses.

She looked at the soil samples and, as expected, they were low in nitrates.

She pulled up mail and started to write a note to Titu and the farmer, suggesting they increase the amount of fertilizer, but stopped. That farmer knew all about fertilizer, it was hard to believe he wouldn't have monitored that.

She gave him a call instead and caught him in the field.

"Some of the soil samples I took show a low nitrate level. When was the last time you applied fertilizer?" she asked.

"A week ago," he responded a little indignantly, "I'll send over the logs."

She disconnected and looked at the logs that appeared. They showed a good farmer. He was watching the levels carefully and applying just enough to keep the plants happy.

Based on the history, the nitrate levels should have been higher when she took the samples.

She looked again at the logs and noticed that the amounts of fertilizer applied had been growing faster than the bio mass of the plants. It wasn't much, or even necessarily significant, but it was unusual.

She looked at the soil analysis again. A bit moist, she thought. She started a soil sample run and wandered off to the bathroom while it ran. When she came back and looked at what was living in the soil it was the usual gang of decomposers and nitrogen fixers and their companions. She scanned down the list and her eyes caught on Pseudomonas Aeruginosa M20991. She looked up its history and properties.

"Got you," she said to the display.

She dissolved another sample in water and spun the container in a centrifuge on a slow speed, poured the clear water into a dish, looked at it under a microscope, and estimated the number Pseudomonas Aeruginosa. They were plentiful.

She drove to the farm and walked into the fields without stopping at the house. She took a spade and turned over the crunchy earth. It was dripping wet at the depth of the sugar beets. The farmer caught up with her and looked at the hole. She looked at him.

He raised his hands defensively, "I haven't irrigated in two weeks, besides, these beets can tolerate a bit of water."

"You've got an aerobic microbe in the soil that has an anaerobic mode. Guess where it gets its oxygen when it can't get it from the air?"

He closed his eyes and rubbed his forehead, "let's see, it splits the nitrate into nitrogen and oxygen?"

Ellie put her finger on her nose.

"OK, I know what to do," he said.

"Good," she said and smiled to soften it. He smiled and said, "Thanks."

Ellie wrote a note to Titu from the truck. She'd write the formal report when she got back to the lab.

She started for the station, expecting to feel good about the day's work, but as she drove, she fidgeted. She looked up at the bluffs and tried to see where the picnic lake was. She looked across the valley and noticed rain clouds closing in.

"Better get home," she said to the truck and managed to beat the storm by a few minutes.

Seventeen

"Barley! Today I make barley," she said when morning came.

She hurried through her morning routine, and then remembered her reports. She dashed off reports for the week including the sugar beets. Since she had no work order for it, she opened one on behalf of the farmer. She hesitated about including a copy of the destruct sequence in the report, but it wouldn't make sense without it, so she included it.

She was standing up to go to the lab when she a courier on the porch. She retrieved the package and found a hand lettered invitation for a fitting at a clothing store she had never heard of. She almost threw it away, but paused looking at the quality of the paper and lettering. She called the address listed on the back and a middle-aged woman answered.

"I just received an invitation...," Ellie began.

"You must be Ms. Waddell," the woman interrupted.

"Yes. I'm a little confused about this invitation..."

"It's an anonymous gift from some members of the community. If we can arrange a time that suits you, simply bring the invitation to the shop, pick out an outfit, and we'll have it tailored for you while you wait."

"I'm grateful, but I'm guessing your line-up may be a little out of my price range even with the free fitting."

"The fitting includes the outfit. There will be absolutely no charge to you."

Ellie started mentally reviewing her wardrobe. She had a church dress and a few cute skirts that she liked, but nothing really for formal occasions. "The party!" she thought with some alarm.

"Miss Waddell, are you still there?" the voice on the other end asked.

"Yes, I'm still here."

"Well, is there a time that would suit you?"

She looked at her watch.

"Is this morning too soon?"

The voice on the other end laughed softly. "That would be fine; is 10:00 acceptable?"

"Yes, that would be fine."

"We look forward to your visit."

At 10:00 her truck was parked in front of the clothing store and the attendant who opened the door eyed it with vague distaste as she let Ellie in.

The lighting inside was subdued except for patches of bright lights accenting various articles of clothing and bright lights in front of a set of mirrors in the back.

A glowing large format book lay open on a table to the right with models walking back and forth on its pages in what Ellie assumed must be the latest fashions.

The voice from the phone greeted Ellie from behind and she turned to see a woman a little shorter than herself but crisply dressed approaching her.

The woman gestured and they sat down at the little table together and exchanged pleasantries. Then the woman said, "So what kind of event are we dressing for today?"

"Well, I'm not completely certain. I've been invited to a house party with some of the farmers, and I was just assuming it was relatively informal, but now I'm not so sure."

The woman smiled a little. "This party wouldn't be at the Alcantar household would it?"

"As a matter of fact, yes."

The woman smiled again and said, "I think it's safe to say that this will be a formal event."

The woman flipped a couple of pages in the book to the formal section and Ellie found herself looking at images of herself walking around in a variety of different dresses. The woman leaned in next to her and said, "Let's see... definitely not." She flicked several of the images off the page with her index finger leaving five which grew larger on the page. "Are there any here that you like?" She asked.

Ellie gestured towards a black dress and a silver one. The other three "Ellies" disappeared and were replaced by six more in outfits similar to the two she had chosen and one that was actually radically different in a completely different direction. The woman leaned in again and dismissively flicked several off the screen and they repeated the process several times until there were five gleaming "Ellies" all wearing beautiful clothing and competing with each other for her attention.

Ellie was just beginning to feel a little weary when an attendant appeared with refreshments. While they ate, the woman said, "I think we should take a look at fabrics next, and make sure the feel and flow is going to be correct." Ellie nodded. The woman gave instructions to the attendant who left and returned with a several small boxes each with sample fabrics in them. The woman hunted through them and brought out several samples which she laid over her arm and gestured for Ellie to feel. When Ellie showed interest in any of them, the woman draped it over Ellie's arm so she could feel the weight. The woman spoke softly to the book and the dresses shifted subtly into what Ellie realized must be representations with these specific fabrics. Ellie narrowed the choice down to two and the woman nodded approvingly, then lead her to a changing room and brought her the two dresses.

She tried them on. They already fit better than anything else she owned, but when she came out, the woman fussed at her as if something was wrong. She had Ellie stand up on a fitting stand in front of the mirrors and made small changes using pins. Ellie was surprised to see that it made a visible difference. When she was done the woman stood and looked at her from every angle. Then she came closer and said, "You know if you want to do something a little more... daring, you've got the figure to pull it off." Ellie looked at her with a puzzled look.

"We could raise the hem a little, shorten the sleeves, drop the neck line a little. Not too much of course, but just enough..."

Ellie smiled and said, "I think it's perfect the way it is." The woman shrugged slightly and returned the smile. They repeated the process with the second dress. It was a creamy silver dress a little longer, and though Ellie harbored some dreamy pretensions about who she might be with such a dress, it was clear to both of them she would choose the first.

While the dress was being tailored, they chose the shoes and accessories. When the dress came out for a final check they put the entire ensemble together and she looked at herself in the mirror. She thought about what the woman had said about her figure, and noticed it had changed slightly since she'd last paid any attention to it. She had lost the last of her adolescent fat and had become more angular and shapely; even her face had more highlights. The woman showed her some different ways to wear her hair that might work well with the dress. Then it was time to go. When she went to put her old clothes on they seemed thin, cheap, even slightly soiled. She shook the feeling off and went to the front counter where the new outfit was wrapped up like so many jewels in shining boxes. She thanked everyone, took her packages and climbed into her truck. As she closed the truck door she thought she caught a glimpse of the attendant watching her. She couldn't blame her. It did seem a bit ridiculous to imagine the girl in the mirror climbing into this lumbering beast of a mud spattered farm truck. As she pictured it she laughed.

It was 3:00 by the time she got back to the station, just time enough to get a snack (so she wouldn't eat like a pig at the dinner), bathe (again) and change into the new outfit.

She was leaving when Titu pulled up in a sedan. He leaned out the window and took a long look at her. Ellie flushed and looked away. Then he said, "Would you like a ride? If you drive your truck, I can't guarantee you won't have to park next to the livestock yard." Ellie weighed her alternatives and finally nodded. Titu hopped out and opened a door for her.

The drive wasn't far. In fact at one time the station and the Alcantar ranch were probably adjacent properties before the land had been improved and further divided.

Titu stopped the car at the front door, gallantly opened her door for her and then took the car back to the garage, leaving her to enter by herself.

The entry way had the same dimensions as the entry way at her station, and as she looked around she could see that both houses shared a basic design from the same era, but the similarity ended there. This house had been completely refurbished on the inside, probably more than once. The door casings were all hand carved wood and the walls were completely plastered and white washed to hide all signs of the old adobe walls that must be under there somewhere. The furniture was tasteful, new, and probably comfortable. Accent lighting spotlighted works of art on the walls and in cabinets, and the air was at least twice as moist as at her house, which made the cream she was wearing feel almost sticky.

Titu's father saw her standing awkwardly at the door, went to her, and brought her into the group introducing her to everyone as they walked. He was clearly in his element, smiling and attending to his guests. Recorded music played softly in the background, the accent of the singers giving them away as old world Americans. The room they were mingling in had been the work area of the old house, but was now thoroughly converted for entertaining. A double doorway had been cut into the outside wall towards what at her house was the vegetable garden, but here was an attached green house, and there were amazing fragrances coming from it. Ellie made small talk with the other guests, but her eyes kept drifting back to the green house. When Titu came in his father hailed him, and said, "I think our young botanist friend might like to see the greenhouse." Ellie looked away to cover her expression and heard the two men laughing.

Titu lead her into the green house and began naming plants for her, but then stopped and said, "Look who's telling you what we have here." "No, go on," she said, "These are a little out of my specialty." With the sun down, the only light in the green house came from small lights on the ceiling that looked like stars and small Japanese lanterns that had been brought in for the party. The fragrance was powerful like perfume, and as Ellie listened to the names of the plants and looked at their leaves, she realized this was no ranch vegetable garden. In fact none of these plants could even be adapted to present conditions. Certainly an adapted plant could be made of them, but it would be such a drastic change that they would be unrecognizable descendants. These were the plants of continents nestled between warm oceans much closer to the sun. "Gardenia, Orchid, Hibiscus," she had seen them all in books during her undergraduate survey courses, and thought she remembered there was a small green house for them somewhere on campus tended by students with very different specialties from her's, but she had never seen them before herself. She felt the smooth leaves between her fingers and smelled the intoxicating perfumes. She looked around. This was not a small green house. It was built from the same kits used to build production green houses. She looked at Titu in frank surprise. He noticed and looked down suddenly just a bit self-conscious. "This is amazing," she said. Titu looked at her and raised his eyebrows in agreement. She was still committing the sight and texture and odor of the plants to memory when the dinner bell sounded. It was a good old common ranch dinner chime, but somehow it didn't seem out of place.

They gathered to their places at the table and Titu's father asked a man to give the prayer. He looked a bit annoyed by the request, but when Titu's father continued looking at him steadily, he didn't protest but offered a short appropriate prayer. Then the food was served. There was some small fowl she didn't quite know, and the usual vegetables and potatoes. There was also a tiny portion of rice which she had never eaten before. "Where did they find someone who knows how to cook it?" she wondered.

Conversation had slacked off when the food first came, but slowly picked up again. Ellie was seated to the right of Titu's mother who had once been beautiful, with high cheek-bones and still surprisingly smooth skin; and to the left of a younger woman wearing a dress with short sleeves that didn't work well with her fleshy arms.

"Tell us about yourself Miss Waddell. Where do you come from?" said Titu's mother.

"Yes do!" chimed in the younger woman.

"I'm from Paititi," Ellie ventured, "I just graduated with a Masters from the University of Paititi in xenobotany, and this is my first real assignment."

Titu's mother opened her mouth to say something but the younger woman jumped in with "Paititi! You must have gone to the shows every week." Ellie was about to respond when the woman went on with, "My Hector here took me to the new Opera house on my birthday and we saw 'The Gondoliers' with Nellie Reid playing that poor Casilda. She did such a good job..." Ellie watched carefully for her turn to speak, but when it didn't come right away she noticed Titu seated across from her keeping his dancing eyes away from the younger woman's face and suppressing a smile. He dared look at Ellie just once during the exchange, then pressed a thumb against his lips, looked down for a second and returned to toying with his food. "... I think that Nellie is so much better than that stuffy old Patricia; you need a younger woman for that role. Don't you think so?" the younger woman said and waited a full second before Ellie realized it was her turn to talk.

"Oh...uh... you would know better than I would. I haven't been to the Opera." The woman's mouth opened and her forehead wrinkled in concern.

"Oh, but you must!" she said, laying a pudgy hand on hers "you must."

Ellie was thinking of a response when Titu's mother interjected, "Have there been any exciting break throughs in botany this year?" Ellie smiled and as she warmed to the topic, the younger woman's eyes glazed over. She looked at her plate, then looked down the table and began offering comments on a conversation happening in the middle of the table.

Titu leaned back a little in his chair, shot a glance at his mother, who saw and studiously ignored it by concentrating on what Ellie was saying. He smiled and shot a glance at Ellie, who also ignored it. Titu then contentedly went back to chewing on the last of his fowl.

When the dinner dishes were cleared, Titu's father stood and said, "I hope you all saved some room. We have a special treat tonight that is truly the FRUIT of our labors this year." Then he sat down. The lights dimmed dramatically and attendants entered with small plates of glowing strawberries for each person. Ellie looked at them quizzically, and when everyone had been served, Titu's father said, "Enjoy." People hesitated before eating them. Ellie cut a small berry in half and examined it before tasting a little. It tasted like a strawberry. It seemed a shame to eat them.

"So, what do you think?" Titu's mother asked.

"It's beautiful. Luciferin?"

"Yes... sort of."

"From fireflies?"

"No. I think they tried that first, but it was just too taxing on the strawberry plant, even with enhanced lighting. In the end they went with foxfire."

Ellie looked at her plate.

"It's so bright!" she said. "I wouldn't have guessed..."

"The first batch wasn't so bright. They ended up adding fluorescence from the Crystal Jelly fish and then they had to create a novel protein that produced particles that absorb the green light from the luciferin and reemit it as blue light to pump the fluorescent protein."

"That must have taken forever."

Titu's mom nodded. "It did, and when they got done with that, it tasted bitter."

"What'd they do?"

"They were about to give up when they realized they'd taken too much of the pathway from foxfire. When they scaled it back, the berries got bigger and the taste came back to normal."

"Too bad they couldn't find a naturally occurring re-emitter."

Titu's mom looked at her.

"If they had found a naturally occurring re-emitter it would have been simply recombinant. You could have gotten by with the basic safety testing instead of the extended impact studies. You're commercializing it, right?"

Titu's mom looked at her with respect. "Yes, the testing is what's holding us up."

Ellie pulled out a tissue. "Do you mind?" she said, gesturing to the strawberry.

"No. Not at all. The preliminary patents have already been granted. Have fun."

Ellie wrapped up a strawberry and put it in her bag. "Thanks."

Titu's mom continued, "If you poke around enough you probably already have the early..." She stopped herself, "... probably have the early advantage on anyone else to understand this stuff."

Ellie smiled at her. Titu's father wrinkled his brow and asked how she was settling in. Titu rolled a strawberry around his plate.

After dinner the music resumed, the lights were kept down a little and people gathered in the room just off the greenhouse. Ellie tried to make small talk with some of the younger wives, but out of the corner of her eye she could see Titu and his parents discussing something in a low voice. They didn't talk long, and she might not have noticed if they hadn't been looking at her during part of the exchange. A little while later Titu approached her group and they stopped talking and looked at him.

"Sorry," he said, "I was wondering if I could borrow Ellie for a minute."

She stood and walked with him toward the greenhouse.

As they walked she heard a small commotion and saw a girl, maybe 17, walking quickly toward the front entry, or maybe the bathroom with her parents in pursuit.

"I hope she's OK." Ellie said, "That can be a tough age."

"Yeah." Titu agreed, looked down, and then looked back into her eyes until she looked away. They continued toward the greenhouse.

The perfume of the flowers became stronger, and as the sounds of conversation faded the music was more noticeable.

"What song is this?" Ellie asked.

"We're going through a classics phase right now. I don't remember the title. Ella Fitzgerald is the singer," he said.

"She doesn't sound Irish."

"American."

There was something hypnotic about the warm tones and quick rhythms of the lyrics, especially blended with the perfume of the flowers. It all seemed to fit.

"So, what did you want to talk to me about?" she asked.

"Nothing really. I wanted to show you something."

The night lights in the canopy of the green house winked like stars as they walked toward the back of the green house. There on one of the last rows of the green house were a dozen or more small orchids with bright green foliage and pure white fragrant flowers.

Titu picked one up and handed it to her. "What do you think of these?"

"They're exquisite," she said.

He picked a miniature greenhouse off of a shelf, took the orchid from her hands, put it in and handed it back to her.

"Take it home with you," he said.

She started to shake her head...

"No, no, it's OK. We're going to try to sell these later this year, but we're not sure we've got the little greenhouses quite right. It'd be like you were testing it for us."

She looked at the enclosure. It was beautiful. Finally she just nodded.

Titu smiled.

They walked slowly back towards the house. The singer was crooning "Fight, fight, fight, fight, fight it with all of your might..." "Fight what?" Ellie thought. The air was heavy with moisture, fragrance, the smell of soil. Titu casually put his warm hand on her shoulder, guiding her away from a cart in the pathway she was in danger of hitting.

The night lights and lantern light reflected off the shiny dark leaves of moist plants. The distant warm light of the house and the barely discernible hum of conversation in the distance created a distinct sense of wellbeing. Titu's eyes also picked up glints of the light and reflected it back. They paused not too far from the door. Ellie felt a little faint, she realized, because she hadn't been breathing normally. Titu looked at her to make sure she was OK, and smiled. He was about to say something when a motion at the door caught his attention. It was his father, standing patiently. He beckoned to him. "Wait here," he said. His father met him halfway and whispered something in his ear. He wasn't the quietest whisperer and Ellie caught the words "situation" and "driveway." Titu looked annoyed, then calm, then came back and said, "Wait here, I'll be back in a minute."

After ten minutes her hands grew weary of holding her bag and the orchid, so she moved back into the main room and sat talking with the other guests. They all admired the orchid as it sat on a table in front of them. When they asked her about it, she said Titu had asked her to test the miniature greenhouse to make sure it would work for casual users. After a second, one of the women said, "Of course dear," blinked, and wandered toward the refreshment table. When Titu came back fifteen minutes later his face was tight and he said, "I'm sorry, that took longer than I thought it would, and it's getting late. Would you mind if one of the hands gave you a ride home?"

"No. Not at all," she said.

"Thanks, I know that's rude of me. I'll try to explain later."

He said goodnight, and started walking towards the residence wing, loosening his tie.

Eighteen

When Ellie woke up it was still dark and her heart was racing. She listened intently, but heard only early morning sounds, little rustles and wind moving through trees. It was too late for the late traffic and too early for the farmer's traffic, and there was nothing that should alarm her. She tried to remember what the sound had been, and then it came back to her. It had been an unworldly howling. Something like a feral dog, but wilder, more primeval. She listened some more but there was nothing. She poked around the old station moving from window to window peering into the darkness, but there was no sign of anything.

She noticed for the first time that the windows of the station, of all the very old stations, were built for defense. They were a little narrower than people would naturally want and never let in as much light as a body craved, but seeing how there were few people and hardly a creature larger than a cricket when those stations were built, that made no sense.

She shook it off, made herself some cocoa and began to be amused with herself. The windows were built that way for heat retention, and conservation of expensive glass, not defense. The worst thing ever accidentally introduced was a biting fly, now mercifully extinct, and the only native species was less frightening than lichen. There were no monsters on Mars. Still she'd ask Cava about it sometime.

By the time she had settled herself, sleep was gone. She wandered into the lab and looked at her orchid. She was tempted to sample it and take a look. She thought about her strawberry in the specimen locker, but even as she considered it she knew it would be the barley.

She worked steadily, and by dawn she had forty nuclei ready and fifty host cells. She could never quite manage to keep from destroying a few hosts during insertion. Yet to her surprise she used only 42 hosts. "Good gear makes a difference," she said out loud.

By the time she was hungry again they were all safely in a bioreactor dividing and maturing. It was ten o'clock. Cava called while she was scavenging around the kitchen trying to put together something edible. "So, do you ever check your mail, or are you especially ignoring me?" she said.

"It's just you," Ellie said as she pulled up the mail through the filthy refrigerator display. "So what's up?"

"I'll wait until you've finished reading my message." Ellie turned around and saw Cava looking in through the kitchen window. "So, are you going to let me in, or do you want to go put your clothes on first?" she saw Cava's lips say slightly out of synch with the sound. Ellie looked down at herself and shook her head. She let Cava in and went to dress. When she got back Cava said, "Late night?"

"No. Early morning. I couldn't sleep, so I baked," Ellie replied and led her back to see her latest creation basking in the reactor.

"Let me guess, no-stink asparagus?"

Ellie looked at her, and flipped on a display.

Cava stared at it for a minute, scrolled through the base pairs, then flipped the display upside down. She looked at it again and said, "I don't read Tibetan, girl," but she was looking at Ellie out of the corner of her eyes.

Ellie rolled her eyes and skipped to the last page with the Latin name, summary descriptions, and proposed version numbers.

"That's better," said Cava. "Barley, huh? Who for?"

"Young couple on the uplands trying to get ahead."

Cava shrugged, but seemed to calm down a little as she switched the display to mail and said gesturing, "What do you make of this?"

There were a series of pictures and a field analyzer readout attached.

Ellie flicked through the pictures and said, "Looks like a bunch of rotten potatoes."

"Keep looking," Cava said.

Ellie switched the view to her glasses and leaned back on the couch staring and clicking.

"You look like some kind of psychotic when you do that," Cava said.

"Shhh! Don't distract me."

Cava rolled her eyes.

Ellie put up her glasses and said, "So, you're telling me that these were freshly dug from living plants, there are no irrigation problems, and the problem covers an acre?"

Cava nodded.

Ellie pulled the glasses back down and started going through the analyzer report.

"Looks like some sort of a decomposer." She clicked softly a few times and the report appeared on the display nearest Cava. After a pause, five species names popped up next to it.

"So which one is it?" Cava asked.

"I can't tell from this. We probably need to run a more detailed analysis. Do you have a sample?"

"It's three days old."

"It should be good enough."

They opened Cava's sample jar, scrapped some of the powdery stuff out and ran it through the sequencer.

While it ran, they went back to the kitchen and Ellie threw together a rough meal of leftovers. She offered Cava some, but she just made a puking face in response. Ellie shrugged and dug in, but when she was finished she didn't feel so well.

Cava caught the expression on her face and laughed at her.

Ellie leaned back in her chair and closed her eyes waiting for the feeling to pass.

"So, I hear you got all dolled up and went to dinner last night," Cava said.

"One hundred and fifty *years of entertainment and half a billion books in the archives and what passes for fun here is answering the burning question, 'Can Ellie wear a dress?'"

"Yeah, pretty much."

"You need to get out more."

"We throw a pretty mean harvest festival. Besides, it's not like you get out much seeing how you had to get a new dress just to go."

"No. I guess not." Ellie said with a sigh of resignation. "Is there ANYTHING that isn't public knowledge around here?"

Cava laughed slightly. "Not much. We know just about everything, and some of it's even true."

"Yes. I went to dinner. It was all a bit more than I'm used to, and they are doing much more amazing things than I ever expected to find on any farm."

"How about Titu? Was he amazing?"

Ellie looked at Cava. She was still smiling, but there was hint of warning in her eyes. Cava was older than Ellie, older than Titu too, but only by a few half-*years. Had she missed something? She cocked her head and narrowed her eyes a little. "Are you and Titu..." she paused looking for the right word and distractedly touched her fingers together.

Cava burst out laughing, "Me and Titu? Seriously?"

Ellie felt her face go white. Cava leaned forward, put her hand on Ellie's shoulder and, stifling a smile said as reassuringly as she could, "It's not Titu I'm worried about girlie!"

Ellie felt the embarrassment fade and turn into something colder and sharper, but she couldn't figure why.

Just then, they heard a completion tone from every device in the house.

"Afraid you'll miss something?" Cava said, still smiling but softer now.

"I didn't set it up that way. The guy who was here before me did that and I haven't taken the time to figure out how to undo it yet."

"I know," said Cava, and Ellie wondered what it knew.

In the lab they pulled up the results. This time there were only two species, with substantial, if only partial, matches on both. She set the system to show only the differences between the two known, and the unknown species, then had it mark all the standard library traits in green and the unknown traits in red. One of the known species became mostly green. She dismissed it and the display adjusted to show only the differences between the one known species and the unknown species. There were only six. She quickly scanned them and they were mostly deletions, base pair flips, and repetitions.

"Looks like it's a mutation of Bacillus Subtilis M21007."

"That's a common enough decomposer." Cava said, "Is it causing this or is it just being an opportunist because something is wrong with the potatoes?"

"I don't know yet."

Ellie pulled up the notes for each changed sequence to see what it did. This bacterium was well documented. She could see it had been done early on and a lot of people had worked on it together. This had been a special project from before the tools had fully matured. She could only imagine how long it must have taken. She felt almost reverent looking through their work. About three of the mutations were common, anticipated by the design team, well understood, and didn't really impact function even in combination. The fourth and fifth had been noticed and described by previous station stewards, investigated at Paititi and found to marginally decrease the ability to break down cellulose, do no other harm, and typically disappear from the population after thirty generations. That left the sixth variation. It wasn't described anywhere. The sequence wasn't a trait per se. It was part of the basic metabolism of the bacteria and played a role in almost a third of the bacteria's functions. It hadn't been tampered with much either. In fact, as she expanded her view to include the whole family of the species and beyond, she found it was a well conserved sequence. She wrinkled her brow and sat back in her chair.

"What is it?" said Cava.

"I don't know, and it's not going to be easy to figure out, but this might be something."

"You going to call it in?"

"Probably, but give me a minute to think about it. I don't want to have to deal with the bureaucrats until I'm sure I have to."

Cava nodded.

Ellie leaned forward again and compared the sequence itself to known pathogens. No matches. She loosened up the match criteria and ran it again and got hundreds of matches. She tightened the criteria slightly and got 53 matches. She tightened them just slightly more and got zero matches. She backed off the criteria again and looked at the 53. They were all very different from each other and from the new mutation. Still they all involved metabolic pathways. She leaned back in her chair and tried to imagine how the mutation would affect function, but it was too complicated.

She started to load the full genome into a simulator and Cava started fidgeting.

Ellie looked at her.

"There's no instance of this mutation in the library, but it smells a little like a lot of other bad actors out there."

"So, if it might be bad why aren't we just calling it in?"

"I want to make sure. I want to try simulating the organism with the mutation and see how it reacts to its environment."

"... and if the simulator doesn't predict any bad reaction then are you comfortable not calling it in?"

"No."

"Then what are we waiting for? The simulator can't be trusted, and this thing has probably already been brewing for six months at least. Do you want to give it another week to spread?"

Ellie opened her mouth, then closed it. She looked at the display. She looked at Cava. She looked at the bio-reactor. She looked out the window. "No. I guess not," she finally said. "But we're not going to get anything done around here for a long time once I call this in."

"Nope. But maybe this is the one thing that we better get done."

They filed a joint report and sent it. Within five minutes Ellie's dad called her.

"Are you sure?" was all he said.

"No," she responded. "But everything in the report is accurate."

"OK. Hold on to your hat. Love ya."

"I love you too," she said and hung up.

"I see how it is," said Cava. "How many men have you got thinking you're their one and only?"

Ellie blushed, "That's my dad!"

"Oh, OK so it's just Titu?"

"Yes! No!" Ellie said.

"Ah, so how many are there?"

"None!" said Ellie, but a flicker of doubt crossed her face.

Cava was satisfied. She'd actually been satisfied since she saw her blush, but why pass up the fun of tormenting her?

"Oh, OK," she said with a knowing look that infuriated Ellie. Before she could formulate a response, Cava said, "Come on. Let's go warn this old farmer about what's about to happen to him. Better he hears it from me."

"Then what you do you need me for?"

"Hey, YOU did this to him."

"WE did this to him. Besides, it's not even really us," said Ellie.

"I know, but that's not how he's going to see it," said Cava.

They climbed into Cava's truck.

When they arrived they found the old man at the rear of the farm manually weeding a bend in an irrigation ditch. When he saw them coming he leaned on his hoe and watched in silence for a long time before finally standing up straight and greeting them.

"Behold the canals of Mars!" he said grandly, gesturing to the irrigation ditch and then smiling at his own joke.

Cava looked it over, smiled faintly and said, "Looks good."

The old farmer's smile faded. He looked over the fields a little too long and when he looked back at them his eyes were moist. "Well, I guess you'll be wanting to go back to the house to talk some."

They both nodded and he began slowly leading the way, but as they walked his back straightened and he picked up speed.

At the house he offered them both cocoa and they accepted and sipped at it while he downed a couple of tall glasses of water. When he had finished he said, "You know I had real cocoa once at a reception for the president." They looked at him expectantly. "I didn't like it. Too strong..." He sat down in a chair next to theirs, looked at his fingernails and then folded his hands and looked at them, waiting.

There was an awkward pause and then Cava said, "We've run some tests on your potatoes and it looks like you might have a new pathogen attacking them." He looked down at the floor and then back up at them. "We've called for help from Paititi and we are waiting for an answer, but the most likely outcome is that they will set a quarantine not only on your property, but on the neighboring properties. If we are right about this, you may be out of business for a couple of *years." He wrinkled his brow and then relaxed back into his chair.

"Well, it's not how I wanted to go out, but I've known for a while that this was serious. I appreciate you ladies coming down here to let me know in person," he said, standing, and shook hands. As they were walking towards the door he added, "I guess the next time I see you I'll be a field hand for the Alcantars."

Cava turned to him and put a hand on his shoulder. "I don't think it will come to that," she said, looking straight into his eyes. He nodded back, but looked down.

"Thanks again," he said.

In the truck on the way home Ellie puzzled over the old man's reaction. It finally dawned on her that the old man didn't expect to live much more than another two *years, but she was still puzzled.

"Cava, why does he think he'll have to turn to the Alcantars for help? He's a steward, not a commercial farmer."

Cava bristled, but didn't say anything. Ellie turned her face towards the passenger window.

"He's afraid he's going to lose his stewardship over this," Cava said quietly.

"Why would he lose his stewardship? There's no way this is his fault."

Cava kept looking out the window and said, "A surprising number of stewardships have been lost in the last couple of *years."

Ellie let this sink in, but couldn't make sense of it. "But why?"

Cava looked at her with an expression of almost tenderness, but finally just shook her head and said, "I don't know for sure."

When they got back to the station, Ellie sat in the truck not moving. Cava let her be, rolled down the window and looked up at the stars. A cold breeze ran through the cab and Ellie shivered a little. It brought her up out of her thoughts.

"I don't want to go in there," she said. They had both shut down their communications links when they left the farmer's house and they each had a fair idea of what would be waiting for them in their respective offices.

"I know what you mean," said Cava.

"Do you have plans tonight?" Ellie asked.

"Honestly, I haven't had any plans in three *years," said Cava.

They both got out of the truck. Ellie picked at her watch, remotely changed her presence to unavailable, closed down the work agents, and shut off the displays in the station.

The station was eerily quiet when they entered, but with the lights on, some popcorn popping and a movie playing, it warmed up. They started watching a comedy, but neither of them liked it. Halfway through they switched to an old romance where all there problems were overcome in ninety minutes and the couple lived happily ever after. When it ended the room lights came up and they were both sitting there with little glints in their eyes.

"This is stupid," Cava offered, wiped her eyes and went to the bathroom.

Sitting in the half dark, in the quiet, Ellie remembered the howling and the hair on her arms stood up.

When Cava came back Ellie said, "Have you ever seen any wild animals out there that aren't in the catalogue?"

"What kind of wild animal?"

"A predator. A large canine predator."

"No. Why?"

"I thought I heard something howling outside my window last night, but it wasn't a dog. I don't know, maybe I dreamed it, except I've never heard a sound like that before."

"The wind does funny things sometimes in this canyon."

"Maybe that was it," Ellie said, but her face didn't relax.

"Unless it was the ChupaCabra," Cava added unhelpfully.

Ellie shook her head and stood up, "Thanks."

"My pleasure," said Cava and stood to go. They gave each other a short hug at the door and then the station was quiet again.

Nineteen

It began with a last minute phone call asking her to pick up two ana-lysts from the 10:00 train. "Simple enough," she thought, grabbed her pack and headed for the train station. One of the "analysts" turned out to be the university instructor that used to rail on her for hogging the equipment, and the other was someone she had never met, but he intro-duced himself as a Department lab technician. They asked surprisingly few questions on the way back to the station. When they got there they found Cava in the kitchen cooking up a brunch.

"I let myself in with the spare key," she said, holding up a thin piece of metal that bore no resemblance to a key.

Ellie got her guests settled into a pair of the small guest rooms off the main work area, helped them stow their gear, showed them the work area she'd cleared out for them, and went into the kitchen to help Cava. There were boxes of fresh food all over the counters. "Thanks Cava," Ellie said and started putting things away. "I didn't even think of this."

"I just didn't want them getting sick from one of those awful con-coctions you make. They might send back a bad report and you might get reassigned to herding sage brush or something."

"Gee Cava, I didn't know you cared so much," Ellie said putting on her big doe eyes.

Cava didn't even look back at her from cooking.

"Yeah well, I just don't want them sending another fat guy out here that'll stink up my truck every time we have to do something together."

When Ellie finished putting things away she approached Cava to see if she could help with the cooking but Cava waved her away with a spatula before Ellie could even get close, so she went into the work area to check on her guests. She found her old instructor eying her equipment.

"How did you manage this?" he said, pointing.

"It was here when I got here."

Then he pointed at the orchid. "Was that tropical flower here when you got here?" he asked.

"No, one of the farmers is planning on selling them later this year and he wanted me to be a kind of a test customer to see if the enclosure was going to work out." He looked at her with a raised eyebrow, but didn't say anything more. They went into the kitchen. The lab analyst was already there and they sat down to a meal together. They joined hands for the prayer, which wasn't as strange as it ought to have been.

They ate quietly at first because everyone was hungry, but as the eating slowed, Cava asked, "So, how long will it take you two to prove we haven't been smoking peyote?" The men chuckled a little and Ellie was relieved to see her old instructor had a sense of humor after all. The lab analyst spoke up and said, "We should have a pretty good idea tonight, but we'll double check everything and send the report tomorrow sometime."

They finished eating and all started to clear dishes, but Ellie put her hand on Cava's shoulder and said, "You cooked. Take a load off." Cava relaxed back into her chair, and the other three cleaned up in short order.

The men gathered their gear and loaded it into the trucks. Ellie followed Cava out to the farm. The old farmer was waiting for them at the gate because Ellie had called ahead. The men put up a GPS beacon and started taking samples from all over the field. Soon she realized there was a pattern to the samples. They were working a grid with the location of each sample being logged as it was taken. Once she realized what they were doing she offered to help, but they shook their heads. "The confirmation has to be independent. You can't be part of it," her old instructor said. With that Ellie went back to Cava and the old farmer by the trucks. All of them were fidgeting. Finally the old farmer said, "Let's go back to the house." At the house the farmer excused himself and went into his office. Cava took over the kitchen table, and Ellie retreated to the couch. When each had finished their correspondence, and Ellie had finished checking her barley remotely, they all found themselves loitering in the kitchen together.

Ellie looked at her companions. Cava had her arms folded and was staring at the spot where the wall met the ceiling with a pained look on her face. The old farmer was half sitting half leaning against the kitchen counter absently looking at the back of his hands, and then at the palms, but he didn't look like he was enjoying it. Ellie started laughing. The other two looked up at her puzzled.

"I'm sorry," she said, "but look at us. We're no good at idle anymore." The old farmer and Cava looked at her for a second and then at each other and a thin smile crept across the farmer's face. Cava just looked away.

"So, have you figured out what you're going to do for the next couple of *years?" Ellie asked the farmer.

"I was thinking about trying livestock. They're not going to let me export anything I grow here for a while, but I could grow feed for my own livestock, and I've got the water. I don't know how much of a return I could make, but it would be better than letting it sit idle." By the time he finished talking, his eyes were distant, seeing things that weren't there yet. He snapped back when Ellie told him she thought it was a good idea.

Before anything else could be said the sound of the men noisily cleaning their boots on the porch interrupted them. One of them knocked on the door, and then poked his head in. "We've got what we need," he said, and disappeared outside. Ellie and Cava said their goodbyes and joined them outside.

Back at the station, the men started the analysis, Cava went home, and Ellie tended to her barley. She moved them out of the bio-reactor and onto growing media and put them in the incubator. Then she went into the orchard and watched the sun go down. When she came back inside the men were lounging in the kitchen picking at left overs. They looked tired. She looked at them, expectantly. They glanced at each other and the lab analyst said, "It's confirmed, Ellie. You've discovered a new species and it's all over that field." Ellie sat down. After a few minutes she called Cava and told her the news. "Did you really doubt it?" was all Cava said.

The next day's last minute request was to pickup truck loads of undergraduates from the train station and to prepare for the arrival of ten other people from the university and Department who would be arriving with their own vehicles. Cava took in a few of them, but most stayed in the station. She and Cava spent the whole day shuttling students out to the farm, making meals, making introductions, cleaning up messes and keeping people out of their projects. The students were sent out with field analyzers for kilometers around the farm to establish how far it had spread. She knew a lot of them at least by sight, and they seemed to look up to her like she was important. They even started referring to the new species as "Waddell's blight," until one of the professors heard it and harshly put that down. By the next day it was clear that it had spread beyond the farm, but only about a kilometer in each direction and two kilometers downstream. "We're lucky this is primarily a soil dweller," said one of the older Department men.

Titu came by on the third day just as the first of the heavy equipment came rolling in.

"I heard there's a little excitement," he said.

Ellie nodded and smiled with relief. She was glad to see him.

"Anything I can do to help?"

Ellie looked over at an undergraduate who was trampling through her little herb garden and said, "Do you think you could take some of these students off my hands for a few days?"

"Done. I'll take all of them off your hands." Ellie smiled again. "Just bring them back for work."

Titu went up on the porch and started introducing himself to everyone and explaining what was going on.

Cava came over with a hard look on her face. "What are you doing?"

"I'm getting us all some sanity back."

Cava watched the students gathering their things. She didn't say much, but it was clear she didn't like it. She seemed to be weighing something in her mind. "Well, I guess it's done now," she said and went back up to the station.

In the afternoon Annabelle stopped by with more eggs from her mother. Ellie introduced her to everyone and insisted she stay and be part of the conversations that were going on. She didn't have to be invited twice. Mostly she just listened until there was work to be done and then found her place, helping with anything that needed doing.

By sundown everything was set to begin the next day. They would sterilize the top six inches of soil for twenty square kilometers using field burning equipment turned up way too high and pulled at one quarter the usual speed. This would be followed by diverting the irrigation canal into culverts across the entire farm to keep run off from reaching it. Then over the next several months the top meter of soil at the farm itself would be dug up and run through a hazardous waste incinerator that was being moved to the site, before being put back in place. Finally, the entire farm and two neighboring properties would be treated with long lasting pre-emergent herbicides to make sure nothing grew on the property for two *years to starve out any remaining bacteria. Ellie would be responsible for long term monitoring, and the university would send up a full survey team twice a *year.

"Well, there go his ranching plans," said Ellie when she heard about the herbicide treatments. The others looked at her puzzled, so she explained what the farmer had been thinking. Finally one of them said, "Yeah, that's out. We can't take the chance."

That night when the station was finally quiet, Ellie sat at her workspace and called up her messages. There were a lot of them. This was a hot topic now, so everyone wanted a part of it. She scanned down the list, looking for something she couldn't quite define, hoping for a personal note of some kind. She thought about calling her father, but it was late. She heard a knock at the door, looked out, saw Titu and opened the door.

"I put the kids to bed. Would you like to go for a walk?" Ellie stared at him for a second and then remembered the students, smiled, and got her jacket.

The nights were still brisk and the bite in the air made Ellie feel alive. The stars were brilliant and twinkling. Orion was high in the night sky and the big dipper leaned towards the opposite horizon. Earth was at its brightest low along the horizon with a faint hint of blue-green and its pale companion. She stared at it a while.

Titu said little. They walked down the side road next to her property line with their hands in their pockets. Occasionally he would look up at the sky too, but more often he was looking at her. She smiled at that and then started running, "Race you to the streetlight," she said over her shoulder, and Titu picked up speed in pursuit. At the streetlight Ellie declared herself the winner. Titu picked up a notebook he found on the street, and started leafing through it. It took Ellie a second before she realized it was hers and started protesting. He held it above her head trying to read it in the faint light, while she pulled at his arm. Finally he handed it to back to her and said, "Nothing interesting."

She took it and protectively put it in her hand on the opposite side from him, just in case.

They walked on slowly. As they walked Titu reached out his hand. She took it.

They walked hand in hand to where the tall trees from an older orchard crowded close to the road and blocked out much of the sky. They stopped. In the distance an owl hooted and she could hear little things scurrying in the leaves. He took her other hand and they stood facing each other.

"I like it when you smile," he said. "Your eyes light up."

He brushed her hair with his fingers. She closed her eyes and when she opened them he was looking straight at her. She smiled. He leaned forward, and kissed her once, but she cut it short and looked down. He kissed the top of her head.

She put her hand on his shoulder and he stopped, but held her. After a moment they started walking back toward the station, slowly, still holding hands. There was a lot to think about, but she would think about it later. When they reached the door to the station, Titu asked, "Should we walk again tomorrow?" Ellie, smiled and squinted at him. She studied his face, brushed a stray lock of hair out of his eyes and finally said, "I don't know yet."

Titu pretended to mope.

Ellie smiled, said, "Good night," and closed the door.

Twenty

The field burning began a little after 10:00 AM, which was later than a lot of people thought it should. By 11:00, smoke hung heavy in the air and crowds of kids on bikes and old men in trucks formed along the roads. The smoke was oppressive, but when a wind picked up in the afternoon the dust made things worse. The old farmer, who had watched stoically all morning, turned and left when he saw the top soil blowing away. By 5:00 p.m. the sun was a blood red ball two fists above the horizon and the crowds had retreated. Everyone left was wearing a filter mask, but it didn't keep the taste of ash out of Ellie's mouth. It was bitter. Her eyes burned. She thought about going back to the station. There was nothing to do on site. Some of the others had gone back to the station and were observing in shifts. "I can't," she finally whispered.

At 9:30 pm the field burners had moved on to the neighboring properties, fire leaping out from underneath them in the darkness like dragons. She felt a hand on her shoulder and turned. Her father was standing behind her quietly watching the fire and her. She buried her face in his shirt and he stroked her hair. After a few moments she straightened and stood beside him. He put his arm around her and they watched the big machines until they shut down an hour later. They stood frozen to the spot listening to the low sound of land cooling, hissing and popping. Finally they walked to her truck. When they got back to the station, everything was quiet.

When they returned in the morning, the field burners were already at the far end of the fields.

Not far from where Cava and Ellie had stood with the old farmer, waiting to break the news to him, a grader was finishing a pad and a doublewide flatbed was waiting to unload the second half of an incinerator. Another truck was waiting further down the road with prefabricated wall panels for a garage. The students were deployed in the fields again with portable scanners sampling soil every ten feet. By lunch it was clear there wasn't much for Ellie to do, so she went back to the station and watched the reports coming in. "Looking good so far," said one of the older men from the Department. Ellie showed her father the barley which had sprouted and was beginning to get its color.

By evening, Ellie felt lost, her strength gone. She sat on the couch pretending to do research while her father caught up on news from men he hadn't seen in a while. She closed her eyes, hoping that when she opened them it would all be over. Her father finished his conversation, came near, and sat down next to her.

"Are you all packed?" he asked. She looked up at him puzzled. "Packed for what?"

"For the memorial, we have to catch the morning train." Ellie looked at him uncomprehendingly.

"Whose memorial?"

Her father waited. Ellie racked her memory. "Billings?" she asked.

Her father nodded amused. "His funeral was weeks ago," she pointed out, and only as she said it began to wonder why her father hadn't attended.

"The funeral is for family and neighbors. They don't need us crashing in on them at a time like that, though if Nora had been alive we probably would have gone. The memorial is for us, all the station stewards. It's always five weeks after the death."

"Why didn't anybody tell me?" asked Ellie.

Her father reflected for a second and then shook his head, "I guess we all just figured that station stewards know these things."

"I can't go. We are in the middle of a crisis here. I never even met him, and..." but Ellie suddenly saw herself on a rocky field, at night, stacking rocks in a pile with a man she barely knew, and the memory made her heart pound.

"And what?" her father prompted after a moment. Tears filled her eyes.

"And I think I already paid my respects," she said looking down.

Her father raised her chin, looked into her eyes and said, "It's important for you to go."

She looked at him, shrugged and said, "OK."

He gave her a hug, and she packed.

In the morning she got up early, took the barley out of the incubator, put it into a cardboard box, wrapped the box in blankets and put it into the truck. The drive to Julie and John's was more peaceful than her first trip. She did not clench up where the road got narrow with a big drop-off, and past that the sun climbed over the horizon and lit the farmland below. She had worried that she might wake them coming so early unannounced, but they were all up and finishing the morning chores when she found them. They invited her to breakfast and she gave them instructions on how to care for the barley and when to plant it and she felt a pang as she handed it over, but she knew she was actually putting it into more capable hands than her own.

She felt hollow, but clean as she drove back to the station. When she arrived the place was humming with activity. Cava was waiting outside the station drinking her cocoa and being quiet. "Ready when you are, girl," she said and smirked at her a little as she went in.

Inside there was tension in the air. Her father was standing about six centimeters from a Department manager staring at him. The older Department men were watching from the sidelines somewhat amused by the whole thing and two old station men were standing behind her father, arms crossed.

"Is there a problem?" Ellie said.

"No problem," her father said without looking at her.

The manager looked at her sharply, then back at her father and said, "No problem," then walked away.

"Let's go," her father said.

Ellie grabbed her things and the four of them jumped into Cava's truck.

They arrived at the station just a few minutes before the north bound train glided to a stop. They boarded and watched the country-side fly by.

In Paititi, they stopped by the house for a late lunch and Ellie remembered the moss spores. She rummaged in a box under her bed, found the ones she was looking for, and stashed them in her pack. She answered a hundred questions from her sisters and then her father's hand on her shoulder signaled it was time to go.

At the port they climbed into the old transport. She felt it shudder as it took off, and then leaned back into her chair as it picked up speed and the lights of the city receded into insignificance. When the attendant came to bring her a drink Ellie recognized her and smiled. The attendant was distracted. Ellie wondered what she was thinking of. Was it her home, her family? When she handed Ellie her glass she noticed the ring was gone.

Her father was asleep, and the others were too far away for quiet conversation. She looked out the window at the blackness below punctuated with points of light.

"In a couple of hours I'll be back," she thought.

Back where? Back in the desert? Back with Jake? Back in a moment which was supposed to stay under glass, complete and nonthreatening?

She couldn't find the right angle to think about it, so she let it go, and relaxed into her chair. Her mind quieted. When she closed her eyes, she saw the desert, smelled damp sagebrush, and kept her eyes closed.

It creeps in, unaware
It fills
It takes your air
It sings and flies around
Catch it!
and throw it to the ground

Twenty-One

Ellie barely remembered the trip from town to Jake's station. It had been late. Her father did not carry her as he had done when she was little, but she had stumbled along behind him.

They let her sleep in the back of the car while they unloaded the few pieces of luggage they had brought. She could hear Jake's voice occasionally and then after an interval of silence she was awake long enough to stumble into a bed she was pointed to.

The morning broke, thin, gray, and full of the muffled sounds of men cooking and bumping around. They did not sit in chairs, but collapsed into them. They did not chat but grumbled, teased and laughed, free for a morning of the requirements to please, regulate, adjudicate and perform.

Ellie looked around the room. She was in a king sized bed, which didn't seem right. There were high windows cut into the eastern wall letting in morning light. The furnishings were old and worn, but they were real pinewood, and must have been something of a luxury when they were new. A mechanical clock ticked on a shelf below the windows. A picture of Jake's parents, young, holding a baby, sat on the dresser. The closet door was ajar, and in the empty closet she could see her bag lying on the floor. She was in Jake's parents' room. As she let this thought roll around her brain, she could see that it made a sort of sense. She couldn't bunk with the men. The men, except for possibly Jake, would never dream of using this room, and it was probably the nicest room in the house so they would want her to have it.

She showered, dressed, and fretted about which shoes to put on. She finally chose the work boots over her newer dress shoes.

When she emerged, things had settled down in the kitchen. They had saved some food for the stragglers and she dug in gratefully.

Jake was on the far end of the living room talking with some of the younger men, and if he had seen her come in, he hadn't shown any sign of it. He had grown a little leaner since she last saw him, but his eyes were bright and his conversation with the others was animated. She had not noticed his smile as much when she had been here before. It was good natured, kind, and tempered. As she watched him his eyes slid up into the kitchen and caught hers. The smile changed, became more contained and focused. She wanted it to go back to what it had been a moment ago. She smiled back at him and then dropped her gaze to her food before looking around the room. When she looked back in his direction he was talking with the others again, but he had changed position so he could glance her way more easily.

She washed her plate, cup and fork and put them in the drying rack with the rest of the dishes. Then she joined the group forming in the living room.

She sat next to her father who was discussing commercialization with a small group. He felt her sit down and reflexively put a hand on her shoulder, and introduced her to the group. They were just beginning to ask her questions when a slightly stooped, white haired gentleman stood up in front of the fireplace and waited patiently for quiet.

When things had quieted down to where she could hear the fire hissing he began to speak.

"Thank you all for making the time to come today. I know many of you had items of concern that made it difficult to come, but some traditions are worth keeping, and I think this is one of them." He paused and looked around the room, then continued, "I think except for maybe Chris's daughter all of you knew Jacob, so there's no need for me to go over the facts and details of his life. He was as independent as they come. He was impatient which was both good and bad. I often disagreed with him, but he was right far more often than I'd like to admit. He loved his wife, and I'm sure it's a relief to him to be with her again. He loved his boy, and I'm sure he's proud of him today. He lived his religion for the most part, and though no one can ever say for sure, I think judgment will be a positive experience for him. Now, I've said enough. I'd like to hear your stories." Then he sat down.

There was an uncomfortable moment of silence and then Ellie's father got up and talked about how he first met Jacob, about the surveys of the area they had taken together as young couples just starting out, and the big plans Jacob and Norah had formulated and shared with them during those trips. Then he said, "I went through reports for the area a little before I came, and it's surprising how many of the things we talked about in tents and on long hikes they actually accomplished." Then he sat down.

Others spoke. One man shared a funny story of a misunderstanding that began with a miss-shipment of fifty kilos of dried peas and ended in a formal apology from the chairman of the senate foreign relations committee, "he never did get his dried peas though."

Another man told a story about the time they switched reports and turned them in to see if anyone would notice. "No one did." Chris got some razing on that one.

Someone else told about how he had hosted his family after a dam burst and undermined their station. The stories went on for a couple of hours.

When it seemed like everyone had said all they wanted, the old man got back up and thanked everyone, then he gestured to a table in the back corner and said, "I guess we'll make the pile on that table over there, if that's alright with you Jake." Jake nodded, the old man nodded back and everyone got up and started moving around. A few men went out into the driveway while others migrated back towards their rooms. A few pulled small packages from their pockets and put them on the table. "What are they doing?" Ellie whispered to her father. "They are bringing seeds from their stewardships, or other gifts, that they think will be useful to the new station steward." Ellie was silent. "Don't worry. I brought something that can be from both of us," he finished. "No, that's OK. I have something," she said and her father smiled as she went back to her room. When she returned and placed the small pouch of moss spores and instructions on the table, she saw many pouches and boxes of different sizes. None of them had tags, but many did have little notes in them, like hers. There were also some big bags of commodity items on the floor around the table including a fifty kilo bag of dried peas. After the pile was formed people stopped by and admired it. One man slapped Jake on the back and said, "There you go boy, it's just like Easter morning."

Men got to work in the kitchen working to some schedule of assignments Ellie couldn't find posted anywhere. She tried to help out, but they just stared at her until she got embarrassed and left them alone. Lunch was served on the lawn in front of the station. Ellie noticed some of the men had changed into heavy work boots and had their gloves stuffed into various pockets, so she took the clue and changed to match during lunch.

After lunch the old man waved everyone over and pulled Jake next to him. Then he said, "Now Jake is gonna tell you where you need to go." And Jake did. He split them up into three groups and set them to work on different projects. Hal showed up with an old battered truck and took one group up to work on a new oasis Jake wanted built around a pond. Another group set to work straitening up the maintenance yard and the herb garden, and Jake led the last and smallest group, with Ellie in it.

They stopped at the barns and picked up boards, posts, resin and tools. Then they went past the experimental plots and up a high ridge beyond it. Ellie recognized the trail they had taken earlier and saw that it deliberately skirted the ridge to avoid going over it. When she looked back at Jake, she saw him shift his attention from her to some of the others in the group before moving on. The ridge was higher than it looked.

Near the top, Jake paused while everyone caught their breath and then said, "I like the view from up here, but the ground gets awful cold.

I was thinking we could build some seats up there." He gestured to the highest point on the ridge.

"Are you sure you don't want to put it someplace higher?" one of the men said straight faced and the others smiled, shouldered their loads and made the final ascent.

At the top Ellie looked around. From that height she could see probably a third of the stewardship, the rest being blocked by mountains and the curvature of the world. To the north she could see little glints of light in the distance that might be the sea. Closer to the station, to the west, she could see undulating sloped hills grooved with canyons and pockmarked with little ponds disappearing into the distance with the road to town next to it. To the east the land became flatter, less wrinkled, and disappeared into the distance, and to the south she could see a small dot of a building with a mountain rising up several kilometers behind it. She didn't have to check a map to know what she was looking at. The others were quiet too for a moment, looking around.

Finally one of them said, "This will make a pretty good survey point."

"Yeah, better than flat old satellite images," another said.

Jake agreed with them and they got to work.

The post holes were the hardest, since the hill was mostly rock, but with everyone working within two hours a bench was installed. The resin they filled the holes with was supposed to be fast setting, but nobody wanted to test it until it had hardened overnight. They gathered their tools and moved towards the trail. By then the sun was lower in the sky and lighting the top of the mountain in the distance dramatically. Jake stood regarding it for a moment while the others looked around and pretended not to notice. Finally he said, "Let's go," and the whole troop starting working their way down the trail.

When they reached the station, the men who had been working in the yard were making dinner. The smell of it greeted them at the door, and they hurried to wash and change, then lounged around on the front lawn talking and waiting for the other group to come back. Ellie's father was with the other group so there was no natural place for Ellie to sit. Jake was apparently still changing or perhaps in the kitchen, but was nowhere to be seen outside. She contented herself to lean against the trunk of a cedar tree and watch the sun sink.

By the time Hal and the others arrived, the food was overdone, but no one cared. They invited Hal to join them for dinner. The conversation was light, the camaraderie real. When the meal was over and the dishes done, they all gathered unbidden in the main room and knelt. The white haired gentleman prayed then, thanking God for meaningful work to do, for having known Jacob, and sincerely asking that His blessings would be on the new steward.

After the prayer the group dispersed. Most went back to their rooms, but a few gathered their things and left to catch the late transport back to Olympia. Jake went out to say goodbye to them. Ellie sat in the great room near the fire. The house quieted. Ellie could hear the whine of a motor moving away and gravel crunching outside, then the door opened and closed. He paused behind the couch and waited a moment. She didn't turn.

"I'm glad you came," he said, then went to his room before Ellie remembered herself enough to respond.

Twenty-Two

The sound of a morning bird woke Ellie, but no light came through the eastern windows. It was still early. No morning bird would sing at that hour. She lay in bed for a while, pondering her situation in the morning clarity. Sleep did not return. She dressed and went outside. All was quiet and cool. The frogs and crickets had given up for the night. The air was still, the sea and the land no longer fighting for control of the wind.

She paused for a while on the porch and then looked in the direction of the ridge where she had worked yesterday. She began walking. Half way up the ridge the stars held her attention so much that she stumbled off the trail twice. At the top she looked over a vast sea of dark punctuated by a few dots of distant light.

She looked towards the bench and froze. There was a form on the bench. It did not move. The hair at the base of her scalp stood up. The form was indistinct in the starlight. It might have been a person. It might have been a rock. She stayed quiet and watched. There was no motion. She relaxed a little and moved more normally. When she did, the form moved. She froze, then took a step backwards.

"Ellie, it's OK," Jake's voice said calmly.

She threw a rock she found clutched in her hand in his general direction.

"You phage!" she said before closing the distance and sitting next to him.

"You scared the pants off me," she added.

"Come on. You of all people know I never commit felonies before breakfast. You're mostly safe."

She ignored him, looked back towards the trail and couldn't make out much of anything.

"What if it hadn't been me? What if it had been some crazy psychopath?" she asked.

"But it was you."

"Yes, but you didn't know that!"

"Yes I did."

"How could you? It's pitch black."

"Well, present company excepted, the only known psychopath in the area is afraid of the dark and locked in his room at this hour."

"Strangers sometimes come here. I was a stranger the last time I came here."

"True, but a stranger would have to have found this path... in the dark... right before dawn."

"It could happen."

"It could."

"How did you know?"

"Let's just say you have a little lighter step than most of the guys that come this way. Besides, I know the sound of your breathing."

She looked at him, relaxed back into the bench and looked up at the stars.

They were dense and sharp enough that as she stared into them she could begin to make out what looked like depth. She could imagine flying or swimming through them. She looked at Jake to regain a sense of orientation. He was looking at them too.

"So, are you really going to be the new steward here?" she asked.

"That's the plan. I applied for it, and all the other stewards say that if a son applies for his father's stewardship it's almost guaranteed... if he's qualified. They said they'd put a good word in for me."

"You're probably overqualified."

"I don't mind, if they don't."

"Is that really what you want, though?"

"I didn't think so before, but yes."

A faint slip of light lit the eastern sky just on the horizon. It wasn't much, but it was enough to see by. Jake was looking at her. His forehead was slightly wrinkled.

"What about you?" he asked. "Have you found your life's work?"

Ellie watched the sky turn a pale pink for a few seconds before the sun rose up over the lip of the horizon and began chasing it away. Now her forehead was wrinkled. She thought about the events of the last few weeks, about barley, strawberries, orchids, sugar beets, orange trees, and potatoes. She thought about her orchard. She thought about picnics, dinners, walks in the dark, and holding Titu's hand.

She looked back at Jake. His brow was smooth now. There were little creases at the edge of his eyes as he squinted to see her clearly against the rising sun. A lock of hair was hanging nearly in front of his eyes. She reached up and brushed it back into place with her fingers. He closed his eyes for a moment longer than a blink but then searched her face.

"Maybe, but it's too soon to be sure," she said.

He nodded, pressed his lips together and looked away toward the sea. When he looked back at her, his eyes were steady, looking through her into some distant time.

She watched him for a moment and then added, "Maybe not."

Twenty-Three

The old stewards were creatures of the morning and by habit somewhat impatient for first light, so the station was already stirring when Jake and Ellie arrived.

They were in time to get a quick breakfast going and greet everyone as they packed up gear and got ready to leave. They worked together on breakfast and this time no one bothered her about being in the kitchen. Seeing them together subtly changed the arithmetic about her from junior steward, and a girl, almost a guest, to something else.

When everyone was gone they worked on, cleaning things up, talking some, but mostly just working. In the middle of putting away glasses Ellie looked up, saw her father standing in the kitchen, and briefly wondered why he was there. Then she saw their bags in his hands and it came back to her. He hadn't said anything. He was just standing there watching them when she happened to look up.

"Better get going," he said softly and went in the direction of the front door.

Ellie put down the glasses and wiped her hands with a dish towel, then faced Jake to say goodbye. She awkwardly stuck out her hand and looked him in the eye. He eyed her hand suspiciously. He took it. He shook it rather formally, and then transferred it to his other hand and held it.

"I'll see you out," he said.

She adjusted her grip slightly, but did not let go.

When they reached her car, he asked, "When will I see you again?"

"I'll need a few weeks to get things settled down again. Then come see me in the valley."

Jake nodded.

Ellie closed the door and Jake watched the car disappear leaving a plume of dust behind it.

At the terminal, Chris and Ellie saw Hal picking up a package.

"Is Jake at home?" he asked when he saw them.

Ellie nodded.

"Good, he's got a letter I need to deliver to him," he said leadingly.

"From whom?" she replied.

"Well, I can't say, but it looks real official," he said and winked at her. They couldn't stay to talk. They were late and the transport had actually been waiting for them, but as she walked away she flashed him a big smile.

"That's a relief," her father said after they found their seats.

"What is?" asked Ellie.

"His letter is."

"I thought that was pretty much a sure thing."

"It should be, but some of the old stewards have been making a point of insisting on it, and that's exactly the wrong thing to do with my boss. One of them even came by the offices and made a bit of a ruckus about it. Ed's capable of turning him down just to make a point. I've been a little worried about it."

"Why didn't you tell me?"

"There was nothing you could do it about it. Besides, I didn't know you cared."

Ellie pressed her lips together. The last words stung. Her father looked at her, puzzled.

She put up a hand defensively and said, "No. You're right. I didn't care."

"But you care now?"

She blanched. "Yes, I care now!"

He chuckled, shook his head, and looked away.

"What?" she demanded.

"Nothing."

"What?"

"You've always cared, Ellie. You just didn't know you cared."

"That's ridiculous."

"Is it?"

"Yes," she said, but with little conviction.

Her father shrugged. "OK," he said and turned his attention to a book, but he was smirking.

"Stop it!" she said.

"Stop what? I'm just reading my book," he replied but his smile got bigger.

She looked out the window.

She watched the desert below her sliding away and imagined herself walking in it, but this time alone.

She imagined herself walking away from her smashed up rock crawler on her own, through the canyon, up past the pond to the wilderness hut alone. She imagined watching the meteors fall, and walking the next day through the morning mist to the station alone. In it, the landscape was flatter, the colors less luminous, the sounds less crisp than they were in her real memory. She imagined walking up to the station, asking to use a phone and Jake opening the door, helpful, but distant and a little sad.

That was probably the way it should have been. The way it might have been, if it had not rained. The thought left her cold. She tried to imagine how her life might have gone from there, but the images wouldn't form.

She looked around the cabin. It was clean, but a little worn. The people in it were getting older too. Her father had permanent wrinkles at the corners of his eyes and mouth.

She closed her eyes and breathed in but there was only the smell of plastic and dust. She relaxed and tried to sleep. She became aware that her father was fidgeting and opened her eyes. His face was tight. Finally he pulled out a small tablet and began fiddling with it. She frowned. They would be back at work soon enough, why start now?

He poked and prodded the device for a few minutes and then was still, reading something. He sat back into his chair, quiet, but not happy.

She watched him for a while, but he was lost in thought. She turned back to the window. She could feel the soreness in her back and arms from the previous day's work. She leaned her forehead against the window and closed her eyes again, willing the desert to come back into her mind, trying to remember it the way she always had before. But it was gone. At length she sat back and accepted the fact. As she did her mind wandered and she remembered Hal at the terminal and in her mind she followed him to his truck, down the dusty road to the station, and up to the door. He knocked. Jake opened the door. The diffuse morning light illuminated him. Hal handed him the package. He smiled and the desert came back to her.

The transport pitched and she opened her eyes. There was an over correction in the opposite direction, then a gentle nudge back into stable flight. She looked out the window and saw cloud cover below her rising up to meet the transport. They were descending. She looked at her father. He smiled weakly, tired. Rain started smattering the window in long streaks. She was gathering her thoughts and remembering where her bags were when her father said,

"He didn't get it."

"Who... what?"

"Jake. He didn't get the stewardship."

"But I saw Hal at the terminal..."

"That was the other kind of letter he was delivering."

She looked doubtful.

"I know what I'm talking about," her father said and held up his tablet.

Twenty-Four

Jake stood on the porch looking at the letter. Hal watched, quietly waiting. When Jake had read it a second time he put it back in its envelope, sat down on the steps and thought.

Hal sat down next to him. A lizard scurried in and out of the stones along the edge of the porch. After a while, Jake looked over at him and said, "Well, I guess I'm still unemployed."

"Anything I can do?" Hal replied.

"I may need some help moving. I have to have everything out in two weeks. Only problem is, I'm not exactly sure what's mine and what belongs to the station."

"Once you've got it figured out, let me know and I'll give you a hand. You can store whatever you want at my place. I've got room."

"Thanks."

"Anything else I can do?"

"Yeah, wait until tomorrow to let everyone know. I'd like to have a day to think it all through."

"You got it."

Hal put a hand on his shoulder, stood up, went to his truck, and drove away.

Jake let the quiet seep into him.

He stretched in the morning light and felt surprisingly good. The tasks he had set out for himself in the morning were now completely pointless, and so he was at leisure.

There were certain parts of the job he had never cared for, and in fact had run as far as he could to avoid. Now he wouldn't have to do them.

He went into the house and looked around. The "pile" was still where it had been built and he decided that it probably belonged to him. His parents' clothes and journals under the bed belonged to him. The pictures on the wall were probably his. His personal gear from school was certainly his. Beyond that, he wasn't sure.

He went outside and looked through the barns and sheds and decided that pretty much all the equipment belonged to the station.

He looked at the mountain in the distance, and briefly wondered who the body at its peak belonged to. He climbed the hill he had descended only a few hours before and looked over the whole area. He could see much of the path he and Ellie had taken weeks before. Those memories were his. "Ours," he corrected himself, and then looked doubtful. He looked again seeing the land around him the way he had imagined it being in the future and realized that future would never happen. It was not his future to plan. He let it go.

He took a long walk and when he returned, he went into his father's office, brushed aside the notes he had been making on water and humidity requirements for various trees and plants and opened his father's archives. Handling them, he decided that the records themselves belonged to the station, but the information was his inheritance. He duplicated all the digital records and uploaded them to his personal storage space. Next he set out imaging the paper files and uploading them.

The paper files were an odd collection. There were small sketches of dams and other structures, handmade graphs, and lists. The margins had one word reminders and even scraps of poetry scrawled on them, and Jake half suspected many of the sheets were kept more for the marginalia than for the contents. There were also a child's drawings, Jake's drawings, from when he was little. He moved them into his room.

He went through the expenses and found that his father had kept detailed records showing which purchases were for the station and which were personal.

"Look, I have furniture," he said out loud, when he found it had been bought as a wedding present for his mother. Further review showed he also had pots and pans, some small appliances that had been discarded *years ago, some old drapes, and the buggy he liked to drive around. His father had salvaged and restored it on his own time and expense. He also found that his mother had left him a small savings account that his father had not touched in all the *years since her death. He was not sure he wanted to touch it either.

At dinner he checked his mail and messages for the first time, dreading it. There was only a message from Ellie, saying "I just found out about your letter. Call me." He could tell by the look on her face that she knew what was in it. He didn't call.

In the evening, he called Hal and asked if he could come help him move things in the morning.

"Make it the day after tomorrow," Hal said.

"OK," Jake replied, then added, "Anybody figure it out yet?"

"Probably, I've had three people ask me if you got your letter and when I wouldn't tell them what you said about it, they got all quiet."

"OK. Thanks. See you in a couple of days."

He went to the living room and leaned back on the sofa to brainstorm possibilities. He fell asleep almost immediately.

In the morning he picked up where he left off, thinking about possibilities. He checked the Department stewardship postings, but the only post open in the last few weeks had been his father's and even that was now marked closed.

He called the Department to see if there was anything coming up. He got a polite but curt, "Nothing at this time," which was very different than the chatty reception he'd gotten before.

He filed an appeal of the decision, but with little hope. The Department had wide discretion in awarding stewardships, largely because they had little discretion in removing appointed stewards.

All that was left was the commercial market. He'd had an interview set up with Empaqueme for the week of his father's funeral, but had cancelled it. He gave them a call. They had filled the position, but asked him to come in anyway.

He was about to scan the general listings when he realized he hadn't packed anything. Hal had been right to put him off a day. He scrounged around in the barn and found some boxes. By evening, everything was packed, and he was at loose ends.

He toyed with answering the message from Ellie, flipping it around on the living room tablet and watching her face rebound off the edges of the screen. He almost pressed it to give her a call, but he hesitated. What if he had been wrong about her as well?

She didn't seem very interested in him. What if he was just a baby bird imprinting on the first things he saw after hatching? Attaching to a job, because it was there at a time he needed a job; attaching to an attractive woman, because it was well past time to be attached. Perhaps it was nothing more than that. He flicked the message one more time, just a little harder than before, watched it settle, then pressed it.

Twenty-Five

When Hal arrived the next morning he had reinforcements from church in tow.

"I thought you had a problem with the church," Jake said.

"No," said Hal scratching his chin, "I like the church OK. I have a problem with being in large groups of people. That's why I stay in the desert."

Jake didn't have much, so everything was packed and moved by noon. Hal had cleared out a section of a barn and things were actually pretty orderly.

Jake thanked everyone and then didn't know what to do with himself. He wandered around town for a while, but he kept running into people telling him how sorry they were, so he retreated to the station.

He paused at the porch and looked out across the landscape. He went to his closet, picked up his boots then put them back. He pulled out a paper journal instead, wrote a few notes, turned the page, and closed the book.

He looked through the job listings again, but it was a small world. Listing jobs was mostly a formality, because everyone who was qualified to do any advanced job generally knew about it from associates and was already known by those looking to fill the job. There was nothing to do but wait until there was an opening.

In the meantime, he had to find something to feed himself with.

"The idle shall not eat the bread nor wear the garments of the laborer," he recited to himself, and brought up the general laborer listings. It became clear that to work and keep any connection to the field he would have to go to the valley, or back to Olympia. Ellie and Empaqueme were in the valley. Most of his contacts were in Olympia.

When he discussed it with Ellie, she said, "I know people here that could probably give you some temporary work, and you could use my equipment to keep sharp. I actually have two sets of equipment so we could even work at the same time."

The Olympia option came together by the end of the next day. His old roommates hadn't found any one they could stand to take his spot yet. There was steady low level work available at the port and they were used to students coming and going. One of his professors had a little grant money and was eager to have him continue some of the work he'd been doing before he graduated.

Ellie wrote again and said a farmer in the area would give him work as a field hand with room and board as most of the pay, and offered again to let him use her equipment for projects.

The new steward arrived two days later. Jake heard the cab pull up and came out in time to see him pay the driver and get out of the cab. He was slightly younger than Jake and pale. He had only one bag, slung over his shoulder. He looked around at the place frowning until he saw Jake on the porch. He adjusted his bag and walked toward him.

They shook hands.

"You must be the new steward," Jake said.

The young man's eyes flicked down before meeting his, then he said, "Yes, Alex. You must be Mr. Billings."

"Call me Jake. Please come in."

Alex came in and stood awkwardly in the main room.

"Let me show you around," Jake offered.

Alex nodded.

Jake showed him around. Alex nodded whenever a response was required, but when they came to the master bedroom and he blurted out, "Where's the bed?"

"It's in storage. It's my personal property." Jake explained. "There's a bed in my old room and another in the office that you can use until you get your own, if you don't want to stay in one of the guest rooms."

Alex nodded, but he didn't seem to hear much during the rest of the tour.

Jake offered to make them dinner. Alex stared at him for a second, said, "Sure, that would be great," then flopped onto the sofa and started reading a magazine.

Jake tried to make conversation from the kitchen, but after the second short answer from Alex, he gave up and concentrated on making something to eat from the remaining supplies using the remaining cookware.

At dinner Jake decided to let Alex lead the discussion. Alex had nothing to say until he had eaten his first serving. Then he looked up and said, "That's not bad."

"Thanks," Jake said.

"I think I'll have a little more," he said as he spooned up a second helping.

After dinner, Alex put his dishes in the sink and went back to the living room. Jake took that as a signal to get down to business so, after putting away the food he followed Alex into the living room and sat down across from him.

Alex looked up from his article to see what Jake wanted.

Jake hesitated, then said, "I'm leaving tomorrow. Do you want to go over the status of the various projects now, or in the morning?"

Alex looked at him a little puzzled, and then said, "It's all in the reports, right?"

Jake said, "Mostly."

Alex shrugged and said, "Then I'll read the reports."

Jake rubbed his forehead and said, "OK."

Alex went back to his article and after a few minutes Jake got up, did the dishes and went to bed in one of the guest rooms.

In the morning, Jake waited for Alex almost an hour before finally making enough breakfast for both of them and leaving out the leftovers.

While he was waiting, he looked Alex up. He had a bachelor's degree in administration with a minor in xenobotany. He had decent grades all through school. He'd been assigned to Department headquarters for the last two *years since graduating. He hadn't published anything. There was no social buzz about him.

When Alex finally emerged at about 8:30, Jake sat down with him while he ate.

"So, what lead you to apply for a transfer out here?" Jake asked.

Alex looked at him and shrugged, but kept watching him.

"Got tired of reading reports, and wanted to get your hands on the real thing?" Jake offered.

"Yeah, something like that," Alex said and went back to eating.

After breakfast, Jake said, "Do you have any questions before I go?"

Alex thought for a second and said, "No, not really. I'll give you a call if I have any later."

Jake said goodbye, got into his rover, and drove towards town.

As he drove, he thought about Olympia and the valley and tried to decide which ticket he should buy. He finally concluded to decide at the ticket window, turned up some music, and drove much too fast.

Tighter grow vines through leaves
weaving closer tender trees
but trees can break when bent too far
or knit too fast
or pulled apart

Twenty-Six

The train slid into the depot. Jake stepped off and looked around. He saw a new enough truck waiting at the curb. The passenger window rolled down and Ellie's voice said, "Are you Mr. Billings?"

Jake smiled and said, "Yes, Ma'am!"

Ellie opened her door and came around to meet him. Stray light leaking through the canopy above lit her hair. He put his bags in the back and she gave him a hug.

In the truck on the way to the Alcantar ranch she said, "I'm afraid I may have brought you into the middle of a firestorm," she frown-smiled, waiting for his reaction. He watched her until she looked back at the road and continued. She frowned for real then. "It looks like I have another pathogen loose. This one is probably airborne. While I was gone and things were quieting down, one of the men from the university went through all the station's old mail and followed up on complaints of possible pathogens. I'd assumed they were irrigation problems, but they found something." She closed her eyes for a second and cleared her throat before looking at him.

"Have they already contacted the Department?" Jake asked.

"Yes. They tried to get a hold of me, but I had everything shut off and they weren't sure when I'd return. They sent the first report about an hour before I got back."

"How bad is it?"

"We don't know yet. They found it pretty entrenched in the

northern end of the district, and the genome looks bad but we're just getting everyone back to start surveying.

"How are you doing?"

She laughed. "Oh, I'm doing a great job! I've missed the signs of two blights and abandoned my post in the middle of it." She looked over, daring him to contradict her.

There was a loud, thud on the front right corner of the truck. Ellie pulled over. The truck was OK. There was a brown and white dog growing still on the side of road behind the truck. Ellie put one hand on a hip and covered her eyes with the other. A few cars passed. Jake could hear the cooling fan in the cab kick on. They walked down the shoulder of the road to the dog and looked at it. A breeze rippled its fur, but it wasn't breathing. It had a collar and a tag. Ellie read the tag and looked up the address while Jake put the dog in the back of the truck.

They made a U-turn and went back to a side road they had passed a moment before and up to a dirty little house with a pack of kids playing in the adjacent pasture. Some of the kids started chasing the truck on bikes. Jake hoped they weren't looking in the back of the truck.

When they pulled up, the front door opened and a short round middle-aged woman stood in the door expectantly.

"Let me do this," Jake said.

"No. This is mine to do," said Ellie.

They got out and Jake stayed back by the truck while Ellie approached and explained what had happened. The short woman followed Ellie over to the truck and peered into the bed with a hard look on her face. Then she turned to the assembled children and said,

"Well kids, it looks like this woman has killed Zipper. Leroy, go get your father."

"Why did you kill Zipper?!" one of the little girls wailed.

"I didn't mean to," Ellie said.

"I'll bet she did!" one of the middle boys said. "I'll bet she did it on purpose!"

"No, honest. I didn't even see him."

The mother, who had been studiously avoiding eye contact by studying the truck, suddenly noticed the Department logo on the truck and added,

"Yeah. I hear there are a lot of things you people don't see until it's too late."

Ellie blinked and opened her mouth, but the woman went on,

"You are going to pay for this dog. You should have been more careful. Don't you realize what that dog meant to these children? It's not like we have that much anyway, and you had to go and take that away."

Ellie opened her mouth again but the woman said, "Well, what do you have to say for yourself?" and folded her arms.

Ellie finally said, "I'm terribly sorry, and of course I will pay to replace the dog."

"How can you talk about replacing a member of the family?!" the woman said.

A girl started crying. One the boys started kicking the truck. Jake took him by the shoulders and moved him away from the truck. At that the woman started screaming, "Don't you touch my boy! Don't you touch my boy!" The older boys started moving in on Jake. Jake was just starting to take up a defensive position when he saw a tall man in work clothes moving towards him.

"What's going on!" he bellowed.

The boys backed off and waited.

The tall man looked at his wife.

"This woman ran over Zipper," she said.

The man flushed and said, "Is that all! Damn it woman, for all the fuss I thought it was one of the kids!"

"It easily could have been," said the woman.

Ellie opened her mouth, but Jake put a hand on her shoulder.

"Go inside!" the man said to the kids. "All of you!" he said, looking at his wife.

They went inside and he turned to face Jake and Ellie.

"So, where's the dog?"

Jake gestured with his head and they all looked into the bed of the truck.

"Figures," the tall man said, shaking his head.

"Where do you want him?" said Jake.

"In the barn."

Jake picked up the dog and followed the man into the barn.

When they got back the man looked calmer.

"How can I make this up to your family?" Ellie asked.

The man just shook his head. "That dumb dog was always chasing cars and darting across the road. I've almost hit it myself a couple of times. You don't owe us anything."

"I'd feel better if I could do something," Ellie said.

He thought for a second, looked at the truck and said,

"Just get this latest thing cleared up before they come to burn our trees and you'll have done more than replace a dog."

"I'll do everything I can think of," Ellie promised.

The man nodded. They shook hands, and Ellie and Jake left.

At the junction with the highway, Ellie hesitated, then turned the opposite way they'd been going earlier. Next she turned onto a back road. Ellie looked at Jake after the final turn. He was relaxed, looking out the window.

"Hungry?" Ellie asked.

"I could eat," Jake replied.

A few minutes later they pulled up to a gray squat adobe building and went in.

It was warm and dark inside. Ellie ordered without looking at the menu. Jake ordered at random from it.

After ordering Ellie closed her eyes and leaned back. Jake could hear the sounds of their meal being prepared in the back. Ellie furrowed her brow. Jake reached across the table and took one of her hands in both of his, rubbing the wrist with his thumbs. Ellie kept her eyes closed, exhaled, and relaxed her forehead. At length she opened her eyes and looked at him with a question on her face.

Jake let go of her hand and sat back. Ellie left her hand on the table for a second before slowly pulling it back to sit with her other hand.

"It's going to be OK," she said, but there was a hint of question in her voice.

Jake opened his mouth to answer, but the waitress arrived with food.

By the time they were finished eating, Ellie's spirits had recovered.

They piled into the truck. On the way Ellie looked over at Jake and said, "You're going to love Titu, your new boss."

"Good," replied Jake.

"He's smart, always helping people out, and they've got some interesting projects going," Ellie continued.

"Good," he said again, watching her more carefully.

They arrived at the Alcantar ranch in the early afternoon. The light was harsh and there was a whiff of chicken manure in the air as they pulled up in front of the small one story building across from the bunk house.

Titu came out of his office and smiled at Ellie.

"So, is this your friend?" Titu asked.

Ellie smiled back and performed the introductions.

"It's good to meet you," Titu said and playfully squeezed Jake's shoulder and bicep, appraising him. "Been behind a desk for a while?"

Jake nodded.

"Well, we'll whip you back into shape," Titu said, and slapped Jake on the back.

Ellie put her hand on Jake's shoulder and said, "Let me know when you're settled and we'll work out some lab time for you."

Jake nodded and Ellie left. When Jake looked back, Titu was watching him. He seemed to conclude a thought, smiled and led Jake to the bunk house.

"I think we'll put you on the afternoon shift, 2-10 p.m. We're a little shorthanded there."

"I appreciate the work," Jake said.

Titu introduced him to the foreman and then left him to unpack. Jake could see Titu and the foreman talking on the porch. Titu was giving instructions. The foreman was smiling. He glanced up at Jake, then turned his back to him.

Jake finished unpacking. The foreman came in, and said, "Ready to get started?"

"Ready enough," Jake said.

The foreman smiled and said, "Alright then."

Twenty-Seven

When Ellie arrived at the station she resumed going over reports from Paititi. The new blight had been identified. It was a mutation of Ewingella Marinera M3714, but the mutation was subtle, not the sort of thing that should make it virulent. They found the most infested area just 100 kilometers outside Paititi and so far the surveys hadn't found any sign of it as far south as the station but it had turned up half way in between. There was still a lot of survey work to do, but the area involved was huge, perhaps as much as a fifth of the productive land in the valley. The debate about how to handle it was already beginning, and was centered on burning the fifty acres most heavily affected and aerial dusting of copper hydroxide over most of the valley.

Ellie looked up from the reports and thought. True containment and eradication was unlikely. Not that they shouldn't try. Even if they only succeeded in keeping the spore counts lower or slowing the spread, it would help. This was shaping up to be a chronic problem to be managed. That idea wasn't expressed outright in the reports. To say it out loud before it was certain was politically foolish, but it was there between the lines. She remembered from her undergraduate survey classes that chronic problems were common on Earth, but here this was a first, and a lot of people weren't going to like it.

She began mulling over the possibility of adapting the trees to resist the blight, when a call came in. She didn't recognize the address. She answered it.

"Ms. Waddell?"

"Yes."

"This is Linda from records extraction."

"Yes."

"We are processing report EW109 concerning a problem with a new species of sugar beet and we need some information about the species."

"Go on."

"Ms. Waddell, my department is responsible for publishing all public domain species developed by the universities and public stewards. This new species doesn't appear to be in the Department's internal database. Are you the author of this species?"

"No."

"Do you know who the author is? We need to clear up ownership."

"My understanding is that the previous steward, Lou Ferris, developed it, but I'm not sure about the ownership. I suspect it belongs to the Alcantar ranch."

"Hold on a moment."

There was silence for a while, then a different voice came on.

"Ms. Waddell, this is Maria Jimenez. I work with Linda. I'd just like to clarify that the new unregistered species was developed by Lou Ferris, the previous steward, but is owned by the Alcantar Ranch. Is that correct?"

"I don't really know. I wasn't here when the species was developed. All I know is that the Alcantar family brought me a memory pearl with the species on it, said that Lou Ferris had helped them develop it, and that they needed help with it. I searched among the station records for a trace of it, but didn't find any."

"Ms. Waddell, would you be willing to submit a sworn affidavit describing the conversation you had with a representative of the Alcantar Ranch?"

"I guess so. What's going on?"

"We just need to determine whether or not this species should be in the public domain."

"OK. Just let me know what you need me to do."

"We would like you to write up a description of the conversation you had with the representative of the Alcantar Ranch and take it to the District Recorder's office. You will be placed under oath and asked to declare that the record submitted is a true account of your conversation. Also, we would like you to turn off all your systems. A technician will be contacting you shortly about examining your equipment. Can you do that?"

"Yes. I'll start right away."

"Thank you Ms. Waddell."

Ellie disconnected and starting shutting down systems. She furrowed her brow as she thought about the call. It seemed like a lot of fuss for a simple extraction to the public domain.

She wrote up her memory of the conversation with Titu and copied it into her watch. She started to stand, but then stopped and opened the Department directory.

"Maria Jimenez," she muttered as she typed and looked through the results.

Maria Jimenez didn't report to anyone in the Extraction group. In fact she was in second level management at the Department. She didn't manage the Extraction group.

"Hmmm," Ellie sighed, then looked at Jimenez's direct reports. She managed only five people. Ellie drilled down into the list and found that the five people included the head of the Audit group, the head of the Legal Affairs group, the head of the Regulatory Compliance group, the head of the Worker Safety group, and Linda, who was the head of the Records Extraction group.

Ellie closed the directory, and shut the system down. She sat there for a moment reflecting. "I guess it's only natural that on a difficult case the head of records extraction would bring her boss into the conversation," she said to herself. Then she left and went to the district recorder's office to swear out her affidavit.

On the way back from the recorder's office she got a call.

"Ms. Waddell?"

"Yes."

"Hi, I'm Ben Amaru. I'm the tech who will be coming out to your station to help you with your equipment."

"It's nice to meet you."

"Would you be available for me to stop by tomorrow morning?"

"Sure, I guess so."

"Would 9:00 a. m. be OK?"

"Sure."

"Great. I'll see you then. Oh, and Ms. Waddell, it's very important that you shut down all your systems and leave them shut down until I arrive."

"They are already shut down."

"Great, thanks."

Ellie puzzled over the conversation. She couldn't remember ever being able to get a tech on site in less than a week. Even remote support usually took a day to get.

She pulled over, put on her glasses, and clicked her way through to the Department directory. Ben Amaru did not work in system maintenance. He worked for the Audit Department as a forensics expert. Ellie leaned back in her chair, puffed out her cheeks and let the air go. Then she said out loud. "Great! I'm getting audited."

On a whim, she took the long way home and drove past the Alcantar Ranch. She didn't see Titu outside anywhere, and she hadn't really expected to. She saw someone about Jake's size shoveling something into a wheelbarrow behind the hen house, but that was fifty meters from the road, and he was wearing a hat and facing the other way so she wasn't sure. She needed to get home and find something to eat, so she sped up and went towards the station.

Twenty-Eight

Jake didn't have to wait long for his instructions. They were immediate and simple, and he thought he detected a particular satisfaction in the foreman's voice when he gave them.

"You need to clean all this crap up and put it in that pile out there," he said, pointing to pile of chicken manure just outside the hen house door. "The skip loader will pick it up in the morning and take it out to the composter. Any questions? "

Jake could see shovels, a wheel barrow, and brooms by the door so he said, "No. I got it."

"Good. And hose the place out when you're done."

Jake nodded and the foreman left.

The hen house was 100 meters long by ten meters wide, with rows of cages filled with chickens. The legs of the cages made it difficult to sweep. Jake found a push broom that was the right width to fit between the legs and began at the northeast corner of the building. He pushed the manure out from under the cages into the walkways until he had a whole section of cages cleared. Then he swept down the aisle until he had a large pile at the end of the section. Then it was time for the shovel and wheelbarrow. When he got done dumping the first load into the pile he went back inside and counted the sections.

"One down, 29 to go," he said and got back to work.

About half way through the barn, when his muscles were starting to complain, the wheelbarrow tipped over just before he got it to the pile. He paused, then loaded the crap back into the wheelbarrow, pushed it five meters and dumped it out. Just then he heard the dinner chime, so he stowed the equipment and made his way to the dining hall attached to the bunk house. He saw others drifting in about the same time. He got his food, considered what he must smell like, and sat off in the corner by himself. The food was good; canned peaches, mashed potatoes, chicken and chicken gravy. Halfway through a bite of chicken he noticed it smelled like chicken. His appetite dimmed some.

He saw the foreman come in and sit across from some men near the serving area. He looked up at Jake a couple of times while he was talking and the men smiled.

Then he waved at Jake and left.

After dinner, Jake realized that if he didn't pick up the pace he wouldn't finish before the end of the shift. He moved faster. By 9:45 p.m. the last load had been moved to the pile. He looked over his work. The chickens at the far end of the hen house had already covered the floor with a thin layer of manure. He remembered he was supposed to hose off the floor. He spotted the hoses with nozzles hung at intervals on both sides of the henhouse and the drain running down the middle. He grabbed the first nozzle and got to work. It was 10:45 before he got back to the bunkhouse, showered and went to bed. The lights were out and the other men were asleep. He manually keyed, "Long day. Talk to you tomorrow," to Ellie, and fell asleep.

Twenty-Nine

Ellie was still awake when Jake's message arrived. She smiled when she read it, imagining the day he must have had.

The stillness of night finally came and took away the whine and hum of a fruitless day. She had the window open a crack and heard the new leaves on her trees in the orchard shivering in the night wind, and that was soothing too. When she slept and dreams finally came, they were filled with colors and kites on the wind and the endless blue of the horizon over the North Sea. And when she awoke in the morning she knew that whatever came, she would be OK.

Jake awoke to the sound of the early shift dressing in the dark. He closed his eyes, and when he opened them again it was light out and there was a low rumble of activity outside. He got up. He showered again, mostly to try to bake away the stiffness in the hot water. He had missed breakfast. At 8:00 he gave Ellie a call.

"Have you eaten breakfast yet?" he asked.

"Yes. Did you want to come and make me some anyway?"

"Yes, but I don't have any food... or a way to get there."

"I'll come get you."

A few minutes later he was in the truck with Ellie. She told him about everything that had happened since she dropped him off, and he gave her a full report on the many aspects of chicken manure. He could smell her hair and lotion. He smiled and she said, "What?"

"Nothing."

"What?"

"I was just thinking that you smell a lot better than chicken crap."

Ellie considered this for a moment and then said, "Thank you."

At the station, they made breakfast together, and were just finishing when Ben Amaru arrived in a white motor pool van, obviously tired. After introductions were made, he set to work with Ellie shadowing him. Jake washed dishes. Ellie showed Ben her systems and Ben nodded until they got to the new sequencers and analyzers. He hadn't expected those.

"Right," he said after a second. "So, we are going to swap out all your equipment, except for this newer equipment. We'll figure out what to do with that in a few minutes."

They trudged back and forth through the kitchen lugging gear for a while and then Ellie and Ben got the replacement systems up and working. Finally Ben turned around, looked at the new equipment, bit his lip for a moment and started opening access panels on them. He looked inside for a while, looked up something on his watch, and finally said, "I don't have any pearls that will fit these units. Can you live without them for a couple of weeks?"

Ellie looked back at the old equipment and replied, "I'd rather not."

Ben thought for a minute, looked back inside the access panel, went to his van, and came back with two clunky boxes and a bag of connectors.

"If you can stand the appearance, I think I can get these working for you."

"I don't care how they look," Ellie said.

Ben smiled and got to work. He removed pearl readers from both systems, leaving the pearls inside them. Then he hooked a jumper from each system to one of the clunky boxes. He took pictures of the serial numbers of each system, and turned the systems on. Ellie made a few test runs and they worked, though they were noticeably slower.

"I'll get these back to you as soon as I can," Ben said.

She walked him out to his van and watched him drive away.

Back inside, Jake was drying his hands in a spotless kitchen. Ellie made a show of running her finger over the counter top and examining her finger tip. "Not bad," she said. Jake nodded and Ellie said, "So what do you want to do to keep your skills up?"

"Let's start with the most pressing problem," he said, "tell me the latest on your blight."

Ellie pulled up the newest reports and they reviewed them together.

"I was thinking, we're not really going to be able to contain this," Ellie said. "Maybe we can slow it down, or lessen the severity, but we aren't going to stop it."

"I agree. We caught it too late. So, if we can't stop it, what do we do?" said Jake.

"Well, if you can't survive the way you are, you have to adapt. So, we're going to have to adapt the trees to the new situation."

"Not just the trees," Jake said, "We're going to have to adjust everything that could be affected by the blight. Do we have a list of affected species?"

"No. So far the field surveys have been looking at trees because it was first found there. At this point they are just trying to figure out how far it's spread."

"Which trees have been mentioned so far?"

They pulled up the reports and skimmed them to get the names of all the trees it had been found in. There were eight species.

"Some of these trees are in different families from each other," Jake said as they looked over their list. "This blight doesn't seem very picky."

"Let's see if we can project anything from its predicted metabolism," Ellie said.

Jake nodded and they moved into the lab, reloaded the genome into the species simulator and drilled down into the metabolic modeling.

"Looks like it likes cellulose for lunch," Ellie said.

"Yeah. It looks like it would be fairly resilient to most toxins plants would use to defend themselves. Run some simulations trying natural compounds in the database under normal conditions."

Ellie started setting up the simulation. She left the environmental conditions at their normal defaults and was about to run the simulation when Jake put his hand on hers.

"Wait," he said. "You need to change the environmental to current conditions."

Ellie looked at him funny. "They're at normal."

"Look again," Jake said.

Ellie went through the parameters one by one. "I don't see anything. These are the parameters we always use, unless we're making something special for a specific region."

"Those default settings are from 14 *years ago. We switched to new default settings at Olympia when I was a freshman."

"Have they really changed that much?" Ellie said.

"We have dumped billions of metric tons of ice, carbon, ammonia, and trace elements from asteroids into the atmosphere over the last 14 *years. If it hasn't changed anything our tax dollars have been seriously wasted," Jake replied.

Ellie did a quick search of academic databases and got conflicting answers on environmental conditions. She flipped over to meteorological records and found a steady increase in temperature, humidity, and pressure over 14 *years.

"Come on," Jake said, and took her by the hand. They went outside. He fiddled with his watch until he had it in the mode he wanted, took it off and held it away from him by the strap. After a few seconds it glowed briefly. He touched it and then held it out again until it glowed.

"Now you do it," Jake said.

Ellie took off her watch and set it to monitor atmospheric conditions, but hers beeped when it had a sample. They each took several samples then went inside and compared results.

"The average is 702 millibars pressure, twenty-two degrees Celsius, and 20% humidity."

Ellie changed the fields in the environmental conditions screen from 625 millibars to 702 millibars.

"That's going to change the dew point a fair amount."

They ran the simulations. The blight was not predicted to be affected by natural plant toxins much. Out of curiosity, Ellie ran the simulations again with the old default settings, but the results were the same.

"So our little error doesn't affect the results," Ellie said.

"No, I guess not. But you should fix it anyway. You're building to the wrong standard."

Jake's watch jiggled. He looked down. "I have to go to work!"

Ellie gave him a ride.

Jake had just enough time to change before the foreman arrived to give him instructions. He had missed lunch.

"Cutting it a little close," the foreman said.

"Yep. But I'm ready."

"All right. You handled the hen house OK, so I want you to take over doing that once every three days. In the meantime, follow me."

The foreman drove him over to another property with a barn on it.

"This is the pharmaceutical goat shed. These goats are kind of touchy, so you have to keep their stalls clean and supplied with hay, you have to be quiet around them, and you have to make sure you only use the hay in that shed over there. If you use any other hay you could affect the quality of the drugs they are making. Understood?"

"Understood."

"All right. Here's your dinner," he said handing him a large sack. "I'll be back for you at the end of the shift. If you have any questions, give me a call."

Jake looked at the goat shed. It was 100 meters by ten meters.

"Is everything standardized?" he wondered and got to work.

Jake liked the goats. He had to keep an eye on them though, because they tried to eat his shirt tails whenever he wasn't watching.

"Careful," he said to one goat that was extra persistent. "We don't want someone's grandpa getting a shot of my shirt."

He stopped to eat about the time they started taking the goats to be milked. He wanted to keep working because it was easier to clean the stalls when they weren't in them, but he was just too hungry.

While he was eating his mind wandered onto the milking. He imagined them being milked the old fashioned way with a pail and two hands, even though he knew they used milking machines. He pictured the milk in the bottom of the pail and he wondered how long it would take to evaporate. As he turned the problem over in his mind, he got stuck working out the density of goat's milk compared to water. Finally, he shook his head and said, "Well anyway, it evaporates a lot slower now than it did 14 *years ago." He shook his head, and froze.

He looked at the shade trees growing by what had been the farm house. He looked at the fields of sprouting hay, and grain. He looked at the pond and the plants growing around it. Then he laughed and called Ellie.

Thirty

Jake managed to get up in time for breakfast, but just barely. He threw on his clothes and ran. He sat down to eat.

One of the men closest to him said, "Do I smell goat?"

"Goats!" his neighbor said and waved a hand in front of his face. Then they laughed.

Jake chuckled along with them. He'd showered before going to bed, but he'd thrown on yesterday's clothes, so he did stink like goats. When they saw him chuckling they waved him over.

"Come on, you can sit with us crap boy."

He moved over next to them and continued eating.

"So, I hear you're some kind of professor that can't find a job, so you're down here shoveling crap for us. That right?"

Jake nodded, "Yeah, pretty much."

The man looked around the table smiling and said, "Now isn't that something." There were nods of appreciation all around.

One of the other men asked, "What's your name?"

"Jake. What's yours?"

"Sam."

"Pleased to meet you."

"Yeah, Sam's pleased to meet you too," said the first man, "Really pleased. Sam's our previous crap boy." Everyone laughed at that.

Jake finished eating, glanced at his watch, and said, "Well it's been fun," and stood up to go.

"Where are you off to in such a hurry?" the first man said. "You got a date or something?"

"Or something," Jake said.

In the shower, he watched the water drip off his hand for a minute and laughed again. Then he threw on clean clothes and called Ellie. Fifteen minutes later he was sitting in the truck with her.

"So you're not making breakfast for me this morning?"

"Nope. If I keep making breakfast for you, I'm going to put you in the poor house."

"I doubt it," Ellie said flatly. Jake shrugged then smiled.

At the station they got straight to business. Ellie pulled up several note pads she'd been sketching on and showed them to Jake.

"Ever since you called I've been going through every species I could. None of them have been engineered to today's environment, and the soil microbes are the worst, because they were first. No soil, no plants. The soil microbes were engineered for an atmospheric pressure of 400-450 millibars with soil moisture at half of today's levels."

Jake sat back, thinking about the implications.

Ellie continued, "So, even if we somehow contained the two current blights, there's no telling how other soil dwellers might adapt. There are over seventy engineered microbes, let alone those that have arisen from them."

Jake thought some more about it.

"It's worse than that," he finally said. "Even if there were no more blights, productivity is going to drop. The plants are going to be unhealthy and then normal decomposers will start working on them. It will be worst for the food crops because they've given up a lot of variability to increase yields. Just as bad, the behavior of the community of soil microbes is going to change unpredictably. Some microbes may make the aerobic/anaerobic switch..."

"It's already happened!" interrupted Ellie. "I saw that at a sugar beet farm last month."

"Then we've got a problem."

"Yeah," agreed Ellie.

They sat around the table in silence for a full minute thinking about the possible consequences, listening to the sound of traffic on the road outside.

Finally they looked at each other. "We've got to write this up and get this out to the whole Department," said Ellie.

"Let's do it," said Jake.

By the time Jake had to leave for work, they had the basic form of the paper written and all the supporting information stuffed in at the right places.

"I'll work on it some more tonight, and we can send it out tomorrow," Ellie said.

Ellie dropped him off at work and he changed into his work clothes.

The foreman was waiting for him when he came out of the bunk house.

"What flavor of crap do you have for me today?" he asked the foreman with a smile.

He saw a half smile cross the foreman's face. "The crap will have to wait until tomorrow. We've got something different for you today."

Jake raised his eyebrows.

"Follow me," the foreman said.

Five minutes later he was seated in a planning room adjacent to Titu's office. Titu was already there looking over documents. The foreman started to leave.

"No. Stay, Robert. I think we'll need you in on this as well," Titu said.

The foreman sat two seats over from Jake.

Titu brought up a satellite image of a farm and orchard with basic statistics displayed in the corner. "It looks like we'll be getting another long term contract to manage a public farm. If all goes well, everything should be signed within a few days."

He touched one of the statistics which brought up an entire report.

"The contract terms are such that most of our profit comes from net revenue and production above the current level, so we'll need to improve both quickly. We should see some immediate improvement due to lower fixed operating costs, but we're also going to need to improve yield, improve management, and change the mix of crops to higher demand items, and that's where you gentlemen come in."

He switched back to the satellite view. "Robert, we're planning to put the green house operations in the current barnyard and garden area, tear down the existing out buildings except for the main barn, shut down the domestic livestock operation, and convert the barn to equipment storage and maintenance. The green house will be 100 meters by ten meters. We'll be scaling up the experimental strawberry project from Greenhouse A by ten times and housing it there along with some regular strawberries."

He touched a different statistic and the farm's water and power supply figures came up. "It looks like we have sufficient water for the greenhouse operations, but it will leave us a little lean for the orchard. Looks like we are short on power, too. Any thoughts?"

The foreman spoke up. "Well, we can bring in some standard arrays and put them up on the barn to bring up power production... May I?" he said, gesturing at the display. Titu nodded.

He looked at the satellite for a minute, zoomed in on a section, switched to a topology map, switched to a geology map. "We'll have to go verify this on site, but I'd take this section out of production and build a rain water catchment dam. We can dig it deep and float balls on it to cut down on evaporation. We'll lose about 2 % of production initially but it'll give us the water we need. What's the irrigation system look like?"

"Check the third item down."

The foreman touched the third item and the farm inventory came up. The foreman shook his head. "That thing is 15 *years old and it wasn't the most efficient even then. There'll be some savings there. We might not even need the pond if you recirculate some of the green house water. It'll depend a lot on crop selection."

"Thanks Robert. Jake, what do you think about crop selection?"

Jake hesitated. "May I?" he said, gesturing to the display. Titu and the foreman nodded. Jake went back through the geology reports, production numbers, varieties planted and age of plants. Then he switched to his watch and glasses and combed through commodity prices and projected yields. There he paused. Titu and his foreman exchanged glances. Robert looked at the ceiling. Titu looked at the floor. Finally Jake said, "Clearly peaches aren't very profitable at average prices over the last five *years. The land will support pretty much anything grown in the valley. You could safely add this small parcel to your existing apple production; pears would be OK too. If you want to go for a new market and take more risk you might try blueberries. There is very little competition." Titu was paying more attention now. "But, I'd leave it in peaches this year. This blight has changed things. There is so much uncertainty that I wouldn't make any investments in new plants this year." Titu looked at the floor and absently drew a figure 8 with his finger on the desktop. When he finally looked up he seemed a little disappointed. "The peaches have to go. We'll give the blueberry idea a look. Thank you." Titu nodded at the foreman.

Jake and the foreman stepped out on the porch.

"What'd I do wrong?" Jake asked.

"Nothing. You're probably right. But you need to be right faster..." The foreman looked over the yard for a moment, looked at Jake, and added, "You might want to compare the Alcantars' current peach production with demand." Then Jake thought he saw him wink before he said loudly, "Come on. I've got some hogs for you to meet."

Thirty-One

Titu sat at his office desk, flipping through images of the new farm absently. He looked through what little data there was on blueberry sales. He checked the price of starter plants, then found himself looking at the Department org chart and Ellie's picture. He looked at the clock. It was after 4:00 p.m. He should call his distributors and see what they thought of blueberries. He should discuss it all with his parents, but it could wait.

He drove to the station. From the porch he could see Ellie working at her desk in the back room. He raised his hand to knock, but waited watching her. She never glanced up. Titu tried to remember being passionate about his work, but could only remember being energetic, being pleased with good results. He knocked. She looked up, distracted. She smiled as she came to the door. Was it a smile of friendship? Courtesy? Joy? Flattery?

It wasn't flattery. She was at the door.

"Looks like you're busy," Titu said.

"Actually, I really am," she said.

Titu waited to see if she would add anything.

"Did you have a quick question I could answer?"

"Yes, two really. First, I've got some new land to develop and I was considering putting it in blueberries. What do you think?"

Ellie thought it over. "I think it's a good idea. They'll grow fine. People seem to like them. It would diversify away from the big ten crops. When were you planning to do it?"

"Right away."

"I'd wait a year," she said.

"Why?"

Ellie hesitated. "I think there will be better varieties out in a year."

"Could I get an improved variety sooner?"

"Probably not. Our response to this blight will be putting every-thing on hold."

"What aren't you telling me?"

Ellie shifted her weight and looked away before answering,

"Things that haven't been confirmed yet." She looked firm.

"So what is your second question?"

"Are you busy for dinner?"

Ellie hesitated.

Titu looked down and raised a hand to wave away the offer.

"It's alright," he said smiling.

"No. I could make it to dinner. It would just have to be a late dinner. I have to finish a few things."

"8:30?"

"8:30."

"I'll pick you up."

When he picked her up she had changed into a dress. They went to a restaurant on the far side of town, not far from the dress shop. Ellie thought of the shimmering dress she'd bought there and briefly won-dered if she should have worn that. The restaurant was set back off the road in a clump of trees. It was dimly lit. They were shown to a table immediately. There were candles on each table. The room had carved wood and clean, well-executed lines. They ordered. Ellie relaxed into her chair. She looked around and thought, "I could get used to this."

She looked at Titu. He had a handsome face, warm brown eyes, high cheeks, finely chiseled mouth and perfect black hair. He smiled at her and she looked away, but when she looked back he was still looking at her, confidently, giving confidence.

They ate. The food was perfect. Ellie talked about her school days. Titu told a story about getting lost in Paititi on one of his father's business trips. Before she was aware of it, it was 10:30. The dishes were cleared. No bill arrived. Titu suggested they take a walk on the patio. When they went out, the patio was filled with the fragrance of orchids. Ellie looked around and saw them lining the walls. She smiled.

"Our first customer," Titu said smiling. Music was playing softly from hidden speakers.

"Do you dance?" Titu asked. Ellie nodded, and they danced slowly. She rested her head on his shoulder, caught herself, looked at him, and kept dancing.

After a while Titu said, "Let's walk in the garden," and led her onto a path. "I'd like to make you an offer," he said. Ellie was quiet. "I'd like you to become a partner at the Alcantar Ranches. You would be a 5% owner. We need someone with your skills and I personally would enjoy seeing you every day."

Ellie remained quiet, thinking about the possibilities.

"If you feel that you've found your life's work at the Department, I completely understand and we can figure out something else, but..."

She looked him in the eyes. "This is sudden," she said. "I need to think about it. Can I give you my answer tomorrow night?"

Titu smiled, "Of course."

They walked on in silence for a while before he took her home.

Thirty-Two

When Jake got up he still smelled like a hog. He had showered for twenty minutes before going to bed but it wasn't enough. He showered again and resorted to cologne.

He arrived in the dining hall just in time for breakfast. When he sat down with the others the red faced one said, "Pig boy smells pretty this morning. I'll bet he's got a date with that brunette who's always picking him up." One of the other others picked up on the thread. "Yeah pig boy; has that pickup got a nice bed on it?" Jake casually got up, smashed the man's face into his potatoes, held him there for a second, let him go and said, "Looks like you got something on your face." He walked out and sat on the porch. The men came out later, looked at him, and went off to work without saying anything. He called Ellie.

While he waited, he looked up the peach production numbers. The Alcantars had been increasing peach production over the previous two and a half *years even though prices had been steadily falling for three *years. Prices were so low he couldn't see how they were making any profit on it. Next he looked at the percentage of production each grower had and found that the number of peach producers had dropped 70% over the past three and half *years. The Alcantars were now one of just eleven peach producers left. Four, including the Alcantars, were large operations. Well, soon there would only be ten. "No wonder," he said out loud and looked up to see Ellie's truck pulling in.

Ellie wrinkled her nose and rolled down the window when he got into the truck. There wasn't much conversation on the way to the station. Ellie was distracted and distant. By lunch time their joint paper was done and transmitted. Ellie had done most of the work the day before.

She threw together an indifferent lunch and invited him to share it. When he sat down next to her she moved to the far side of the table. "You seriously smell bad," she said.

They finished eating and he cleaned up the dishes. When he came back to her she was staring out the window, absently fingering a locket. They sat in silence for a while. Finally he said, "Are you OK?" She looked at him, startled, and then her face softened as comprehension settled in.

"Yes. I'm fine. I just have to make a big decision today."

Jake stayed quiet but tilted his head.

"I got a great job offer yesterday."

"If it's great, why haven't you taken it already?"

"I should. I probably will. I just need to think it through," she said, and frowned.

"I don't think you really want it."

"Maybe you just don't want me to want it," she countered, staring at him defiantly.

"I don't even know what it is!" he said, speaking distinctly and raising his voice a little.

"If you don't know anything about it, then what makes you think you could have anything to say about it?"

"Because I know you!" he said.

"Look Jake. You're a nice enough boy, and I like you, but you really don't know me."

"I think I do."

"That must be nice," she said curtly and stopped talking.

Jake was looking out the window. "I think I should get going. Thanks for lunch."

"I'll give you a ride," she said, softening.

"That's OK," he said, "It's not that far."

Outside, Jake enjoyed feeling his legs moving under him, taking him away from the station. About half way from the station to the ranch he heard a truck slow down and stop next to him. He looked up and saw Titu smiling at him.

"Need a ride?"

Jake considered his options, nodded and climbed in.

Titu didn't say anything for a while, but it seemed to Jake that he was driving slower than necessary. Finally Titu chuckled and said, "You have the look of a man with girl problems."

Jake just looked out the front window.

That was all the confirmation Titu needed and he chuckled again. "Yeah, I've sat in your seat a few times..."

Jake looked at him out of the corner of his eye but let the awkward silence stand. He could see the gate to the ranch ahead and saw relief coming. Titu drove, if anything, slower.

"Look. I know you don't want to talk about it, and I don't blame you. But let me just say this: you can't blame the girl for not wanting the future you're offering right now. I mean, you live in a bunk house and clean pens for a living. Maybe you need to put your focus on changing that before you go after the girl."

They pulled up to the bunk house. Jake said, "Thanks for the ride," and hopped out. After he'd changed into his work clothes, the foreman said, "It's chicken day again." Jake nodded and walked towards the hen house.

Thirty-Three

Ellie refused to watch Jake go, but once he was gone the station was too quiet.

She went to her desk, sat, and drew up a pro/con chart for taking the Alcantar job.

There were plenty of "pros." A five percent stake was valuable. The projects were interesting. There was enough funding to do things right. There would be fewer interruptions.

"The con's," she said, thought for a moment and then threw the chart away.

She thought back to when Titu made the offer, trying to remember the details. Five percent ownership, orchids, candle light, dancing, romantic walks. A strange business deal indeed. It was more of a proposal, except it wasn't. But the implication was there. Wasn't it?

"The question is really 'do I want to be an Alcantar, partially now, perhaps fully later?'"

"But what if I worked there five *years and he never actually proposed?"

"What if he did propose?"

A call came in. She looked at the address.

"Hello Cava."

"Hello Ellie. Did I catch you day dreaming about your two boyfriends or writing another paper that upsets absolutely everyone?"

Ellie hung up.

Cava called back and Ellie looked at the display trying to decide whether or not to answer.

She was about to answer when it went to mail. When the message came in, it just said, "Call me."

She selected "Return call."

Cava answered.

"I'm sorry," Ellie said, "It's just not a good time to be yanking me around."

"Was it the boyfriends crack, or the paper?"

"Both."

"I'm sorry about the boyfriends, but you deserve it on the paper."

"What? Was there something wrong with it?"

"Well other than that you're predicting the end of the world and nobody can find anything wrong with it, it's great. Ellie, I'm getting panicked calls from people hoping I can tell them you're crazy."

"Am I?"

"No! That's what really scares them."

"Maybe I am."

"Now we're back to boyfriends, aren't we?"

"I don't know."

"Did Titu make his move?"

"What do you mean?"

"I mean did Titu make you a vague promise of a perfect life that was a little short on actual commitment?"

"Why... why would you say that?"

"Oh, honey, I've been trying to tell you. You wouldn't be the first he's done that to."

There was silence.

"I... I need to go."

"Ellie, if you need me, call me. I don't care what time."

"I understand. Thank you."

Ellie sat quietly. "Cava is my friend," she said out loud, "but Cava can be wrong."

She looked down and shook her head.

Others called about the paper. Her face sagged answering the same questions over and over. She almost called Jake to get him to take some of the calls, but he was probably covered in some sort of fecal matter and probably not speaking to her.

When 5:30 p.m. rolled around she heard Titu's feet on the porch. She switched her presence to unavailable and answered the door. Titu was dressed in his casual but nothing out of place outfit. She let him in and they sat at the kitchen table.

There was an awkward silence after they sat.

"Did you have a chance to consider my offer?" he asked softly.

"Yes, I did."

Titu chuckled softly at her tone. "Well I guess I know your answer," he said.

Then looked her in the eyes and said, "Is there anything I can say to change your mind?"

Ellie thought for a moment then said, "Couldn't you even let me say it?"

"Say it."

"After careful consideration I'm afraid I can't accept your offer... you ass!"

Titu started laughing.

Ellie stood speechless.

"I told my mother you would never accept such an offer. I told her you were too sharp for that."

"What has your mother got to do with this?"

"Look, my parents never, and I mean never, tell me what to do. They don't even try, but where the business is concerned they know everything that I do."

"So, this is business then," Ellie said.

"Ellie, in one way or another, everything is business, but this is honestly something more."

"What is this?"

"Ellie, I'm willing to up my offer from 5% to 25%, half my share, with no vesting period and only one condition."

Ellie was silent.

"The condition is that you will marry me."

He lifted his hand off the table and his mother's ancient wedding ring sat on the table.

Thirty-Four

After Titu left and the room was quiet again, Ellie could feel her pulse beating. She went to bed, but didn't sleep. What answer should she give? She closed her eyes and pictured their picnic on the hill; saw Titu alone in his office. There were ways she could help him grow to his potential, be happier. She could help the business as well. It would be an interesting life. Being an Alcantar had its privileges.

"Do I love Titu?" she said into the darkness. She saw his warm eyes and strong hands. She could smell his skin and feel his arms around her as they danced, and these were good feelings.

She wondered what Jake would say she should do, but how could she even ask?

She got up, threw on some clothes and went into her orchard to walk and listen to leaves rustle and young frogs calling out for companionship. The breeze felt good on her face. She decided she could imagine a life as Titu's wife and actual partner. She could use the wealth and influence of his family to help people and Titu would approve. They already helped their neighbors.

She sat and looked at the stars twinkling in the cooling night and felt calm.

She found a quiet place and knelt and told the Lord about her decision and asked if it was right. There was no real answer but an amused assurance that she would know.

"I need more time," she said, but she knew Titu well enough to know he wouldn't wait forever.

She went back to bed and looked at the ceiling. After fifteen minutes she called her father. He was in his car coming back from the Temple. He pulled over and asked, "Is everything OK?"

"I don't know what to do."

"Is this about your paper? I haven't read it yet."

"No. Titu asked me to marry him."

"Do you love him?"

"Yes, I think so."

"Do you respect him?"

"Yes."

"Is he kind to you?"

"Yes."

"Is he kind to his family?"

"Yes."

"Is he kind to those he has power over?"

"Yes."

"Does he love God and obey His commandments?"

"I think so."

"Do you want to be a better person when you are with him?"

"I guess so."

"When you're pregnant, nauseous, unemployed, and broke at 3:00 a.m. with ten loads of dirty laundry, is he the man you want standing by you?"

"That's not easy to imagine."

"Well, get some sleep. We can talk more about it in the morning."

And she did sleep.

Thirty-Five

Jake woke early and walked through the fields away from the bunk house. He walked steadily, not pausing much and after half an hour he looked around; noticing the landmarks and seeing what he had been walking through. He breathed in the air and let it go. He recognized a small mesa shaped hill in the distance and wondered if he wasn't walking into the satellite photo he had seen two days before. He walked in that direction and found himself in a peach orchard. He looked at the trees as if he had never seen them before, the knowledge that they would probably be gone soon flickering behind his eyes.

When he reached the hill, he climbed it and looked over the land, and it was the land he had seen, but real. He turned and started to descend when a call came in.

"Hi Steve," he said.

"Hello Jake. We still don't have any openings, but if you can come by tomorrow, we'd like to talk about a possible opening in a few months. Would that work?"

"Absolutely. What time?" said Jake.

"How about 9:00 A.M.?"

"I'll see you then."

Jake closed the call, and rubbed the bridge of his nose. He turned to descend again, when he heard shouting from below the hill. In fact a man was yelling at him. The words were indistinct, except for "Get down here!" repeated at intervals. The man looked a bit unsteady. At length the man swore softly and quieted down. Jake climbed down and approached him.

"You one of Alcantar's men?"

"Yes."

The answer seemed to surprise the man and he stumbled over his next few words but finally got out, "He sent you to spy on me!"

"No, I just got tired of the smell of the hen house and went for a walk."

"The hell you did. Don't lie to me. You know he sent you. Do you get paid extra or is this your regular work?"

"He didn't send me. I just needed to get away from work. I'm sorry I intruded."

"Admit it! You're part of his planning team to take over."

Jake realized with a start that he was part of the planning team to take over.

The man saw the hesitation.

"I knew it. You get the hell off my property. You hear me!? Get, and tell Alcantar I'll shoot the next man he sends in here. You got that? Answer me!"

Jake did not answer. He simply started walking in the direction he had come with the man trailing slowly after him shouting. When he had left the man behind and gotten clear of the property, he stopped. He looked in the direction of the Alcantar ranch and exhaled sharply. He turned and walked north instead toward what he expected would be the main road. He thought of home as he walked, and pictured the wide open country where you could walk for days and not encounter anyone to yell at you. He considered making a break for it and just going home. They could deny him the stewardship of the land, but not the joy of walking it. He started to reflexively lay out the logistics. He could probably stay with Hal for a while and save up until he had enough money for equipment to freelance... but while thinking on it he hit the road and had to decide which way to go.

He realized that he was only about 100 meters from Ellie's station.

The pull of the hills seemed even stronger. He checked the time, shrugged it off, and began walking towards the station.

Ellie had been up since dawn. She enjoyed the quiet and for a half hour she did not think about her situation. "Why is this a 'situation'?" she asked herself when she did think of it. She didn't answer. She decided that if she stopped thinking about it for a while, then maybe she wouldn't get so tangled up in the loops of her own thoughts and the answer might come to her. She left her status as unavailable and worked on some of the backlog of ordinary station work she had neglected in the emergency. As she did, her pace quickened and she caught herself smiling. She had finished off several of the more pressing items when she heard a knock at the door. She looked out and saw Jake standing there. He looked tired. She remembered the previous day and winced a little. He had not meant to offend her, no matter how high handed he might have been.

She let him in. Their greetings were awkward. After a moment of silence, Jake said, "Are you OK?"

Ellie's eyes filled with tears, and she felt her head shaking no. Jake stepped closer and held her close for a long time until she stopped crying.

They sat down in the kitchen and Ellie told him everything and ended by saying, "I don't know what to do." And then cried again briefly, and looked embarrassed.

Jake took her hand in both of his and rubbed her wrist softly with his thumbs while he thought. He looked up from his thoughts into her eyes.

"Ellie I love you, so I want you to be happy. You know that or you wouldn't be telling me about this. If marrying Titu will make you the happiest, best Ellie you can be, I want you to do it. I have doubts that marrying him will do that, but I have to tell you that even though those doubts seem well founded to me, my judgment may be clouded, because not only do I love you, I am in love with you and I have been for a while. I didn't want to say this now or in this way. I don't want to add to the struggle you are going through, but if I don't say this now I may never get the chance."

Ellie's face registered alarm.

"Ellie, I can't promise you much, but ..."

Ellie pulled her hands free, stood and said, "Jake! No! Don't say it."

Jake looked at her steadily.

"Ellie, I know what your answer will be, but I have to ask. Will you marry me?"

Anger, then hurt flashed in her eyes. She looked down and said nothing.

She sat. She cried quietly.

Jake scooted his chair closer and put an arm around her.

She turned towards him and buried her face in his shirt.

He stroked her hair until she was quiet again.

She looked up at him and said, "I won't answer you now and if you press me, I'll say no. But when I do answer you, whatever I answer, don't go away. Be my friend."

Jake looked at her and said, "I will always love you, but I can't be the close friend of another man's wife, especially if it's you."

They sat quietly huddled together until a chime told them it was time for Jake to go to work and even then they sat until it was almost too late and then she drove him to work and they said nothing when they parted.

At work Jake shoveled robotically.

At the station Ellie went out to her rock in the orchard and sat very still until the sun was low in the sky. Then she went inside and tried to eat, but couldn't get much down.

Jake ate his sack dinner sitting under a tree watching the sun go down. When he had finished he exhaled sharply, smiled grimly, and got back to work.

Ellie said her prayers and went to bed early, exhausted.

She dreamed she was lost in a maze of slot canyons and every time she thought she recognized a landmark and moved towards it she became more hopelessly lost. Finally she came to a narrow flooded canyon and sat down and looked at it because she was afraid to swim it. She was about to turn back, but then saw a dark form moving in the canyon twilight behind her. She watched more carefully. It was moving toward her. She edged away from it toward the water. It slowed and moved into the shadows on the edge of the canyon, but it was still coming. It was large and powerful and it had her scent and was closing. She turned and ran the last few steps to the water, then jumped out over the water and as she did she heard an unearthly howling that woke her from her sleep. The hair on her arms was standing up and she listened trying to decide if the howl was a part of the real world that entered her dream, or part of her dream that hung in the air after waking. There was silence. Her stomach tightened and she ran to the bathroom, a wave of nausea overcoming her.

She vomited bile and what little dinner she had eaten into the toilet and then rested the side of her head on the cool porcelain. As she laid there her father's words came back to her. "Who would I want next to me at three in the morning when I'm vomiting?" she wondered.

"Jake," she said out loud. She closed her eyes, and shook her head to get rid of the thought, but it wouldn't go. She tried to imagine Titu there with her, strong and holding her head up, but whenever her focus weakened it was Jake cradling her in his arms. Finally, she stopped fighting it and fell asleep on the bathroom floor.

She woke before dawn to the sound of a morning bird and smiled in recognition. Her mind was clear. She would see Titu and give him her answer. What she would say to Jake was less clear.

Thirty-Six

Titu's smile remained fixed when he saw Ellie come into his office. It didn't fade, but the edges of it hardened. Ellie's motions were hesitant, but resolute. She paused before entering boldly. She thought before accepting the offered seat. She looked down before meeting and holding his gaze. With each of her actions Titu calibrated his expectations. He calmly accepted her praise of his virtues, each enumeration adding weight to the inevitable "but." When it came time for the "but," she simply stopped talking. Titu waited a full thirty seconds in silence, and finally began to gesture, preparing to speak, when she held up a hand and he was silent again.

"Titu, I need to actually say it. I won't marry you. I'm not going to be a partner in the ranch. It may be the biggest mistake of my life, but I don't think it is. I'm grateful for the offer. It forced me to figure out what matters most to me, and it would be wrong for me to mislead you to gain the advantages you offer."

Titu looked at her, a real but sardonic smile beginning to play around the edges of his mouth. "What if I don't mind the deception?" he said, leaning his head to one side. "Would that make it better? Nothing in life is absolutely pure. We all make trade-offs. The miserable can't accept that; the happy do. We would not be perfect together; no relationship is. But I think it would be worth it."

Ellie paused for a long time before answering. "You're right that everything is a trade-off and nothing is perfect, but it's the ranking of our priorities that defines who we are. I show what really matters to me, not by what I say, or even by what I like or dislike, but by what I give my time and attention to. I have realized that the many good things a life with you would offer aren't what matter most to me."

Titu nodded defeat. "I understand. There are no hard feelings here. I hope we can still be friends."

Ellie nodded and said, "I hope so too."

Titu escorted her to the door, smiled, and said goodbye.

He sat in his chair thinking for a while. He stood up, shut off the light, went to his truck and drove into the countryside.

Ellie went back to the station and looked at the displays around the station with dread. There was bound to be a lot of backed up work and unpleasant questions to be dealt with inside those displays. The thought of dealing with them was overwhelming. She fled outside, but the sun was getting high and a little harsh even among the trees. She finally went back inside and sat in the cool quiet of her office with the lights out.

Relief began to seep in. It was done. She wanted to call Jake but waited until it was almost time for him to start work. When she did call, he didn't answer.

"He must have started work early," she said to herself, but then realized this was his day off. "Why didn't he call? She began to think, and then remembered their last conversation.

Fly away
Climb high to fall away
Torch it to the ground
A goodbye missed and found

Thirty-Seven

At Empaqueme he only had to wait in the lobby a few minutes before Steve came down for him. He took Jake to a conference room where another man was waiting.

"Jake, this is Mike. He's leading a special project we think you might be a fit for."

They exchanged pleasantries and Steve said, "I wish you had applied earlier. I think we would have hired you on the spot, but as it is we are fully staffed and looking at probable funding cuts as the growers face lower profits over the next few *years. However, Mike has a special project that, if it goes through, will have its own funding. It would only be contract work, but hopefully by the time it was completed we could figure something out. Mike, would you tell Jake about the project?"

"Sure. First I'll need you to sign these nondisclosures."

Jake signed them.

"For some time we have been working on a joint venture with TruGro, a North American custom bio-engineering firm that doesn't merely adapt existing flora and fauna, but designs novel creatures from scratch. They are looking to expand into new markets, and Mars looks attractive to them. They have all the right equipment and personnel to accomplish in months what it takes us a *year to complete, but they don't understand the Martian market and can't seem to produce any-thing we want here. We've tried working with them remotely, but the round trip communication delay makes conferencing ridiculous and we can't seem to get them to understand our needs through mail. About a *year ago they proposed we send them one of our engineers to work with their team at their expense, but funding has been hung up ever since. The transit window between earth and Mars is coming up in two months and will be closed in three months for another *year; two years their time. Our partners have been able to use that deadline to at least fund flight training an engineer, and getting him strong enough for occasional visits to Earth's surface. Most of the work would be done in a lab they will lease on a LEO space station spun up to simulate Martian gravity. That's where they will test possible products before putting them on the market. There is no guarantee that the rest of the funding will come through so this job might be quite short. On the other hand, once you launch, you're guaranteed at least 120 weeks of employment. I've got a good feeling about the project. I think now that they've got some money invested they will probably go through with it, but there are no guarantees. Also, wages are bit higher on Earth than here so we were able to get you roughly double the starting salary."

Mike closed his book and looked at Steve.

"Does this sound like something you might be interested in?" Steve said.

Jake paused. "It's different than I was expecting, but it is interesting work and I think I could do it well." Jake frowned for a moment, his thoughts far away, "But I need to think about it. When do you need an answer?"

"The flight training is only six weeks, but the weight training would need to start almost immediately and continue during the flight. We'd also like to have you spend at least four weeks with the staff here before leaving for the training center. So, we really need an answer in the next three days."

"I'll get back to you by then, and I appreciate this opportunity," Jake said.

When Jake left the building he was dazed. The opportunity was more than he had hoped for. He would learn techniques that no one on Mars knew. It was also an opportunity to see the old world at no expense and to maybe understand his ancestors a little better. And yet, it would take him away for over a Martian year with no possibility of return before that.

He had three hours before the next train would leave, so he walked to a restaurant and ate on the patio looking up at the gleaming low rise suburban office buildings. There was nothing holding him here. He had no family left. No job worth having. No home to care for. There were no projects he needed to finish. He briefly wondered if he had time to go downtown and visit the university, but rejected the thought. Ellie had made it clear she didn't think of him in any way that implied a real future together. He closed his eyes remembering the feeling of sitting close to her one last time. "She loves me," he thought, "but that doesn't matter if she loves something or someone else more." He shifted in his seat, uneasy with the thought, paid for his meal and left.

On the train, he wandered the aisles, and changed seats a few times. He almost called Ellie twice, but then realized that he had already pushed things farther than he should have. She would have to call him.

By early afternoon, Ellie was answering mail again and hating it. A lot of the mail seemed to be people trying to poke holes in her and Jake's report. She answered as best she could and concluded each email with, "I hope you are right."

There were several messages from her father and one later from her mother, but she didn't feel like answering them yet.

There was a message from, the upland barley farmers, with pictures of the first fuzzy green test field. She smiled at that.

In the evening she decided to call Jake, but she didn't know what to say. She called anyway, but it went straight to mail.

Jake was riding in a taxi mentally saying goodbye to everything even though he had decided not to decide until morning.

When he arrived at the ranch he saw Titu coming out of his office much later than usual. The two men stopped and looked at each other. Both were tired. Each stared nakedly at the other trying to understand something before giving up. Then Titu said softly, "I need you on the day shift tomorrow if you can make it."

Jake nodded. "What are we doing?"

Titu thought for a second and shifted his weight before saying, "Some transition and planning work. We can talk about it in the morning."

Jake nodded.

At breakfast the next morning Jake saw Sam wearing smellier clothes than usual. He eyed Jake with a lazy and unfocused anger, before walking out towards the chicken house. Jake shrugged to himself.

After breakfast Jake, the foreman and three other men assembled on the porch of Titu's office.

"What's going on?" Jake asked the foreman.

"The final contract came through yesterday to take over the operation of that ranch we discussed. He needs us there to make sure nothing important is missing and finish characterizing the place."

Nobody talked much.

Jake finally asked, "Will they still be there when we get there?"

The foreman shrugged. "They shouldn't be. Yesterday was their deadline to be out. The sheriff is coming just in case."

When Titu came out, they climbed into two trucks and went to the new property. The sheriff had arrived first and was on the back porch of the farmhouse talking to the farmer's wife and daughter. The wife had her arms folded and wasn't saying much. The daughter was crying. When the sheriff saw Titu coming, he walked over to meet him.

"Looks like the old man never told his family. They haven't even started packing," the sheriff said.

"I could get some men down here to help..." Titu offered before the sheriff waved off the suggestion.

"Look, these people have been here fifteen *years, I think you can wait another day or two."

"And who's to say they'll be any more packed in two days?" Titu countered. "If you're not going to do your duty," he said waving the contract, "I'll find someone who will."

"Good luck with that," the sheriff snorted. "It's not going to hurt your operations to let these people stay in their house a few more days.

Your men can take charge of the rest of the property and start getting things in order."

"All right. Where's the old man? I don't want him interfering with my men."

"They haven't seen him since early this morning. He probably took off rather than watch this, but I'll leave a man behind just in case."

"I don't like this much," Titu said.

"Yeah, well they don't either," said the sheriff looking at the two women on the porch.

Ellie noticed the commotion and came out on her back porch. When she saw Anabelle crying she crossed the street and went to her. When Anabelle told her what was happening, Ellie looked at Titu and Jake with a hurt puzzled expression before turning and leading the women inside.

Titu signaled the foreman to go on while he finished with the sheriff. The five men fanned out into the barn yard checking equipment as they went. The foreman went into the barn and stopped. He stopped so suddenly that Jake ran into him. Jake looked up, following the foreman's gaze, and saw the farmer's body hanging by a rope from the rafters.

Thirty-Eight

The foreman swore softly under his breath and walked quickly out of the barn towards the sheriff. Jake stood looking at the body for a moment. The breeze from the door opening caused it to sway on the rope a bit. He recognized him from two days ago, but just barely. There were broken canning jars shattered here and there near the walls and a distinct smell of peach brandy and fecal matter. Jake turned and left the barn as the others approached it. The women had noticed the change in activity and were back on the porch. The old woman watched the body language of the men coming out of the barn and sank down on the steps, clutching her belly with both arms. Anabelle looked around confused. Ellie looked at Jake when he came close enough. He looked back and just shook his head. Ellie put her arm around Anabelle and tried to move her back to the doorway, but she broke loose and ran for the barn. When she got there she hesitated, then opened the big door wide. She stood for a moment staring uncomprehendingly, then she wailed out a "No!" and her voice broke. "No!" she said again. Then she started picking up rocks and throwing them at the body. She hit it twice before anyone could stop her, and then she just sobbed as they hustled her back to the house. The old woman stood silently when they brought Annabelle back to her, glared at the barn, glared at Titu and went inside.

The sheriff was on the phone talking to someone. Ellie went inside. Jake took off his gloves, threw them on the ground and sat on the porch with his head in his hand. Titu started towards the truck and motioned for the men to follow.

"Come on Jake. We'll finish this later." Jake raised his eyes and shook his head.

"I'm done."

Titu considered this for a moment, nodded and said, "If you change your mind come see me." He left.

When Ellie came out an hour later, Jake was still sitting on the steps. Ellie looked at him, saw his gloves still lying on the ground, didn't see any vehicles but the sheriff's and an ambulance which was just leaving.

"Tell your boss they aren't staying here tonight," she said.

Jake shook his head, "I don't work for him anymore. You can tell him yourself."

Ellie sat down next to him, "I don't think I'll be seeing him anytime soon..." she said.

Jake looked at her but didn't say anything.

"I'd like to help them if I can," he finally said.

"Probably the best thing is to be gone before they come out," she said.

Jake said nothing, but picked up his gloves and stood awkwardly before leaving the property. He lingered in the area long enough to see Ellie leading the two women with their luggage to the station, then turned towards the ranch to retrieve his belongings from the bunk house.

The foreman cashed him out, but there was barely enough to pay for train tickets, clothes, and the things he would need for his new job. He slept under the stars in some one's orchard that night and wished the stars were clearer. He wished they were like the stars he had known when he was younger, and then it occurred to him that he would soon see them clearer than ever, and get his fill of seeing them too.

Thirty-Nine

Ellie gave Matilda her room and Annabelle a smaller room next to it. Her room had a larger bed, and the private bathroom. Once they were settled with clean towels and linens, she set to work cooking a real lunch and cookies.

The sheriff came to get statements from Matilda and Anabelle. After he left Matilda showered for over an hour.

Anabelle sat at a table where she could see her house through the window and stared at it.

The food got cold and nobody ate, so Ellie put the cookies out on a plate and packed away the food.

Annabelle picked at the cookies absent mindedly from time to time.

When evening came, the house seemed cold. Ellie looked at the fire place and wished she had ordered some gas for it.

Matilda emerged from the room and sat with Annabelle. They leaned against each other. Then Annabelle started to cry. Matilda stroked her back. Ellie gave them their privacy.

In the morning relatives from Paititi came, helped them pack up the most important things, and took them home.

Only when the house was empty again did it occur to her to wonder about Jake. She called him.

"Come have brunch with me," she said. He arrived a half hour later and only when she saw him at the door did she remember he didn't have a car here. He set his things down in the kitchen.

"Do you mind if I use your guest facilities to get cleaned up?" he asked.

"That's fine. Do you have any laundry that needs doing?"

He nodded. "Can I use the machines?"

"I'll do it for you while you clean up," she said.

"You don't need to. I can do it."

"Go shower. I'll take care of it."

Jake pulled out the cleanest of his clothes and his toiletry kit and disappeared into the guest bath.

Ellie sorted the rest of the clothes and put the first load through. As she worked she could hear the water bouncing off him in the shower and the slight sound of his movement. She moved back to the kitchen. She was heating up leftovers when he came back to the kitchen. She turned and startled slightly.

"I didn't hear you come in," she said.

They sat down and ate.

Ellie watched him. He was a little thinner than when they first met. His cheeks seemed hollower, his eyes softer. He didn't say much.

"It's my day off today," said Ellie, "Spend it with me."

"I ..." Jake began, shaking his head, "I should probably go."

"Why?" asked Ellie.

He looked at her, distressed.

"You know how I feel about you. I can't just shut that off. I can't just be your friend."

"I see," said Ellie with studied seriousness, but her eyes were dancing.

"So, I'll just go," he said, and started to rise.

"You should wait for your laundry," Ellie said.

Jake sat.

"Besides, you asked me a question a couple of days ago and I didn't really answer you."

Jake put up a hand defensively, "You were clear enough."

"No, Jake. I wasn't clear. I was completely confused."

Jake watched her carefully now.

"But I'm not confused anymore," she said slowly. "Jake, I will marry you on one condition. You have to propose to me again when the time is right. Until then, nothing's official. Deal?"

For the first time in four days Jake smiled. "Deal," he said.

Ellie softened, teared up. They hugged for a long time until the laundry machines signaled the first load was done. Then Jake said, "I think I will spend the day with you."

They folded laundry together and Ellie thought, "I don't know why people complain about doing laundry."

When the laundry was done, they drove randomly around the valley enjoying the sites and the secret knowledge they shared. They stopped for ice cream at some old stand along the highway and watched the traffic go by.

In the evening, they began to discuss next steps. Jake told her about the job offer. Neither knew what to do. Professionally it was obviously the right thing to do, but the thought of being apart that long seemed impossible.

"I'll just find something in Olympia instead. I've got friends there," he said, but the words fell flat.

"Maybe I could get a leave of absence, borrow some money from my parents and come with you," she said. "I'd like to see the old world and there are worse ways to start a marriage."

"That would mean we would have to get married in the next three months and spend our 1st month of married life together on a cargo ship."

"I can do that," Ellie said.

They looked up the costs. The travel costs were outrageous. The housing costs on a LEO space station for 100 weeks were crippling.

"I'll just tell them 'No, thank you'. Something will turn up," Jake said.

Ellie reluctantly agreed and then said, "We should pray about this." They knelt together for the first time as a couple. It felt good to be united, but there was no confirmation. They began a fast together. Jake booked a room at a nearby motel using a credit account one of the new commercial banks had foolishly given him in college. Ellie said it wasn't necessary.

"We're both stewards. This is a station. It has guest quarters. I've stayed in the guest quarters at your station. I'll be good. I promise."

"Three problems with that:

One, I'm not technically a steward anymore.

Two, Your father and about fifteen grizzly old men were in the station with us.

Three, I don't promise I can be good. Besides, this is a small town and you know what people will assume."

Ellie relented and drove him to the motel. They shared a long kiss at the door before Ellie pulled herself away and went home.

The next morning she picked him up and they went to church together.

In the afternoon Ellie's Dad called. She went into her room to talk. Jake could hear snatches of conversation whenever she raised her voice, and smiled as he speculated about what they were saying.

When she came out he asked,

"So, did you tell him?"

"No. It's not official until you really ask me."

Jake pretended not to care about the rest of the conversation. It was transparent, but she added anyway, "I told him I turned down Titu and he said he was relieved. He hadn't wanted to interfere, but he was relieved. Then I told him I was seeing you, but that you might be taking a job off-world for 108 weeks in a few months.

Jake winced a little.

"I signed a nondisclosure agreement. There's only one place a person could be going off world for 108 weeks leaving in a few months."

"True, but he doesn't know with whom or why. In fact you didn't even tell me who the partner is."

"Good enough I guess. So, was he still relieved when you told him we were seeing each other?"

"I think so. He seemed happy at first, but then he got all quiet."

Jake considered this for a moment, then moved on. Time stretched out. Ellie kept looking at him and he looked right back.

Ellie's stomach rumbled and they both smiled. "I think it's time we broke this fast," Jake said.

They knelt beside each other and each said his own prayer. They were quiet a long time. Finally Jake looked up at Ellie who was quiet a while longer and then looked at him.

"Did you get anything?" Jake asked. Ellie nodded a bit wide eyed. Jake knew what it was by her expression and it matched his own impression. He looked down, shook his head and looked vaguely distressed.

"Was it clear?" he asked. She nodded. He looked down again, and closed his eyes.

"I don't want to go," he finally said.

"It will be OK," she said, putting a hand on his shoulder. "I'll be here when you get back."

He nodded still, looking down.

She lifted his chin with one finger, looked him straight in the eyes and repeated slowly, "I'll be here." He smiled and they closed their eyes leaned forward and pressed their foreheads together for a long time. Jake's stomach rumbled and they both laughed, made dinner and ate.

They talked with the ease of a long last talk.

They talked late into the night. When Ellie dropped him off at the motel, she lingered at his door. They were all talked out. He looked at her to say good night and she looked back at him steadily. He leaned toward her and she leaned towards him and they kissed. Then he tucked her head under his chin and held her for a long time, and then she left.

Jake slept well that night. In the morning he called his contact and said, "It looks like we've got a deal."

Forty

Jake stood outside Empaqueme for a second before entering. It was a bright morning. He was early. He plunged through the front door. He was too early. No one was there to meet him. The guard had him wait in the lobby. He leaned back in his chair, his foot tapping out some rhythm on its own. He watched the place wake up. The receptionist arrived. Employees started coming in. Steve came in and took him to security to get scanned for access. Once that was done, doors politely unlocked for him whenever he approached. Steve settled him in a temporary work space and said he'd be back to introduce him to the team in about an hour.

Jake looked out the window and noticed his own reflection looking back at him. He studied the stranger. The contrast from how he saw himself at his last job was a little startling, yet he was the same person.

The security scan had noticed his personal equipment too, because he found he had access to Empaqueme information. He got caught up on the discussion his and Ellie's paper had spawned. There was a growing consensus that it was only a matter of time before things got worse. A couple of university professors had volunteered to start mapping which species would likely be most vulnerable and several others were redirecting efforts to see if there were any new threats unnoticed in existing studies. A separate thread had been started to discuss what ought to be done. They had already sent out an alert to update the default setting in all the emulators, and an ad hoc group was working on setting up an automatic update for default settings based on field measurements. Others argued that all defaults should be disabled and every simulation should have all parameters manually set at each run.

The soil microbes would have to be engineered first of course, but there was also a growing consensus that the annual crops should be next to be re-engineered, since it would take *years to get benefit from new trees. Some disagreed for the same reason, saying they should get to work on the trees first because the rest could be changed in a single *year if needed.

Jake heard someone approaching, lifted his glasses and saw Steve. They visited the labs and he was introduced to several of the researchers. The equipment was recent enough, but Jake noticed that the flooring and furniture were a bit worn and the walls could use fresh paint.

"Jake, this is Lou Ferris. He was our newest employee until you. We got him from your old stomping grounds."

Jake first thought of the desert, but then realized he meant Ellie's station.

"It's good to meet you," Jake said. "Did you like working up valley?"

"Yes. It was a good opportunity. It's what got me here. I understand you worked for the Alcantars. Is that right?"

"Yes, but it was just temporary ranch work."

"Well, the Alcantars can be very generous."

Jake hesitated; then said, "Yes. They can be."

Lou smiled and said, "You can usually find me in here if you need me." Then he turned and went to the far end of the lab.

Jake looked at Steve. Steve shrugged imperceptibly and they visited the other members of the team in their work spaces. Jake set up a time to work with each of them, not because they needed help, but to get to know them and their habits. It would help when collaborating from a distance.

A bunch of them took lunch together in the break room. Most of them were from the valley, farm boys who had gone to school. When they found out he was from the desert they began dredging up stories of their adventures there, mostly from when they were in scouts or on family camping trips. Jake smiled and nodded politely. He told them about a few trips he and his father had taken that didn't go so well, but he didn't tell them about his lone roaming as a teenager, and he didn't tell them about a crashed rock crawler he once found.

In the afternoon he did some library work for the lead engineers. At the end of the day he stopped by Steve's office on the way out to say thanks. Steve thanked him in return and told him to check his account. "There should be a little signing bonus in there to help you get set up."

He walked back to the hotel. The days were getting long enough for there to be light after work, a low warmer light. In his room he checked his account and there was enough there to cover his expenses until he got paid. He warmed up some food, and called Ellie.

Forty-One

Hal studied the young man standing in front of him. "You want to rent a rock crawler?"

The young man shrugged, and said, "Yeah. You rent them right?"

Hal went back to straightening various objects in his office while he thought.

"Who are you again?" Hal asked, but he was preoccupied, and seemingly uninterested in the answer.

"I'm the new steward over at the station."

Hal nodded acknowledgment without really looking at him.

"You ever drive one of these before?"

The young man shrugged, looked over at the water cooler and said, "Yeah."

Hal looked at him and snorted. "Yeah, sure you have."

The young man looked straight at him and said, "You calling me a liar?"

Hal shrugged, mocking him, and said, "Yeah... pretty much."

"Are you going to rent me the thing or not?"

"Yeah, I'll rent it to you. But you're taking out double the insurance and you have to sign this." He handed him a release form. "It says you understand that if you get in a wreck, help may not come for days or might not come at all."

He took it and signed it. He accepted the insurance.

"Where's your stuff?"

The young man started to shrug, checked himself and said, "Right here," and then shrugged anyway. All he had was a jacket.

"No. I mean where is your tent, sleeping bag, backup oxygen, coat, food and water?"

"I'm just going out for the day. I'll be back before dark."

"Did you even read the document you just signed?"

He looked at him blankly, "Yeah."

"So what is it? Do you just want to die or something?"

Alex looked at him disdainfully, "No. I just want you to rent me a crawler so I can get out of here. So, are you going to do it, or not?"

Hal looked at him for a minute. "Not. I don't really like you, but I'm not sending you out to get killed. Come back when you've got the right gear for this country."

Alex glared at him, said, "Fine. Be that way!" and slammed the door on his way out.

He came back the next day with proper gear. Hal winced a little when he saw Jake's sleeping bag. Hal looked him over, saw that he had a satellite link as well, and then handed him the key.

"Call if you're going to be late, or there's an extra charge."

Alex barely nodded and went out to the rock crawler. It was sleek and lovely, the latest model to come out of Olympia. It seemed a little too good for a dump like this. He climbed in and set out across the desert. "What a god forsaken dried up old crust of landscape," he said out loud and sped up a little. He smiled at himself. At least this was better than sitting around the station listening to the heater turn off and on. He flipped some switches trying to get music, but didn't find any.

He had intended to go to the top of the first small mountain he could see from Hal's place, but about half way there he came over a rise a little too fast and caught some air. When he got over the surprise he grinned and circled back around to the top of the rise. From the top he looked around and smiled. The hill he had come over was part of a series of closely spaced hills. If he had been going just a little faster he would have landed on the far side of the next hill and come down it like a ramp. If he got it just right he might have enough speed to use that hill as a jump too. He looked around for something a little more open to mess around first and found a flat space to his left. He took the crawler down and started going in circles as fast as he could, then in figure 8s. Then he started jumping little ravines. After ten minutes he was laughing so hard he could barely see where he was going. Finally he decided it was time. He lined the crawler up with the first hill, tightened his straps and shoved both controllers full forward. He cleared the swale between the first and second hills and came down on the far side as planned. He had to concentrate to keep his controllers straight when he got to the bottom of the second swale and started climbing the third hill. It worked. He still had enough speed when he cleared the third hill to catch air, but when the crawler nosed over he saw that this swale was lower than the other two. His stomach flipped. He hit hard. He did a mental check. He was still in one piece. He looked around. The crawler appeared to be in one piece. He started laughing again. He pulled all the way back on the right controller and pushed the left one full forward to make a hard right turn that would take him up and out of the swale, but after an initial bump and whine of motors the crawler went silent and red warning lights lit on the console in front of him. He reset the system and tried again with the same result. He reset the system again and tried going left, but the lights went red immediately and the motors didn't even try.

He got out and looked the crawler over. The frame seemed OK, but both the front wheels were pointed at odd angles to the other wheels. He climbed back to the top of the hill, looked around and then sat down and tossed pebbles down at the crawler. He rubbed his shoulders where the straps had dug in. They were bruised pretty well and he felt achy all over. He tried to call Hal and shook his head remembering there was no terrestrial service out here. He tried to pair his watch with the sat link on his belt, but it wouldn't pair. He pulled out the sat link and looked at it. It looked alright to him. It had power. He reset it and tried to pair it again. Nothing. He shrugged. "Cheap piece of crap," he said and stuck it back in its holder.

A breeze came up and he felt chilly. He went back down to the crawler and put his jacket on. The crawler still had power, so it had presumably sent its coordinates and problems to Hal. Someone should be coming for him anytime. He grabbed his food bag and went back up top to watch for rescuers. When the food was all gone he stood and began to pace. "Where are they?" he said scowling. "They should be here by now." His mind flitted to the acknowledgment he had signed. "That's just legal language," he thought and sat down again. The breeze tapered off, but the shadows grew long. He sat on the top of the rise watching for rescuers until it was too dark to see. Even then he still sat there trying to make out forms in the darkness until he was shivering so violently he had to stand and move around.

He got into the cab of the crawler. It wasn't much warmer. He found his sleeping bag and fiddled with it until he got it open and slipped in. He still wasn't warm, but at least he wasn't getting colder. He licked his lips and looked for his water bottle. It was empty. He closed his eyes and lay still for a while, then turned and reached for the bottle. He opened the cap and held it upside down over his mouth shaking it. A drop reached his tongue. He put the cap back on, put it away and laid back. He closed his eyes. After a minute he opened them again and stared out the windshield of the crawler at the sky. Brilliant stars filled it. He searched for dark areas in the sky that might indicate clouds, but he didn't find any.

He closed his eyes again and tried to remember how long a person could go without water. They had said something about it before he quit scouts, but he couldn't remember what. "More than a day," he finally said to himself, irritated, and turned his face away from the window. He slept for a while, but woke up with his arm numb. The seats of the crawler weren't meant for sleeping in. He thought about setting up the tent, but it was dark and cold out there. Ice was forming on the inside of the crawler's windows. "Not so warm in here either," he said to himself.

He wondered if anyone would come for him after all. That guy who rented him the crawler didn't seem to like him much. He was an outsider. Maybe they would just leave him out here. "Yeah, right," he said touching the brand new dashboard of the crawler. "Leave your brand new baby out in the desert so you can stick it to the new guy." He rolled his eyes, but the thought didn't leave him entirely.

When he woke again the sun was sparkling off a layer of frost on the inside of the windshield. He licked his lips and pictured licking the window. Instead he took out his water bottle and scraped the frost into it. When he had scraped all he could he put the lid on and pulled the bottle into his sleeping bag with him and dozed a little. When he opened his eyes again he pulled out the bottle and looked at it. It had about a millimeter of water in the bottom of it. He smiled. It was a real smile. Then he mocked himself. "Thrilled by a half swallow of spit water." But he smiled again and drank the water.

He got up and went outside. The cold cut through his jacket like a knife. He hesitated and looked at the crawler, then headed down the gully toward a nearby ravine. He found the lowest part of the ravine he could see and started digging with a small flat rock. The top layer was course sand stuck together in a kind of crust. Below that the soil was moist, but he didn't find any water. Still, it showed the idea wasn't crazy. He looked more carefully at the crust. The sun was just high enough that he could hold it up and watch the different grains sparkle their different colors.

He looked around for a better place to dig, but didn't see any nearby. He made a mental note to stick close to the ravine if he had to try to walk out. He walked to the top of the hill and looked out. He didn't see anyone. He wasn't exactly sure where town was, but he reasoned that he could follow his own tracks, at least as long as the wind hadn't erased them. He followed them with his eyes as far as he could see and they angled away from the ravine.

He went back to the crawler and looked through the storage compartments. In the back he found two bottles of water, nutrition bars, and a worthless blanket. He ate one of the bars and sipped a little of the water. He took out his tent and practiced setting it up and putting it away. The tent was surprisingly warm inside.

He went back up the hill and looked over the terrain again. No sign of anyone. He thought about sitting down, but the ground was cold. He looked at his water supply again. He was hungry, but it was the water he worried about. He looked at the sky. No clouds in site. It had rained three times since he'd been here, keeping him inside the gloomy old station house, but now that he needed it, there was nothing.

He began walking along the rim of the ravine trying to imagine where water would be hidden. The air was relatively dry, but the soil had been moist just a few centimeters down. His eyes started resting on every shadow and hollow in the ravine. Most of the deepest holes showed exposed rock at the bottom. At a bend in the ravine he saw a hollow in the side of the bank. He dropped down into the ravine and looked at the hole. It was on the outside bank of a turn where an eddy would be when the ravine was flowing. Water had carried away the dirt revealing a meter wide crack in the rock disappearing below the surface.

He found a rock and started digging. Six centimeters down the soil was moist. He paused to breathe. He was surprised at how easily he tired. He looked at the small rolls of fat bulging from his shirt and shook his head. He went back to digging. At fifteen centimeters a little water pooled at the bottom of the hole. He stuck his fingers in the murky puddle and licked them. The water was tangy, but he liked the taste. He dug some more. At thirty centimeters he had a puddle deep enough that he could have dipped a bottle in it. He cupped his hands and drank. He smiled. The hole refilled to the level it had been before and the water was slightly clearer. He thought about his empty bottle back at the crawler and decided he had better get it before this dried up. He drank as much as he could, then carefully covered the hole with flat rocks and came up out of the ravine. He froze, looking at the little hills near the ravine. He had no idea which one his crawler was behind. There were dozens of them. He started following the ravine upstream. He started to breathe easier whenever he saw one of his own footsteps along the way. The he froze again and turned around. What if he couldn't find his well again? He back tracked until he found the place and piled rocks up on the near bank. Then he headed back towards the crawler. Hungry as he was, his mind was working. He smiled again. After a while he noticed something scurrying under a sage brush plant. He kicked the plant and a lizard ran out the other side, stopped, and watched him. He let it go, but tucked the information away. After a while, the ravine seemed unfamiliar. He didn't see any more of his own footprints either. He stopped, looked around, and started retracing his steps. Near the sage brush clump with the lizard he could see where foot prints were heading up over a rise. He piled up some rocks where the path turned from the ravine and followed the foot prints to the top of the rise and there was the crawler. He scrambled down and got his empty bottle and his half empty bottle and scrambled back up to the top of the rise. He started walking towards his well, then saw a cloud of dust moving roughly towards him. He watched it for a minute. It wasn't moving straight for him, but more towards the rover. He started cutting cross country until he came to his rover tracks from the day before. He looked up at the cloud of dust and it seemed like it was heading towards him. He stood still. After a long two minutes a sheriff's rover came over a small rise and slowed as it approached. The sheriff's deputy opened a side window and said,

"Are you Alex Lundy?"

Alex nodded "yes," eagerly.

"Need a ride?"

"Yes!"

A door opened and Alex got in. They went to the crawler and got his stuff. The deputy took some pictures and climbed inside. He looked at the control panel, flipped some switches and came out shaking his head. "Did you fiddle with the switches on the control panel?"

"No." Alex said reflexively. Then shook his head, and said, "Yes. I did."

The deputy shook his head and said, "Well today was your lucky day. You turned off the location tracker. If the wind had blown any harder, we might not have found you for days."

Alex didn't say much on the way back into town. He saw the

pile of rocks marking his well as they passed by. As the joy of being rescued receded it was replaced with an impulse to open the door of the deputy's vehicle and run back to his well and camp. He looked at his hand sitting next to the door latch, but it didn't move.

Hal didn't have much to say. He'd already seen the photos and was filling out the insurance forms for him when he came in. Alex signed. As he left, Hal said, "I'm glad you're alright," without looking up. Alex stood outside the door for a minute then went back inside. Hal looked up surprised. "You saved my butt yesterday. Thanks."

Hal nodded at him, and Alex went back outside.

Forty-Two

In the morning Ellie drove up-canyon to visit Julie and her barley. When she rounded the corner she could see lush grey-green fields of spring wheat rolling into the distance. Julie took her around back to the test fields. The barley was tall and green. It rippled when a breeze played across it. Ellie ran her hand across the barley tops as Julie told her about their plans.

"We're just going to go for it." Julie said. "We're not even going to try any selection on the first round, we're just going to put it all in during second planting."

Ellie smiled, "Counting your chickens before they hatch, huh?"

Julie said, "Just taking a gamble."

Ellie took some samples and packed them in her case to go. On her way out to the truck she saw the kids in their sandbox playing some noisy game that involved shrieks and crashes. They were growing as quickly as the barley. She thought they seemed taller, but decided they were merely leaning as they got farther from winter.

When she got back to the station it was mostly committee work again.

The next day she was off to check blight monitoring points which took all day. She worked into the evening correlating the results and making her report. The blight was spreading steadily. They would have to increase the number or monitoring points. She had just sent the report when Jake called and they talked for an hour about nothing.

The next day she went on rounds with Cava.

"I hear you've been a busy girl," Cava said smirking when Ellie slid into the cab of her truck.

"Yes, I have!" Ellie said.

Cava shook her head. "Well, I'm not sure I should be seen with a cold hearted, incompetent, hussy like you." Cava said matter-of-factly.

"What?" Ellie said.

"Why are you surprised? You just confirmed you've been busy like everyone says," Cava said with an air of supreme patience.

Ellie sighed. "OK, I'll bite. What are they saying?"

"Nothing much. Just that you jilted the most eligible bachelor in the valley so you could sleep with one of his ranch hands at some sleazy motel. Oh, and that if you hadn't been so busy trying to reel him in just to jilt him, maybe you would have done your job and stopped this blight before it started. There's even a theory going around that your father must have abused you to make you such a man hater. Don't worry, I defended your father and said you must be naturally bad. "

"Gee, thanks."

"Don't mention it."

Ellie sat looking out the side window with her forehead wrinkled.

Cava glanced at her and said, "Don't worry about it, girl. By next week they'll have moved on to the next news. Besides, half of them are relieved because he's back on the market."

When Ellie didn't respond, Cava put her hand on her knee, and said, "You did the right thing, but honestly, did you think there wouldn't be any blowback? You'll get through it."

At several stops Ellie could see at least some of what Cava had been saying behind the eyes of people they spoke with. Cava did most of the talking at those houses.

By the end of the day she was bushed. "Wanna do a girls night out?" Cava asked.

Ellie shook her head, went inside, and waited for Jake to call.

At church on Sunday Ellie could feel eyes boring into the back of her head. Some people weren't talking to her and others were going out of their way to talk to her. Between meetings she went to the bathroom mostly to be alone. While she pretended to fuss with her hair a young woman she vaguely recognized came in, stood next to her and adjusted her perfect makeup. Ellie was about to go when, the girl said,

"I bet you thought you were smart."

Ellie paused and finally said, "If you have something to say, just say it."

"That's all I've got to say, but if you thought a ranch hand would make Titu jealous enough to propose to you, you aren't as smart as you thought you were."

"I've never wanted to be that kind of smart."

"I'll bet that's what you'd be telling that ranch hand of yours if he hadn't skipped town," the girl said, smiled, and left the bathroom.

Half way through the next meeting Ellie finally remembered the girl's face. She had stormed out of the dinner party at Titu's.

After the meetings were over Ellie made a bee line for the parking lot, but the bishop happened to be in her path. He greeted her and asked if she had a moment. She reluctantly assented and they went to his office.

"I'm sorry I didn't have you in when you first got here," he said.

"That's OK. I know you're busy."

"I am, but not that busy. If you need to discuss anything, anything at all, I'm here," he said and sat back expectantly.

Ellie involuntarily rolled her eyes and sighed. The bishop laughed. "Yeah, I didn't think so," he said.

"Just for the record," Ellie said, "Titu did propose to me, I did turn him down, and the 'Ranch Hand' is actually my soon to be fiancé who was out of work and took a menial job here just to be near me, and no I have nothing to confess."

"Good. Things might be a little difficult for you over the next few weeks. The Alcantars have a lot of friends and a lot of people who want to be their friends. If it gets overwhelming and you need to talk, feel free to call me."

"Thank you."

"Oh, also, we'd like you to teach the Fourteen half-*year olds in Sunday school. Will that be OK?"

"Sure... but is that going to create a problem for you?"

"I like trouble. Besides what are they going to do, get me released? I need the vacation."

He smiled wearily, stood, shook her hand and walked her to the door.

Ellie went home and locked herself inside. She didn't want to go out. Jake had moved to the Olympus training facility and would be out of contact most of the next month.

She pulled up a book, started to read, and quieted. By late afternoon she was back to herself and decided to go for a walk. She drove beyond the last ranch and walked in the empty country. The days were starting to be long enough to feel a little warmth from the sun in the late afternoon and she relaxed to the touch of it. In another month the fields of wheat and dune grass she saw stretching out in the distance would start to change from bright grey-green to more of an olive color. "And I won't be here to see it," she said absently to herself then stopped walking. She shook her head but her first words stayed with her. She continued walking but more slowly, thinking. Finally she shrugged and moved back in the general direction of the truck. By the time she reached it, she was calm and ready for whatever was coming in the week ahead.

Forty-Three

Ellie didn't have to tabulate results to know things were getting worse. All she had to do was look at the trees and the faces of the farmers. It was already clear there would be no apple harvest this year in the northern half of the valley, and most of the other tree crops weren't faring much better. In the southern upper part of the valley, fruit buds were at least forming but the line between north and south was hardly sharp and fixed. The farmers were fighting it with everything the Department could suggest and anything they could think of. Some were spraying the trees with mixtures of copper sulfide. Others used worse things. Several of the northern farmers were burning the most infected portions of their orchards on their own trying to save the remaining trees. The most damning sign was that most of the stewards had stopped studying trees and started focusing on annual crops. When one of them noticed and complained about it, another steward pointedly replied, "It'll take two full *years at least to get new mature trees, do you want to eat while their growing?" In reality, the grain crops seemed healthy enough, but there wouldn't be enough to offset all the fruit losses. They would be dipping into the stockpiles this year. The only questions were how much, and how long the stockpiles could hold.

A conference in a couple of weeks would finalize the strategy. Ellie sat looking through her own list of suggestions and concerns. She put the list down, closed her eyes and rubbed her temples. She wished Jake were here to talk it over with, but from his messages it was clear he wasn't aware of how bad it had gotten. His most recent message was full of rocket flights and exotic food. She hadn't mentioned the situation in her own messages because without access to information he couldn't help anyway and it wouldn't help to distract him.

"It'll have to wait until his break," she said. Training would be over soon and he would be back in the valley for a month before departure.

She was nearly done feeling sorry for herself when there was a knock at her front door. She approached cautiously since everyone used her back door. She saw a formally dressed man on the porch.

"Can I help you?"

"Are you Miss Elisa P. Waddell?"

"Yes," Ellie said warily.

The man handed her an envelope. "You are hereby summoned to appear in court on June 34th," he said, and walked away.

Ellie opened the envelope. At the top of the letter it said, "Alcantar enterprises V. Department of Agriculture, Elisa P. Waddell, et al." Beneath that was a summary of the case. Ellie scanned it.

- *"The plaintiff contends that Miss Waddell used her position with the Department of Agriculture to illegally obtain Alcantar intellectual property and did conspire with the Department of Agriculture to illegally place that property into the public domain."*

"The sugar beets..." she said to herself, then after reading more carefully added, "and the strawberries."

They were seeking an injunction barring the Department from posting the sequences, barring anyone from using them if they already had them, and seeking monetary damages to cover legal costs, lost revenues, and damage to reputation.

Ellie called the legal hotline and found herself instantly talking to a Department lawyer, which meant they already knew about it.

"I assume you've seen this?" Ellie said.

"We haven't seen anything, but we expected there might be trouble. Did you get summoned?"

"I've been summoned and named in the law suit," Ellie said.

"They named you personally?"

"Yes."

"We didn't expect that. They must be taking it personally. Don't worry about it too much. Unless you broke the law in any way, and we don't think you did, you're pretty much bullet proof."

"So does that mean I don't have to appear?"

"No. You have to appear. Don't worry. We'll be there with you."

"What exactly is going on?"

"Based on your statements and evidence we found on the memory pearls in your equipment we believe the Alcantars were attempting to patent designs made at public expense by a public employee. We've started an administrative procedure to formally put the designs into the public domain where we believe they belong. It looks like the Alcantars are filing suit to stop that before it happens."

"Is there anything I should do to prepare?"

"We already have your statement. You should review it and make sure you remember everything in it. If you have anything else that would support the case, let me know. Above all do not have any contact with the Alcantars. If they contact you, don't say anything to them except to refer them to me. Also don't talk to anyone in the area about the case. You never know how people will twist what you say. Any other questions?"

"No."

"We've got a good case. I'm confident we will prevail."

"Thanks," Ellie said and closed the call. Then she looked at the calendar and laughed. "Well I guess I don't have to worry about the conference." The hearing started at the exact same time.

Ellie finished preparing her remarks anyway. Even if she couldn't be there, she wanted to be represented.

When she had finished she flipped through her requests queue. It was eerily quiet given all that was happening. She answered the few questions that were there, set a couple of appointments and went out on monitoring rounds. She focused on the edges of the blight trying to see how it was moving and changing. There were few farmers to greet her. They were busy helping their neighbors try to fight off the blight so it wouldn't come to them next.

In the late afternoon when she was about to return to the station she saw it: a reddish brown tinge out of the corner of her eye. It wasn't near any of the monitoring points. She just saw it on the way from one to another. She stopped the truck, clutched her sample bag, and thought about not turning to look at it. If she didn't look at it she could just drive on. She looked out the back window and it was still there. She opened the truck door and walked to the edge of the wheat field. It was still there. The blight had infected a quarter acre of spring wheat. It made no sense. How could a single pathogen target such different species and spread so quickly? She stood staring at it for several seconds and then started collecting samples and estimating the size of the outbreak. She was starting to edge around to the far side of it when she heard a truck door slam on the road. A large boy about seventeen, was moving towards her in a hurry. When he was within shouting distance he yelled,

"What are you doing in our field?"

Ellie waited until he was a little closer, but he repeated,

"What are you doing in our fields?"

Ellie wordlessly gestured to the infected wheat. But standing just inches from her he shouted,

"I asked you a question!"

She pointed again and said, "I'm checking to see what's wrong with the wheat." He didn't look to see where she was pointing.

"There's nothing wrong with this wheat! You need to move along. You need to get out of here right now."

There was the sound of more doors opening and closing along the side of the road. They both looked over to see a middle aged man moving towards them quickly, shoulders hunched. Two other men stood at the edge of the field looking around and Ellie heard one of them say, "Oh Lord!" when he finally saw what Ellie had been looking at.

"Pa, I caught her nosing around our fields!"

The older man waited until he was closer and said, "What brings you here today Miss Waddell?"

Ellie gestured towards the wheat, "I have to see if this is what I think it is."

"There's nothing wrong with this wheat," he said, looking straight at her without even glancing at the wheat. "You need to leave, and don't come back without making an appointment."

"You didn't even look at it," Ellie said.

"I don't need to, and if you go saying otherwise, maybe it doesn't go so well for you. Now go!"

Ellie made her way back to the truck. The men on the side of the road didn't look at her. Instead they started unloading torches. She sat in the cab, shaken, and logged the location. She went back to the station, locked the doors, and wrote her report. When that was done, she began sequencing the latest samples.

Late that night she compared the sequences of every affected species. Even later, she found the common sequence that made tighter leaf pores in every food crop planted in the entire world, and realized there would be no stopping the blight.

She sat blindly at her kitchen table, not thinking. Her eyes fell on a bag of bread resting on the shelf. She looked at it until her eyes got dry, blinked painfully, and went back to summarizing her findings and updating her report. When she finished at 2:30 a.m., she crashed into bed.

Forty-Four

Jake's transport glided down over the sandalwood shrubs towards the bulky grit of the port. In Olympia the port was the total transit hub, sea, air, rail, everything but the spaceport, and even that was accessed from there. As he waited to climb down the stairs he breathed deeply, smelling the incongruous mixture of sandalwood oil being boiled at the edge of the port, sea salt, and methane exhaust from the engines around him. "We're in Olympia alright," he said to anyone listening and there were smiles from a few other passengers.

The air was fresher on the stairs and the light came in filtered grey by an overcast sky. He moved quickly into the terminal building. It was a different building than he was used to and he smirked at the display over the main exit, a huge Kalachakra Mandala made of fine wood oddly placed next to a large analog clock. No one else would notice but he was amused. He moved on to the street and walked two industrial blocks to drop into the subway. He changed trains in the old underground town the first colonists built, and breathed the butter tea, momos, and mutton smells coming from the food court before moving on to the smell of ozone coming from train motors. He came up out of the subway among a nondescript set of buildings not far from the university. He had to hunt to find the front door, then checked in at the front desk and waited.

In orientation they handed in all their communication devices. They would get messages twice a day just like on the real flight. After orientation they had their medical exams, then went to lunch.

In the afternoon, they moved into the tiny simulated guest quarters of a cycler ship. The real cyclers, hollowed out asteroids, were actually quite large, but the space allotted to passengers depended on the amount of cargo making the trip and the program assumed the worst. There were six small rooms to a pod and Jake briefly greeted his pod mates in the common area between the rooms, then retreated to his personal space. He glanced at his journal, but then lay down in his bunk and listened to music.

They were scheduled to start weight training in the morning, preparing for the increased gravity of earth, but he already felt heavier. The next day he dutifully went to training. He stayed positive, because he knew they were watching for any sign of depression that might make him a problem on a long voyage. He did well. After three weeks of training they went as a group to the port and took the train up the side of Mount Olympus to the spaceport. He watched from the windows of the train as the city shrank. At the halfway point they changed into their pressure suits as a safety precaution. When he finished dressing he looked out the window again and noticed the horizon was slightly bowed. He pointed it out to his seat mate. Who stared for a while and then nodded. Jake had expected to see the massive rail gun from a distance, but it didn't appear until they crested a small rim near the top of the mountain.

The rail gun was 120 kilometers long running across the high plateau of Mt. Olympus. It curved slightly upward from the beginning, but the angle increased more rapidly to 45 degrees over the last sixteen kilometers of track. Jake could see the back of the solar covering that coated the entire southern face of the launcher through the structure. Their practice launch would be a single orbit in a large training pod that fit all twelve members of their group. The real launch would be alone so they could achieve sufficient altitude to meet the fast utility shuttle that would take them to the cycler.

When the train stopped, they picked up their helmets and personal bags and got off in the pressurized station. The man who met them was short and thick and talked with an old world, possibly American accent. "I'll be your captain when we launch next month. If there's anyone here who doesn't feel up to this, say so now, because we don't put up with anything on the real trip. If you cause a problem, I'll have you sedated and locked in your cabin until we arrive." He paused and watched to see if anyone would speak up. No one did. "Good. Anil will be your crew chief both today and during the actual voyage. You do exactly as he says, and you probably won't get hurt." The captain nodded at Anil and left.

Anil lead the group up to a room just below the low end of the rail gun where they put on their helmets, checked the seals and walked out onto the platform. The platform was pressurized and on the warehouse floor below the platform, Jake saw dock workers in short sleeves moving cargo. In fact, the gun was busy launching the cargo that would be traveling with them and lining it up in orbit. The shuttles were already collecting it and starting to move it out to the cycler. Their real launch would be among the last. They stepped into the training pod. It had been rigged to look like the real pods inside, so he couldn't see any of the other travelers. They would each go through all the manual launch procedures just in case they had to do it on their own launches, and even though they wouldn't really be controlling this POD every command would be recorded and a report generated. The procedure was actually very simple, so no one was worried.

A voice in Jake's helmet said, "Standby for launch in thirty seconds." A loud whistle sounded up and down the track for five seconds, with flashing lights. The lights continued flashing after the whistle stopped and the pod moved smoothly down the rail out of the loading area onto the open track. Jake could see the lights winking down the track. He glanced up and saw the stars shining through the purple sky. "Launch in five seconds," the voice said again. Jake felt the pod lurch forward. Over five seconds the pressure built to where he could barely breathe and stayed that way for nearly a minute then suddenly he was light as a feather. "Ramp cleared," the voice in his helmet said. Then "Prepare for primary ignition." Jake saw the sky grow black then the voice said, "Ignition in 5 seconds, 4, 3, 2, 1," Jake flipped the switch, even though he knew it did nothing and felt the kick of the rocket engine slam him into his seat as though he had ignited it. "Engine shut down in 2 seconds, 1, shut down," the voice said. Jake flipped his switch back and the engine quieted.

The stars shone down sharp and unblinking, so deep and detailed a field of dots that staring into it was almost hypnotic. He stared for half an hour until the stars began to dim a little and some of the smaller dots disappeared. Then the voice in his helmet said, "Prepare to deploy feather." Jake found the feather handle and put his hand on it.

"Deploy feather in 5 seconds, 4, 3, 2, 1, deploy."

Jake pulled and twisted the handle. The nose of the pod pitched up, angling the belly of the pod into the thin air ahead of the ship. He felt the gentle pressure of the seat against him. The pressure grew stronger over the next twenty minutes, but the view outside his window was changing. The light from the sun slipped out of site and Mars was cold and dark below him. Suddenly a long curving crescent of light erupted directly in front of him, brilliant white, then widened and fractured into the colors of the rainbow for a split second before the sky resolved itself into a deep purple all around him and the ground erupted into a corrugated montage of browns, whites, greys, and deep blacks.

"Prepare to unfeather," said the voice, and Jake put his hand back on the lever. "5, 4, 3, 2, 1, unfeather." He twisted and pushed the lever in. The pod angled downward.

In the distance he could see the bulk of Mt. Olympus growing larger. "Prepare to fire retrorockets." Jake found that switch, uncovered it, and put his finger under it. "Fire." He flipped the switch and felt the blood rush to his head as the straps dug in. After three minutes, Mt. Olympus was huge and moving slowly underneath the ship. "Retro rocket shut down in 5 seconds, 4, 3, 2, 1, shut down." Only after he flipped the switch off did he realize he had held his hand on the switch the entire three and a half minutes and his fingers were going numb. Mt. Olympus was stationary below the pod, but was rising quickly up to meet it. "Prepare to fire landing rockets in 3, 2, 1, fire." Jake flipped the switch and felt his seat catch him. The ground slowed. "Deploy struts." Jake hunted along the instrument panel for the button, found it and heard the struts deploy just as he was about to press the button. He pressed it anyway. "Reduce landing rocket thrust to 50% in 3,2,1, throttle down." "Cut landing rockets in 3, 2, 1, cut off." He flipped the landing rocket switch back into position just as he felt the struts hit the ground. "Safe all systems," the voice said, and Jake pressed the big friendly "Safe" button and watched until a green confirmation light lit.

A flatbed truck that had been waiting at a respectful distance backed towards them and slid under the pod. Evidently, the driver now had control of the pod because the struts retracted on their own when he was in position. Jake closed his eyes as the truck rumbled along. It took a half hour to get back to the prep station, which was a little up track of the warehouse they had started at.

When they climbed out onto the platform, Anil was there taking off his helmet and waiting for them. By the time they gathered around him he was looking at a hand held display and flicking the data around. He looked at each of them to see the look in their eyes then said, "Billings, get those struts out a little quicker." Jake nodded. "You passed though. Any questions?" No one said anything. "Good." Anil said, "Let's get off this mountain and get something to eat."

Two hours later they were seated in a restaurant Jake had never heard of when he was a student. The group was starting to loosen up, and starting to talk about the flight. Jake looked around, noticed a fair number of uniforms, and decided it was some sort of flyboy hangout.

Anil noticed him looking around and said, "Some of the guys like to hang out here, but don't come down here without me. Some of them don't really like you being here." Jake noticed a lot of the shorter men going in and out of a doorway towards the back.

"What's in there?"

"Don't even think of going in there, that's the bar. They don't even like me going in there."

Jake knew of a bar down by the port where some of the dockworkers liked to go. A few of his college friends had tried to crash it, but the dock workers kicked the crap out them, stuck them in a taxi and told the driver to take them back to preschool.

"Why? Are they going to fight me if I do?"

Anil thought for a minute, "Probably not this close to a flight, but they have other ways to get even with you. There's nothing for you in there anyway."

Jake heard a couple of men laughing a little too loudly in the bar and looked back at Anil convinced. Anil smirked and looked into his glass.

"Well, is the food good?"

"That's why we're here." Anil said, "That and no one pays any attention when you talk about firing rockets."

"What's good to eat?"

"Just let me do the ordering. It's going to be expensive, and you guys are paying for it, but you'll thank me later."

"What are you going to order?" Jake asked, looking through the menu.

"It's not on the menu... This is our place so we make sure there's always a little food from the old world that finds its way here in various nooks and crannies of the ships. That way the short folks get to have a taste of home while they're stuck here. I figure since you guys are going to be stuck there for a *year, you might as well get a taste of it. Besides, these guys know how to cook it."

When the food came, everyone looked at it and then looked at Anil. Jake tried to cut the meat with the side of his fork, but it was a little too tough for that. He picked up a knife, cut a small piece, put it in his mouth, and closed his eyes.

"This is good," he said.

"This is steak," said Anil. "Any questions?"

Jake shook his head and chewed.

"Good," said Anil and put a piece in his own mouth.

When they were done eating, someone at the end of the table said, "No wonder they're all fat on Earth."

Anil shook his head, "They aren't fat, well... at least not all of them. They just look that way to us."

"Well, I'm going to get fat," the man said.

"You better bulk up those knobby knees of yours first," Anil said, "or they'll snap off like twigs." Everyone smiled at that, because he did have knobby knees. They stayed a while longer and tried a few other things like lemons and canned water chestnuts, but the steak was the winner.

In the evening, they waddled out to the street and hailed taxis. In the morning half of them were sick, but aside from being a bit irregular Jake felt fine. It didn't matter. They had the day off.

When Jake and his roommates arrived in their classroom the next morning, only the assistant was there. Once everyone was seated the assistant said,

"Most of your instructors have been called back to the port for meetings so they won't be joining us today. We're not sure when they will be back, and you're ready for flight, so we'll skip ahead and take the final exam today, then you'll be free for the rest of the week."

A happy murmur spread through the classroom, but Jake stared at the assistant with a question on his face. The class settled down and started studying. After a few hours they quit and took the tests.

An hour later the assistant said, "Congratulations to all of you. We'll send you your certificates at your registered addresses. You are dismissed."

As the others filed out Jake approached the assistant and said, "What's going on?"

The assistant looked at him for a second, softened, and said, "It looks like the central government is taking control of the next three cycler shipments in both directions. The port authority is scrambling to figure out how to make all the changes." Jake's face went blank, then he suddenly came to life, thanked the instructor and rushed to get his gear.

As he ran he called Ellie, but there was no answer. Her status showed unavailable. He sent her a quick note and made a break for the port. On the way, he got into the Stewards' Forum and then it was obvious what was going on. He read all the way to the port, booked the first flight for Paititi and read some more in the waiting room and on the transport.

Only when he landed did he think to make sure his hotel room would be available. He was jumping into a taxi when a new message for him came in from the Department. He read it in the back of the cab. It asked him to report to the Department the next day. It wasn't until he was in his room that he finally heard from Ellie.

"Where are you?" she asked.

"Paititi," he said.

"Me to," she said. "I want to see you."

He picked her up at her parents' house and they went to a little shop Ellie knew near the campus with books on the wall.

Forty-Five

Earlier, that morning, Ellie had woken up to pounding on her back door. It took a few hazy seconds to begin wondering what was happening. She looked at the clock, 10:30 a.m. She looked out the door and saw a sheriff's deputy. "What now?" she thought.

"Miss, are you OK?"

"Yes, I was just up late last night."

"May I come in?"

"Sure." Ellie opened the door wide.

The deputy took off his hat as he entered and said, "The Department asked me to check on you when they couldn't contact you this morning." Ellie wrinkled her forehead trying to figure out why they couldn't reach her, then remembered she had set her status to unavailable while working on the report.

"Oh," she said and changed the status back. "I forgot to switch this back last night."

"Miss, the Department would like you to check in and they've asked me to wait here while you do."

Ellie stiffened a little at that. The Department obviously knew she had been working late by the time stamp on her report. How could they doubt her like this?

"OK."

She called her coordinator and was immediately routed to the main office.

"Ellie," her father said, "Is everything OK?"

"Yes. What's going on? I worked late last night and now there's a Sheriff's deputy in my living room."

"Ellie, the Department has received several threats against you, and they seem credible. Pack your things and come home. The deputy will escort you to the depot."

"Dad. I don't think this is necessary. People are upset, they say things..."

"Do you really think you're so indispensable that it's worth the risk? Come home. We'll sort it out when you get here."

"Dad. If I leave now, it's going to look like I ran away and then it will be very difficult to ever come back. I'm staying put."

"Ms. Waddell, this is a formal transfer. Leave your station within the hour, and report to the main office by 10:00 a.m. tomorrow morning."

"Yes, sir," Ellie said, and disconnected. She looked at the deputy daring him to say something but he wisely studied the floor, so she turned and packed her things.

At the depot in Paititi she toyed with getting a hotel room, but her anger was spent. She caught a taxi and went home. Her old room seemed smaller than she remembered. The paint she had picked out seemed too bright and she felt mildly embarrassed to remember the intense feelings she had felt over nothing in that room. Her parents were careful with her, and even that seemed silly. Only after she had unpacked did she notice Jake's messages.

At dinner they were both too tired to say much, but there was companionship in the silence. Outside the streets were wet from an early summer shower. They walked arm in arm down the streets that had once been her home. Ellie shuddered as she began to relax. Jake pulled her closer and warmed her hands in his.

"Ask me to marry you, Jake," she said.

He looked at her for a second, smiled, and shook his head, "Not tonight."

"When?"

He looked into the middle distance and then back at her and said, "Soon enough."

She shook her head and said, "Not soon enough!" But she didn't say anything more about it.

They walked for an hour more and then he took her home. They kissed for a long time on her father's doorstep. She lost track of time. She found herself wanting more, and then he was gone.

In the morning they met at the main office and waited together in the break room. Ed Lundy came in and called Ellie into his office. When she came back there was still a hint of annoyance on her face, but the wheels in her head were turning something over.

"What happened?"

"I'll tell you afterwards. You better get in there. He wants to see you next."

"What does he want with me?"

"How should I know? Probably the same thing he wanted with me. Just go find out."

Jake entered Ed's office. He had a fine wood desk that seemed a bit much for the small office. Ed offered Jake a seat and sat down behind the desk.

"Jake, I was sorry to hear about your father's passing."

"Thank you."

"I know you've had your share of disappointments this year, and I'm sorry to say I'm going to have to hand you another one."

Jake looked at him expectantly.

"The central government will be declaring a state of emergency tomorrow morning. Among other things, that means that all off world travel by essential personnel will be restricted."

"Mr. Lundy, I don't work for the Department of Agriculture."

"Starting tomorrow morning you do. We will be buying out your contract with Empaqueme and you will be working for the Department under me. We are initiating a number of special projects to deal with the current crisis. You will be working with Dr. Erwin, some students, and several station stewards on creating new blight resistant apple trees." He handed him a briefing folder. "You'll get a soft copy as soon as this becomes public. Get registered in our system before you leave today and report to the address in your folder tomorrow morning to get started."

"How long does this assignment last?"

"Until the emergency has passed."

"What's my pay?"

"It's all in the packet. If you have any other questions, give me a call. I have a meeting I have to attend," he said, and showed Jake to the door.

Jake wandered back into the break room and saw Ellie smirking at him. "So, what did you get?"

"Apples," Jake said. "You?"

"I'm on wheat."

Jake was still fuming about the high handed treatment he had received when he noticed Ellie was smiling. "What are you so cheerful about?" he asked.

"Where are you working?" she asked. He opened the folder, looked at it, and showed it to her. She opened up her folder and lined up the address of her work place next to his. They were adjacent buildings on the university campus. She watched him, waiting for recognition to spark.

He looked at her, sat back in his chair, rested his chin on his hand and said, "I guess this changes things a bit, Miss Waddell."

"Yes. Yes it does."

Then Ellie noticed his salary.

"Hey, that's not fair. I've got more experience than you do."

"You're right. I guess it's not so bad being press-ganged into service after all, especially when your new employer works for the folks that print the money."

Since they had the afternoon off Ellie said, "Come on, I've got a delivery to make." They went back to her parents' house and she picked up a carton with little green shoots sticking up out of it.

"Where are we going?" Jake asked after Ellie had given the cab driver the address.

"You'll see," she said beaming.

The driver dropped them off and they walked slowly towards a house. Ellie was looking a little pensive as they approached the door and knocked. A plump older woman answered the door and Ellie asked for Matilda. The lady disappeared and Jake braced himself. In a few moments Matilda came to the door. She saw Jake first and stiffened, but relaxed a little when she saw Ellie.

"Come in," she said, opening the door wider.

When they were in the entry hall, Ellie said, "Matilda, these are clones of your orange tree. I thought you would want them." She lifted the box towards Matilda.

Matilda shook her head, clenched her jaw and was silent for a moment before saying, "That's very kind of you. But I don't want them. Please take them away." She turned and retreated down the hall. Ellie and Jake stood frozen for a few seconds, then turned and let themselves out. Jake got busy calling a cab and Ellie was fighting back tears when there was the sound of a door closing behind them. Ellie turned to see Annabelle jogging toward them.

"Ellie! I'm sorry about mama."

Ellie shook her head and smiled. "It's OK. I should have thought it through more."

"I know mama doesn't want them, but can I have them?"

Ellie nodded, "Of course," and handed her the box, but Annabelle wasn't done.

She gave Ellie a big hug. "My father was a lot of things, but this," she said hefting the box, "was one of the good things."

Ellie gave Annabelle a hug. Then she turned and went back into the house leaving Jake and Ellie alone.

Falling paths unwind
Sure hands entwine
New life ignites
Old loss sprouts delight

Forty-Six

Jake and Ellie met for breakfast the next morning, and every morning, while they worked on successive generations of blight resistant crops. The barley team broke out ahead of the rest when they realized Ellie's barley was already blight resistant. They quickly bought up all the barley Julie and her husband could produce to provide seed worldwide.

Ellie's court day came and went uneventfully. The Department lawyers successfully argued that since the administrative procedure had yet to be completed, there were no grounds for a law suit. When the suit was filed again after the Alcantars lost their administrative case, Ellie was not individually named.

One morning when they met for breakfast, Jake took Ellie's hands and said, "Let's skip work today." Ellie looked up started to shake her head, but Jake caught her gaze and she said, "OK."

They rode up onto the bench above town, past the temple to the end of the road. At the end of the peninsula separating the bay from the ocean, they climbed a steep trail up the bluff to a point where they could see in all directions. The wind had a bite in it, so they stood very close to each other to keep warm. Ellie watched the white caps forming on the waves and the ships far out at sea. The seagulls far below danced on the air currents and the distant line between sea and sky was indistinct. All sense of place, season, and time faded, leaving only the moment floating unbounded.

Ellie felt Jake lean into her as he shifted his weight, moving his free hand. She did not look over, but only felt him close to her. She closed her eyes and when she opened them again he was looking at her, studying her face. She smiled at him and brushed the hair out of his face. He leaned his forehead into the caress for a moment and then pulled back again to look at her.

He opened his mouth, and said, "I like having breakfast with you." She smiled, but said nothing. "I like having lunch with you." He said. "I like having dinner with you and working with you, and playing with you." She narrowed her eyes watching him to see what he would say next. "I like talking to you. I want to go on big adventures with you." He paused to see her response, but she only watched him, calmly, waiting for her turn to speak. "I'd like to ask you out on another date. Would that be OK?"

She nodded, watching him carefully. "If you have time this fall, I'd like you to marry me. What do you say?" She kissed him then, and after she kissed him she said, "What time will you get me home?"

"Never."

"What should I wear?"

"Something white... I hope!"

She narrowed her eyes at him.

"And this," he said pressing a small box into her hand. She opened it and a stone on a platinum band made little rainbows in the palm of her hand. She smiled and kissed him again, and when he opened his eyes she was slipping the ring on her finger.

He took her left hand in his right, interlacing the fingers and said, "Well, what do you say?"

She looked up at him and nodded rapidly.

"No. You have to actually say it for it to hold up in court."

"I, Elisa P. Waddell, will marry you, Jacob W. Billings II this fall. Will that do?"

He wrapped his arms around her waist and said, "That will do."

The late summer and early fall were full of preparations. Ellie took a ride on the train with her mother and sisters up valley to visit the only dress maker she knew. The miles of open farm land that passed by the windows looked very different without any trees. The scorched black earth was softened by a green fuzz of fall wheat, barley, and soybeans and it was a darker green than Ellie had seen before. Closer to her old station there were still some trees, but they were forlorn looking things empty of fruit and waiting for renewal.

Cava met them at the depot and drove them to the shop. The woman there greeted them warmly and started the ritual of looking through the dress book with them. At the break she had chocolate chip cookies and milk in honor of her sisters. In a few hours, once Ellie had discouraged some of her bolder proposals, she was standing in the most stunning dress Ellie could have imagined for her wedding. In the end, even the dress maker had to admit that, "Simple can be very powerful... when it fits right."

Next they worked on dresses for the attendants.

"Look at you, Cava," Ellie said smiling, "You can wear a dress after all."

Cava didn't take the bait.

When they went to leave, the dress maker wouldn't accept payment. "Go. Get married and make lots of Ellies to come here and save us from the next blight." Ellie tried to say thank you, but her voice broke.

On the way back to the depot, Cava told exaggerated stories about Ellie to her mother and sisters. Ellie just looked out the window to avoid being drawn in. At an intersection a block from the depot, she saw Titu sitting in his truck waiting for the light to change. He had already seen her. She looked at him. He nodded then drove away.

The day of the wedding was unseasonably warm for October. The sun was low, on its autumn path, providing golden light all day. A light breeze kept the flags outside the temple flapping contentedly as they arrived.

Jake woke up that morning suddenly unsure, not of Ellie, but of himself. His success so far was pretty much a fluke. Could he keep the commitments he would make? Would he be what he ought to be through all the twisted obstacles and the long days? He was uneasy, but then he saw her there waiting for him just inside the temple gates and he knew he could do it, not because he was strong or clever or wise, but because she would be there to help him.

The ceremony was deep and simple, and when he kissed her again as her husband, his mind was clear and calm.

They spent the first two nights in Paititi, then caught the first flight to their honeymoon spot. In flight Jake pointed towards the north polar sea and said, "You're sure you don't want to 'swim in the hot, carbonated seas formed after asteroid strikes'?" Referring to a travel ad she had instantly vetoed three weeks before.

She leaned against him, smiled and shook her head slightly.

When they landed, Hal picked them up and took them back to his place for lunch. After lunch they went out to Hal's barn and sorted through Jake's things looking for gear.

"I guess we ought to get this stuff out of your barn soon," Jake said.

"Take your time," was all Hal would say.

Once they had enough gear, Hal drove them out almost to the wilderness hut and dropped them off. They hiked the rest of the way intentionally knocking shoulders from time to time. They had brought a good dinner with them, but in the tradition of the hut they left it on the shelves and made a meal of the oldest food there. It was not good, but they did not care. A wind kicked up in the evening and they cuddled on the bottom bunk, listened to it for a while, and then explored each other.

In the morning, the sun came out clear and bright. They made breakfast and amused themselves reading the log until they came to their own entries.

"You read mine out loud, then I'll read yours out loud," Ellie suggested.

Jake hesitated, then read.

"March 43, 0076 – Elisa P. Waddell and Jacob W. Billings II - Sunny & cool on the 42nd, followed by wind and snow in the early hours of the 43rd and heavy rain during the day.

Ellie – I came to the badlands of Arabia Terra soul searching and looking for my future. Instead of finding it, I crashed my rock crawler in a wadi and found a wild man raving in the wilderness."

Jake sighed and said, "I guess I was a bit of a wild man, but raving? Babbling maybe, but raving?"

"I only wrote that because I was sure you were going to read it when you wrote yours, even though you said you wouldn't," Ellie said.

"So what would you have written if you had known I wouldn't read it until now?"

Ellie thought for moment and said, "I came to the badlands searching for something special, and he found me."

Jake looked at her out of the corner of his eyes and said, "Really? You would have written that then?"

Ellie laughed and said, "No. Probably not. But I think I knew even then. I wouldn't admit it, especially to myself, but I think I knew."

"I knew," Jake said.

"No, you didn't," Ellie said.

"Read my entry," Jake said.

Ellie gave him an uncertain look, cleared her throat and read.

"My father died and I buried him on the mountain. Sometimes I think I see him out of the corner of my eye and I turn to tell him something but he isn't there. He shaped this place. He will always be a part of it. He shaped me. He will always be a part of me. Someday many years from now, I hope to turn and see him standing there for real, come to take me with him.

On the way home from the mountain I found Ellie alone and in trouble. I helped her, then she helped me.

I came back to this place to say goodbye, to close a chapter of my life, and turn my back on this place forever. But as the miles unwind this place calls me home, and chapters I had not anticipated open."

Then below the main entry was added,

"I can't tell her now, but someday I will marry Ellie and we will have

children together and make this desert into a beautiful forest. ...if I can convince her to speak to me again."

Ellie stopped reading and looked at him.

"You did know. Why didn't you say anything?"

"Because you would have run home, bolted the door, and filed a restraining order against me."

Ellie considered this for a moment, nodded and said, "That sounds about right."

"I missed on a couple of things though," he said. "We don't have any children, and we won't shape this land."

"Forecasting a forest here was a bit wild. But I think if we try real hard, we can do something about the other part," Ellie said very soberly.

Jake considered this for a moment, nodded and said, "That sounds about right." Then he chased her back to the bunk.

Over the next few days, they retraced their steps to the wadi and to what was left of the crawler and to the place were Jake first found Ellie. He took her to the mountain top and showed her his father's grave, and told her about the cottonwood trees his father made him promise to plant. They stayed late on the mountain using oxygen masks and waiting until the stars came out, and Jake described the view from orbit.

They made a circuit around the lower fifth of what had been Jakes father's stewardship, going slowly and growing more used to each other. Everywhere Jake went he could still see the forest. He did not mention it much, even tried to pick topics that lead away from it, but Ellie could see the look in his eyes. "Are you sorry we came?" she asked when they were on the way back to where Hal would pick them up.

"No," he said. "Not all ghosts are unwelcome. I think this land will someday look the way I imagine it. It doesn't matter that someone else will make it that way."

Ellie hugged him and they walked on side by side. They had dinner with Hal at a sandwich shop near the terminal. They wanted to take him some place nicer, but that was where Hal wanted to go, and restaurants only got to a certain level of nice in town anyway. Hal had a grilled cheese sandwich and tomato soup. He was so enthusiastic about it that they ordered it too.

When they arrived in Paititi they went straight home to Jake's place. He unlocked the door and gestured for Ellie to go inside. It felt a little strange to follow her in and lock the door behind them. The living room was full of boxes of Ellie's things that her family had brought over while they were gone. Their wedding presents were piled in the dining area. They kissed in the kitchen. It was getting late. Finally Ellie said, "This is ridiculous," grabbed him by the belt, towed him to the bedroom and closed the door.

Forty-Seven

Titu folded his arms and looked at a spot just over his father's left shoulder while he waited for his father to stop speaking. Whenever he did this, his father hesitated slightly longer between one word and the next. Then the muscles at the corners of Titu's mouth twitched nearly imperceptibly, which made his father pause again. Titu had been playing this game for nearly fifteen minutes when his mother came in and put a stop to it.

"I'm sure Titu understands your point Urco," she said, taking a seat.

"I don't think he does," Titu's father said.

"Titu, do you understand what your father has been trying to tell you?"

"Yes. He is saying that if I had been more careful at executing our goals we wouldn't be in the trouble we are in now."

"Then why do you think this is funny?" his father said.

Titu finally looked him in the eye and said, "Because I executed as perfectly as I can and it still didn't work. I'm not the problem here."

"Are you implying I'm the problem?" his father bellowed, turning slightly red.

"We made the wrong goals, and we had some bad luck."

"You see! You never fully committed."

"We tried to expand too fast - much too fast. We were doing fine before, and we should have grown at a more careful pace."

"You see that!" Urco said to his wife, "The boy lacks the courage to strike when the opportunity presents itself. I don't know why I let you talk me into making him a full partner."

"Titu doesn't lack courage. He merely lacks the vision to see what he is destined to be. He doesn't care as much about wealth as you do, and he doesn't see that wealth is just the first step to greatness and that you have to acquire it early to have time for the rest of the steps. He has forgotten that he is a descendant of kings..."

Titu held up his hand in a stop sign. "I haven't forgotten. I'd have to have something organically wrong with my brain to have forgotten that since you mention it at least three times a week."

His mother started to respond, but he held up his hand again.

"The fact is I think Dad is right, but not in the way he thinks he is. I don't lack courage in taking risks in business, or with my reputation, or any other competition. In fact, I think I'm pretty good at it. I lack the courage to tell you who I really am, and what I really want."

"You've never been shy about that!" his mother said, "and all those things are fine, but you have a greater destiny to fulfill, you have..."

"No. Those are your plans. I don't need as much. I don't think I even want as much. It's time for us to unwind this."

"To unwind what?" his father said.

"To unwind this partnership."

"How can you talk like that, especially right now when we need to pull together?"

"We will pull together, and we will get through this, but when we are done I won't be part of Alcantar Enterprises anymore."

His father started to object, but Titu shook his head. "My mind is made up." He turned to go and then almost didn't when he saw the look on his mother's face. The old man was hurt, but he was almost proud of him. She might not ever forgive him. He turned and left anyway.

Outside, the smell of smoke was strong as the burning in the southern end of the valley was getting up to speed, but Titu walked lightly. He smiled at some of the ranch hands on the way to his truck, and they paused and watched him go. He drove up to a little rise where he could look out over the ranches and watched them burn. Then he reached behind the passenger seat, pulled out a guitar and began practicing an old folk song about eagles soaring, and several others. He sat back and watched the sky turn red then gold, closed his eyes, and slept.

Forty-Eight

Chris was reviewing steward requests for grants when he heard Ed start patrolling the hall. Most of the requests were straightforward and would be granted. Fortunately, most stewards had been returning profits to the Department as agreed for *years so even though almost every steward was making a request, and the drain would be heavy, everyone would get what they needed and there would still be reserves for next year.

There were also several offers from commercial banks to sell farm land to the Department. Chris was familiar with some of the property, major chunks of the Simmons, Alcantar, and Call ranches, but there were a dozen or so that he was not familiar with. The Department would probably buy some of them since the banks were desperate, the prices low, and the Department solvent. Still, Mars was one of the few places where the old real estate adage "They aren't making more land," was completely false. The Department made hundreds of acres a year of new arable land, which was usually enough to meet the needs of young farmers entering the program. In a year like this though, they might not have enough. The Department was already cancelling its contracted stewardships to have more to assign. The commercial farms, seeing no chance for a profit under the terms were only too happy to get part of their upfront money back to try to save their main properties from foreclosure. In the end, the decision to buy or not would be made by others.

Ed was back in the office from wherever he had gone and was walking faster than normal. He suddenly filled the frame of Chris's door.

"You set me up!" he said, his face flushed.

Chris rearranged documents on his desktop for a moment, then looked up at him.

"I didn't set you up Ed. I documented what you set up."

"You S.O.B.! How could you do that after all I did for you and your family? How could you do that when I was willing to look the other way after your whore daughter nearly crashed our entire economy with her incompetence? I was looking out for you and all our friends and you pulled this?"

"Ed, what you were doing was wrong. It risked destroying the trust that the Department needs to function, and it was probably illegal. I tried to reason with you."

"You shut your pious hole and listen to me. You're not the only one who can write reports. You're going down with me and everyone connected to you. Do you hear me Waddell? You're going down."

Ed left sputtering. Chris collected his thoughts for a second and shook his head. Then he pressed a few icons on his desktop saving the day's office recordings off site and amending his report to include them.

Back in his office, Ed sat scrolling through his inbox, more as an outlet than with any intent to do anything. He rested his head in his hands for a minute, then wiped the sweat off his forehead with his sleeves. When he looked back at his inbox a request caught his eye. It was from a friend's boy, the Alcantar kid. He was requesting to enter the program as a steward for one of his father's cancelled contracts.

"Well," Ed said, "I still have the authority for now. I might as well use it to help a friend one last time."

Ed approved the request and hand walked it through the system, then cleaned out his office.

Forty-Nine

The fall wheat and barley harvests were good enough that when the first relief shipment arrived from Earth it was tucked away into storage without touching much of it. Anxiety began to give way to tedium. The fields were frosted over now, too cold to grow anything. In a few months the farmers would break ground for the spring crop, but for now all was quiet.

Ellie's belly was beginning to show a little, but it took a sharp eye to spot it. Most of those that did weren't sure enough to risk saying anything, and Ellie didn't tell them. But her mother cried when she saw it. Jake liked to hug her from behind and put his hands on her belly.

Their life settled into a routine. They still ate breakfast together every morning, and went to work together. They had each moved on to new projects. He was working on tomatoes, and she was working on squash. They teased each other about their team's performance. If Jake's team was closer to being finished, he'd say "some teams are just faster than others." If Ellie tried the same trick with him when they were behind, he would say "Well, some teams care about quality more than others." It became a regular feature of breakfast until it was condensed down to one saying "Speed," and the other, "Quality." The work was fulfilling. Each new release was eagerly awaited and they got to stay with each project all the way through the first field trials before handing the product over to the seed producers. There was work enough to last *years. Then one morning breakfast was interrupted by a courier at the door. Back at the table, Jake and Ellie stared at the letter. It was from the Department, which was strange, since they had nearly daily contact with the head office. It was addressed to Jake, and Jake just kept looking at. "Open it already!" Ellie said. He did. Read it, then laid it on the table for Ellie to read.

"Dear Mr. Billings: We are pleased to inform you that your appeal in the case of the AT14 stewardship is granted. It is the opinion of the Department that the stewardship should have been awarded to you on your first application and that the appointment of the current steward was defective and will be vacated on your request."

When she looked up at him, he was watching her, his face a mask. "What should I answer?" he asked.

Ellie's eyes were sparkling as she said, "Oh, I don't think you really want to go back there, do you?"

Jake pressed his lips together and looked at her until she couldn't hold back the smile anymore. Then he smiled, and then they laughed and then he said, "Are you sure? It can be a lonely place, the pay is minimal, and there's never any recognition."

"Jake I have never ever felt lonely there, and I wouldn't miss an opportunity to build a whole diverse forest to make row crops for the rest of my life."

He hugged her close. They held on for a while and then sent a response saying, "Count us in."

It took two weeks to make all the arrangements and then they were standing in the yard of the station house. It was unchanged. The yard had drifts of snow covering it half a meter deep.

Hal was waiting in the driveway just in case no one was home, or there was trouble. They walked up to the door together and knocked. Alex opened the door on the third knock and stared at them blankly, until they felt uncomfortable. Then he broke out in a grin.

"Finally," he said, "Please come in." When they stepped into the front room they saw his bags packed and waiting by the door. He looked thinner than the last time Jake had seen him. He invited them to sit down and started briefing them on the situation. "I haven't been able to do much," he said. "I even actually tried the last few months before the snows came, but all I could really do is document the decline in everything."

Jake and Ellie looked at each other and chuckled.

"No, I really did. I just don't have the training for this sort of thing."

"It's not that," Ellie said. "We just know a thing or two about documenting decline."

"There really wasn't anything you could do," Jake added. "Even if Ellie and I had been here we couldn't have saved this environment. It's the wrong analog now. Conditions have changed too much and too quickly."

Alex perked up a little. "Well, I leave it in your hands then."

"What are you going to do now?" Ellie asked.

"I'm not sure. I've gotten pretty good at exploring wild places over the last few months. I'm thinking about joining the southern pioneer teams for a few seasons."

"I hear they could use a good man," Jake said.

"I hope so," Alex responded.

They said their goodbyes. Hal looked visibly relieved when everyone came out smiling and opened the door to take Alex back to the terminal.

When they were gone, Ellie and Jake went back inside and stood silently looking around; unsure what to do next. Finally they plopped down on the sofa, turned on the fireplace, cuddled up and fell asleep.

Moss grew
Grass grew
Trees grew
Babies grew
Birthdays fade
Long days
Short weeks
Years that will not stay

Fifty

Ellie ran to the bathroom in the dark and vomited in the toilet. Jake was sound asleep. She rested her head against the cool porcelain and wondered what was wrong. She had never been sick a day with her previous pregnancies. She flushed the toilet and washed up. Jake stirred in their bed. When she slid back into the covers he mumbled, "Everything OK?" but slid back into sleep faster than she could answer.

She turned her back to him and stared into the darkness. Dawn was only a few hours away, but she refused to think about the day to come. She kept her mind quiet. She closed her eyes. When she opened them again, Jake was in the shower and she could hear little kids climbing the counters in the kitchen. She looked at the clock and a thrill of panic ran through her stomach. She had less than 45 minutes to get everyone to school.

She threw on a robe and ran into the kitchen. Mary and Sam, her three and four half-*year olds, were still in their pajamas feeding themselves breakfast cereal and leaving plenty on the floor, table, and counters for the dog to eat.

Ellie clutched her hair with both hands and said, "Go get your clothes on!"

Sam said, "But we're eating breakfast!"

"I see that, but we're running late. Go!"

They went.

She went down the hall to find the older kids, Ada and Jacob, the sixteen and fifteen half-*year olds, were still in bed. "GET UP!" she shouted, shook them until they sat up, then went down the hall to check on Cava and Chris, the middle kids. They were up, dressed and ready to go. "Thank goodness!" she said, "Go help Mary and Sam get their clothes on then get in the car."

They sulked and moved slowly down the hall.

"There's five dollars in it for you," she hollered after them.

They moved quicker. She went back into Jacob's room and shook him again.

"You're going to be late!" she said.

He growled at her and covered his head as she left.

Ada wasn't up either. "What is the matter with you people?" she said. Ada got up in a huff and started dressing. Ellie went back to Jacob's room. He was faking sleep.

"You're out of time," she said.

"I'm not going," he said flatly.

"You are going," she said.

"No."

"Then you'll be on restriction and you'll be required to work all day."

"Fine, but I won't work."

"Then you'll be on restriction and minimum meals until you do work, AND go back to school."

"Fine."

"Fine," Ellie said, clenching her jaw and forcing a smile.

Jake was in the hall when she came out.

"He won't go to school. He won't work. He doesn't care if he's on restriction. I can't work with him. You deal with him!" she said, and went to throw on her clothes.

Jake went into Jacob's room. "So, you're not going to school today?"

"No."

"That must mean you'll be working today."

"No."

"Well, I suggest you get your clothes on then."

"No, I don't think I will."

"Well you can't stay here. If you want to go out in your underwear that's your business," Jake said and left the room.

Ellie left in a blur with three of the kids in hot pursuit. Jake put out a proper meal for the two littlest kids and went to check on Jacob. He was sulking in the dark. Jake went around the house locking the doors and windows, except the front door. Then he went into Jacob's room, picked him up, and threw him out the front door in his underwear. A few minutes later he threw some clothes out the back door for him. Jacob picked them up indignantly and moved towards one of the barns.

Jake yelled out the window, "If you're headed to the barn, you're headed for work." Jacob considered his options for a moment then moved out towards the open country side.

The little kids were done eating, and running around the living room when Ellie got back.

"Are you taking him to school?" she asked.

"No."

"Well I'm not!" Ellie said.

"So he won't go today."

"He has to go."

"Not today."

Ellie looked out the window. She was stiff as a board. Jake rubbed her shoulders and felt her soften a little.

The littlest kids were leaving a wake of destruction behind them. After Mary knocked over a lamp, Ellie focused on them. She inhaled and exhaled slowly, and walked towards them.

She sat down in the middle of the floor and shook her arms and head until her cheeks flapped while burbling. The kids broke into peals of laughter and ran around her.

Jake looked at her, smirking. She looked up in time to see it and smiled.

Jake went outside and walked among the trees nearest the house. They were not yet full grown, but they were already the tallest trees in the world. They even had to put a chain across the driveway to keep the odd visitor from driving up to the station at all hours of the day and night to take a look at them.

Beyond the station the trees thinned out and weren't as tall yet. The grass of the meadows was dressed in its September brown. The rabbits watched him coming, alert, but not afraid. If little Cava had been with him they would have actually started following them. Soon it would be time to introduce bobcats or coyotes (if Ellie would let him). He sat by the pond and dangled his fingers in the water. The trout nibbled his fingers and he slowly exhaled.

When he got back to the house, the younger kids were having another snack and Ellie was organizing their morning lesson. She had saved a muffin for him. He ate it.

He looked through the calendar, and started getting his things together.

"Going up river?" Ellie asked.

"Yeah, I'm worried about the forest on the west bank below Crawler Hole. I think too much underbrush is accumulating. We probably should have tried to burn it over the summer, but it'll never burn now."

"Is this where we have our goat discussion again?"

"No. This is where I say 'white tailed deer' and leave quickly before you can think of an answer."

He gave her a peck on the cheek and opened the door.

"Don't forget our date," she said as he went out.

"I won't," he said, closing the door.

By 12:30, the kids' lessons were done and they were getting cranky. Ellie put them down for a nap, tied her hair back and fired up the equipment in the lab. Jake came in a few minutes later, hung up his things, kissed her and said, "What are we making today?"

"I was thinking about wild sweet peas to help with the nitrogen fixing on the back side of the mountain. The lupine just isn't cutting it anymore."

"Sounds good," Jake said, and rolled up his sleeves. Jake started bringing up the trait library and arranging it while Ellie went through three varieties of wild sweet pea deciding which one to use as a starting point. Once Jake had the libraries open to the right places, he started preparing the blanks and warming up a bio-reactor. By the time he had finished, Ellie was nearly done inserting traits. He stood behind her looking at the display.

"What do you think?" she asked when she was done. He scrolled through the design and finally said, "I like the original purple flowers better. "

"You'll get your purple flowers," she said, pointing at a specific set of sequences, "You just won't get them every time."

This had become Ellie's thing lately. She liked putting little surprises into ordinary things. The environment had changed enough that most organisms only needed slight tweaks, and the surprises kept it interesting.

Jake wrapped his arms around her from behind, pressed up against her pushing forward and said, "I think you like to leave your mark on everything."

Ellie smiled and pushed his arms off. "Get to work," she said as she hit the encoding button. Within 45 minutes Jake had the young plants snuggly tucked into their bioreactor. Then they walked down the rows of reactors and young plants under lights checking on their work from previous days, and then out into the barns.

"We need to talk about the underbrush," Jake said.

"Ah, the white tailed deer..."

"Yes. The rabbits won't eat the underbrush and they're starting to over graze the softer meadow plants by the creek... which brings up the need for predators to check the rabbits."

"We can split the rabbits and move them a few more times before we need to get predators."

"Yes, but if they get too far ahead of the predators, we're going to have a problem."

"No coyotes!" she said.

"All right, no coyotes, yet. I was thinking bobcats. They're relatively shy and they can take on a bunny pretty easily.

Ellie considered her options and finally relented, "OK, but we don't release them until the spring."

"Agreed."

"And far from the house."

"OK, now what about the deer."

"I'm not sure the deer will really eat the underbrush, they'll probably just go for the grass like the rabbits."

"They'll eat the underbrush when it's young. We need more variety in our herbivores."

"And when we get too many deer..."

"Then we'll need some large predators."

"No wolves!"

"Eventually we will need wolves... but we could probably start with some cougars, though I don't see how that's better."

Ellie nodded. "Go ahead and order the bobcats. We can talk more about the deer later."

Jake looked at the clock. "I'll get the kids," he said, and went for the car.

Half way to the school he saw Jacob walking along the road. He slowed and pulled up beside him.

Jacob didn't look at him, but got into the car.

"Have a good walk?"

Jacob shrugged.

They drove in silence.

Jake looked out over the hills he must have been walking through. He couldn't recognize his old haunts, even when he knew where they were.

"I know why I roamed these hills. Why do you?"

Jacob didn't say anything, but just looked out the window. Jake let the silence hang. At school Jacob went to pick up assignments from his teachers while Jake gathered the other kids. When Jacob got back, the front most seats were taken. He glowered at everyone as he worked his way to the back, and the happy chatter stopped. Just before sitting down he punched Chris hard on the shoulder for looking at him and then the fight was on. Jake jumped out of the driver's seat, opened the back hatch, and pulled them both out through it by the back of their shirts. He set them down on the curb and then stood there, curbing his own anger. "What is the matter with you?" he finally asked.

"He hit me first."

"You had it coming," Jacob said, and moved quickly toward him just to see him jump.

"Chris, get back in the car."

Jacob bristled.

"Chris isn't the problem here."

"He always gives me attitude when you aren't looking. You don't know."

"You've been pissed all day. Is thumping little kids how you feel better?"

"Yeah, I guess it is."

"You're just digging it deeper, aren't you?"

"Yeah, I guess I am."

Jake looked into the distance, then looked back at him and said, "We'll finish this at home."

Nobody said much on the way home. When they got to the station everyone split up pretty quickly.

Jacob tried to slip away too, but Jake collared him.

"We're not through."

"Yes we are."

Jake looked at the barn where he knew there was plenty of manure that needed shoveling, but then looked at the hills. "Come on," he said.

Jacob suppressed a look of surprise and followed. Jake walked fast and Jacob struggled to keep up after the first kilometer, but Jake didn't slow down. They slipped through side canyons Jacob didn't know were there and around hills he would have gone over. Only once when he came to a flooded gulley did Jake hesitate, but only for a moment and then he was moving forcefully again.

After two hours, the sun was getting low in the sky and Jacob was starting to look worried. They started trudging up an incline and when the trail finally leveled out it wound around the shoulder of a small mountain and out to a protected hollow in the mountain that looked out to the southwest. The view was so sudden and stunning that Jacob just stopped when they rounded the corner.

"This was my best spot," Jake said.

Jacob sat down.

They sat in silence for a long time as the sun got low in the sky.

Finally Jake said, "You've been pretty difficult lately. What's eating you?"

Jacob didn't look up but shrugged almost imperceptibly.

Jake waited. Jacob said nothing, but he was looking out over the horizon now.

"Are you tired of school?" Jake guessed.

Jacob looked away disgusted.

"Well then, what?" Jake said.

"You wouldn't understand," Jacob said.

"Try me."

"Leave me alone. I'm not like you. You wouldn't get it."

Jake laughed, "Oh, yes of course, we're nothing alike. Your experience is so different; I could never possibly understand it." He laughed again.

Jacob stood up, "You see. It's like I said. You drag me all the way up here thinking I'd spill my guts or something. You don't know me. You don't know me at all and you never will." He turned and stormed back the way they had come.

Jake followed, keeping about ten meters between them. After fifteen minutes Jacob's pace slowed a little at junctures. After a half an hour he was hunched and pausing at every decision point in the trail. At one point he sat down on a rock overlooking the trail ahead and Jake took the opportunity to look down long enough to text Ellie. When he looked up again, Jacob was gone. A momentary thrill shot through his gut, but he started moving immediately. He caught sight of him two minutes later and closed his stalking distance to seven meters.

"Why are you following me old man?" Jacob said without looking back.

"Because you don't know what you're doing ," Jake said.

Jacob huffed in derision. "Yeah, I'm the one who doesn't know what he's doing."

"Yup," said Jake.

"I know what I want," Jacob said. "You just won't let me."

"How do you know until you ask?"

"Why should I have to ask? It's my life."

"Because you don't know what you're doing."

"Of course you'd think that. You think I'm an idiot."

"I don't think you're an idiot. You're very smart and you're a fool."

Jacob huffed again. "Yeah, that makes sense."

"I never said you didn't know what you wanted to do. I just said you don't know what you're doing. You don't know how to get where you want to go and you think all this descent and posturing is going to get you there somehow."

Jacob tensed up. "I know where I'm going," he said and picked up his pace, plunging down one fork in the trail after another.

After ten minutes his pace slowed again.

"So you know how to get where you're going and you don't need any help from an old man. Is that it?"

"Yeah. So leave me alone."

"OK," Jake said, and disappeared through a shadow between two rocks.

"Finally!" Jacob said loudly enough for anyone within fifty meters to hear, but he shivered.

The sun had gone down and the first stars were coming out. The air was getting cold. He shivered again. He looked at the land around him. Grass, moss, pine needles... the only bare patches of ground were shiny rock reflecting the last light. The rock pinnacles around him blocked his view of the horizon. He climbed to the top of one of them and looked around to get his bearings. There were no lights, or familiar sites. He looked back the way they had come, but shook his head, sat down and drew his knees to his chest to conserve heat and think. He decided not to panic, cleared his head and looked up at the stars. He knew that if he went north long enough he'd hit the road between their house and town… unless he was farther east than he thought he was and then he'd hit the ocean a day or two later.

He checked the stars again and started walking north northwest, but there was no way to hold the course without a distant object to walk towards. He crested a ridge, stopped, scanned the horizon again, and then slumped down behind a rock. The last of the night wind blew across him and he shivered. He looked at the cheap watch he was wearing. "If I had a real watch," he muttered, "this wouldn't be a problem." He tried to picture his father glancing at his watch every few minutes as they had walked out to "his spot," but he couldn't. He hadn't. "Probably doesn't even know how to work a watch," he thought, and then winced. It was a cheap shot and it wouldn't hold. "I'll just wait until morning. Then I'll be able to see." But he was entirely unprepared to spend the night.

"What kind of a father leaves his kid in the wilderness without supplies or a good watch?!" he shouted at no one. But as the sound was swallowed up by rocks and trees, frustration gave way to shame. He shook it off and sat calmly looking over the dark landscape wondering which rock his father was hiding behind. Finally he sighed and called out, "I need help, dad. I give up. You win."

He waited and listened, but heard nothing.

"I said you win!"

Silence.

"I admit it. I'm lost, now help me."

He waited for almost a minute then exhaled and was surprised he had been holding his breath.

For the first time actual fear began to spread across his belly and chest.

He looked at his watch and sent a text to his father, "I'm lost."

He was about to despair when his watch clicked. There was a one word message. "Saturn."

He looked and scanned the skies. Saturn was high enough in the sky that he could see it but low enough to take a bearing. Then he found the place half way between that and Polaris and looked for any formation close to the horizon. He found a cluster of three stars and walked toward them. When he had walked an hour the stars had drifted below the horizon, so he repeated the process and found a new target. He continued like that until three in the morning when he hit the road. He stood in the middle of it and looked both directions. He felt the pull of town and faced that way, not daring to take a step. Finally he turned and began walking towards home. After 45 minutes of walking he could see it. The lights were on. Ellie let him in and pointed him towards the kitchen where soup was waiting

Fifty-One

Jake woke up suddenly aware that he was alone in the bed. The light coming through the windows was too white and the shadows too short. He had overslept. When he ventured out of the bedroom, the house was already in motion. Ada and Cava were on their Friday schedule and were shadowing Ellie in the kitchen. In a few minutes they would help teach the younger children. In the afternoon they would work with her in the lab, and in the late afternoon it would be back to the books.

Ellie had already taken Jacob into town to work at the Woolwrights' store, but Chris was sitting at the kitchen table catching up on homework and waiting for Jake to come out. Jake watched him from down the hall for a moment. Chris had his grandfather's ability to work quietly and enjoy his own insights as he found them. Jake almost envied him for a moment, then smiled and walked down the hall.

"Sorry I'm late."

Chris smiled at him and shrugged. "It's OK."

Ellie handed him some leftovers from breakfast and gave him a kiss on the cheek before getting back to work.

When he had finished eating, Jake and Chris grabbed their gear and jumped in the rover. They took the main road for about fifty meters then cut up a side road through tall trees and into the back country. They didn't talk much, just took in the air and the scenery until they came over a rise and Jake parked the rover.

They pulled out binoculars, flopped down on their bellies at the top of the rise, and surveyed the valley below. They watched for about twenty minutes and then Chris logged the number of rabbits he saw and their distribution. He stood and measured the relative height of the trees and recorded it, and then they walked down into the valley. The rabbits watched them but didn't disperse. They checked the counting frames looking at the number and variety of plants and insects. Chris wrote it all down. Then they walked around just looking at things to see if they noticed anything unusual before returning to the rover. At the rover Chris compiled his observations, then pulled up a report comparing the situation with previous observations.

"Well?" said Jake.

Chris slid the display over to Jake and said, "What do you think?"

"It's your valley. What do you think?" Jake said.

Chris shrugged. "Not much change. The younger rabbits are maturing. No new rabbits. There are several missing, but nothing statistically significant. The plants haven't grown much or spread much since the last survey and there's no significant change in the distribution of plant species. Basically, it's at equilibrium and slowing down as the days get shorter."

Jake nodded. "Sounds about right to me."

They drove to some other sites, checking on them, then took the long drive to a hill overlooking the fringe. Jake and Ellie had aerially seeded it with dune grass which had taken hold here and there. There was still plenty of sagebrush, and little fingers of plant life had followed streams down into the fringe, but otherwise they hadn't altered it much yet. They looked at it in silence for a while. Then Jake said, "What do you think?"

Chris thought it over for a while and said, "I think this side of the mountains will need to follow a different analog than our side of the mountain. There isn't as much rain on this side, but there is still enough winter snow and run off to keep it from being totally arid. I'm thinking maybe a Russian Steppe model."

Jake nodded. "Your mom and I were thinking of a Great Plains model, mostly because I like the idea of herds of buffalo roaming through here, better than trying to burn it all every fall, but you're right, the Russian Steppe model might be a closer fit. Why don't you put together a study comparing both models and the current environment? Include a management plan for both of them. Then we'll get the whole family together and discuss it before we file a final plan with the Department. Chris's eyes widened a little and he said, "OK."

When they got back to the station the girls were singing and fooling around as they came out of the lab.

"What's that all about?" Jake said.

Ellie responded, "Ada and Cavita managed to build a novel clover, slip it into a bio-reactor and get it out into one of the green houses without me noticing it. I found it today and gave them hell about it, but I haven't destroyed it yet, so they're feeling pretty triumphant."

"What did they do to it?"

"They took the stock variety we've been using and made it so 90% of the stalks have four leaves and they glow a subtle green for about three hours after dark."

"Is it toxic?"

"I don't know. I just barely found it."

"It would be kind of fun to plant a whole valley in it and watch it grow," Jake said.

"We'd have to get approval before we released something like that. I don't know if we've got enough budget for that kind of testing this year. I suppose we could do our own tests first to see if it might pass..." Ellie said.

"Something tells me we'd better decide one way or the other soon or there might be an 'accidental' release before we can do anything about it."

Ellie sighed, "I guess so. Let's figure it out after dinner."

"I have to do visits after dinner."

"Do them on Sunday! No one wants to see you on a Friday night."

"Hal's coming over here on Sunday. Besides, I think Brother Stevens could use a little help in his yard more than a lesson and I can't do that on Sunday."

A little before dinner, Jacob came home and harrumphed his way to his room.

Ada and Cavita were busy making dinner and Chris had his hands full getting Mary and Sam to set the table.

Ellie waited a few minutes and then went to check on Jacob.

"Did you have a good day at the Woolwrights'?"

"Same as usual."

"If you don't like it, you can always change to something else."

Jacob rolled his eyes, "I'm not coming back here."

"No one said anything about coming back here."

"No, but that's what you want, right?!"

"I honestly don't care. I'm just saying you don't have to work at the Woolwrights' if you hate it."

"Yeah, well, I have to do something."

"It doesn't have to be that."

"Just drop it. It's fine. OK?"

"OK."

Ellie left him alone and came back into the kitchen muttering. Jake looked at her.

"I don't know why that kid keeps learning a job he hates instead of finding one he likes. It's not really fair to the Woolwrights, either."

"Three reasons," said Jake barely looking up from an article he was reading.

"One: it's not here. Two: there aren't any opportunities he likes in this area. Three: the Woolwrights store is two blocks from the terminal."

Ellie closed her eyes and shook her head. "Of course. Why doesn't he apply to apprentice at the terminal?"

"The Matheson kid's got that all sewed up for the next six months. Besides, the terminal employees won't let Jacob or any other kid anywhere near the transport maintenance shed. Even if they did, all the real work is done in Paititi or Olympia. They just make occasional urgent repairs here."

"Does Jacob know that?"

"Yes, he told me. I checked it out though. He's right."

Ellie exhaled, threw up her hands and went to go check on dinner.

After dinner Jake and Jacob went on visits. Jacob sat with his head leaned up against the window. "I hate going on these," he said, but Jake could see he had relaxed some just getting out of the house.

At the first two houses they delivered a short message on forgiveness. Jacob delivered it at the second house and he managed not to sulk doing it but there wasn't much enthusiasm. As they pulled up to the Steven's house Jacob said, "What a dump." Jake gave him a look, and Jacob said, "What? You're thinking it too. "

"No, I'm thinking they could use a little help with the yard. They're both getting older now."

They gave an even shorter version of the message than at the other houses and then asked if they could help out in the yard.

"No, that's OK," Brother Stevens said, "I'll get it tomorrow."

"Are you sure? Jacob and I could get the lawn and that would free you up to work on the bushes tomorrow."

Brother Stevens got kind of an icy look in his eye and said, "I'm sure. Now Brother Billings would you say the prayer?"

When they were back in the car Jacob said, "Real smooth, dad!"

"Hey, I was trying. Give me a break."

Jacob shook his head and looked out the window.

They stopped for sherbert on the way home. The sherbert place was across the street from the terminal and Jake caught Jacob eyeing it.

"Did you get anywhere with them today?"

"Nope."

"You gonna try again next week?"

"Yep."

"Good luck with that."

Jacob eyed him suspiciously for a second, then said, "Thanks."

When they got home everyone was sitting down to watch a movie. Mary and Sam had picked it out so Jacob just groaned and went to his room.

Fifty-Two

For once, everyone was up on time. Ellie sat at the kitchen table and watched Jake finish making breakfast. Even Jacob was quietly waiting for his food. She leaned back in her chair and exhaled deeply. The girls chattered about what someone at school had said. Sam was making a tower by stacking utensils and Chris was lost in thought. Jake had widened the window by the table a few weeks ago and Ellie closed her eyes and felt the feeble warmth of the sunlight on her face.

The moment passed and soon they were hurrying off to church. The first hour was peaceful. Hal conducted the meeting and the speakers were well prepared. During the second hour Ellie went off to teach the fourteen and fifteen half-*year old girls, including Cava. Ellie gave a lesson on the At-one-ment and despite two of the girls refusing to sit in their assigned seats, the lesson went well, and she could see new light in the eyes of several girls.

By the time they got home, the boys were ready to burst. While they were changing out of their Sunday clothes a chase started down the main hall with Chris chasing Sam and Jacob down the hall in his underwear trying to get a book back. It ended with Chris standing in the middle of the kitchen with all the girls staring at him and Sam and Jacob laughing until Chris stomped back into his room.

In the afternoon Hal stopped by with Paul, one of Chris's friends from church, and delivered a lesson. After the lesson, Hal motioned for Jacob to stick around while the others left.

"I hear you like mechanics."

Jacob smirked a little but said, "I like fixing things."

"I could use some help on Fridays keeping my rental vehicles in good shape. Are you interested?"

"That depends; do any of your rental vehicles fly?"

Hal glanced at Ellie and said, "They're not supposed to."

"Then no. I'm not interested," Jacob said. Looking at his father he added, "Can I go now?"

Jake nodded and then shook his head after Jacob had left.

"I'm sorry about that, Hal. Thanks for making the offer."

"No problem. I really could have used the help."

"How's Sarah?"

"She's fine. She wants to get together with you guys for a barbecue before the weather gets too bad."

"Say the day."

"I'll have her call Ellie and sync calendars."

Jake walked Hal to the door and watched him drive away.

In the evening, Jake and Ellie herded all the kids into the living room for prayers. Ada offered a prayer asking, among other things, that Jacob could find an internship he liked.

On Wednesday the family gathered to discuss Chris's report about the back side of the mountain. In the end they all agreed the Russian Steppe was a better analog.

"Don't worry, dad," Chris said. "Who says there can't be some buffalo on the steppes?"

"American Bison?"

"Sure. It's an analog, not a copy."

The family, even Jacob, also voted that Chris should lead the program.

"It still has to be your mother and me on all the paper work," said Jake. "But it's yours."

After the meeting Chris was smiling a lot, but he didn't say much. Jacob watched him silently, and Jake watched Jacob. Jacob seemed genuinely happy for Chris. He watched silently from the edges of the group until things started to break up, then he gave Chris a pat on the back while crossing the room to the front door and going outside.

After fifteen minutes Jake went outside and found Jacob leaning against a tree in the front yard looking towards town. Jacob glanced at him as he approached and the two of them stood there silently for a while.

"You alright?" Jake asked.

"I'm fine." Then after a pause he added, "That's great about Chris."

"Yeah. He's got a long a way to go, but it's a big step," Jake said.

"Did Ada turn in her college applications yet?"

"Yes."

"Where did she apply to?"

"Paititi, Olympia, Stanford, and as a backup, Arabia Terra Tech."

Jacob nodded.

"I always kind of pictured you as an Olympia guy?" Jake said.

Jacob gave a short laugh. "Yeah, like that's going to happen."

"Why not? You're smart enough, and Olympia's got the Astronautics program."

Jacob shook his head. "School and I don't mix. I'd be lucky to get into ATT."

"You've got a *year left. You could pull up your grades. If it isn't enough you could start at ATT and then transfer to Olympia."

Jacob shook his head but didn't say anything. After a few minutes he said, "I'm tired. I'm going inside."

In bed that night Jake told Ellie, "I had a talk with Jacob tonight. I think maybe I got him thinking about fixing his grades."

"Really? That would be great."

The next day Jacob went to school without any fuss. After school he went to his room and was busy working.

On Friday he went to the Woolwrights' without any fuss and when they picked him up, Mr. Woolright mentioned what a great job he did that day.

In the afternoon everyone was in a perfect mood for a barbecue. Even the weather cooperated with a cool clear autumn afternoon.

Hal and Sarah brought the meat. Jake fired up the wood barbecue he'd just bought, and Ellie and the girls brought out fruit and potato salad while the boys set up tables.

After dinner they gathered around a fire and Hal told a tall tale about a tow truck driver who saved the world. Jake laughed a little more than the rest because he recognized the real story underneath the one Hal was telling. Hal winked at him so no one else would see.

A few of the kids offered stories of their own and as the night started to get a little too cold and the moment to break up was approaching, Ada stood and said,

"I have an announcement. I've been accepted to Stanford with a full ride scholarship, and, if we can finance the travel costs, I'll be leaving on the spring cycler."

There was a moment of stunned silence and then everyone started congratulating her. Jake looked at Ellie with a puzzled look, but Ellie just looked at him out of the corner of her eye with a barely perceptible smile at the corner of her mouth.

Jacob joined his siblings giving Ada a group hug, and then quietly slipped away from the group.

Fifty-Three

Saturday dawned colder than usual. Ellie frowned. The family had been planning to go to the river after chores and now it might be too cold. They would go anyway. The winters were long, and this would be the last time for a long time that they would all go together.

She dragged herself out of bed, turned on the fireplace and warmed herself. Jake got up and gave her a hug from behind.

"That's better," she said, "You're my hot water bottle."

"Is that all I am."

"Yep. Pretty much."

They gave each other a smack, said their prayers, and got going. The kids were having a tough time getting up too.

Jake started playing some nameless brass band marching tune as loud as possible on the house PA system, while Ellie got some bacon cooking and wafted the smell towards the bedrooms.

Jake marched loudly up and down the hallway pounding on bedroom doors in time with the music and bellowing, "Get up!" One by one they came straggling out of their rooms and sat at the table in various states of dress. Ada, completely ready, sat in the corner seat watching the others drift in, amused. Cava glared at her father, while Mary just laid her head on the table. When everyone was present except for Jacob, Jake made a show of pretending to kick in his door, then opened it, went in, and didn't come out. The brass band song ended and no one played another one. No one said anything.

Jake came out of the room with a paper in his hand and gave it to Ellie. Ellie quickly scanned it.

"What's going on?" Ada asked.

"He's gone," Jake said.

Fifty-Four

When the shock had worn off, Chris asked, "Where did he go?"

"It doesn't say," Jake said, gesturing to the paper Ellie was holding. "It just says he's OK. He's gone. He doesn't want us to follow him, and he'll come home if he gets in too much trouble. Did any of you know about this?"

Sam looked down and covered his face.

"Sam, what do you know about this?" Ellie asked.

Sam looked at Jake with a "save me" expression, but getting no encouragement looked back at Ellie and said, "Last night he said he was going away, but not to say anything. He said if I was good and didn't say anything, he'd bring me a real shooting star when he came back."

Jake and Ellie looked at each other. "Was there really any doubt where he'd be headed?" Ellie asked.

"Where?" demanded Chris.

"Olympia. He's going to try to get into the Astronaut Corps," said Jake.

"What time was it when he said goodbye?" Jake asked Sam.

"I don't know," said Sam.

"Was it in the middle of the night or right after we went to bed?" asked Jake.

"I hadn't gone to sleep yet, but everyone was being quiet," Sam said.

"So that would be about 9:30 or 10:00..." Ellie said.

"There's an 11:00 p.m. transport to Paititi," Jake said," but I think he would wait for the morning run to Olympia."

Ellie sent the kids to get dressed and Jake went outside. He came back two minutes later.

"The rover's gone. I'm going to town," he said and went back outside.

In town, Jake drove straight to the terminal and found the rover parked nearby.

He peppered the ticket agent with questions and once the agent understood what he was asking, he checked the passenger list, said there was no Jacob Billings on it, and said there had been no last minute bookings.

Jake asked to speak with the maintenance supervisor. After a few minutes an annoyed looking man said, "What can I help you with?"

"I suspect my son may have stowed away on last night's transport to Paititi. Have you seen anything this morning or last night that might confirm that?"

The man muttered and said, "Yeah, looks like he busted into the maintenance shack and stole a ground crew uniform. I was just about to call it in."

Jake bought a ticket for the afternoon Paititi flight and called his in-laws and Ellie before returning home to pack.

When she got the call, Ellie sprang into action organizing the kids and charging Ada and Chris with taking care of things.

When Jake got home she cornered him and said, "I'm going with you." Jake put his hands up and said, "OK."

By afternoon Ellie and Jake had everything arranged. They'd gotten their first report back from the Waddell's saying there had been some sort of disturbance at the terminal but no one could say if it involved Jacob. The police hadn't run into him, but they would put out a bulletin.

When they left, they took Chris with them to drive the van back so he and Ada could use it.

Once the transport was in the air there was nothing to do but think. After a while Jake got restless and started texting old contacts in Olympia to see if anyone had seen him. No one had, but everyone would keep an eye out. He contacted the police and the port authority in Olympia and sent a picture. No one had seen him. Finally he sat back in his seat and simply worried for the rest of the flight.

In Paititi they spoke with the Terminal Authority and learned that there had been an incident that morning at one of the landing pads involving someone dressed in a ground crew uniform, but the person got away. They were pretty certain he hadn't boarded any other transports but had no idea where he might be.

They cruised the streets between the terminal and the sea ports slowly watching for any sign of him.

Jake spoke with a man at the Port Authority who spent the conversation leaned back in his chair watching a fly buzz around the office. When Jake finished explaining the situation, the man looked at him and said, "We get kids coming in here all the time. We always turn them away if they're under eighteen unless we can verify they have permission from their parents. That's our policy. That's always been our policy. We'll let you know if he contacts us."

Jake and the man sat there looking at each other for a second. The man got up to show him the door.

"Aren't you forgetting something?" said Jake.

"What?" asked the man tiredly.

"My address, so you can let us know if he contacts you," said Jake.

"Oh yeah, uh, just write it on this," the man said and slid him a napkin and a pen.

Jake looked at him hard, wrote down his address and left.

They spent the evening randomly driving around the downtown area trying to guess where to look for him. The cheap motels wouldn't even talk to them. "We don't rent to kids," was all they would say.

Around midnight they finally turned in. In the morning they decided to split up. Jake caught a transport to Olympia and Ellie stayed in Paititi.

Jake repeated the whole exercise in Olympia and found nothing. Finally he went the offices of the Astronautics Corps and explained the situation to the director there. The director listened carefully with a gleam in his eye. "Sounds like a kid after my own heart," he said after

Jake had finished, "but don't worry. We would never accept him without your approval. We like a kid with spirit, but we can't use them till they've learned to respect authority. I'll put copies of this picture out on the watch list to all departments and we'll let you know if he contacts us. In fact, if he comes here we'll figure a way to stall him till you can pick him up."

"I appreciate it," Jake said.

"No problem. " They shook hands and Jake left.

After that there wasn't much to do. He wandered the streets hoping to catch site of him. He haunted places he used to go as a student. He thought about visiting old friends, but he didn't feel like it.

Ellie fell to doing similar things in Paititi, but she did visit her friends, and they all pledged to help in any way they could. She went to the temple and did a session. Afterwards she drove out to the point and climbed up a hill looking over the bay and ocean. She watched the seagulls play in the air currents and the ships far out at sea and wondered where the little boy was that had been part of the half formed plans made long ago.

Land, Air, Sea, Stars
A boy runs where half-men are
Pull him close then send him far

Fifty-Five

Jacob pushed the rover far enough from the house to drive it without waking anyone. The light in his parents' room was still on, but no one came out.

He drove to the terminal and parked a block away. He'd been watching the maintenance shack for weeks and knew security was non-existent beyond a padlock. He quickly broke the hasp leaving the lock in place, slipped in, grabbed a uniform and put it on.

He stood in the shadows behind the maintenance shack, peering around the corner toward the transport. His heart was thumping. The distance from the maintenance shack to the transport was at least a 45 second walk. He could get there quicker if he ran, but that would draw too much attention. There were two men working on the ground crew. One was refueling the transport while the second had finished pulling the cargo container out of its belly with the lift and was driving it towards the terminal building. Jacob had to get into the belly of the transport before the second crewman came back with the container for the return trip, and he had to find a place where he wouldn't get crushed by the container. He couldn't make his move with the first crewman standing where he would see him scramble up into the pay-load bay. He waited. The first crewman was in no hurry refueling. He stood watching the gauges with one hand on the shutoff valve and one on in his pocket. With the transports engines shut down, the terminal was quiet at night. Jacob heard the second crewman drop the container in the terminal and start maneuvering to pick up the other.

"No guts no glory," Jacob said to himself, and started walking briskly towards the transport. He tried to angle his approach to make it look like he was coming from the terminal, but also to keep the landing gear between him and the first crewman. He was three quarters of the way to the transport when he heard the second crewman finish lifting the new container and start for the door of the transport. Jacob resisted the urge to run.

Just as he came into clear view of the first crewman the crewman flipped the shutoff valve and turned his back to purge the other end of the line. Jacob scrambled up into the payload bay as fast as he could, sandwiched himself between two hydraulic pump cabinets and listened. At first he could only hear his heart beating, but after fifteen long seconds he heard the lift position itself under the payload bay. Then suddenly the cargo container was rising slowly in front of him. He pulled his knees close to his chest to make sure they didn't get hit. Before the payload bay doors were shut, he noticed there was a whole meter of clearance between top of the container and the top of the payload bay. He stifled a laugh. "All that for nothing," he muttered, felt his way around to the door of the cargo container, climbed up it and laid on its roof. "No dashing across the landing pad for me. I'm going to be delivered in style," he said.

Then he waited, and waited some more. It felt like days before all the passengers were loaded and the engines finally sprang to life, roaring louder than was comfortable. After a few minutes the cold set in. The cargo bay was heated... to keep things from freezing, not for comfort. Just when he thought he couldn't take the cold anymore, turbulence started. If he had been in a soft seat, it might have been the fun kind of turbulence that puts a thrill in the bottom of your stomach, but lying prone on top of a cargo container it had a different effect. By the time transport had altered its speed and altitude to smooth out the bumps, Jacob's chest, the undersides of his arms and the front of his legs had bruises that would take weeks to heal. Jacob breathed in and out slowly to see if his ribs were broken. "Just bruised," he reassured himself. His eyes began to close on their own, but the pain from the bruises spiked each time the transport made any small flight correction and his eyes opened again. The engines changed tone, then a strange thing happened. The payload bay seemed much too hot. Jacob wanted to strip off his clothes, but there wasn't room, and he didn't have the energy. The bay continued to get hotter, until suddenly he was shivering from cold. "This doesn't make any sense," he chanted to himself through chattering teeth until that chattering was replaced with the painful rattling of the whole transport as the exhaust from the engines created its own turbulence bouncing off the ground and slamming back into the underside of the transport. A few seconds passed then there was silence except for the sound of turbines winding down.

Jacob tried to think clearly. Soon he heard voices and machines beneath the transport. The payload doors opened. The lift whined for a second and bumped the cargo container. Jacob winced and that cleared his head. "Oh yeah, delivered in style. Keep low so they can't see you." Catches released and the container settled a little, then started descending. Only once the cargo container had clicked into its secure position and started moving towards the terminal did he notice that he was looking up at the cockpit of the transport. "He might not look back here," he thought, "stay calm." Then he looked over and noticed that this Terminal was two stories tall. He could see a little kid about Sam's age tugging on his mother's coat and pointing at him through the window. "Not good," he thought, "stay calm," he got up on his knees and acted like he was inspecting something, then very businesslike, backed his way to the door and started climbing down. He managed to land on his feet then started walking beside the container on the opposite side from the Terminal. Just as they were almost to the Terminal warehouse, he heard a radio squawk in the cab of the lift. A few seconds later, he saw the driver looking at him through the side mirror. Jacob slowly drifted back towards the rear of the container, cut behind it and started moving toward a man door in the Terminal. Halfway to the door he noticed five or six ground crewmen moving towards him. Three meters from the door he noticed the door had no external doorknob. "Stay calm," he thought and kept walking toward the door, eyes darting to find some other exit. Just as he reached the door, it opened, and a crewman walked out adjusting his bright orange ear protectors. Jacob slid past him and closed the door tightly behind him. He was in a corridor. He went to the right walking quickly and unzipping his jump suit. At the next door he paused, stepped out of the jump suit, kicked it into the corner and stepped through the door. He found himself in baggage claim. A smile slipped across his lips. He walked across baggage claim, out the door and into a waiting cab. The cabbie eyed him suspiciously.

"You got any money?"

"Sure, plenty."

The cabbie considered this for a second and said, "The flag drop is $5, you pay that before we leave."

Jacob put on his most insulted look and handed the cabbie one fourth of his life's savings. The cabbie pulled out of the airport saying, "Where to?"

Jacob's face went completely blank. The plan had been to switch to a cargo container headed for Olympia. Jake remembered there was a train in Paititi, but he didn't know where it went and there was a pretty big mountain between Paititi and Olympia.

"Hey kid, I said, where to?"

"The port," Jacob said without thinking.

The cabbie chuckled, "Any particular pier or just the port?"

Jake looked at the meter and said, "The closest pier."

The cabbie chuckled again and said, "You got it."

Fortunately, with tip, the trip only cost Jacob half his life savings.

"Good luck, kid," the driver said as he drove away.

Jacob looked down the long straight street with row after row of identical buildings facing it. If he hadn't been able to smell the ocean beyond the buildings he would have assumed the cabbie had cheated him. Ports were supposed to be long piers with boats tied to them, not rows of building separated by fences. He decided he had better get moving before the cabbie told someone where he was, but where?

He started walking. When he got to the fences between the

buildings, he realized they were gates and that beyond them were the piers he had expected. The buildings were warehouses and offices. After a kilometer he came to a pier and warehouse that had been converted into a shopping center. He went down its pier and saw ships tied to various piers up and down the water front. He sat on a bench and looked around. It was still dark. None of the shops were open yet, but the merchants were getting them ready. His ribs hurt, and he was suddenly very, very tired.

When he woke up it was midmorning and he was curled up on the bench. He sat up quickly and looked around. No one seemed to have noticed him. He tried to think of a cover story in case someone asked him what he was doing, but nothing seemed believable. He scanned the pier. There were gift shops, restaurants, fruit stands, import/export shops, an information booth...

Jacob jumped off the bench and went to it. It turned out the pier for passenger ships was next door, and for only $150 he could be in Olympia by tomorrow afternoon. He thanked the lady and went back to his bench to think.

After a while he walked to the passenger pier and started studying the ships. He found the one bound for Olympia and watched it. He could imagine slipping up the ropes or the anchor chains to get on board, but there were large round shields in the middle of each to prevent that, and even if you succeeded there were plenty of folks and on the pier that would see you doing it.

Another ship was boarding. Jacob watched the passengers. Each one paused in front of a machine and waited for a light to turn green before boarding. Not much opportunity there. He was wondering how they moved cargo on and off the ships when he noticed someone standing beside him.

Jacob stood stiffly looking straight ahead at nothing.

He turned to casually move on, but the man said, "Are you interested in ships?"

Jacob looked at him.

"Ever been on one?"

"No," Jacob said.

"The man looked across the water. I've been at sea most of my life since I was about your age. I like it."

Jacob didn't say anything, but kept watching the man.

"So what brings you to the water front today? Going on a trip?"

Jacob eyed him for a second and said.

"I haven't got the money."

"So you want to go on a trip but you don't have the money?"

"Yeah."

"Where are you headed?"

"Olympia."

"Forget about sneaking on. They'll catch you. There is a way though. Buy me breakfast and I'll tell you."

Jake considered his options and agreed.

"There's a place over at the end of the pier I like," the man said. Jake was relieved to see it was churro stand. They each ordered a churro and a hot cocoa and settled in at a table. The man extended a hand and said, "Ernie's my name. What's yours?"

"Steve," said Jacob.

"Good to meet you Steve, and thanks for breakfast." Ernie ate a few bites and then said, "Um that's good. I always get one of these when I'm in port." Ernie put the churro down and seemed to forget about it as he talked. "See here's the thing. In a way, it's lucky that you don't have the money for one of those fancy passenger ships. You don't really get to know anything about the sea on one of those. You spend all your time at shows and different things they've got to keep you busy, and they travel so fast you hardly have time to experience the sea anyway. Plus they're so tall you don't get an ocean level view. No, those ships are for old people who want to relax. Not for adventurers that want to experience new things. Let me look at you." Ernie leaned back and looked at him, felt his arm and shoulder. "Nope. You're not that kind. You're strong and want to see the world. Right?"

Jacob nodded.

"Sure you are. So, the way to do that is on a freighter. You don't make much money, heck on your first couple of runs you don't make anything, but they feed you and you get where you're going for free and you get to see things on the way. Who knows? You might decide you want to be a real seaman."

"I'm not going to be a seaman. I'm going to be an astronaut."

"You see, I knew that the minute I saw you," Ernie said, "I knew you were an adventurer and it don't make no difference if that's in the sky or on the sea, it's the same thing. But if you're partial to the sky, I respect that. I myself, I couldn't give up the salt air no matter how good the view is, but I respect the astronauts. So is that why you're going to Olympia?"

Jacob nodded.

"Of course it is. They got their head office there and their school there and everything. Of course you know where you're going. Your folks know where you're going?"

Jacob stiffened.

"You ran off, didn't you! Don't worry. I'm not gonna tell anyone. I did the same thing *years ago. Best thing I ever did. But it can be kinda hard at first, till you get to know your way around and all."

Jacob relaxed a little. "Yeah, I suppose, but I'm going straight for the Astronautics Corps, so all I've got to do is get to Olympia."

"I can see you've got this whole thing thought out. I respect that. You remind me of myself at your age, so I'm going to help you get there if that's alright with you. Besides, I owe you for breakfast and I like to help young men get their start."

"How?" asked Jacob.

"See I'm the Crew Chief on the North Sea Star. We're shovin' off this afternoon and we'll be getting to Olympia in a few days, but we got to make some other stops on the way and we're kinda going the long way, but we'll get there. Since I'm the Chief I get to take a steward along, kind of like an apprentice if I want, but the shipping line they don't like tourists or nothing, so if we go, you gotta say you're interested in the sea and everything and then when we get to Olympia, I'll just tell them it didn't work out or something. What do you say?"

Jacob thought about it for a few seconds and said, "I guess so. Thanks."

"Alright. So get your stuff and let's go."

"This is it," Jacob said gesturing to his backpack.

"I like a man who travels light."

"I just have to use the restroom first," Jacob said.

"I'll be right here."

Jacob walked to the bathroom. When he entered, a wiry looking young guy followed him in. Jacob went into a stall. The wiry guy went into the stall next to him and sat on the toilet, but he didn't seem to be doing anything. Jacob could see him peeking through a crack in the stall at him.

"What are you doing?" said Jacob.

"Nothing," said the guy.

"Stop looking at me."

"I'm not looking at you. Not like that," said the guy.

"Then just don't look at me."

"OK. OK."

After a few seconds the guy said, "That guy you were talking to at the table."

"Ernie."

"Yeah, Ernie, I guess. He offered to get you a job on a ship right?"

"Were you watching us?"

"No, nothing like that. Listen, don't go with him."

"Why not?"

"He's on a chicken run."

"So, why do I care if he wants chicken?"

"Because you're the chicken."

"I'm not scared."

"Geeze, you really are green. Look, just don't go with him. You'll be sorry. If you want to get somewhere just go down to pier 28 and sign up. They're always looking for help and don't go with the North Star Line, those guys are creeps, stay with True North or Mermaid lines."

"How do I get by him?"

"Just walk past him. It's not like he's going to chase you."

"How do I know you're not just messing with me?"

"I'm not. Just get out of here."

Jacob thought about it for a minute.

"Or don't then, I don't care," the guy said, and left.

Jacob cleaned up, washed his face in the sink and looked at himself in the mirror.

He looked out the doorway and saw Ernie, waiting, eager.

He walked out of the men's room. Ernie rose to meet him. Jacob just kept walking, fast.

"Where are you going?" Ernie yelled after him. "You're blowing it kid. You don't work with me, you won't work at all!"

Jacob caught a glimpse of him as he turned the corner onto the main street; he was looking at his watch and cursing softly.

The man at True North looked him over with only slight curiosity. "What brings you to the sea?"

"I've got to get to Olympia."

"What's in Olympia?"

"A job I hope."

The man seemed to check something off in his mind and smiled a little.

"Passage isn't free. You'll be doing the jobs experienced hands don't want to do. And you won't be going directly to Olympia. This is a cargo ship. We stop at all the little outposts, moving things that are too heavy, too big, or too worthless to spend aviation fuel on. You understand that?"

"I do."

"Welcome aboard then."

Fifty-Six

Ellie flew home alone. The transport was dusty and half empty. She looked at the empty seat next to her then looked down at the hands on her belly. She could feel the firm little bump under her hands. She looked out the window. Low clouds clung to the landscape obscuring the ground below. She looked around the transport. It was getting old. The run from Paititi to Spring Creek wasn't a particularly profitable one and the condition of the transport showed it. Everything was still working, but storage doors didn't close quite as tight as they should. Replacement parts weren't quite the right color to match the rest of the interior. The carpet was worn. Things just generally seemed to squeak and rattle more than they should.

She looked down at her belly again and at her hands. The skin across the back of her hands was still smooth enough, but she could see it starting to change. She rubbed her thumb across her ring.

The transport arrived without incident. Ada was waiting for her and gave her a ride home. Ellie watched the dark land roll by her window under heavy clouds. She knew the land almost as well as Jake by now, knew its history, what they had done to it, and how it had surprised them. She looked at the clouds, not seeing the water in them, just letting them be clouds.

When they got home the house was a mess. Ada and Chris had enforced enough discipline to keep the dishes from piling up and had even gotten the kitchen and living room straightened before leaving for the terminal, but Chris had gone off to his room to read, and the little ones had trashed the kitchen again making a snack for themselves.

When Ellie entered the room, the little ones yelled out and ran to her. She hugged them and they hung on to her as she surveyed the wreck of her kitchen. Then she picked up her bags and went into her room.

Ada began marshaling the little ones to clean up. Ellie closed her door.

She didn't bother to put her things away. She took a hot shower and went to bed.

She woke up. The house was dark and absolutely silent. Her belly hurt. Suddenly she jumped out of bed and ran to the bathroom. She pinched her lips tight lifted to toilet lid and started lean over it to throw up, then changed her mind and sat on it instead, doubled over. The wave of nausea passed and was replaced by a hard cramping. She felt something pass, and when her mind finally grasped what it was, she slumped onto the floor unconscious.

After a while she opened her eyes. The house was quiet. She lay still, listening to the silence until it was broken by a faint moaning sound. She listened until she found the source deep in her own chest, and then she cried.

She got up and cleaned herself, being careful not to a certain place on the floor. She splashed her face and looked into her own eyes in the mirror. She breathed deeply, went to the spot on the floor by the toilet and looked at the smooth gray little shape lying there. She wrapped it in paper and cradled it in the palm of one hand, her other hand covering it, carried it into the lab. She put it in a sample box and slid it into a refrigerator.

She washed her hands in the sink slowly, then pressed them against her forehead and let the water run.

She went back to sleep. When she woke up again it was midmorning. She could hear Jake in the living room issuing orders in his tight frustrated voice. She put the pillow over her head to block the sound, but couldn't sleep. When she took the pillow off, she could no longer hear his voice, but she knew from the sound of things he was still out there, setting the house in order with laser-like concentration. Dishes banged; cupboard doors closed with too much force. The kids were moving through the hall quicker and heavier than normal. She waited for the sounds to subside, and voices to return to normal.

Jake stuck his head in the door and looked at her. "You're awake," he said.

She looked at his face. It was not a particularly kind face. His hair looked funny.

"Yes," she said looking away.

"I didn't find any sign of him," Jake said.

"I figured," Ellie said, not looking up.

"I just got in. I didn't want to wake you."

"Thanks," she said.

He closed the door softly.

She watched the door close. Watched for a while to see if it would open again, then turned towards the wall.

When she came out for lunch Jake gave her a perfunctory hug, but she held onto his arm and buried her face in his shoulder. He held onto her until she suddenly broke free and turned her back to him.

"You should have come home yesterday," she said.

"I was a little busy looking for Jacob yesterday," Jake said tightly.

"Did you find him?"

"No. You know I didn't."

"Then you should have come home."

"That doesn't even make sense. If anything, I should have stayed until I did found him."

"No. You should have been here."

"I'm here now."

"I don't need you here now! Go back to Olympia, find Jacob and bring him back," she said her voice breaking.

Jake watched her carefully but didn't say anything.

Finally she threw her hands in the air, said, "You're useless!" and marched back to bed.

Jake didn't follow her.

Ellie waited on the bed listening for his footsteps, watching the door, but he didn't come. She covered her face with the pillow and screamed.

Fifty-Seven

Weeks passed. After the first week everyone but Sam stopped mentioning Jacob. After two weeks Jake finally realized the baby was gone too. When he asked Ellie about it she only said, "I wondered when you would notice." Jake found the box in the lab refrigerator, ran a sample through the scanner, then quietly buried it in the backyard.

He took to sitting up on the overlook every evening when work was done, looking over the horizon. Ellie did her work quietly. Chris noticed the creases around Jake's eyes when he would come out of the office on Friday mornings to work with him. Sometimes he heard him yelling at people on the phone.

After three weeks, life resumed a semblance of order. There were a few jokes around the dinner table. Ellie found time to test the glowing clover and concluded it would probably pass an environmental review. Chris finished laying out a detailed timeline for the far side of the mountain and started pricing embryos and laying specifications for plants. They took their final trip to the river but no one would go in because it was too cold. Finally Jake stood up and said, "Oh for crying out loud," and jumped into the nearest pool. Mary and Sam followed him a split second later. When the three of them broke surface and everyone got a look at their faces, no one else went in. Once they'd dried off and had a fire going, the teasing started. They got a cheese pot going on the fire and watched the sun going down. Jake forgot to check his messages until they started for home.

The following Monday morning, Jake came out of his office in a hurry moving straight for the lab. He found Ellie, and simply said, "They've got him."

Fifty-Eight

Jacob's bunk on the "Witch of the North" was in a separate cabin from the regular crew. There were three other kids about his age in his cabin. Eddie was a little older and he was all for the sea. Quan was younger and quieter.

"Great, another @#@!$#@ tourist," was all Eddie said when Jacob told him he was going to be an astronaut.

"Do you think they'll take you?" Quan asked.

"They aren't gonna take him," Eddie said in disgust. "There are five kids a year come through here trying to be astronauts and they never take them."

"You hear from any of those kids?" Jacob asked.

"No. Why would I want to hear from them?" Eddie answered.

"Then how do you know they didn't take them?"

"'Cause they never take them."

"How do you know?"

"'Cause everyone knows."

"You ever see one come back on the ship?"

"No, their parents come and get them."

"How do you know?"

"I just know," Eddie said.

"They probably just tell you that so you won't jump ship. They just want to keep you slaving away down here instead of flying among the stars."

"#@!$#@!" Eddie said with feeling.

"Can't take it, can you," Jacob said.

"I can take a lot more than a #$%#@ tourist like you."

Quan watched all this with a thin smile on his face. There wasn't a lot of free time, but when there was, any entertainment was valuable.

"Think you can back that up?" Jacob said.

"Any day," Eddie said.

The hatch in the bulk head opened and the boys lined up to get their assignments.

"Eddie," the Assistant Crew Chief said, "you're on first mate's watch."

"Aye, Aye," said Eddie and smirked at the other two.

"Quan, you're on forward trash hauling. Report to Wilson in the forward galley."

"Aye, Aye," said Quan.

"Steve, you're on aft bilge clean up. Report to Perez in the aft galley."

"Aye, Aye," said Jacob and left. In the hall Eddie shoved him into the wall with his shoulder on the way forward, but he didn't say anything. The Assistant Crew Chief came out about that time. He looked at them both, then moved forward.

Jacob moved aft to the galley, got his breakfast and a checklist of stations he was to clean. When Jacob entered his first station, he quickly covered his mouth and nose with his sleeve. "This is worse than yesterday," he said. "The bilge" wasn't actually seawater. The hull was tight so no water could get in. "The bilge" was freshwater that condensed on the sides of the hull and then slid down to the lower levels and pooled up in sumps. Automatic pumps kept it from getting deep enough to reach the deck grates, but every kind of gunk you could imagine liked growing in the sumps. "Why don't they pump a little seawater in there to kill all the gunk before it stinks?" he wondered out loud to himself, but he half suspected they liked keeping these smelly holes around to torture "tourists." Talking to yourself was one of the few perks of bilge duty. No one wanted to be there, so everyone left you alone. Once you got used to the stink, you couldn't smell it anymore, so it wasn't bad.

Jacob finished cleaning all his stations before lunch. After lunch the Assistant Chief patted him on the back and gave him deck duty cleaning up after the seagulls. "We'll leave the forward bilge to give you something to look forward to tomorrow," he said with a wink.

There was very little seagull mess to clean up, so Jacob worked slowly and watched the sea change colors with changes of depth and angle of sunlight. The sea was beautiful when it wasn't trying to kill you.

His first day aboard had been one of those "trying to kill you" days. Four hours out of Paititi a sudden storm kicked up. Eddie had been called on deck to free up more experienced hands, but Jacob and Quan had been confined to quarters. Jacob spent the whole time curled around the head, turning colors and puking while Quan just laughed at him. It wasn't until the second day that Quan showed him where the anti-nausea medicine was stored. There hadn't been a serious storm since then, and the little ones hadn't bothered Jacob since during both he happened to be above deck.

On days like today, Jacob could see what Eddie loved about the sea. On one side of the ship it rolled away towards the horizon glittering and larger than anything Jacob could imagine; seemingly larger than all Arabia Terra, and more alive, and constantly moving. To look at it was to be large and moving yourself. On the other side of the ship the coast was never too far away. As he worked Jacob imagined scenarios where he was forced to swim ashore and wondered if he could really make it. Jacob saw a fish jump and recognized it. "Oncorhychus Martis," he said reflexively and then added silently, "That water is colder than it looks." He shook his head. "Why would an astronaut know that?" He looked over the railing in a different direction, towards a house full of people that wondered where he was. He got back to work and let the alternating blues and greens of different depths of water on the shore side of the ship take away all thoughts.

That night at dinner he told Eddie, "I think I understand what you like about the sea."

Quan chimed in, "He likes the fact that his ex-girlfriend can't find him. That's what he likes."

Eddie watched Quan until he looked away and then looked back warily at Jacob.

"So, you think you got me all figured out, do you?"

"No. I just mean there are things I like about it, too."

"So are you still getting off at Olympia?"

"Yes."

"Then why do I care if you like it?"

After dinner Jacob took his personal time on deck. He looked out over the dark water and listened to it slipping by the hull. The ship was almost silent except for a faint vibration coming from somewhere aft. He thought about his conversation with Eddie. "I don't blame him," he thought.

He felt the wind on his face, closed his eyes and tilted his face up slightly. He could almost imagine himself staying, but then he opened his eyes and saw the stars above him in all their sharp detail and kept looking. "You will never visit any of them. Not really," he thought to himself. Other than the sun, the nearest star was 300 earth years away with the most powerful "Star" drive available and if the telescopes were to be believed, once you got there the closest thing to an inhabitable world had double the gravity, was frozen solid and bathed in the radiation field of its gas giant parent. If cryogenics had worked out... maybe it would have been worth visiting.

"I'm still going," he said defiantly to no one, and went below.

The next morning he got the dreaded "Forward bilge" duty and Eddie smirked at him again, but only when the Assistant Chief wasn't looking. In the afternoon, he was ordered to report to the engine room. When he arrived, the engine room was disappointingly clean. The Mechanic's Assistant saw him come in and stop.

"What? Were you expecting coal?"

"Nothing. I wasn't expecting anything."

The assistant looked him over and nodded, then gestured him over to a series of large tubes entering the room from forward and moving down in parallel before recombining and entering what appeared to be the engine itself.

"These are the sea water intakes for engine number one. We need to clean the fine filters every three operating hours. It's been three operating hours. I'll do the first one, you watch."

He pulled up a checklist on a screen above the pipes, pressed a button on the checklist and heard the sound of the pipes shift to a higher pitch. He watched until an indicator turned green, then pressed the next item in the list and a hatch opened in the top of one of the pipes. A membrane in a frame rose up out of the pipe. It was greenish brown on one side and shimmered a rainbow moray pattern on the engine side. The assistant looked it over carefully.

"It's not enough to clean them. You've got to look 'em over carefully and make sure they aren't torn or anything."

When he was satisfied he lifted the frame out of its holder and put a clean filter in its place.

"Watch the little arrows on the top of the frame. If you put it in backwards it'll clog up in ten seconds flat and then the engine will overheat and we're limping back to port at half speed."

He pressed the "next" button and the screen disappeared back into the pipe. An indicator changed color and he pressed the next item in the check list. The sound of the pipes changed back to the lower rush they had been before and an indicator on the screen changed.

"We're not done," the assistant said.

Then he took the dirty filter over to a pipe the same size in a corner of the room and inserted it for ten minutes. When he pulled it out, it was white where it had been brown-green.

"We're still not done," the assistant said, then stood there examining the filter carefully. Finally he nodded and said, "Now we're done. Your turn." He handed him the filter.

Jacob studied the screen and found the place to switch to the next pipe. Then he started clicking down the check list. When he went to put the new filter in he noticed that the bottom of the filter was keyed, so it wouldn't fit in the slot the wrong way anyway. He looked at the assistant. The assistant shrugged slightly. Jacob finished the procedure, then cleaned the filter he'd pulled out. Looking at the arrangement he realized he probably couldn't have messed up the engine anyway.

The system could obviously keep running with one inlet down, and it wouldn't let him proceed to the next inlet until the one he was working on was operating normally. He looked at the assistant trying to decide if he knew that and was just messing with him, or if he really believed what he told him. The assistant just met his gaze, and Jacob said nothing. Finally, the assistant said, "I'm going to go take a break. Tell me when you're done with the rest of these," went back into his office and put his feet up on the desk.

When Jacob was done, he reported back.

"All the filters looked good?"

"Yeah."

"Good. Stick around; it'll need to be done again in another three hours. In the meantime, read this." He tossed him a thick paper manual for the engine.

"Paper?" Jacob questioned.

"Yeah, it's nice to have when the reactor goes into safe mode and all the auxiliary power is going into attitude control."

Jacob nodded, found a corner and started reading. At first he balanced on one elbow and read slowly, but as he read he found himself reading faster. Realization began to dawn on him that this engine wasn't very different in principal from plasma engines on an asteroid tug. The main difference was that instead of ionizing hydrogen as a reaction mass, the ship was using its radio emitters to heat seawater into steam as a reaction mass. The chamber sizes and frequencies were different, but the principle was the same. When he got done reading he looked at the engine with new respect. He caught the assistant looking at him, then the assistant said, "Stop grinning, it's time to clean them again."

Jacob finished in half the time of his first try and reported back.

"Done already?" the assistant said, "You know you don't get any extra credit for going fast. There aren't any tears in the filters, are there?"

"No. I checked them."

The assistant said, "Alright, wait a minute then." Jacob could see him examining flow images downstream of the filters, which meant there was really no need for inspection at all.

The assistant saw the look on his face and said, "We're supposed to inspect them manually. The camera doesn't catch everything. OK, we're done here. You can take the rest of the shift off."

Jacob gave him an "Aye, aye," and started for the door.

The assistant called after him. "Hey Steve, what's your real name anyway?" Jacob thought for a second and said, "Jacob. But don't tell anyone."

"All right Steve, I won't."

The next morning they had Jacob scraping rust from a forward weather mast and repainting it. Once again he was finished by lunch and in the afternoon he worked in the engine room again. The assistant had some more detailed manuals for him to read between cleanings, and Jacob inhaled them.

When he got back to his bunk he was quiet. The others were either asleep or being quiet too. He stared at the bunk above him for nearly an hour. His eyes flitted open sometime in the early morning. The sound of the water whishing past the hull had changed and become less urgent. Usually this meant they were coming up on yet another piss hole port somewhere along the coast. Jake had already seen eight of them in the last two weeks. Nine if you counted the one back home. He realized now that it would have been far easier to just runaway on one of these buckets than the stunt he played at the terminal, but until the last two weeks the thought of people being on these ships hadn't crossed his mind. Then again, they would have found the rover and caught him at the next port, so it was probably for the best.

Jacob had avoided spending too much time topside during the first week. He peaked out when he could, but there was never much to see - usually just some old guy with a truck on a skinny one lane pier jutting out from the shore. There never seemed to be a town next to the shore, just a pier and a narrow road running off into the distance. After the first week he ventured on shore at a couple of ports, looked around for a minute and got back on the ship. This time he lay in his bunk, lazy-like, guessing the amount of time before they pulled into port. After a few minutes the ship stopped completely. It was so quiet that Jacob could hear the little maneuvering thrusters keeping the ship's orientation correct. Jacob sat up. Eddie heard him.

"Lie down; they're just bringing the harbor pilot on board. We won't be in port for another twenty minutes at least."

Jacob lay down. This was new.

"Where are we?"

"We're at your stop, star boy."

Jacob was silent for a minute and then sat up. He opened his locker. His uniform was on the right, his street clothes were on the left. He hesitated, then grabbed his street clothes and put them on. Eddie turned over and put his back toward Jacob.

Jacob grabbed the few things he had collected since he left and put them in his backpack. He started to go upstairs, then stopped. He went back to Eddie's bunk and shook him. Eddie raised one hand to brush him off.

"Hey Eddie: my real name's Jacob Billings III. Remember me. I'll write and tell you whether or not I get in."

"Piss off," Eddie said without turning over, but after Jacob left Eddie wrote something short in his personal log.

On deck, Jacob saw the sun slip over the horizon and light up the harbor. It was a big harbor; larger than Paititi which had seemed pretty large. The town behind the harbor began to light up too as the sun rose higher and Jake could see buildings spreading back from the sea towards the mountain range behind it. A set of tracks going up the side of the largest mountain gave off an occasional glint of the morning sun as they approached. Jacob's face flushed when he saw it. He went to the duty station to let them now he was debarking. The assistant crew chief was there going over assignments for the day when Jacob entered.

"Getting off?" he said without looking up.

Jake nodded and said, "Yes."

The Assistant Crew Chief chuckled.

"I thought you would," he said, looking up.

He pulled out his wallet and said, "You'll need your final pay then."

"I thought there wasn't any pay on the first run," Jacob said.

"There isn't, but you'll need it anyway," he said, and gave him $10.

"Thank you," Jake said and nearly ran back to the loading ramps.

Jake fidgeted for the ten minutes it took to arrive at the dock. He paced for the fifteen minutes it took to tie off and lower the ramps, but then he was there, standing on the dock looking up at Mount Olympus.

He asked around and found out the end of the subway line was four blocks away. At first he walked until he was out of view of the dock. Then he ran. He smiled as he felt his legs moving underneath him. He wasn't even winded when he arrived, studied the maps, bought his tickets and boarded. He looked around the subway car. It was mostly empty. The screens that wrapped around the inside of the car were chipped and some of the pixels weren't lighting. Forty-five minutes later he was standing at the top of the subway stairs looking up the street towards the gleaming dome of the Astronautics headquarters. He walked past it once casually to make sure it was the right place. Then he smoothly turned around and went right up to the door, which was locked. He waved his cheap watch over the door to try to get their hours, gave up and looked it up manually. He was an hour early. He went down to the park and waited under a mulberry tree. "Morus Martis," he said, and smiled at himself ruefully.

When the hour was up he went back, marched into the lobby, walked up to the guard at the desk and announced, "I'm here to join the Corps."

The old man barely looked at him and pointed down the hall. Jacob walked down the hall to a waiting area and waited for the clerk to come to the window. When he came, Jacob walked to the window and announced, "I'm here to join the Corps."

"The middle aged man in the window looked at him, looked at something on the wall next to the window and said, "Great. What's your name?" Jacob hesitated.

"Your real name." the man prodded, "you can't fool the iris scan that comes next."

"Jacob Billings III," Jacob said.

"Welcome, Mr. Billings," the clerk said. We have some forms for you to fill out. Come on back.

The clerk pressed a button, and a door swung open that matched the paneling so well Jacob hadn't noticed it. The clerk steered him toward an exam room, sat him down with a tablet, and instructed him to fill everything in. Then he closed the door, took a piece of paper off the wall, set it face down on the counter and went down the hall. Ten minutes later he still wasn't back. Jacob came out of the office with the completed form and looked around. No one was there, so he left the door open and sat down. Another clerk came into the room, took off his jacket, and poured himself some tea. Jacob waited patiently to be noticed, but the clerk was ignoring him. Finally Jacob worked up the nerve to approach him. The man closed his eyes like his head hurt; when Jacob announced, "I'm done!"

He turned and looked at him, "Done with what?"

"My application."

The man glanced up at the wall by the window. Jacob followed his gaze, but neither of them saw anything interesting.

"Let me see it," the clerk said.

He looked it over and shook his head. "You're missing the first page," he said and arrowed back. Jacob sat down and looked at the first page. It had two entries.

"Enter one of the following:

1) Name and date of graduation from astronautics training course, or

2) Name and signature of sponsoring astronaut."

Jacob looked at it for a minute and then asked the clerk, "What do they want here?"

"Just what it says."

Jacob just looked at him.

"Let me guess. You're another kid that can't get through school and thinks they can just walk in here and sign up. Have I got that right?"

"No. I've got a sponsor. I just didn't know I needed his signature. Give me a copy of this and I'll go get it."

The clerk shrugged and sent him the file.

Jacob checked to make sure he had it and stormed out of the building.

The first clerk came back five minutes later and said, "Where's the kid?"

"He left."

"Why did you let him leave?"

"Why shouldn't I? He was getting on my nerves anyway."

The first clerk flipped over the paper on the counter with Jacob's face on it and said, "That's why!"

"I didn't know," the clerk said, putting his hands up.

"Great, I already notified his parents. Come on, let's go look for him."

Fifty-Nine

"They don't have him," Jake said, looking at his watch and fumbling for a larger screen.

"What?" Ellie said.

"They messed up and he left."

"How could they do that?"

"I don't know. The main thing is he was OK an hour ago."

Jake checked his watch. "The shuttle to Olympia doesn't leave for another six hours."

"I'm coming with you."

"Stay here. I know Olympia better than you do. Besides what if he comes back here?"

Ellie nodded. "OK, but keep me informed."

"OK, OK."

Jake called the Astronautics Corps and got as much information from them as he could.

He packed his things. Ellie drove him to the terminal and dropped him off.

Sixty

Jacob walked blindly when he left Corps headquarters. He found himself in the park he had waited in before. He wondered if the ship had left port yet, then dismissed the idea. Minutes passed. He exhaled, and began thinking. He needed a signature, the signature of an astronaut. He didn't know any astronauts.

"I don't have to know any astronauts," he finally said.

"I just have to know where an astronaut is."

He took the subway to the airport. Then walked to the spaceport terminal and watched people come and go. The cycler wouldn't be in for months, so traffic was light. It didn't take long to figure out which people were crew, which were administration and which were astronauts. They were wearing uniforms, after all.

Jacob nearly approached three groups of astronauts. Finally he saw a younger one leaving the terminal and marched up to him.

"Are you an astronaut?"

"Yeah," the astronaut said.

"I want to be an astronaut too."

"That's nice."

"But I need some help, I need a signature."

"Forget it kid. Go to school."

"Seriously, I need the signature."

"Seriously, get away from me."

He tried two more with about the same success.

The security guards were starting to look at him so he let the next two groups go by.

He approached the next set.

"Are you astronauts?"

"Yes."

"I need one of you to sign this."

They looked at his watch and shook their heads.

"It's not happening," one of them said.

"No listen, seriously, I will give you half my first year's pay if you'll just sign this."

"We can't do that."

"Then half my first two year's pay."

"Kid, I'd have to be drunk to sign that. We can only sponsor two people in our whole careers. And if you get caught selling a signature, you're grounded permanently, as in career over."

Jacob stood silently pleading.

"Just go to school. It's not that long. Just go."

The other astronaut rolled his eyes and signaled with his head they should go and they left.

One of the security guards was getting up from his seat, so Jacob went outside and walked down the street to get away from him before he got too close.

He slumped against a wall of the terminal and watched astronauts come and go. Some of them disappeared down the subway entrance but others jumped into taxis, usually in groups. After a while, Jacob stood up and walked to the first taxi in line. He got in. The cabbie eyed him.

"Where to?"

"Where are the astronauts going?"

"Most of them are headed to the bar," the cabbie said.

"Take me there."

"They won't let you in."

"Take me there anyway."

The cabbie just looked at him.

"Yes, I have the money," Jacob said exasperatedly and handed him a $5 bill.

"Suit yourself," the cabbie said.

When they got to the site, the cabbie pointed at a pair of double doors and said, "That's the place."

Jacob crossed the street and watched the door a while. It was getting late, so the place was starting to fill up.

Jacob figured his chances would be better if he let them drink a while, like the astronaut had said, so he waited.

After a couple of hours he started seeing some people leave. He stood up, straitened his clothes, crossed the street and pushed open the door. Inside, people were eating and talking a bit too loud. A man at the door looked at him expectantly. Jacob looked past him scanning the room.

"Can I help you find someone?"

"Yeah, I'm looking for my friend."

"What's your friend's name?"

"Steve."

"What's his last name?"

"I don't know. We just met. He said he'd be here."

"Do you see him?"

"No."

"Maybe he's in the bar. You can't go in there. Give me your name and I'll see if he's in there."

"Jacob."

"OK, wait here."

The man went across the room and through a curtain into another room.

Jacob scanned the room, picked the table with the most laughter, and moved towards it.

It took a second for the men to look up at him. When they did he said, "Can I sit down?"

"What's this about?"

"I want to know what it's like to be an astronaut."

"Steve here is the only astronaut at this table. "

A slow smile spread across Jacob's face. "It's good to meet you."

The man from the door came out of the bar, saw Jacob, and watched for a minute until Steve waved him off.

"What do you want to know?"

"What's launch like?"

"It's like the fastest car you've ever driven, and then it gets all quiet and the stars come out."

"Do you get lonely?"

"Some people do. I don't. I like the quiet."

"How did you become an astronaut?"

Now a slow smile spread across Steve's face as he looked into his drink thinking.

"I'm not sure that's a good story to tell a kid," was all he finally said.

"I'm going to be an astronaut too."

Steve looked at him steadily.

"I've just got to find a way in."

Nobody said anything.

Finally, not looking up from his drink, Steve said, "Go home kid."

Jacob just sat there.

Steve finally looked at him. "Go home!"

Jacob just sat there. Steve signaled the man at the door and stood up.

"I guess I'm going to call it a night boys," he said, got up, paid his bill and left.

The man from the door came and stood by the table.

"Time to go, kid."

"I'm not going anywhere."

"Yes, you are."

The man from the door picked him up by the neck, bent his wrist behind his back and pushed him to the door.

"Let me go."

"Yeah, OK, kid." The man said and shoved him hard through the door. He collided with a customer coming in.

Jacob spun to get clear of the customer, but couldn't get loose.

The man grabbed him hard by the shoulders. Jacob looked up. It was his father.

Sixty-One

Jacob froze.

He looked up and down the street, then finally looked back up at Jake and relaxed.

"How did you find me?"

"A hunch. Have you eaten?"

"Not since this morning."

"Let's get something to eat."

They walked around the corner and down the street till they found a restaurant. Jake keyed a few words into his watch while they waited for their food to come.

Jacob ate as though he hadn't eaten in weeks.

Jake ate little.

When Jacob slowed down, Jake asked, "How have you been?"

Jacob didn't look at him. "Fine."

"I see you made it to Olympia."

"Yep."

"Are you hurt?"

"No. I haven't been in any danger since I left."

"What do we do now?"

"*We* don't do anything."

"What are you going to do?"

Jacob closed his eyes, and after a few seconds said, "Whatever I have to do."

Jake said nothing. He picked at his french fries.

Jacob put his head down on the table.

"Have you been to the Astronautics Corps?"

"Yes."

"How did that go?"

"I started an application."

"When do you enlist?"

Jacob stopped talking and looked away. He closed his eyes. There was silence for a long time.

"I guess, I guess I don't. I guess I'll go back to the freighter lines."

"Is that what you want?"

"That's what I've got."

"Let me see that application."

Jacob bumped his watch against Jake's and Jake lowered his glasses. He scrolled around with his eyes then slowly keyed something in through his watch. When he was done, he raised his glasses and bumped watches with Jacob again. Jacob scrolled through the application, then stopped. In the second field on the first page it said, "Jacob Billings II" and his father's signature was attached.

Jacob looked at Jake with a puzzled look on his face.

"I've only made one orbit, but by the rules at the time, I am technically an astronaut."

Cold rules
Then gives way
Life grows
and flies away

Sixty-Two

Ellie was ice when Jake walked through the door. "How could you do that without even talking to me first?"

"There wasn't time."

"There's always time if you make it."

"No. He would have been gone the first time I turned my back."

"You don't know that."

"I do know that. Besides, what was there for him here? Flunking out, working at the Woolwrights'?"

"It wasn't your decision to make!"

"Was it yours?"

"It was our decision to make."

"No. It never really was."

He tried to give her a hug, but she shoved him away.

"You were wrong," she said, and walked out of the room.

Jake left his things by the door and went outside. He looked around the yard and at each building. He looked down at his shiny "go-to-meeting" shoes and realized he wasn't going to get anything done without changing his clothes, and he wasn't changing his clothes without going back in the house, and he wasn't going back in the house without running into Ellie, so he wasn't going to get anything done. He went around the side of the house where Ellie couldn't see him, and sat on a bench.

He looked for one of the kids, but they were on Tuesday schedule and only the littlest ones were home, and inside, so, same problem.

He shook his head. "I should have taken the later flight," he said.

He sat in silence for a long time and finally got up, walked out into the woods, and fell asleep under a large white spruce he had planted five *years ago.

He opened his eyes because something cold was on his face, and smelled rain. The sky was dark and he was cold. Fat drops were hitting him in the face and drumming the ground all around him. The rabbits scampered back to their holes, and Jake stood up and moved closer to the tree trunk. He glanced at his watch and was surprised to see it was evening. When the rain subsided a little, Jake made a dash for the house.

His things were still by the door when he entered. Ellie was feeding the kids when he came in. She eyed him coolly. He served himself dinner and sat at the table. What little chatter had been going on stopped.

After a few minutes, Ellie put her dishes in the sink and went to her room saying, "You can clean up dinner."

There was a collective exhale, followed by Ada asking how Jacob was doing.

"He looks OK, but he didn't say much."

"Is he really going to be an astronaut?" Sam asked.

"Not right away. He'll have to finish school and training, but yeah, he'll be an astronaut."

"Do we get to see him?" Sam asked.

"Not for a while. You can write, though. He gets to retrieve his mail once a week."

"How did he get from Paititi to Olympia?" Chris asked.

"Looks like he went by ship."

A door down the hall slammed shut.

Everyone was quiet for a minute. Finally Ada said, "I think you did the right thing."

Some of the other kids nodded their heads slightly.

Jake looked down the hall, and said, "Well, that doesn't mean I don't need to apologize for it."

Sixty-Three

The first snow frosted the ground a few days later. Jake stood in the maintenance yard and looked at it. He went to the shed, got tools, and fixed things that had broken during the summer and been ignored or slapped together enough to finish the work. At about 10:00 AM, he poked his head out the shed door. The sun had chased the snow away, and he could see Mary and Sam staking out the new orchard they had been working on all spring and summer. Soon they would plant the fruit trees they had grown. Ellie was walking with them and watching them.

He had been officially forgiven the day before, but she was still cool to him. He didn't press it.

He went back to work and by evening had most of the vehicle work caught up. The next day he worked on fixing implements, but in the midafternoon he abruptly stopped and went into the house. He found Ellie in a corner of the living room reading. "Do you want to go on a picnic with me?" he asked. "If we dress for it, I don't think it's too cold yet."

Ellie put her book down and said, "Sure," with a shrug. Jake put together a basket while Ellie got her warm clothes on and they walked out past the old experimental plots, beyond the pond and onto the trail towards the wilderness hut. They followed the trail for a mile, then cut down into a meadow by a small stream. The grass was brown, and they could see their own breath as steam when they breathed out. The ground was cold. They blessed the food and ate it. The meadow was quiet. In the summer they would have heard frogs croaking and in the evening crickets chirping and the sounds of small things moving through the underbrush, but they had all gone to sleep except a few blue jays watching for an opportunity to snatch food. Ellie threw them the crust of her sandwich and watched them pounce.

"I wish I had been here for you... I wish you had told me when I first got home." Jake said.

Ellie leaned on one elbow and kept watching the blue jays. "At first I didn't tell you because you weren't here when it happened, so it was my grief, not ours, not yours. Later, I just didn't want to feel it again."

Jake thought about that.

Ellie threw some more crust to the birds. "... and I was mad at you so I didn't care if you had a right to know. And you have been gone a lot lately."

"I never go anywhere and I work right here."

"That's not what I mean. I mean you're absent a lot. You stay busy with your tasks and I stay busy with mine. Even when we go out to do something together it's like we're just checking off another task. Sometimes I wish it could be like it was when we were younger."

"That was crazy busy too," Jake said.

"Yeah, but it was our crazy. 'Jake and Ellie' crazy, Not 'Mr. and Mrs. Billings Incorporated' busy."

Jake considered that for a moment, then finally said, "I don't know how to be younger. I don't know what responsibilities to ignore. If I ignore the forest, then I'm a bad steward. If I ignore the kids, then I'm a bad father. If I ignore my callings, then I'm a bad person. If I ignore you, then I'm a bad husband."

"See that's just it. I don't want to be another of your responsibilities. It takes all the fun out of it."

"Weren't we just talking about how I failed you and have been failing you."

"I don't want you to be by my side so you won't be a failure. I want you to be by my side because you want to be... because you love me."

"I do love you. Why do you think I do the things I do?"

"Because you're supposed to love me! But you don't enjoy loving me, do you!?"

"I don't know. I don't think about it that way."

"You used to."

"I don't know how to fix this."

"Don't fix it!"

"Then I don't know what I'm supposed to do."

"Don't do anything. Just pretend I didn't say anything and feed these stupid birds with me."

Jake got a box of crackers, lay down beside her, and they took turns throwing them at the blue Jays and watching them squabble over them. As the afternoon got cooler, they cuddled and were calm.

Sixty-Four

In November, Mary and Sam planted their fruit trees. In late November Jake and Ellie heard that Jacob had been in town for several days doing grunt work for the terminal crew, but he was gone before they heard about it. They wrote to him, but he never answered. Occasionally he would send a short note to Ada or a small present to Sam, but he ignored the rest of the family.

In mid-December they got a Christmas card from him and on Christmas Eve they opened the door to find him standing there. He was a good two inches taller than when they had last seen him, though part of that was the boots he was wearing.

He didn't say much, but the week after Christmas he joined in with the rest of the family doing chores, and he volunteered for the worst ones. He was still there the second week after Christmas when approval for Chris's management plan came. He congratulated Chris. When it came time to go, he gave everyone a long hug and then left for the terminal without looking back.

He wrote letters to the whole family after that.

In April, a little before Easter, the first of Chris' seeds and embryos arrived. The buffalo embryo's would have to come on the cycler from Earth, but that was fine, it would give the grasses time to take hold before the buffalo tore it up.

Ada started her weight training and centrifuge training in late April. When she came home in May for a week, Jake playfully felt her biceps and said, "I've got a wood pile I'd like you to meet."

"Bring it on," Ada said, and split an eighth of a cord of spruce before anyone could stop her.

The last week in May they accompanied Ada to Olympia and rode the train together to the plateau at the top of Mount Olympus. On the way, Jake pointed out the curvature of the world to the kids, but they seemed unimpressed. He proceeded to point it out to Ellie who made a big show of being impressed just to get the kids to laugh.

At the Cycler briefing they were surprised to see Jacob walk in. He called the small group of travelers and their families together and announced that he would be their co-pilot on the launch vehicle. He went over what they should expect, then showed a short video describing the trip. He gave the travelers a few minutes to say goodbye. While they were saying goodbye, Jake approached Jacob and said, "I'm impressed they trust you with passengers so early."

Jacob chuckled and said, "They don't trust me with anything yet. They're just being nice and letting me go with my sister. These flights don't need copilots. I'm just extra weight."

"Still, they trust you not to do something stupid and cause a crash."

"Maybe that much," Jacob said.

There were hugs and hurried words, and then they were all gone through a door.

An hour later, the catapult heaved and a sliver of metal disappeared into the deep blue afternoon sky.

Sixty-Five

The ground fell away beneath the ascent vehicle in an eerie quiet that shattered when the engines fired a moment later.

Ada watched the stars come out, eyes wide trying to see everything.

In LEO they transferred to a shuttle. Ada was surprised when Jacob buckled in beside her.

"Shouldn't you be up front?"

"I'm not part of the shuttle crew," Jacob said.

Ada felt herself settle into her seat as the shuttle engines quietly pushed them in wider and wider loops away from home, until they broke orbit.

The captain asked the passengers to recheck their harnesses. Then the crew followed up, pushing people into position and pulling on straps.

When the crew started strapping in, Jacob leaned over and whispered, "Hold on to your shorts."

A light at the front of the cabin changed colors. A distant hum coming from the rear of the shuttle grew audible, and Ada felt herself pushed firmly against the seat. Then methane engines roared to life pushing her against the seat so hard that it was difficult to breathe for several minutes. The roaring stopped. The humming continued and the chair felt hard, but at least she could breathe. When the pressure eased, Jacob smiled at her.

"You should feel it on a cargo run. On a cargo run we have to go retrograde against the cycler, then turn around and catch up with it."

On board the cycler, Ada began to drop her appearance of calm as the reality of what she was doing settled in. When it was time for Jacob to go, she grabbed his arms and said, "Promise me you'll look out for Mom and Dad while I'm gone." Jacob looked at her. Tears were forming and she was staring straight at him.

"They are perfectly able to look after themselves," he said.

"You never know what will happen. Promise me!"

"We both know it will be Chris when the time comes."

"I don't care. Promise me!"

He looked at her for a long time and finally nodded, "OK, OK. I promise."

Ada nodded, and let him go. "I love you little brother," she said. He looked uncomfortable for a second, patted her shoulder, and retreated without looking back at her.

On the ground, Jacob was quieter than usual.

The next day, his pod mate punched him in the shoulder and said, "The new assignments are up." Jacob shrugged and went back to reading until his pod mate pretended to ignore him, then he strolled slowly out to the bulletin board. He waited behind a mob of cadets until he could get close enough to see what he got. The last list hadn't gone well for him. He had been stuck doing remedial work with just an occasional trip up to orbit to help with watching the tugs while the cycler crews unloaded them.

The crowd thinned and he scanned the list. Next to his name he saw a ship name; a real ship, the Astral 4. He ran to his quarters, closed the door and downloaded the details. It was a Fifteen *year old asteroid tug going out to the belt to carry a passenger and cargo that would arrive from Earth on the inbound cycler. They were for a research facility on Ceres. Once they got done babysitting, they were to grab a small asteroid and start nudging it towards home. The "Astral 4" wasn't powerful, but it was a real ship, on a real mission. The crew list was still blank. He refreshed the page about a dozen times, then gave up and went into the hall.

He kept his face expressionless, but he was flush, his skin glowing.

Guys from his class that had already taken their first voyages either congratulated him or punched him in the shoulder when they saw him. Most did both. He wandered into the dining hall, grabbed one of the bag dinners left out for the late comers, and looked for a place to sit. A girl with red hair was sitting at his favorite table by the window. She was looking out at the garden, watching the dusk gather over it, and eating ice cream from the machine that was supposedly shut down after dinner. He hesitated. He recognized her from some of his classes, but couldn't remember her name. After a full minute and without looking up she said, "You can sit here if you want." When he still hesitated, she looked up at him, watched him for a moment, then shrugged slightly and went back to eating her ice cream. He sat down. "How did you get the ice cream?" he asked. She held up a hairpin. He smiled and started unwrapping his sandwich.

"Did you finally get a ship?" she asked.

"Yes," he said. "How did you know?"

"You're beaming so bright I had to look away."

He felt his face get hot and she laughed softly.

"What about you? Seems like you've been around here as long as I have."

"As a matter of fact I did get a ship, that's why I'm celebrating," she said, gesturing to her ice cream bowl with her spoon.

"What ship?"

She pushed a button on her watch and an image of the girl's dorm assignment list appeared above the table.

Jacob skimmed it hoping to recognize her name as he went. He didn't. On his third skim she shook her head and said, "You don't know what my name is, do you?"

Jacob looked up at her like a rabbit caught in the headlights, then smiled and said, "I have absolutely no idea."

She set her mouth firmly in mock gravity and shook her head, but there was a flash of something else. "It's Val. Val Kyria. You know, the girl who beat you on every test," she said with a hint of actual annoyance. Jacob shrugged slightly and studied the list. Just as she shut it off, he saw her assignment, and started laughing.

Val shifted in her seat uncomfortably. Jacob laughed again.

"I suppose you did better?" she said defensively.

Jacob shook his head and said, "No. I did exactly as well."

She looked at him, still miffed, for a second. He looked straight back at her, waiting for comprehension. Her face softened, then hardened. Then she said, "I have to go. I'll see you tomorrow," turned and left.

Jacob sat back in his chair and watched her go.

Sixty-Six

Ada watched Jacob walk away, then stood tall and followed the others into orientation. The passenger liaison, Julie, gave them a virtual tour of the ship, stressing the off limits section of the ship several times, showing them where to find the schedule of passenger activities and introduced them to their pod mates. Ada was with a girl named Lorie from the uplands of Mariner Valley and a short girl named Deidre who said she was from "@#$%! Earth."

After orientation, they walked to their pod together and stowed their gear. Deidre stripped off her clothes, watch, glasses, and earring, and threw them into the trash. She sprawled naked on the couch and switched the "window" to a club scene. Lorie and Ada stared. Deidre looked at them for a second and said, "What? Do you want some?"

Lorie and Ada looked at each other then Lorie said, "Want some what?"

Deidre laughed and said, "I didn't think so. You girls need to loosen up a little. This is an Earth ship. You can do what you want. You're free now."

"How come you threw away your wearables? They were pretty good ones."

Deidre pointed at her head, "My implants work here. They work everywhere on Earth. I'll never need that crap again."

"Can I have them? " Lorie asked.

"Take them, I don't care. But the ship's got a pretty good implant center. You should get it done now so you'll be all adjusted before we get to Earth."

"Why would we want to put a bunch of graphene and nanotubes in our heads?" Ada asked.

"So you won't look like losers."

Ada and Lorie just stood there. Deidre's face softened a little and said, "Besides you can access information a lot faster with implants. It's more like remembering than looking stuff up. It gives you an advantage, and you can't get verisimilis on wearables. The best you can do with wearables is immersive."

Deidre looked at Lorie and Ada who had blank expressions on their faces. Deidre rolled her eyes, "Verisimilis is fake experience, but it seems totally real. It's like a lucid dream."

"Wouldn't that be a hallucination?"

"You can get that too," Deidre said laughing. "No, because you know you're doing it. I mean you don't think it's a hallucination when you play an immersive game, do you?"

"No. I guess not," Lorie conceded.

"You should do it. I've got a couple of verisims I could share with you." Deidre said with a glint in her eyes.

"So do Terrans spend all their time naked?" Ada asked.

"No. I mean some do, but not most people. I mean where would the style be in that? We like clothes, but we aren't ashamed of our bodies like you Martians."

"I'm not ashamed of my body," Ada said.

"OK then, strip," Deidre said.

Ada flushed and said, "No."

"I thought not," Deidre said.

"You wouldn't understand."

"Don't I? I've been on Mars for two earth years. You're going to tell me your body's holy and that you don't share it with everyone or some crap like that. If that's really it, then you're just being selfish. So which is it, are you ashamed or selfish?"

Ada flushed again. "I'm done," she said, then went to her bunk area and started unpacking.

"I win. I'm the winner," Deidre said.

"Or your maybe you're just an ass," Lorie said, and joined Ada in the bunk area.

Deidre laughed, and said, "Yeah, I'm an ass, and I've got a great ass if I do say so myself."

After unpacking, Ada and Lorie left Deidre on the couch and wandered the cycler aimlessly. The great blessing and curse of the cycler was time.

The rear of the cycler had the cargo hold, docking facilities and the observation deck.

The forward section contained passenger pods and was much newer than the rest of the ship. The original layout had been replaced by a large spinning cylinder that provided something like gravity. The lighting in the maintenance and storage areas was constant, but inside the cylinder and on the observation deck it was arranged to simulate a day night cycle.

Above the Cylinder were the bridge and other "Crew Only" areas.

After an hour and a half of exploring, and 45 minutes of watching Mars grow small through the observation deck window, Lorie suddenly said, "I'm hungry."

When they got back to the passenger section they could smell food coming from the dining room. They got food, looked around for a place to sit and saw Deidre sitting by a "window" that was showing the same view they had seen on the observation deck. She was wearing a shimmering impossibly tight black dress that seemed to adjust so it never puckered when she changed positions.

"I see you put some clothes on," Ada said.

Deidre laughed, "Yeah, sorry about that. I've been playing by Martian rules for longer than I wanted to. I just needed to let loose a little. I didn't mean to be too nasty. It was fun watching your faces though. But seriously, you've got to do something about those outfits before we arrive. If you want to stick with wearables, that's your thing. Maybe you can make it into a retro style. It could work, but your clothes are a problem. Let me help you?"

Ada and Lorie looked at each other and shrugged. "I guess we could give it a try," Lorie said.

"Great. We'll start tomorrow."

After dinner they worked out a schedule for who got to pick the pod window view. On Ada's days the window usually showed either a tourist version of Arabia Terra, or a view overlooking the campus in Palo Alto. Lorrie preferred views of the Eiffel Tower and old European cities. Deidre surprised them with views of vast prairies, and meadows filled with wild flowers, and the Flat Iron Range of the Rockies in Colorado.

Life fell into a rhythm. Most of their day to day activities were in the passenger area, but Ada's favorite spot was the observation deck. Ada liked to go there late at night when it was empty, place herself in the exact center of the deck, then twist slightly to put her body into a slow spin, and look out the window into the deep star field beyond it.

The bulk of her time was spent studying. There were a number of topics she would need a grasp of at Stanford that school hadn't pre-pared her for. For example, they had all taken a basic Earth History, but as Ada dug into the source materials she found it was a lot more complicated than she had imagined. Also, materials from different eras had different flavors to them. The 18th and 19th century American and European materials were all about expansion and growth. They were full of self-certainty and the inevitability of progress. They were also flowery in some ways and formulaic in others. Much of the second half of the 20th century and the entire 21st century were different. The self-certainty was still there, but it was all about undoing things the previous centuries had built up. It was about collective guilt and the pursuit of personal enhancement, seemingly through self-degradation. The styles varied wildly, passing through ecstatic, to simplistic, to nearly sterile, and then looping back into highly detailed descriptions of the mundane. The official records were worse. They had their own flowery formulaic constructions that used as many words as possible to say as little as possible. Records meant to offend few, and enlighten even fewer.

Sixty-Seven

When Jacob arrived at the briefing room, Val was already there.

"Hi there, shipmate," he said as he sat down. She watched him coolly, like a cat watching a boy, then smiled.

Neither spoke until their commander came in. They stood. He was one of their old class instructors.

He sat down and gestured for them to sit.

"Going out for a walk, sir?" Jacob said.

The Commander smiled, but otherwise ignored the comment.

Val studied Jacob disapprovingly, but he didn't look at her and the Commander projected a model of the solar system over the desk, saying, "As you know, we are headed for Ceres. Unfortunately for us, by the time our cargo arrives, Ceres and Mars will be out of alignment, so we'll have to take the long way around." The Commander gestured to show the course they would take around the sun and a dotted line appeared. He set the model in motion and a dot traveled between the planet and the planetoid. "Once there, we will need to unload and refuel as quickly as possible to bring back the biggest portion of an asteroid we can. Every day we delay is another 600,000 KM of chasing Mars and that means more asteroid for reaction mass, and less for Mars. We leave in fifteen days as soon as the inbound cycler is unloaded. I want a copy of your flight plan, fuel consumption profile, and crew rotation in my mailbox by 8:00 am tomorrow. I've already sent you the cargo weight. Any questions?"

"Are you sure you want us to write the flight plan? Neither of us has flown a real mission before," Val said.

"It's like Billings said, I'm just going on a walk to keep my commander's wings. I don't want to actually do anything," the Commander said.

Val blinked. "What if we miscalculate?"

"That would be very bad," the Commander said, "I recommend you not do that."

"How do you want us to split up the work, sir?" Jacob asked.

"I don't care," the Commander said. "Any other questions?"

No one spoke.

"Good. Dismissed," the Commander said, gathered his things and left the room.

Val leaned her forehead against her hand and groaned.

Jacob just chuckled a little.

Val peaked up at him with one eye. "What's so funny?"

"Don't worry so much. It's not like he's really going to let us get him killed."

"Are you sure? He seems pretty complacent."

Jacob nodded. "I'm pretty sure. He's made trips like this a hundred times. He'll know if we screwed it up without even reading the whole thing."

"I guess you're right. It won't matter if we make a mistake."

"I didn't say that. We mess up that flight plan and we'll be back to babysitting tugs in orbit."

"How should we do it?" Val asked.

"Let's both write our own flight plan and budget and then compare them before we turn one in."

Val nodded and got to work. Jacob spun his glasses around on the table for a few minutes, just thinking.

Val looked up at him and said, "I thought we were both doing this?"

"We are," Jacob said, "I do my best work messing around."

Val squinted her eyes a little and went back to work. Eventually Jacob put his glasses on and began typing on the table top.

After a few minutes he took off his glasses and put them in his pocket.

Val looked up at him. "Done already?"

"Yeah."

"How?" she asked.

"It's just orbital mechanics. It's not like it's a novel problem every time."

"The values change every time, Val insisted."

"I wrote a program for class. I just changed the variables and reran it."

"You're cheating," she said.

"This isn't class, besides no one said we couldn't use a program, they just said we couldn't use anyone else's work, like a program."

Val started to open her mouth, but then closed it and shrugged. She finished her work and they sat next to each other and projected both plans over the table at the same time.

They were similar. Val's was more detailed, but they both projected arrival time and fuel consumption within 2% of each other, and they were both based on a single long burn leaving Mars, midcourse coasting, and a single long burn into Ceres orbit.

"You left out solar wind, and you didn't include the gravitational pull of the other asteroids around Ceres," Val complained.

"So mine overestimates fuel consumption out bound slightly, and puts perigee a half a kilometer farther from Ceres than we intended, but it's all negligible."

"What about the return trip?" she asked. "It would underestimate fuel consumption on the return trip and decrease perigee. Were you planning to aero brake?"

"We'll be parked on top of a huge fuel reserve and it would only be something like a half a kilometer difference out of 200 kilometers. I wouldn't call that aero braking. Besides we can't plan the return trip until we know when we are leaving and what we are hauling back."

Val shook her head. "Your model is too simplistic. It doesn't give the right answer."

"My model is simple enough I can do it with a pencil and paper in real time, and it's close enough."

"Getting the answer quickly may get your homework done faster, but how does it help us here?"

"It gets us to lunch quicker."

"Are you taking this seriously at all?" Val asked.

"Yes. I'm very hungry."

Val balled her fists up and Jacob laughed at her and said, "OK, OK, we'll use yours."

"OK then," she said.

They spent the next fifteen minutes working up the crew rotation. They would each take five hour shifts on the bridge, overlapping the shifts one hour, and let the A. I. watch the ship overnight. They would each run a full diagnostic at the beginning of each shift and check their position against pulsars at the beginning and middle of each shift. In addition, Jacob would do a manual inspection of the engine room every day, and Val would check the guidance and communication systems every day. They gave the Commander the first shift, Val the second, and Jacob the third, then sent the information to the Commander and went to lunch.

Sixty-Eight

The next morning Val and Jacob got a quick note from the Commander accepting their flight plan, and directing them to Deimos Hangar Bay One by the first available launch to check out the ship. They met at breakfast and agreed to take the morning train after they ate. Val got whipped cream from her cocoa on her nose. Jacob pretended not to see it for a full three minutes, smiling, before he finally gestured for her to wipe it off.

They boarded the train a little before 9:00 a. m. Three quarters of the way up, they starting pulling on their pressure suits. Jacob's eyes flicked over from time to time as Val adjusted the tight fitting suit. Val noticed, but didn't say anything. When they reached the launch ramp the crew strapped them into a light two-seater and fired them off the end of the ramp less than half an hour later. The dark blue closed in around them. The engines fired right on cue, then the hum of the ion engines took over for the long slow pursuit of Deimos. They double checked their speed, inclination, and projected path. Satisfied, they settled in. Jacob opened a bag of candies and lined the individual pieces up in a row floating just above his head, then flicked them back at Val. One bounced off her visor. She raised her visor and loosened her straps. Jacob flicked the next one. She bobbed up and caught it in her mouth. He did it again and she caught it again. He flicked the third one and she deflected it forward again so that it bounced off the canopy and caught Jacob in the cheek. He winced. "OK, no more candy for you," he said, grabbed the remaining candies and shoved them into his own mouth. She shrugged and looked out the canopy at the hard brilliant stars. Ceres was visible for part of the flight, if you knew where to look, but it was just one of many flecks of light. They chatted about school, and differences between the girls' and boys' dorms. Jacob told stories about some especially good pranks they'd played. Val told him how the girls in a section that had been converted for girls use had put potted plants in the urinals and watered them by flushing. Periodically they rechecked their course, but the autopilot was very good and gave them no reason for worry.

When they got close, Val transferred the controls to her console and started slowing their approach with deft little bursts of the thrusters. The ascent vehicle slid into the hangar like it was naturally falling there. They slid along the hangar following directional signs to the nearest available bay and docked. The bay door slid closed behind them and the bay started pressurizing. A series of lights lit along the top of the console. Jacob waited for them all to light, then pressed a button that opened the canopy.

They slipped out of their restraints and pushed up out of the cockpit toward the grab bars overhead, then pulled themselves hand-over-hand toward the small man-hatch at the front of the bay. As they went, a small inspection ball popped out of the wall and started puffing its way slowly toward their vehicle.

"Uh oh," Jacob said, "I wonder what's wrong with our ride."

"Nothing," he heard Val say. "This is AV #7. I've ridden it up three times, and every time the fuel door on it sticks."

They opened the man hatch and started kicking down the corridor to Bay One on the other end of the hangar. After five minutes, they stopped in front of another man hatch and typed in their access code. The grimy screen changed to "Please wait," then the door slid open and let them in. Once they cleared the hatch, they both froze. Jacob could hear Val inhale suddenly over their shared Com link. The Astral 4 loomed up in front of them so close Jacob could touch it. He did touch it, softly. They were so close it filled their entire field of vision.

"Everybody shape up. The kids are here," said a large man in blue deck suit that was a little too tight for him.

The other crewmen kept at their work but glanced up from time to time to watch the reactions.

Jacob nodded and worked his way down to the man. Val watched for a moment then pulled herself around to glide over the surface of the ship slowly.

When Jacob reached him, the large man said, "So are you going to bring her back to me in one piece? We just barely got done fixing her up after the last set of runts banged her up."

Jacob looked at him calmly until the man moved a little then said, "No. I'll probably hit something. It gets a little crowded in the belt. You put any decent shielding on this thing?"

"Of course. Why do you think they let you drive it?"

"'Cause I'm so handsome."

The large man slapped him on the shoulder and said, "Get your boots. I'll give you the tour." Then he paused and pointed at Val flitting over the hull, "Does your girlfriend want to come?"

"Do you mean Cadet First Class Kyria?" Jacob asked.

"Yeah, the firefly skimming over the hull threatening to bend the deflector array."

"She'll let you know when she's done with her inspection."

Jacob pulled on magnetic boots and the Crew Chief showed him around the exterior of the ship, pointing out the standard features and where they'd made modifications.

There were a lot of modifications. The ship still had large impact scars on the more heavily armored belly. The holes were fixed but the carbon smears from the heat of impact had been ignored except were they had to clean them to get good welds. Val caught up with them in the engine room. When he saw the engine Jacob dropped all pretense of cool and smiled from ear to ear.

"You like that, do you?" the Crew Chief said, nodding his head slightly. "We pulled that out of a class B tug some of your classmates banged up last year. Don't get too excited. The reactor and couplers are Mark VII's but you've still got the standard emitters and thrust chambers. So you don't actually have any extra speed or thrust; maybe next overhaul we can get those in. In the mean time you can run your hair dryer all you want."

They checked out the cargo hold, communications system, navigation, crew quarters, everything until the crew chief got bored. "I've got work to do. Call me if you need anything, and make sure you sign the log before you go," he said and left them on the command deck. "And don't touch the thrusters," he added as he left. Val and Jacob sat in the chairs on either side of the Commander's chair and looked out the forward window.

"Sit in the Commander's chair," Jacob said.

Val looked at him.

"Why not? You're going to be sitting in it every day for two and a half months; you might as well give it a try."

Val shrugged and hopped over into it.

"How does it feel?"

"Like an old chair," she said, but she was smiling.

They sat there for a while, signed the log book, and worked their way back to the ascent vehicle. It was waiting for them, all refueled. They climbed in, let go, and fell out of the sky.

Sixty-Nine

The only response from the Commander to their reports on the ship was a one line message: "Good job," with a one week pass attached for each of them.

They met at breakfast and Jacob asked, "What will you do with your pass?"

"First I'm going to get my hair fixed by someone who hasn't spent the last ten *years cutting boy's hair, and then I'm going home. My folks are throwing a big barbecue in honor of my first real assignment and all my siblings and neighbors are coming. What about you?"

"I don't know yet," Jacob said with a strange smile. "I'll probably end up going home too, but I haven't made up my mind yet."

"Why not? Aren't your folks happy about your assignment?"

"I haven't told them yet," Jacob said.

"Why not? Will they be upset or something?"

Jacob considered this for a moment and said, "No, I don't think so. I think they'll be happy for me."

"Then what?"

"My sister just left on the outbound cycler so I think they're kind of done with goodbyes for now, and I think the way I left home has probably left a bad taste about all things astronautic. I don't know. It just seems like a lot of trouble for a few awkward moments that leave everyone less happy."

"I vote you go," Val said. "I think you're just being chicken, but I can respect that."

"I probably will. But you have to be the one to have a good time so we'll have some good stories on the trip."

"Deal."

Jacob missed the direct flight from Olympia, so he had some time to kill. He checked out and went to the astronaut bar, ordered a "hamburger" and "french fries" and wondered what Ada was eating. After that he ordered a "BifSteak" and had them flash freeze it for his dad. He didn't know what to get his mother, but he already had presents for his siblings bouncing around in a small pouch in his front pocket.

He caught a late afternoon transport to Paititi and traced his water route from Paititi to Olympia from the air with his eye. As he did, he suddenly yearned to be on one of those ships instead of flying home.

His transfer in Paititi went smoothly and before long he was landing in the dusty old town he had been too happy to leave. He hadn't told anyone he was coming, so there was no one to meet him.

"It'll make a nice surprise," he said to himself with no conviction.

There was a new taxi on duty at the terminal. He took that. His funds were fading fast, but what did it matter? In a few days he would be where there wasn't anything to buy and they would still keep dumping money into his account the whole time he was gone. Plus, he already knew he was career. Fourteen *years of this, then a nice pension with occasional consulting work. Money didn't matter. He had chosen a simple life. He looked out across the forests in the failing light and the trees mocked him. He changed the topic with himself and mused about what he would do if no one were home. He would leave his gifts and a nice note and head back. It'd be better that way anyway. Even in the dark the forest mocked him, even when he couldn't directly see it. "They'll be home," he muttered to himself. He left the other thoughts alone.

When they pulled into the driveway the lights were on. He noticed the road seemed too quiet and realized they'd paved the driveway since he left. He paid the cabbie and knocked on the door. After a while, he heard footsteps and then the door opened. Jake grabbed him and held him tight without saying a word for twenty seconds. Jacob startled a little, then relaxed and hugged him back. Jake had already eaten, but they fried the beef steak up anyway. He ate again, making a big show of not sharing any of it with the kids, though Ellie got several pieces slipped onto her plate.

Jacob got a pouch out of his pocket and called Sam over. Then he pulled a piece of dark gray rock in a transparent sleeve out of his pouch and gave it to him. "Here is the shooting star I promised you. It's actually a part of Deimos I grabbed for you when I was there."

"Does it glow?" Sam asked.

"Only while it's falling fast through the atmosphere and believe me, if it didn't glow while I was bringing it back, the ship did."

He then passed out various small hunks of metal and ceramic to the other kids. They turned them over in their hands and looked at Jacob for an explanation. "These are parts of my ship that aren't being used anymore. I got assigned to a ship and we are headed to the asteroid belt next week. This way you can have a part of the ship I'm on the whole time I'm on it."

At first there was only silence, but then everyone congratulated him. "Why didn't you tell us?" Chris asked.

"I wanted to tell you myself," Jacob lied.

Ellie gave him a hug and a kiss and said she was proud of him, but then excused herself for a while. Someone got some snacks and a movie going.

Chris took a call from the new station that bordered their station and Cava shouted out, "Say 'hi' to your girlfriend Chris."

Chris blushed, muted the phone, and said, "Shut up, she's not my girlfriend. This is business."

As soon as he got back on the phone Cava, Sam and Mary chanted, "Girlfriend! Girlfriend! Girlfriend!" until he left the room. Jacob looked at his dad, who shook his head a little.

"Not really. She's the right age and he likes her, but mainly he's just coordinating with her dad because the section he's managing bumps up against their station."

After the movie Jacob went for a walk. The shadows of the trees seemed taller, if that was possible, and he missed the gravel on the driveway. He saw the rover he'd stolen the night he left parked behind the station. It looked like his dad had been tinkering with it again. He looked at the sky. Saturn was rising. He heard the front door open and close softly and braced himself. He kept looking at the sky. He involuntarily shuddered when he realized someone was already standing beside him on the edge of his peripheral vision.

"I didn't mean to startle you," Ellie said.

"It's OK."

"So, this assignment is a big deal for you?"

"Yes. It means they are starting to trust me to do real work. If they hadn't assigned me to a real ship sometime in the next year, it would have been a subtle signal to resign."

"Wouldn't they just terminate you?"

"Not usually."

They were silent for a while.

"Sorry I took off without saying anything," he offered.

Ellie nodded.

He thought for a second then shook his head, "I'm not sorry I went. I'm not sorry I didn't say anything at the time, but I am sorry for the pain I caused people."

"If you had leveled with us, we could have worked something out. You still could have been an astronaut."

"That's just it. If I had leveled with you, you would have worked something out. This was something I had to do. Maybe I didn't do it the best way, but I did it."

"Yes," Ellie said, hesitated, then said, "Goodnight," and went back to the house.

In the morning they took the day off and went to the creek. The water was still too cold to go in, but that didn't stop Cava or Sam from trying. Jacob laughed at them, a good open laugh. Jake looked at him and smiled but didn't say anything.

"What? A guy can't laugh? They're funny once you forget they're your siblings."

Ellie watched all this but said nothing.

They ate and went home a little before dusk. Jake got busy putting things away in one of the sheds while Jacob wandered towards the house. Ellie walked beside him.

"Being an astronaut seems to agree with you," Ellie said. "Are you growing in all the ways you should be?"

Jacob controlled his face. "I am growing. I'm probably not growing in all the ways you want me to, but I'm not hurting anyone, and I'm not doing anything that you would be ashamed of."

Ellie looked him in the face. Jacob started to pull back but stopped himself.

"You will always be my little boy. You will always be a part of me. That means I can never really let go all the way. I will always love you even when I don't want to see your face. Please don't hurt me again, and I'll try not to put so many expectations on you."

Jacob nodded.

Ellie nodded.

They hugged briefly then walked back to the house.

Uncertain
but not unwanted
Wanting
but not alone
Until the sky shatters
and calls us home

Seventy

Val got back from leave a half day early and spent it under a tree on the lawn in front of the Corps headquarters. It was a spot set back from the road and to the left of the entrance twenty meters so she could see everyone come and go, but people mostly left her alone.

She had a book that she looked at occasionally. Mostly she leaned back with eyes closed, smelling the air and listening to the sounds of wind, insects and the chatter of humans.

She drifted into sleep several times, but as the shadows moved and left her in sunlight she woke up and moved with them. After one move, she looked up to see her lanky shipmate walking toward the front doors. She watched him, watched the way he moved with that combination of utter confidence and constant alertness that first caught her attention. She didn't speak to him. She let him pass, not seeing her.

She smiled at herself and closed her eyes to listen again, soaking up the sounds and smells. After fifteen minutes, she closed her book and walked around the long way to the back door of the women's dormitory and to her room. She checked her hair, straightened her clothes and picked little stray bits of grass off of them. She reapplied her lipstick, and then walked casually into the cafeteria.

He was there of course, sitting at their table. The boy was always hungry.

"Was leave good?" she asked, sitting down.

He thought for a second and said, "I guess so. It was nothing like I feared it would be. It wasn't exactly fun, but I'm glad I went. How was your party?"

"It was great. My nieces and nephews came and I got to play "Auntie" for a day and everyone got to be proud of me for getting a ship. And the food was amazing."

"I see you got your hair cut."

"I did. Do you like it?" she said, batting her eye lashes.

"It's good. I think I liked it better when it was longer, but it's good."

Val pretended to frown, then shrugged. "It's easier to take care of during the weightless phase this way."

After dinner they officially checked in, even though the system had noticed them the minute they stepped through the doors. Tradition.

They both turned in early.

The next morning they met on the train to the port. Neither one had much to say. They helped each other with their pressure suits on the way up, and then watched the world go by the windows.

At Deimos Station they found the Commander literally crawling through the ship. When he saw them, he climbed out of an engine room service hatch and called them to attention.

"Billings, you're on engineering for launch. Kyria: you're pilot and navigation for launch. We leave in an hour. Get to your stations and prep for launch."

Val went to the bathroom, then strapped herself into the right hand seat on the command deck. She ran diagnostics and preflight checks, though she could see from the logs they had already been done that morning.

Jacob went down to the engine room and visually inspected everything. He powered on the control systems and radio emitters and put his hands on them to feel the vibrations. Finally he ran the local diagnostics before joining Val on the command deck, strapping into the left hand seat and running the full system diagnostics and preflight checks. When they were both done, there wasn't much to do but sit and watch the ground crew securing their cargo in the hold.

At one point, they caught a glimpse of the Commander escorting someone to look at the cargo. He was taller and thinner than most old worlders.

"Think that's our passenger?" Jake asked.

"I guess. Who else would want to see the cargo?" Val said.

They were surprised a couple of minutes later to see the Commander hanging in the doorway with the man they had seen on the monitors.

"Mr. Ottis, this is my crew. Miss Kyria is in the pilot's seat, and Mr. Billings is at the engineering console."

Val and Jacob each gave a crisp short salute and said, "Welcome aboard, sir," when they were introduced.

Mr. Ottis said, "Please call me Will. It's going to be a long flight," he had a fairly thick old world accent that Jacob recognized as northern European of some kind.

"Thank you, sir," they both said simultaneously.

Will shook his head, but the Commander smiled at them.

"I'll get our guest situated on the observation deck," the Commander said.

When he came back, he strapped himself into the center chair. Jacob noticed that even with the Commander between them, he could still look directly at Val. He looked at the floor and saw the Commander's chair was set back a half meter to make sure they could all see each other. He smiled.

When the Commander had strapped in he said, "Reports."

Jacob responded, "All generation, propulsion, environmental, and hull protection systems normal and ready for launch."

Val responded, "All control, navigation, and communications systems normal and ready for launch."

The Commander nodded, checked his orders for any updates, then said, "Miss Kyria, prepare for departure."

Val opened her external com link and said, "Hangar control, this is Astral 4. Preparing for departure."

"Copy. Astral 4 preparing for departure."

Valerie pressed two icons and her console reported back the maneuvering thrusters were pressurized. She clicked two more icons. The running lights came on all around the ship and a warning strobe began flashing. She sent a command to the hangar and it sounded a claxon.

The hangar crew performed their checks then opened the hangar door and released the docking clamps.

"Astral 4, requesting permission to depart."

"Astral 4, permission to depart granted."

"Astral 4, departing."

"God speed Astral 4."

Val fired the maneuvering jets tentatively and eased Astral 4 back very, very slowly. When it was fully into the main cavern, the crew closed the bay door and turned off the lights.

Val continued backing into the darkness, the ship's running lights creating moving pools of light on the cavern walls. When the ship emerged into sunlight, Val increased speed until Deimos was a gray gap in the star field.

Jacob began touching icons and the space around Astral 4 began to shimmer in the dark, then shifted to a dull blue color.

Val reoriented the ship so it was facing the direction of travel, calculated a trajectory, entered the parameters in the flight controller and reported, "Ready to break orbit sir."

"Break orbit Miss Kyria."

"Breaking orbit."

Val pressed a blinking red icon and the engines began firing with a dull electric hum. The acceleration pressed them back into their seats.

".1 G achieved," Val reported.

"All systems normal," Jacob reported.

Mars grew continually smaller out the port window over the next hour until it began to slip behind the ship and Val called out, "Escape velocity achieved."

Val flipped screens to a representation of the planned course and waited for the computer to get a fix on their location from six well known pulsars. Seconds passed and their current course was displayed over the planned one. She grimaced. "I missed," she said puzzled.

"Deimos?" Jacob suggested. "It wasn't in your model."

"Negligible," Val said.

"So Deimos is negligible, but the solar wind and the asteroids aren't?" Jacob said.

The Commander chuckled. "She's right. Deimos is negligible. It's late spring in the Northern Hemisphere..."

"Atmospheric expansion..." Val and Jacob said together.

The Commander nodded and said, "Gold star for each of you."

Val increased thrust slightly until the projected lines came back together,

then announced ".11 G."

The Commander watched for another half hour and then said, "Miss Kyria, you have the bridge." He reoriented his chair, unstrapped and began walking down the wall to the observation deck.

As soon as the Commander was out of ear shot, Val called out, "Status report, Mr. Billings."

Jacob looked at her for a second, looked through his screens, and said, "All systems normal."

Val smirked a little and said, "Mr. Billings, please run a full diagnostic."

Jacob looked at her for a second and a half, then turned to his screen and began running the diagnostics.

After a few minutes he reported back, "All systems normal."

After a few seconds, Val said, "Mr. Billings, sing the Astronautics Corps fight song."

Jacob looked at her for three seconds, then cleared his throat and began singing a nearly monotone, apathetic rendition of the fight song. He only got two lines into it before Val started laughing and said,

"Mr. Billings, belay my last order."

"Permission to speak freely ma'am?" Jacob asked.

"Granted."

"I'll remember this when the Commander leaves me in charge of the flight deck."

"Noted, Cadet," Val said with mock seriousness.

"Mr. Billings."

"Yes, ma'am."

"Pass the cookies."

"Yes, ma'am."

They set the flight deck environment to observation. The lights went out and the monitors switched to a dull red output. As their eyes adjusted they began to really see the sharp edged stars burning in their various colors, sizes and intensities in all directions.

"I wonder what they look like without the glass," Jacob said.

"Shall we put on suits and go see?"

"No, that would just be replacing quartz glass with tinted nano-engineered polycrystalline glass. I mean, I wonder what it looks like with nothing but your own eyes."

"Do you want me to flush you out the airlock and then you could come back and tell us?" Val said.

Jacob smiled and said, "No thanks."

They sat in silence a while.

"Do the stars ever make you feel small?" Val asked.

After a moment Jacob said, "No. They always make me feel bigger, like I'm part of something larger."

"Me too," Val said. "I had this substitute teacher in school who kept throwing out numbers about how large the universe was and what a small part of it we are. His pet name for anyone that gave him a hard time was 'rounding error.' Towards the end of the second week one of my classmates was explaining why his essay was late and this teacher made the "yakety yak" sign with his hands and said 'Go look at the stars tonight and see how much the universe cares about your problems.' That never made sense to me. When I look at them my problems get smaller, but I don't feel smaller."

"What a weirdo," Jacob said.

"Yeah, I think the administration thought that. He never came back after that."

"Maybe he hanged himself," Jacob suggested.

"That's not funny."

"No, I mean it. If he's so insignificant, why not?"

Val reflected and said, "I don't think people do that because they feel small. I think they do that because they think their problems are too big to solve."

"I think it's both."

"Maybe."

The Commander walked in and said, "What is this, a lounge?"

"Observation mode," Val said.

"Lounge mode," the Commander corrected, took his chair and reoriented. But he didn't change the lighting back to normal.

The three of them sat in silence. Jacob looked at Val from time to time, but couldn't think of anything to say. Once when he looked over he saw her looking back at him. But she didn't say anything either. Once he glanced at the Commander. He had his usual complacent mask of a face on, but Jacob thought he could see the edges of a smirk on his face. The Commander looked back at him and raised his eyebrows a little. Jacob looked away. They sat in awkward silence the rest of the day.

Finally the Commander said, "Check everything." They ran all their checks and reported all normal.

"Good. Activate the A. I.." Jacob activated it and ran a few checks to make sure it was sane. "A. I. is nominal."

"Excellent. We'll start the normal crew rotation tomorrow. Get some rest. Dismissed."

Seventy-One

Life clicked into a pattern on board. Val and Jacob ate breakfast together, then hung out in the break room until it was time for Val's shift. After that Jacob would go talk to Will and roam the ship. Then he'd work with Val for an hour till her shift was over, and start his own shift. The shifts were quiet with lots of time for thinking. At the end of each shift he'd crawl through the engine room looking for signs of trouble. Then he'd get a snack and go to bed.

Twelve days into the flight they shut down the thrusters and everything started floating around the cabins again. Val didn't come to breakfast for two days after that and looked a little green when she appeared in the break room later. "Look, it's a Martian," Jacob said. Val glared at him and he laughed. By day three she was back to normal.

At breakfast, there was still fresh fruit from the valley greenhouses, so they ate that. "When we get back, the first real field fresh fruit will be coming out. My folks have friends in the valley that send us a ton of fresh fruit every summer and for the first few weeks, my folks stop cooking altogether and we just gorge on it."

"What do your folks do?" Val asked.

"They're old style stewards running a station in Arabia Terra. But they do their own genetic work."

"What are they like?"

"Pretty boring. They work. They raise kids. Once a week they go out on a 'date' which mostly means they do the dishes together and fall asleep on the couch watching a movie. Once a month they go to Paititi and do temple work. They're church people so they're always doing things for church. They're pretty sure they're right about everything and everyone. I don't think they have any real ambition or dreams or anything. They just plod along."

He looked at Val hesitantly.

"They sound like awful people," Val said, holding back a smile.

"Not awful, just boring and bossy."

"So they didn't want you to be an astronaut?" Val asked.

"No. Not really. I mean they'd have preferred I went to college, but they're OK with the astronaut thing."

Val just looked at him.

"I think they just didn't like that it was my idea and not theirs. You just have to know them for it to make sense."

Val shrugged and went back to eating her fruit.

"What are your folks like?" Jacob asked.

"They're perfect, just like me," Val said. When Jacob didn't bite she continued.

"Dad works as a clerk for a shipping company. Mom works at Paititi Communications. The whole family is very proud of me except for my next oldest sister. She had to take over all my chores when I got accepted. She thinks I'm a turd."

After Val started her shift, Jacob floated down to the observation room to see what their passenger was doing. When he arrived, Will wasn't there. Jacob found him in the cargo hold bolting equipment to a table.

"What are we doing today?" Jacob asked.

"*We* are pretending to rerun a scale model of our experiment to recheck my calculations, but we are actually just bored and fooling around with cool toys," Will said.

"Oh good, my favorite thing; breaking stuff for no good reason," Jacob said, and gave his full attention.

Will smiled a little, put away his wrench and patted two palm sized cylinders with dense foam tips on tubes sticking out of a rack. "Compressed air 'rockets,'" Will said. Then he patted a clunky machine pointing up at an angle. "Anti-Higgs field generator." Next he pointed at a small commercial instrument pointed straight up. "Radar gun," he said.

Jacob interrupted, "Did you say anti-Higgs field generator?"

"Yes."

"I thought the anti-Higgs field was just a theory... just equations that probably described something impossible."

"It was, until eight earth years ago," Will said.

"Why haven't I heard about this?"

"We kept it quiet for the first year because we didn't want to get laughed at if we were wrong. We kept it quiet for the next three years because we were seeking private funding. But four earth years ago we published and the work was replicated within three months. Congress debated it for three months before granting funds, so the last three earth years of ignorance are your fault," Will said.

They fired the rockets a few times and watched them bounce off the ceiling and spin around till air currents got a hold of them. Usually they ended up stuck on the return air grate and Jacob would turn off his boots and go get them. When Will was satisfied he had his radar gun and rockets aimed correctly he said, "OK, three more times to get a baseline, then we turn on the generator."

Jacob frowned. "Do you think we should turn it on in here? I mean what if the hull suddenly disintegrates or weakens and breaks open?"

Will rolled his eyes in frustration. "This is the same crap we got from Congress. We wanted to do this experiment on Earth's moon, but everyone got all nervous about it, so now we have to go all the way to Ceres to do what we could have done perfectly safely a day and half from home."

Jacob waited till he stopped talking.

Will ran his hand through his hair and said, "I'm sorry. It's a legitimate question, but this is perfectly safe. This particular generator is very low power. It only diminishes the Higgs field in a one cubic meter of space and then it only diminishes it slightly. You could probably put your hand in the beam and it would just feel funny, but don't put your hand in the filed.. We've safely operated a generator with fifty times the power this one has on Earth. That one," he said pointing to a large box in the hold, "is 10,000 times as powerful."

Jacob considered this and said, "Fields don't just stop on some sharp boundary. They just get weaker exponentially over distance."

Will faked a benevolent smile, "You're thinking of electromagnetic fields and it's true for the anti-Higgs field as well, but not practically speaking. Practically speaking the effects are small in a one cubic meter area, and immeasurably small a meter beyond that."

"Sorry. I still have to speak to the Commander before you turn that on."

"You have no spirit of adventure, do you? Fine, call him."

Jacob called the Commander who responded with, "We discussed this early in the flight. It's OK. In fact, I want to see this."

Soon the Commander and Val were in the cargo hold, and Will was in professor mode.

Will recapped what he had told Jacob and then switched on the generator. At first it made an audible whining noise which increased in pitch and faded as it warmed up. Val caught Jacob glancing at the cabinet where the space suits were stored and smiled.

Once the generator was silent, Will double checked everything and fired the rockets one after another. It didn't look particularly interesting. The rockets just flew up like they normally would.

Val and the Commander looked at Will. "Did it work?"

Will looked through at a chart on his tablet and said, "Yes. Each of the test flights with the generator on show a slight acceleration as the front of the rocket enters the field and before the nozzle of the rocket has reached it, and none of the runs without the generator on show that." He turned the tablet around to show them the graph, but Jacob had turned off his boots and was getting a closer look at the rockets. They had bounced at a slightly different angle and only one of them was stuck against the return air grate. The other two had ended up in little eddies in a corner. He retrieved the rockets and said, "Let's do it again."

Will shrugged and said, "OK."

Jacob watched more carefully this time. After the second rocket launched he smiled and said, "Did you hear that?"

"What?" Val said.

"The sound the air makes coming out of the rockets changes as it enters the field," Jacob said.

Will thought about it for a second and said, "No. That's not possible. The mass of the nozzle and the air passing through it will change at the same rate as they enter the field, so there would be no change in pitch. All the acceleration happens because the front of the rocket loses mass before the air going out the nozzle does."

"Fire the third rocket," Jacob said.

Will did it.

"I heard it too. The pitch drops," Val said.

"I didn't hear anything," the Commander said.

Jacob collected the rockets again. This time they were all in the eddy. They launched them again.

Jacob and Val nodded their heads after every launch, while Will took on the expression of the patient teacher and explained that it simply wasn't possible.

The Commander smirked at the three of them, said, "I'm going to lunch," and left.

Jacob thought for a minute and then brightened up. "If the molecules of the nozzle are less massive they will be less tightly bound to each other, right?"

Will shook his head, "Not really. Ionic bonds are holding that nozzle together far more than gravitation."

"OK, but if gravitational attraction is diminished, then the nozzle might expand slightly, wouldn't it?"

"Not enough to hear it at all."

"Not enough for old guys to hear," Jacob said and high-fived Val.

Will shook his head and turned off the generator.

Val went back to the flight deck to finish her shift.

Jacob helped Will put his gear away. "So are you going to be firing rockets off Ceres?" Jacob asked.

"No. We're done with that. A couple of your brethren towed some small asteroids into a circular orbit around Ceres. Once we install this gear in the buildings the construction crews put up, we'll fire a beam in the path of the asteroids and measure the deflection of their orbit."

"What new data will that give you?"

"Mostly it's a proof of concept. The asteroids are the size and mass of a practical ship that could hold a reactor large enough to power a big enough generator. Doing it from the surface of Ceres allows us to do it with existing techniques and materials before investing in the new engineering and materials science required to build an actual ship."

"So this is engineering, not science."

"It's a little of both. It's practical science. Once we prove this concept, private industry will do the rest, and we get a share."

"What's the goal, faster ships, cheaper ships?"

"The goal is very fast ships for solar system travel and near light speed ships for interstellar travel. Imagine two weeks from Mars to Earth, or a month if you have to travel out of season. No more cyclers. Imagine six earth years to the planets of Alpha Centauri, and if we do it right it will only seem like four earth years to the crew. Our first probe to Alpha Centauri will probably pass the pulsed-fusion probe that was launched ten *years ago and get there first. Imagine moving cargoes the size of entire cyclers directly from Earth to Mars with little more than a solar tug pulling them."

"A solar tug with a reactor to power the generator?"

"OK, so it wouldn't be a solar tug, but you get the idea."

"No, you're right. That would be amazing. In fact, I want one of those ships as soon as possible."

"Well, in a few weeks, we'll all know if you're going to get one, and in a few *years we'll know how soon."

"Will it work?"

"It'll work. We'd never have gotten the funding if there was any real doubt."

"Well, let's get there and get you set up."

Seventy-Two

At breakfast the next day Jacob told Val about what Will had said. She listened respectfully, but didn't offer much in response.

"Aren't you excited?!" Jacob said.

"Yeah, it is pretty amazing," she said flatly.

"No, but really..."

"I guess so."

"Don't you want to visit Earth, and see new worlds?" Jacob persisted.

"Well, yes."

Jacob looked at her for long second and said, "I don't get why you're not more excited about this."

"Well... suppose we did go to a new World. It would be interesting, but it wouldn't change life much."

"It would change everything!" Jacob said.

"Not really. It might change society a little, but that's mostly governed by human nature. It would probably change how we work at certain things, like farming and mining and manufacture might be different on a different world. But it couldn't be very different or the world would be uninhabitable for humans. We won't be very different just because we are on a different world. We will be doing basically the same things, and thinking basically the same thoughts, and wanting basically the same things. We would just be doing all that in a different place. So it doesn't matter that much."

Jacob shook his head. "So, living on a different world wouldn't change us, wouldn't change our institutions, wouldn't pique our curiosity and lead us to new discoveries?"

"Are you saying that Martians and Terrans are extremely different?" Val asked.

"We are different!"

"Not enough to matter. Martians can live on Earth with just a little conditioning and within a year it's like they were born there. Terrans can live on Mars with no adjustment, as long as they stay out of the mountains. We use similar styles of government, similar ceremonies, and the ceremonies are for all the same events in life; birth, growing up, marriage, and death to say the obvious ones. We speak accents of each other's languages. We share all our technologies. The place hasn't made that much of a difference."

Jacob retorted, "Our people are taller and thinner on average, better educated on average, and we have less crime. We make more discoveries per capita, we haven't had a war in over 80 *years and that was more of a skirmish than a war, while Earth has had a third World War and is constantly having low level conflicts. How can you say we aren't different?"

Val exhaled and said, "The height difference is largely the result of founder's syndrome, not gravity differences like people think. By accident our ancestors were taller than most people. The differences in performance and behavior aren't caused by the planet. They are caused by a selection bias that seeded Mars with more people with a particular view of things. They are caused by a shared belief system, world view, and economic system all supported and maintained by a widely accepted religion. Everything seen on Mars is seen on Earth. What differences there are, are differences in emphasis.

"So having to spend most of our resources terraforming a planet hasn't changed how we do things and see things?"

"It probably has, but not as much as you think," Val said.

"Even if that's true, wouldn't you miss exploring new worlds and seeing new things?" he asked.

"Yes. And I'd probably go if I didn't have to leave too much behind. But if I don't get the chance, I'll just go in the next life."

"Do you really believe all that?" Jacob asked.

"Yes."

"It all seems so remote. I'm living here and now," he said.

"So am I, but that doesn't make the future, however distant, any less real."

Jacob didn't answer but stared at her intently. She held his stare and returned it.

Finally, Jacob shook his head and walked out.

Later on the flight deck Val ran diagnostics, checked logs, checked their position, and projected their flight path. They had been coasting for days so she didn't expect large deviations and there weren't any. She looked out the viewing window towards their destination. It was visible, a bright star in a dark patch of sky a little to starboard.

Bored, her eyes fell on a chest the Commander had brought aboard. She opened it and found a replica of an 18th century sextant. In class he had demonstrated how early astronauts used them to check their position and orientation. She gave it a try. "Close enough," she said when she compared the results to their actual location. She exhaled, put the sextant back, and continued looking at the stars. Her thoughts shifted. After a few minutes she exhaled heavily and said, "Who is that boy?"

A few days later at briefing, the Commander surprised them by taking half of Val's shift.

When Jacob caught up with Val in the break room, she ignored him and looked for breakfast.

"Are you mad at me or something?"

"No," she said, found a box of raisins, staked out a corner near the ceiling, and starting lining up raisins in a row. When she had them arranged, she tapped the wall with her toe and slowly glided forward eating them out of the air one at a time, except the last two which hit her in the face. By the time she'd finished with the raisins, she was moving very slowly through the middle of the room.

"Dang it," she said. Jacob looked at her and laughed when he saw she was stuck.

"Don't worry. You'll get to the other side in a couple of hours," Jacob said helpfully.

"More like five minutes, but I don't want to wait that long."

Val tried swimming with her arms but it mostly made her turn sideways.

Jacob pulled some popcorn out of the microwave and watched, amused.

"Very nice," Val said.

"Thank you," said Jacob.

She tried turning on her boots, but the distance to the wall was too far it to make a difference. Finally she said, "Oh well, I needed a nap anyway," folded her arms, and pretended to sleep.

Jacob watched for another ten seconds then set his popcorn aside, pushed off the floor and pushed her to the nearest wall. Val's head hit the wall a little harder than he expected.

"You OK?" He asked.

She didn't respond.

"You OK?" he repeated and shook her slightly.

She didn't respond.

"Oh crap!" he said, turned on his boots and started towing her to the table. On the way she started shaking, so he hurried. When they got to the table he turned to look at her and realized she was laughing at him.

"That's funny," he said flatly.

"I thought so."

They finished eating and Val tracked down the missing raisins so they wouldn't stink up the cabin.

"What do you want to do with your extra time today?" Jacob asked.

Val thought about it and said, "Tomorrow we start deceleration so I think it would be fun to explore the ship while we are still weightless."

"Sounds good," Jacob said.

They went to engineering and got some helmets, then started playing a game of tag throughout the ship. They started in the parts they already knew. Then Jacob showed her areas he'd found, and she showed him the areas she'd found. Then they just explored. When it was almost time for Val to report for duty, Val noticed a corridor going perpendicular to the thrust line towards the upper hull.

"Ever been up there?" she asked.

"No. I never even noticed that corridor before."

They followed it to a door.

"Should we open it?" Val asked.

"It's an internal door so it should be OK."

"It looks like a pressure door though."

"It is, but it's not set up like an airlock. Besides I know where all the airlocks are. I can look it up in the schematics," Jacob offered.

"No. That would be cheating."

"You are a strange person, but I like that."

They cranked on the manual latch until it unlocked, then swung the door inward and floated into a tiny domed room that was dusty. It was so small that two people had to stand closer than normal to fit in. The dome was slightly shiny on the inside.

"Quartz glass," Val said.

"I can't see anything so it must have a cover," Jacob said.

He rotated to fiddle with the controls and knocked into Val a few times. After a moment some lights lit on a console near the door. Jacob pressed one of them and the cover over the dome split in two and retracted. They were at the highest point of the ship surrounded on all sides but one by stars. It was a little dizzying.

Jacob slid up next to Val silently and whispered, "What is it for?"

"It's an observatory," Val whispered back.

"Like an observation room?"

"No... for taking bearings... for navigation."

"Oh," Jacob said. "How did you know that?"

"I don't know," Val whispered back.

"Why are we whispering?" asked Jacob.

"I don't know, but let's keep doing it."

Seventy-Three

At briefing the next morning Jacob and Val watched the Commander explain, then show an animation of the deceleration maneuver they would perform that morning. Then Jacob and Val glided to their positions while the Commander went to make sure all of Will's gear was properly stored and that Will was strapped into his chair on the observation deck.

Jacob brought the reactor up to 50% power and preheated the plasma generators. Then Jacob and Val each independently double checked the ship's position and orientation in the inertial navigation system against both the Pulsar Positioning System and key guide stars using the ship's sextant. Val wrote a firing sequence into the helm and passed it to Jacob to review. He looked at it and nodded.

The Commander glided in, put his manual sextant into its box and strapped in.

"What's with the sextant?" Jacob asked.

"Never trust a robot with your life," was all the Commander would answer.

The Commander went over Val and Jacob's work then said,

"Initiate rotation."

"Aye aye," responded Val and pressed the friendly green "Initiate" icon.

The sound of gas thrusters firing short bursts at different points on the ship vibrated into the flight deck and the star field outside the window began to slide slowly to port. Ceres disappeared and after eighty seconds a distant Earth slid into view and the thrusters fired another volley of bursts. Then the star field held still. There was silence for a second then a few thrusters fired again and all stayed silent.

"Check orientation," the Commander barked.

Jacob and Val both checked their orientation in the Inertial Guidance System, then against the pulsars and guide stars and each reported back, "Orientation as expected."

The Commander switched his headset to ship wide communication and after an alert tone sounded said, "Prepare for deceleration."

Then he switched off ship wide and said, "Initiate deceleration."

Val slid her finger forward slowly on the controls and they felt heavy again. When the readout in front of him said, ".1" Jacob called out, "Nominal deceleration."

They reoriented their chairs and consoles, and the ceiling of the flight deck began glowing with an aft view of the ship.

"Verify flight path," the Commander said.

Jacob and Val checked their projected path against the planned path and each responded, "As expected."

"Good," the Commander responded. He unstrapped, and said, "Mr. Billings, you have the bridge."

"Aye," responded Jacob.

When the Commander was gone, Jacob said, "Miss Kyria, status report."

"All systems nominal," responded Val.

"Miss Kyria, recite the alphabet."

Val recited the alphabet.

"Miss Kyria, again backwards."

Val recited it backwards getting x and w reversed, but correcting herself.

"Miss Kyria, recite your favorite Shakespearean sonnet."

"Let me not to the marriage of true minds admit impediments. Love is not love which alters when it alteration finds, or bends with the remover to remove: O, no! It is an ever fixed mark that looks on tempests and is never

shaken; it is the star to every wandering bark, whose worth's unknown, although his height be taken. Love's not time's fool, though rosy lips and cheek within his bending sickle's compass come: Love alters not with his brief hours and weeks, but bears it out even to the edge of doom. If this be error and upon me proved, I never writ, nor no man ever loved."

"Wow," said Jacob.

"It's the only one I know," Val said.

Jacob let the silence hang for half minute, then said,

"Miss Kyria, perhaps you might recite that to me again someday."

"Perhaps," Val said with a smile.

They sat in silence for twenty minutes, neither of them looking at the other.

When the Commander came back he was in a curiously good mood, and smelled better.

"The good news is," he said, "the full flow showers and flush toilets are back online. The bad news is that someone forgot to turn on the dehumidifier in the break room last night and now all that slime from the ceiling and walls is dripping on the floor."

Nobody said anything.

"Go take care of it."

"Aye sir," they responded in unison, unstrapped, and left the flight deck.

Seventy-Four

Jacob eyed the mop closet with exaggerated disdain as he walked into the break room the next morning, which made Val blow punch through her nose.

Neither of them had forgotten the hours it took to clean the stink off of the floor the day before.

"I'm not cleaning THAT up!" Jacob said, pointing to the spatter across the table.

"OK, OK, OK, I got it," she said, mopping it up with a napkin.

"You missed a spot," Jacob said with studied severity.

She cleaned it up with exaggerated movements.

"There," she said, "good as new."

Jacob looked away with the disinterest of a cat, and said, "I guess it will do."

Then he smiled and looked her in the eyes until she looked away, which took a while.

"I like talking to you, Val." Jacob said.

"I like talking to you, too," Val said, but then she looked at the ceiling.

"What? Did I miss a spot?"

She shook her head and looked down. "I just don't know where we are going."

"Why do we have to know where we are going?" Jacob said, and looked at her earnestly.

Val leaned across the table and looked into his eyes.

"Because I'm a woman, Jacob. And if I let myself, I'll fall in love with you in pretty short order. And if this isn't going anywhere, or if it's going the wrong place, I'm going to be seriously hurt."

Jacob looked troubled. "What are you afraid I might do? I'm not a saint, but I'd never hurt you."

"I don't think you'd ever harm me on purpose, but that doesn't mean you wouldn't hurt me."

"That doesn't even make sense," Jacob said.

"It makes perfect sense."

"How?"

"Because I'm pretty sure we are going in different directions, and then I'd either have to give you up, or give up everything I hold dear and either way it'll hurt," Val said.

"How are we going in different directions? We're both astronauts, we both love exploration, we're both pretty good at what we do."

"Do you ever see yourself raising a family?" Val asked.

"I don't think about it much, but when the time is right I think that would be great."

"Will you raise your family the way your family raised you?" Val asked.

"No! God knows I'd never do that to my kids."

"That's just it. You complain about your family every time it comes up and every time I think, that's exactly the kind of family I wish I had. Don't get me wrong... I love my family and they love me. But all the things you complain about your family doing, I wish we had done."

"See, but that's the difference, your family loves and supports you. They don't spend all their time trying to hold you back," Jacob said.

"What did they do to hold you back?"

Jacob paused, his face got red, "Lots of things. You don't know. You weren't there."

"No, but you were."

"Mostly they just wanted to fill up my schedule to the point where I didn't have a choice about anything, and most of it was school, and work, and a lot of church."

"What about church? What do you believe in? What will you teach your children?" Val persisted.

"I believe we should be kind to each other and stay out of people's business. I'll teach my kids what they want to learn, and then I'll let them make up their own minds about things. I won't try to stuff it down their throats."

"So, you don't see church being a big part of your life?"

"I don't think it will be. I mean, I'm not opposed to it or anything, I just want to do my own thing."

Val closed her eyes for a second, opened them and said, "Then I don't want to get in the way of that. I don't want to make you miserable. I'm too much like your parents." Jacob stared at her. She looked at him, hesitated, and left the room.

Jacob sat in silence for a moment then spread out his fingers on the table in frustration. He took a breath and let it out in a long slow stream. "Women!" he finally said, got up, threw away his half eaten breakfast, and went into the corridor.

He looked up and down the hall and finally decided to go see what Will was doing.

Will was sitting in a chair with all the lights dimmed, viewing window open to its widest and "Sweeney Todd" playing at full volume. Jacob stood in the doorway watching him conduct the invisible orchestra until he noticed him and waved him in to sit down. When the song had finished, Will shut off the music and turned to Jacob.

"So, what is my favorite astronaut up to today?" Will asked.

"Just looking for trouble," Jacob answered. "What were you doing?"

"Staving off insanity," replied Will. "I've been stuck in one sort of box or another for four months now and I could break at any moment."

Jacob laughed. Will looked at him with mock seriousness, got up and poured himself a drink.

"Can I interest you in some trouble?" he said lifting the glass in his direction.

Jacob shook his head.

"No. I didn't think so," Will said shaking his head ruefully. I haven't had a decent drinking companion since I offended the maintenance chief on the cycler."

"How did you offend the maintenance chief?"

"Never mind about that. What kind of trouble are you looking for today?"

"Anything not involving women..."

"Ah. Let's see... who could he be talking about? It couldn't be the Commander, he's much too butch. It couldn't be me... I mean I've had my moments, but not here. It must be Val."

Jacob's ears were red. "Never mind," Jacob said and turned to go.

Will grabbed him in a head lock and rubbed his hair, "So sensitive... sit down."

Jacob sat down.

"I noticed you two were getting a little cozy."

"It's not like that... at least I don't think it's like that... if it was like that, it isn't now." Jacob put his head down and covered it.

"Oh. I get it. She's your first. Kind of late in life to be having a first, isn't it?"

"No. It's really not like that. We're not that cozy."

Will shrugged and took another drink. "So... she will be your first. That's kind of sweet."

He looked out the window for a while. When he looked back, Jacob was sitting back in his chair watching him.

"Oh, don't be so morose," Will said. "I already told you I've been cooped up in boxes for four months. You can't blame me for having a little fun with you."

Jacob relaxed.

"So, what's the trouble in paradise?"

Jacob looked at him for a minute and said, "She's getting all religious on me."

Will started laughing. "SHE is getting all religious on YOU!? That's rich. That's perfect."

Jacob got up to leave. "No. Stay, stay. I'll be good. I promise."

He sat down again, looked up somberly at the red haired English-man and Will burst out laughing again, then covered his mouth.

"Sorry, sorry," he said, and composed himself.

Jacob sat back in his chair resolved to wait it out.

"OK. So what do you mean she's getting all religious on you?"

"We were just having breakfast…"

"All-nighter eh?"

"Behave yourself…"

"OK, OK, sorry. You were having breakfast…"

"Yeah, we were just having breakfast together and suddenly she gets all serious and says she doesn't know where things are going and then she starts talking about wanting to have a family that does all of the church stuff, and I said I didn't know if I wanted to do that, and she kind of broke up with me, though I don't know how you do that when we weren't even going out."

"You people are fascinating."

"Gee, thanks."

"No I mean it. I need to write this down somewhere."

"You know, you're no help at all."

"OK. OK. Let's back up. So you two are serious about settling down and breeding or something?"

"I don't know. I like her and all, but I hadn't gotten that far thinking about it."

"Jacob, seriously, you're telling me you've seen her, spent time with her, and haven't thought about doing that…"

"Jacob rolled his eyes. I mean I hadn't got around to thinking about a future or anything. And I try not to think too much about the other either."

"Why? I've thought about it plenty and I don't even have a chance with her."

Jacob put his hand up and closed his eyes, "Just shut up for a minute. It's going to take days to get that image out of my head."

Will waited respectfully while Jacob collected himself. When Jacob opened his eyes, Will had a small smile on his face.

"I'm afraid this is serious, Jacob," Will said softly running his finger over the rim of his glass.

"You feel more for this girl than you want to admit. You're a romantic."

"What would you do in my situation?"

"I've never been in your situation. But I would probably let her think I agreed with her, then I'd bang her for the rest of the trip and make a run for it when I got home."

Jacob stared at him.

Will looked up at him and said, "But that's not what you're going to do. No. You are either going to get serious about your religion, or you're going to break up with her. Take my advice. Do the latter. She did you a favor telling you what she's all about. Now you don't have to go through all that. You don't really want to be tied down, at least not yet. You're young, relatively unjaded, and the whole world of women or whatever turns you on is open to you. And if Mars is too tight a fit for you, come back with me to Earth after the demonstration is over. I can introduce you around. We are going to be so busy building and testing ships, that I'm sure I can get you a job. I'll bet we can even get guaranteed return passage as part of the deal."

Jacob sat and looked at his hands while Will was silent except for the clinking of ice in his glass.

"I'm not sure I want to do either. Can't I just be myself? Can't I just fly ships and flirt with girls and not take everything so seriously?"

"You can do whatever you want. If you want to come to earth and be pious there are pockets of zealots like yourself in most major cities. In fact, we have a pretty good collection of different kinds of zealots to choose from. You can live with them and help us build and fly our ships and be as chaste as a monk. But honestly, what is the point of flirting if you aren't going to bed them?"

"Because it's fun. It doesn't have to have a point. You're as bad as she is."

"Touché."

"What?"

"It's a fencing term... point well taken..."

"What kind of fences do you build on Earth?"

"Never mind. I may be the wrong person to ask. Have you spoken to your commander? He seems like the solid, "salt of the Earth" kind of guy you would need."

"No. I think I know what he would say."

"So, there's your answer. You don't want all that."

"No. I guess I don't."

"This is lot to take in. Why don't you think about it? My offer will still be there when we get done with the demonstration. You can join me on the cycler if you want to go."

"Thanks."

"Don't mention it."

Seventy-Five

Jacob and Val continued eating breakfast together most mornings. She always had her book with her at breakfast. Sometimes she would be reading it when he came in, but she always put it away when she saw him and gave him a smile. She didn't look at him in quite the same way she had before. They didn't discuss it.

After breakfast, instead of spending time exploring or bantering, they each went their separate ways. She usually went to her quarters. Jacob would roam the halls. It was two days before he realized he was avoiding Will.

At briefings, the Commander tried kidding them a little but was met with such a wall of ice that he left off it.

After a while Jacob found himself going to the old observatory more and more. At first he thought maybe it had something to do with Val, but it didn't.

One morning at breakfast, Jacob suddenly looked at Val and said, "Why does it have to be all or nothing?"

Val looked at him for a second and said, "Because halfway hurts more than nothing. It's like sniffing the frosting and never eating the cake. "

Jacob pressed his lips together and remained silent.

One afternoon just before his shift he called home. It was later there, evening by the looks of it.

His sister answered and ran screaming around the house for everyone to come.

The tribe assembled around a monitor and Jacob suddenly had

nothing to say. He answered their questions until it was almost time for his shift, then he said, "I'd like to talk to dad for a while." Sam groaned but they all said goodbye.

Jacob did his best to look his father in the eye and said, "I don't want you to take this wrong, but why did you push me so hard?"

Jake looked puzzled. "Why did I push you so hard on what?"

"On everything!"

"I didn't think I was pushing hard."

Jacob pressed his lips together. Jake waited.

"There was never time for me to just do what I wanted. There was always some activity to go to, or some meeting to attend, or some family function, or some chore to do," Jacob said.

Jake hesitated, then said, "I remember things differently. There were a lot of activities, but I thought you enjoyed those, and I remember you spending a lot of time in your room and out roaming the hills."

"Before every activity, I told you I didn't want to go and you always made me go anyway. And when I did roam the hills, you always made me feel guilty for it by pointing out chores I hadn't finished, or that you thought I hadn't finished."

"I remember many times you said you didn't want to go, but then you always came home happy. I thought you just had trouble getting going. As far as chores go, you almost never did them the last *year you were home. I was trying to teach you how to work, and it seems like you learned."

They stared at each other through a radio link stretching millions of kilometers and lengthening.

"I'm sorry if I pushed too hard," Jake finally said. "I was trying to include you in my life. I was trying to make sure that you had every-thing I had."

"But you never asked what I wanted," Jacob said pointedly.

"I asked but you never answered."

Jacob gritted his teeth. "Because I knew you didn't want to hear it."

"How did you know?" Jake asked.

"Because you tried to make me learn all about being a steward, you tried to make me do all the work of a steward, and because you were so obviously pleased with Chris whenever I was around to see it?"

"Chris and I share a passion for the same work. Just because I enjoy talking to him about it and planning it doesn't mean I'm not happy for you to find a different passion."

"Then why did I have to run away to follow it?"

Jake raised his voice a little. "You didn't have to. I would have taken you to Olympia myself after graduation if I had known that's what you wanted."

Jacob looked at the clock in the corner of the monitor and said, "I have to go. My shift is starting."

He went to sever the call, but paused and said, "Thanks for talking to me." Then he cut the call.

That evening, after his shift, Jacob went to the old observatory and looked out at the universe.

Saturn was glowing brightly in the distance. Mars was a reddish star and Earth was a pale binary disappearing around the bright edge of the sun. "I wonder were Ada is right now," he said and listened to his voice bounce of the quartz glass. He tried to calculate it, but gave up.

After an hour on the cramped foldout seat his feet tingled. He got up, shook his feet back to life and sat again.

Ceres was glowing brightly. "The whole future of humanity might hinge on what might happen there in a few days," he thought and then scrunched his face with doubt.

He looked away from the galactic disk into the distant stars and looked for answers written in them, but didn't see any.

He stared until his eyes got tired, then he climbed down the ladder and closed the hatch behind him.

Seventy-Six

Jacob found himself standing in the orchard behind his parent's station. He was dressed in work clothes and had a shovel in his hand. The sky was dark. Great dark clouds reaching up to the stratosphere piled thicker and thicker above him and the orchard lost all color in the gloom. The tree in front of him had curled yellow leaves and not many of them. Jacob looked at the tree, at a loss to know what to do for it.

Thunder boomed. Jacob felt a hand on his shoulder. He turned to look and his father's eyes bored into him.

"Why have you brought this?" His father said.

"I didn't," Jacob replied.

His father stared even deeper and he repeated, "Why have you brought this?"

"Brought what? What did I bring?" His father broke his gaze and scanned the sky. Jacob looked too. The clouds were unnatural, swirling with purple colors, lightning flashing. He looked back at his father and said, "I didn't mean to."

His father's eyes drilled into his soul. Then he said, "I know," and embraced him.

Jacob woke to the familiar sound of a recirculating pump thumping somewhere beneath his quarters. He stretched and lay there for a while before getting out of bed. He looked around his room and saw the book his parents had given him on the table next to the bed. He picked it up and scrolled through the titles on it.

"Of course," he said when he found the scriptures on it, and set it down.

He showered, got dressed and brought the book with him to breakfast.

Val was reading when he came in. She looked up and smiled when she heard him come in. He put his book down on the table and rummaged through the storage containers. They hadn't been following the menus at all so they were starting to run out of his favorite foods.

Val heard his hesitation and said, "Getting ready to break into the emergency supplies in the hold?"

"Just about," Jacob said. "I like protein bars."

He mixed up some oatmeal and an apple flavored drink and sat across from Val.

"So you like oatmeal now?" Val said.

"No, but I'm too lazy to go down to the cargo hold."

Jacob started eating.

"What are you reading?" Val asked.

"Nothing yet."

"Then why did you bring your book?"

"I thought I would read with you."

Val looked at him cautiously. "What do you want to read?"

"The same thing you're reading every morning."

"Are you sure?" Val asked.

"I'm not saying I'll want to everyday, but I thought I'd give it a try. Where are you reading?"

"I was just about to start over in Genesis."

Jacob turned his book on, flipped to Genesis and waited.

"Let's take turns. I'm tired of hearing my own voice in my head," Val said.

Jacob inhaled, and began.

"In the beginning God created the heaven and the earth. And the earth was without form, and void; and darkness was upon the face of the deep. And the Spirit of God moved upon the face of the waters. And God said, Let there

be light: and there was light. And God saw the light, that it was good: and God divided the light from the darkness."

Val picked it up and read.

"And God called the light Day, and the darkness he called Night. And the evening and the morning were the first day. And God said, Let there be a firmament in the midst of the waters, and let it divide the waters from the waters. And God made the firmament, and divided the waters which were under the firmament from the waters which were above the firmament: and it was so. And God called the firmament Heaven. And the evening and the morning were the second day."

Jacob asked, "Didn't the first astronauts read that orbiting their first new world?"

"I don't know," Val said, "but I kind of hope so."

"Do you think it really happened that way?" Jacob said.

"What way?"

"Do you think He actually made it, or do you think He just found it and fixed it like we did Mars?"

"So you think there was a "He" involved?"

"Just for argument's sake, if there is a "He," do you think he found it or made it?"

"I think He made it, but I think He made it out of stuff he found, not like we fixed Mars, more like baking a cake from scratch."

"Do you think he made it in a few days like it says?"

"I don't know. What is a day any way on a world with no people on it? What's a day on this ship?"

"A day is one revolution of the world on its axis," Jacob said.

"One revolution of which world? Mars? Earth? Neither of them was fully a world yet. Saturn?"

Jacob considered this. "I guess it would have to be a standard day of some sort, like we use on the ship."

"Or maybe they're just construction phases from the project plan. You know, "Day one" activities, "Day two" activities.

Jacob nodded. "Maybe," he smiled a little. "Was scripture study like this at your house?"

"We didn't do it much until just before I left home, and no, usually we'd just read a few verses and go to bed. What about at your home?"

Jacob shook his head and then paused, trying to remember.

"You know I think they used to be that way, but as I got older they got shorter, and then I found ways to avoid it altogether."

"If you like it, why did you avoid it?"

"Dad was always so serious about it, and... well, actually when I was younger he wasn't as serious. Anyway they always wanted to do it at some weird time like early in the morning, or when I was hungry or when I had other things to do and I got tired of being pushed around."

Val looked at him, but said nothing. She looked at the clock and said; "I've got a review with the Commander." Then she paused.

Jacob looked at her. "Go. We'll read again tomorrow."

Val smiled, stood awkwardly for a second, then walked toward the flight deck.

Seventy-Seven

Ceres loomed large on the ceiling of the flight deck. Val glanced past the Commander to look at Jacob. He was paying full attention to the image, his face lit as much by the image as by the room lights.

"Look alive Miss Kyria!" the Commander admonished.

"1,928 KM and closing. Velocity 20,626 KM per hour and slowing." Val called out.

"Mr. Billings, bring the reactor to 70% power."

"Reactor at 70%" Jacob called out.

The Commander switched his headset to all decks. "All hands prepare for braking maneuvers."

"1,757 KM and closing. Velocity 19,361 KM per hour and slowing."

"Mr. Billings, prepare to bring engines to 75%," the Commander said.

"Standing by, sir."

"Engines to 75%."

"Engines at 75%"

They sank back into their cushions.

".75 G sir," Val called out

"1,441 KM and closing. Velocity 18,567 KM per hour and slowing."

"Engines to 100% Mr. Billings."

"Engines at 100%."

"1 G sir," Val said and chanted out the distances and velocities.

"1,150 KM and closing. 16,449 KM per hour and slowing."

"893 KM and closing. 14,331 KM per hour and slowing."

"672 KM and closing. 12,213 KM per hour."

" 486 KM and closing. 10,095 KM per hour."

"335 KM and closing. 7,977 KM per hour."

"220 KM and closing. 5,859 KM per hour."

"140 KM and closing. 3,740 KM per hour."

"Engines to 25%," the Commander said.

"Engines at 25%."

 "92 KM and closing. 2,019 KM per hour."

"All stop, Mr. Billings."

"All stop."

" 0 G, 84 KM and closing. 1,810 KM per hour, and... Capture. We are in elliptical orbit around Ceres. Perigee 82 KM, Apogee 467 KM," Val said.

"Round it out, Miss Kyria," the Commander said.

"Mr. Billings, prepare to fire main engines at 100% power for 25 seconds on my mark," Val said.

"Standing by."

"Fire."

 "Firing complete."

"Perigee 82 KM, Apogee 83 KM," Val said.

"Close enough," the Commander said. He switched his headset to ship to ship and said, "Ceres control, this is Astral 4."

"Welcome, Astral 4."

"Please transmit landing coordinates."

"Transmitting."

The display showed the landing coordinates.

"Received."

The Commander switched back to internal. "Mr. Billings, Miss Kyria, reorient the cabin."

They reoriented their chairs to look out the large window in front of them as the shield opened. Val squinted a little.

"Miss Kyria, line us up to pass over the landing site."

"Adjusting inclination," Val said, and began firing maneuvering thrusters.

The three of them squinted to get a better look at the landing site.

The Commander switched to ship to ship and called out, "Ceres control, please light the guide lights."

"Copy. Lighting guide lights."

"Miss Kyria, take us in."

"Aye, Aye sir. Mr. Billings, preheat forward thrusters and descent engines and transfer control to my station," Val said.

"Preheating... Preheated and transferred."

Val began a steady burn of the forward thrusters.

"Ease up, Miss Kyria," the Commander said.

Val pulled the throttle back 2%.

"Ease up, Miss Kyria," the Commander repeated.

Val pulled the throttle back an additional 3%"

"Val, pull back 5%," the Commander barked.

Val pulled back 5%.

The ship was arcing rapidly towards the landing pad; Val cut the forward thrusters and throttled up the landing engines to 50%.

"200 meters," Jacob said.

"Landing engines to full throttle," the Commander said.

Val throttled up to full power.

"75 meters," Jacob said.

"Maneuvering thrusters to full ascent," the Commander said with an edge in his voice.

Val pushed the maneuvering thrusters to full ascent.

"10 meters," Jacob said. A proximity alert sounded briefly before Jacob silenced it.

"Brace for impact," the Commander said over ship wide communications.

The ship hit the pad and everyone was thrown against their restraints. Val shut down the engines. A sickening shudder vibrated up the frame of the ship and it tilted forward and to starboard. Alarm lights were blinking.

Val closed her eyes.

Ground crews started scrambling.

"Status, Mr. Billings," the Commander said.

"Hull is intact. Reactor stable. Engines normal. Communications normal. We are listing 1% to starboard and 2% to bow. We have lost communications to grapple two. Grapple four has lost hydraulic pressure and grapple four servo 7 is in an alarm state. Grapple six is extended 48%, but appears to be normal. All other grapples reporting normal and extended 50%."

"Ceres control, Astral 4."

"Go ahead control."

"Do you require assistance?"

"Standby, control."

The Commander switched his com to person to person and said, Mr. Ottis what is your condition?"

"A little sore."

"Do you require medical assistance?"

After a pause Will said, "No. I'm fine."

"Val, are you OK?"

Val nodded.

"Jacob?"

"I'm OK."

"Astral 4, Ceres control."

"Go ahead Astral 4."

"We're OK. We may need some help with damage assessment. Looks like we may have collapsed or partially collapsed a couple of grapples."

"You punched your right forward grapple right through the landing pad."

"Anything look bent?"

"Doesn't look like it from here. I'll have the crew chief give you a report from the ground."

"Very well. Thanks for the assistance."

"Mr. Billings, suit up and get grapple 4 operational. Miss Kyria, go with him and assist."

"Aye, Aye," they both said.

The Commander switched to person to person "Mr. Ottis, Please sit tight while we stabilize the situation. I don't think your cargo is at any risk, but there will be a delay in unloading."

"Understood, Commander."

The Commander flipped through different camera views of each grapple and as he did the creases in his forehead started to smooth out. After three minutes he sat down, looked around to see if he was alone and started chuckling and shaking his head.

"What's so funny?" Jacob's voice sounded in his ear.

The Commander looked down at his selector switch in surprise, then responded, "Nothing, Mr. Billings," switched off his microphone, and laughed out loud.

Seventy-Eight

Jacob and Val had grapple 4 back online in about two hours.

Jacob took a few minutes to pull his helmet off, grab a bite to eat, and drain and resupply the suit. Then they went forward to the number two grapple. Val sat at a console near the hatch and linked to the communication system.

Jacob prepared the airlock then stepped into it and slowly depressurized.

He examined the external door for damage but didn't find any problems.

"Equalized and opening," he called out, unlatched the door and opened it. Just inside the doorway he found a connector hanging.

"I think I found our communications problem," he said and plugged the connector back in.

The grapple began to jerk. Jacob quickly unplugged it.

"Val, can you put the grapple in safe mode?"

"Standby," Val said."OK. Go ahead."

Jacob plugged the connector back in and the grapple stayed quiet.

"Thanks," Jacob said. "Are you seeing anything?"

"Tons. As soon as you plugged it in it started sending all its cached alarms. I'll send it to your suit."

"Thanks," said Jacob and scrolled through all the alarms. "Looks like most of the servos are burnt. The secondary hydraulics held, and the grapple is fully extended. That's weird. Why would it fully extend?"

"One way communication," Val said, "I'm looking at the ship

diagnostics. It saw communications up but it didn't get any response from the grapple so it kept sending "extend" orders the leg obeyed them until it reached its limit."

Jacob looked at the connector again. One of the locking tabs had broken off.

"I'm going to disconnect the grapple for a second," he said.

"Go ahead."

Jacob pulled the connector apart and looked at it. The broken locking tab was on the transmit side.

He plugged it back in, wrapped the connector with tape, and tightened the cable restraints on each side of the connector.

Jacob worked his way to the bottom of the grapple and inspected it. It looked straight. He replaced the fried servos, repaired and refilled the primary hydraulics and inspected the secondary hydraulics.

When he was satisfied, he climbed back up the inside of the grapple to the airlock and reentered the ship.

Val helped him take his suit off and stow it.

When they got back to the flight deck, the Commander was talking to the Crew Chief over coms. When he finished, he turned to Val and Jacob and said, "How do the grapples look?"

"They look OK on the inside, and all the alarms have cleared." Jacob said.

The Commander nodded. "We've decided to try to pull grapple two up, so strap in."

Jacob took the controls. Over the next ten minutes he swly pulled the grapple free, then leveled out the ship.

"Excellent. Go ahead and set us down, Mr. Billings," said the Commander.

Jacob retracted all the grapples to 5% simultaneously, which put the cargo hold deck a meter above the landing pad, then he locked the controls.

The Commander informed control, and the ground crew moved in and inspected the pad, then grapple 2.

"Looks like you lost a few talons, but nothing too bad. The crew is tired. Let's unload at 8:00 a. m. Mars standard."

"Agreed."

"In the meantime, the Base Commander extends an invitation to a late dinner."

"Thanks and much appreciated." He turned to Val and Jacob and said, "Shut us down for the night."

Val and Jacob put all systems into hibernation mode.

"Mr. Billings, good work. You are dismissed."

"Thank you sir," he said and left.

"Miss Kyria, Ceres isn't just any asteroid, it's the asteroid. It actually has some gravity. Where did you make your mistake?"

"I decelerated too quickly and as a result fired the descent engines at too low an altitude. Also I should have gone to full power on the descent engines immediately."

"That's all true, but it's the wrong answer. Your mistake was not realizing it earlier and aborting the landing. Everyone makes mistakes. The best of us recognize them early and correct them early. Do you understand?"

"Yes, sir."

"You did mess up though."

"Yes, sir."

"So you'll babysit the ship while we go to dinner."

"Yes, sir."

Seventy-Nine

Val woke up and stared at the deck above her. It was morning, some-where... in Paititi. Here the feeble sun had been shining when she went to bed and it had already been morning twice since then. The only in-dication inside her quarters, deep inside the ship was that the lighting had been gradually increasing over the last half hour. She dressed and went to the break room. Jacob was already there looking a bit groggy while he re-laced his boots.

"How was dinner?"

He sat up and tried to focus. "Well, our food is fresher. I guess they haven't bothered much with the green house that was built for them. The conversations were interesting at first, but as it got later everyone got louder and the conversations got stupider. They were still at it when the Commander finally announced we had to go and that was after midnight standard."

"Well, I guess they're celebrating."

"I guess so."

They ate, then pulled out their books and puzzled over "light cleaves to light and darkness to darkness...." for about fifteen minutes. By then it was time for briefing, which they held informally in the hall just outside the break room.

The Commander looked more tired than they had seen him before. "Miss Kyria, I need you on the flight deck. Settle the ship on its belly to make unloading easier. Mr. Billings, suit up. I need you supervising the cargo bay while they unload. Keep them from banging up the hatch or we'll be stuck here for months. Any questions?"

Val and Jacob were silent.

"Dismissed."

They each turned to their duties. Jacob was still suiting up when a clunking crunching sound vibrated up the ship as its belly touched the surface.

"You ready?" Val's voice said in Jacob's ear.

"Not quite," he answered.

"Hurry up. They're already assembled out on the pad."

Jacob slid his helmet on, sealed it, dropped pressure on the deck slightly and checked for leaks.

When he was sure he said, "OK, ready."

Lights started flashing, a claxon sounded as Val started depressurizing the deck while Jacob stood by the abort button. Thirty seconds later there was an explosion behind one of the cargo pods.

Jacob hit the abort button.

"What's wrong?" Val asked.

"Something went boom. I'm going to check it out."

"Turn your camera on, so I can tell if you get in trouble."

"Oh, yeah, sorry," Jacob said and turned it on. He walked around the cargo pod and held his breath for a second, then started laughing.

"What is that?" Val asked.

"It's blood!" Jacob said.

"Seriously what is it?"

Jacob walked over to a table Will had set up behind the cargo pod, picked up a shattered bottle and held it to the camera.

"Ketchup! Hungry?" Jacob asked.

"I guess we really ought to take a walk around the cargo bay before we depressurize in the future. What if Will had been back there eating?"

"Will's with the Commander on the observation deck."

"I know, but..."

"You're right, you're right," Jacob said, and took a walk around the room. He went back to his position by the abort button and strapped in. "We're good."

"OK."

The lights started flashing again, the horn sounded, and Jacob felt his suit subtly stiffening.

After another thirty seconds the door opened and startling sunlight filled the bay. Jacob's visor darkened reflexively.

The crew moved in. After thirty minutes the bay was empty. Jacob had Val close the hatch ¾ and partially repressurize the bay to blow all the trash out onto the pad.

"Litterbug," he heard Val say in his ear.

"Hey I don't hear you volunteering to sweep up."

In the afternoon they moved the ship fifty meters farther down the pad and set down. Val raised the broken grapple a meter off the ground and they both suited up and went out with the tool cart.

Working together, it took just over three hours to disconnect and replace three of the talons with spares, but that left a fourth broken talon with no spares left. Jacob picked through the broken ones and decided he could salvage one of them.

"Let's get back to the ship. I'll fix this one up and we'll put it on tomorrow."

Val hesitated, then stretched her arms out and turned around and around in the fading light of sunset.

"This is the first time I've been out of the ship in weeks."

Jacob gathered the tools and broken parts onto the cart and then went over and stood by her.

Neither said anything for a while. Then Jacob asked, "Want to fly?"

Val looked at him suspiciously.

Jacob went behind her, grabbed her by the waist with both hands and threw her into the sky gently. She vaulted about three meters then came down with a slight thud and laughed. Jacob squatted down then jumped as hard as he could and was standing next to her a second later. They both took a long last look around, then trudged back to the ship.

They helped each other pull off the bulky suits then lay around in their short sleeved flight suits on packing blankets in an empty container sharing a bag of potato chips. Jacob could feel the clammy moisture that covered his skin in the suit start to evaporate. Then he noticed that Val was leaning against his chest. He had one arm wrapped around her with his hand on her stomach. She seemed to become aware of it at the same time, but she didn't move. They ate quietly for a few moments, then went to get a real lunch.

After lunch, Val reported to the flight deck and Jacob went to the machine shop to fabricate replacement talons. By dinner time he was done.

Dinner was quiet. After dinner they put on a movie and the three of them watched it; the Commander sat between Val and Jacob.

Eighty

Midmorning Val and Jacob took advantage of the noon day light to install the last talon. Then they joined the Commander at the Ceres Base Cartography Room to go over potential asteroids they could lug home. They were all asteroids they had considered in flight, but Ceres Base had higher resolution maps of their current positions. They finally settled on one 1,500 Kilometers away that was just the right size and composition. Leaving cartography, they ran into a breathless Will in the main hall.

"It's all installed! They're calibrating it tonight. Tomorrow morning we make history! I hope you'll join us in the Command Center as my guest."

Jacob and Val looked at the Commander. He looked at Will and said, "It will be our pleasure."

The Commander retired early that night, but Jacob and Val wandered the ship, talking and goofing around. They ate "ice cream" in the break room. Then they practiced trying to run on the walls of the corridor until the Commander's voice finally came over the P.A. and said, "Knock it off."

They still weren't sleepy, but Jacob walked Val back to her quarters. They stood in the doorway to her room a long time, talking and pausing a lot. Sometimes Jacob would stop talking in the middle of a sentence and just stare at her.

"What?" she asked after the third time.

He shook his head and said, "I'm just tired."

They said goodnight.

The next day the three of them arrived at the control center together. They stood next to Will, who got them some seats, but didn't use his own. There was a large screen on the left of the main window depicting the path of two small asteroids orbiting Ceres. To the right of the Window there was another screen with video of the reactor building and each emitter, plus a telescopic image of the space above the emitters. Above the window there was a narrow screen with fluctuating numbers describing the orbits of the asteroids and below the screen there was real-time information about the performance of the reactor and emitters. As they watched, an asteroid passed into view on the screen to the right and then slid off it. Looking out the main window Val could see two tiny coppery glints of light when the sun broke the horizon. They were on either side of the window and seemingly about five kilometers away, though it was hard to know the real distance. Will was pacing and chattering with someone through his earpiece. Finally he looked up at the screens and said, "Good, Good. Lock it down." He stood still, waiting for something. Then he nodded, switched off his mike, and clapped his hands for attention.

"Alright everyone, we are ready. Let's start at 1% power on the next pass of #2. Mark, are you ready?"

"Standing by."

"Power up."

The numbers at the bottom of the screen changed and everyone held their breath watching the upper screen. Val saw an asteroid pass by on the right hand screen and the room erupted in cheers.

"Power down," Will yelled over the cheers and Mark powered down the emitters.

Val glanced a question at Jacob.

"You have to look at the orbital numbers above the screen," Jacob whispered. "The asteroid's orbit was deflected 1/10th of a percent."

"Couldn't that just be a random change?" Val whispered back.

Jacob shrugged.

They waited 45 minutes.

"Mark take us to 2% power on the next pass of #1."

"Powering to 2%... power at 2%."

This time Val watched the upper screen and saw that the orbit had changed by 2/10ths of a percent.

Cheers went up again.

Val leaned over to Jacob and said, "Looks like it's a linear response."

Jacob nodded agreement.

"Power down. Steve, did we get all the data?"

"We got it."

"Great, everyone, let's do a quick analysis, file a report and then take it to the next level."

The Commander stood and approached Will. Jacob and Val took the cue and followed.

"Congratulations, Will. Thanks for letting us witness this."

"Thank you. Are you sure you won't stay longer?" Will asked.

"We'd like to, but if we delay too long we'll have to target a smaller asteroid."

"I understand. I'm glad you were here so these two lovebirds will be able to tell their grand babies about it."

Val examined her hands. The tips of Jacob's ears reddened, but Will just winked at him and turned back to his work.

The three of them didn't say much to each other on the way back.

Strapped into their chairs on the flight deck, the Commander ventured, "Mr. Billings, you don't seem as excited about this breakthrough as I thought you would be."

"No. I am. I really am," Jacob said unconvincingly.

The Commander chuckled and said, "Alright then. Miss Kyria, take us up and find us a good refueling site."

"Yes sir," replied Val as she released the grapples and lifted off gently.

Val eased them into an equatorial orbit and they had to go around three times before they spotted a broad smooth plain to the south.

"There you go Miss Kyria... a nice impact crater lake frozen solid."

On the next go round Val dropped smoothly out of orbit and hovered over the expanse.

Jacob read out readings indicating ice depth until they found the deepest spot and Val set the ship down.

Jacob slowly extended the grapples and dug in the talons.

"Insert proboscis," the Commander called out.

Jacob opened the proboscis doors, turned on the preheaters, and slowly lowered the proboscis towards the ice. When it made contact, a hole in the ice appeared and Jacob eased the proboscis deeper and deeper into the hole. When it was fully inserted Jacob called out, "We are at eighteen meters sir."

"Excellent, not one rock. Begin extraction," the Commander said.

"Yes, sir,"

Jacob turned on a series of pumps forcing hot water down the proboscis and sucking cold water back into the holding tanks.

"Extraction under way. Tanks at 42% and rising."

"Mr. Billings, you have the bridge. I'll be in the gym. Call me when the tanks get to 90%," the Commander said.

"Yes sir."

The Commander unstrapped and went down the hall.

Jacob looked at Val and said, "This will take hours, you don't have to sit there the whole time."

"I'm good for now," Val said.

They looked out the window towards the distant hills that ringed the ice rink they were parked on and saw the great cloud of the Milky Way looming like an incoming storm. It was one thing to visually swim it in open space, and another to see it pressing against a local reference like hills. It was unnaturally beautiful and powerful. For a long time neither felt like speaking.

"How long do you think it will be before we reach one of those stars?" Jacob asked.

"Do you mean mankind, or you and me?"

Jacob looked at her confused. "I guess mankind, because on the wild chance that we are selected to be the first, then we will be representing mankind, so either mankind gets there before we do, or at the same time."

"What if we weren't representing mankind when we went? What if we were no longer part of any nation or planet when we went?"

"That would be a neat trick. Are you planning to build a starship in your garden?"

Val looked at him for a minute, decided something and said, "About fifty earth years and then it will probably be to Alpha Centauri Proxima."

"I think it could be sooner," Jacob said. "It looks like this technology works. I bet they have a probe based on it in ten earth years and a complete starship in twenty."

Val bit her lower lip and said, "You may be right, but I think it will be longer," she squirmed a little and said, "I've got to go to the restroom. Do you want me to bring you a snack when I come back?"

"Yes, please."

With Val gone, Jacob stared out the window and puzzled over what she had said. After a while he gave up.

He checked the tankage. It was at 53% and still rising at the same rate. He got bored and started thinking about how to hurry the process along. There wasn't any safe way to speed up extraction. He looked at his cold Attitude Control Thruster reserves. They were at 25%. Val had burned through it at an alarming rate on landing. He checked the reaction mass tanks. They were at 55%. Jacob decided to start splitting water before the extraction process was complete. There was plenty of power, and they were separate subsystems anyway. That way they wouldn't have to top off the tanks again after conversion, and since conversion was slower than extraction it would save a little time. About the time he'd finished setting that in motion, Val appeared with some of the protein bars he liked from the emergency supplies and a sippy cup of hot cocoa for him.

"Thanks."

They ate and Val took a shift while Jacob stretched his legs and went to the bathroom.

When he got back they both started fidgeting. Jacob started messing with the Com system trying to see if he could pull in the low power UHF stream coming from the bunker.

"You're not going to find it," Val said.

Jacob glanced at her and kept hunting.

"There's a whole big water rich globe between us and them, and this rock doesn't have an ionosphere to bounce the signal off of. Heck, it doesn't even have a magnetosphere."

Jacob just kept hunting until he found an unnatural wave form and then started running Fourier transforms against it until he could hear a distorted version of Will's voice coming over the speakers.

"How did you do that?" Val asked.

"I don't know, but I'm guessing the signal is bouncing off nearby asteroids and coming back to us all garbled."

Will's voice sounded tired, but enthusiastic. "Power to 30% on the next pass of #1." They could hear Mark repeating the commands and reading out the results.

"Sounds like it's going well," Jacob said.

"Yeah. I wonder why he's pushing so hard though. Seems like there should be more breaks in the procedure."

"They are all climbing the walls over there. They've been waiting to do this testing for months."

They left the broadcast running at a low volume in the background. Sometimes they could make out what was being said, other times it was just a clatter of staccato voice sounds.

Jacob checked the reserves. The attitude control thrusters were fully replenished. The reaction mass tanks were up to 70% and the reserve water tanks were at 60%.

"Do you think I'd be brought up on charges if I turned the A. I. on and played racquetball in the cargo hold?" Jacob asked.

"Probably, but you could leave me here and go do it."

"No. That wouldn't be fair."

Val rummaged through the bin in her chair and found an emergency pee sponge and batted it leisurely towards Jacob's head. He saw it at the last second and batted it back towards her. They kept a pretty good volley going for several minutes until the sponge finally hit Jacob in the eye and Val broke out laughing.

"That hurt," Jacob said.

"At least it wasn't used," Val retorted.

In the background they could hear Will saying they were up to 35% power. The Milky Way had risen well above the horizon and was almost overhead.

They settled back into their chairs and waited.

"I wonder why this seems so much longer here when it's really no worse than our shifts on the way." Jacob mused.

"I think it's because we aren't moving."

"It's not like we could feel the movement out there."

"No, but we knew we were moving towards our goal. Here we are just waiting until we get on with the next phase."

"I guess," Jacob admitted.

The Commander's voice came over their headsets, "Status, Mr. Billings."

Jacob looked at the monitor and reported, "ACS thrusters at full reserve, reaction mass tanks at 80%, water storage at 65%."

"Very good. I'll be in my quarters. Let me know when we are ready to withdraw the proboscis."

"Yes, sir," Jacob said and then asked Val, "Do you think he was working out this whole time?"

"No. He was in the break room when I got our snacks."

"What do you think he does when he's in his quarters?"

"I know he reads a lot. He sends a message home every day; I see it in the logs."

"It's weird to think of him having a family and a personal life. I can't imagine him sitting around in shorts."

"Yeah, one time I saw my fifth grade teacher in the grocery store and it was just awkward."

In the afternoon Val fell asleep in her chair. Jacob watched her sleep and listened to Will in the background like a baseball game on a Saturday afternoon.

By the time the tanks were full, Will was running 70% power tests and Val was drooling on her uniform. Jacob found the sponge and threw it at her. It hit her in the chest and she opened her eyes blinking.

"Wake up. I'm going to call the boss."

Val adjusted her position, looked down to find the sponge and then started wiping off her uniform.

"Commander, this is the flight deck. We are 100% on all tanks and ready to retract the proboscis."

"On my way, Mr. Billings," the Commander said.

"Power to 75% on the next pass of #2," said Will in the background. They heard Mark repeat the command, then start to say "Power at..." when the signal broke up again.

Jacob found himself holding his breath waiting for the signal to come back, but it resolved itself into silence. He fiddled with the receiver, but there was no signal to be seen. He looked at Val. She shrugged.

Jacob opened his Mic and said, "Commander, be aware that..."

The ship lurched and the landscape around the ship exploded into fragments of ice refracting sunlight into tiny rainbows.

Then they both slipped into silence.

To go
or stay
To try
or run away
Broken things
and twisted ways
Leave one thing to do
and nothing to say

Eighty-One

Val was at her graduation dinner. She saw her parents, her brother and sisters, her friends. Her father rose, raised a crystal glass full of sparkling cider, and said, "To our daughter the graduate and future astronaut."

They each clinked their glasses together, then clinked them again harder and their glasses shattered.

Val opened her eyes. She could still hear the glasses tinkling. She shifted in her seat till the restraints hit her shoulders, and winced. She looked around the flight deck. It was dark except for red emergency lights glowing over blank screens and controls. Jacob was slumped in his seat. She thought she could see his chest move in the dim light, but she wasn't sure. She became aware of the tinkling sound again and looked at the window. She shifted her head trying to see better. The window glinted red light back at her along a fine meandering line in the window. Beyond it she could see the stars spinning in a slow ballet. Small chunks of ice and rock were slamming into the window at intervals making the sound. The deck was eerily quiet. No sound of instruments, or even air moving through ducts.

She put her hands on the controls but nothing lit up. She closed her eyes, breathed deep, then unstrapped and drifted gently to the window being careful not to touch it. She opened a box on the wall by the window, pulled out a short rod with a handle, inserted it in a hole labeled #1 and began cranking. Slowly the metal shield on the outside of the window slid over the window. After about thirty seconds it covered the entire window, but Val kept cranking until a dark line drawn ten centimeters up from the bottom of the shield was even with the bottom of the screen, then she pulled the rod out and stuck into the hole labeled #2 and began cranking. After about ten seconds of cranking, the ratchet in the hole made a slipping, pinging sound every time she cranked it. She pulled the rod out, stowed it, and let her arms go limp. After a few seconds she pushed her way to Jacob. He was breathing slowly. There were no marks on him. She pushed her way to the back of the flight deck and closed the hatch into the rest of the ship, then went back to Jacob, pulled an oxygen mask out of the arm in his chair, cracked the valve open and started to put it on his face. As soon as the mask touched him, he grabbed her wrist, and stared at her fiercely before recognizing her, blinking, and letting go of her wrist. He took the mask, pushed it over his nose and breathed in deeply several times before looking around.

"What happened?" he asked.

Val shook her head, "I don't know. There was an explosion. We are in freefall and spinning around our bow-to-stern axis at about three RPM. The bridge has lost primary, secondary and battery power, except for emergency lighting. I suspect life support is offline."

"Why is the shield closed?"

"The window is cracked. We were getting peppered with blast debris, which means the forward deflectors are down. That's not surprising though since we were sitting on the surface with them shutoff."

"How long was I out?"

"I don't know. About seven minutes longer than I was."

She looked at her watch. It was blank. "...And my watch is dead."

Jacob looked at his, "So is mine. That's not a good sign."

He looked at the hatch behind them and saw it was closed. "Did we lose pressure?"

Val shrugged. "The corridor to crew quarters still had pressure when I closed the hatch."

"Well let's see what we've got," Jacob said, unstrapped and started pulling panels off of the wall.

"I'll see how our air is holding up," Val said. She opened the emergency kit and pulled out a palm sized device with a rainbow scale on the far right. She pushed a slider switch to "on" and a rainbow lit up next to the scale. She breathed on the box and watched the spectral lines shift, then shift back.

"Air looks OK. We must not have been out for too long. Without fans, the air in here will get bad pretty quick."

Jacob had his face in the cabinet and called out, "All of the circuit breakers and relays are tripped. I mean all of them." Jacob flipped several levers inside the cabinet and the consoles next to Val's chair lit up. Val hovered over them. "Do you see anything?" Jacob asked.

"Navigation and flight panels have lit, but the readouts are all flat."

"It's probably isolated from all the real equipment down in engineering... if there is an engineering."

He thought for a second about what he had just said and went back to work. He flipped some more levers and the consoles next to his chair lit up. He hovered over them.

"The good news is engineering is still there. " He flipped through different displays, "The bad news is almost everything is offline." He flipped through a few more displays, paused, and said, "Uh oh."

"What?"

Jacob's hands were flying. "We're venting water. The proboscis was still extended."

Jacob stopped sending commands and watched, breathing shallow, for several seconds.

"We're OK, it's stopped. We've still got 60% water storage." He switched displays, "and all of our reaction mass and ACS propellant. Now let's get some real power in here." He flipped through animated views of the ship's power system starting from the reactor and working back towards the bridge. "Reactor's OK. All the breakers are tripped up and down the line on both primary and secondary power." Jacob started commanding each breaker to re-enable in order, from the reactor up. At mid-deck the breaker would trip the second he re-enabled it. He tried two or three times then gave up. "Well, we have power to the bottom two decks. I'll try the secondary." The very first breaker on the secondary refused to re-enable. "I'll try to cross feed on the second floor," Jacob said, and lit up the cross connect, then re-enabled breakers up to the bridge on the secondary. All of the consoles shut down. Jacob re-enabled the consoles next to his chair, then Val's, then turned them all on. The main lights came on and the emergency lights flickered off.

Jacob looked at Val. "The rest is hard. Do we want life support or navigation or flight control first?"

"I vote for navigation. We are falling blind and who knows what we might be falling into."

"Makes sense."

Jacob started re-enabling the communication path to engineering. "This won't be complete when it comes up. A lot of stuff is offline down there." He finished the reconnect and the proximity alarm went off. Val and Jacob hurriedly strapped into their seats. Jacob nervously eyed the loose panels he had left floating around the cabin, started trying to restore flight controls while calling out "Where is it?"

"Everywhere," Val said throwing up her hands, "It's everywhere," she silenced the alarm and thought for a second. "We're in the middle of a debris field."

"I just restored ACS control."

"I don't dare use it. All I've got is proximity sensors. If I start moving the ship blind, we're going to hit stuff."

Jacob absorbed what she was saying, nodded, and went back to sensors. After fifteen minutes he had three forward cameras, radar, and gyroscopes back online. As each instrument came back, Val poured over the data.

"That's the best I can do from here," Jacob said. "How does it look?"

"Not too bad," Val said, and projected a map on the ceiling. Nothing big will hit us for at least six hours, and when we decide to pull out, I can do it on ACS alone this way. She drew a line through the field forward. "Of course, once we are free of the debris field I don't know which way we should go."

"We should probably get life support and main engines restored before trying to pull out of here," Jacob said.

Val looked distracted.

"What's the matter?" Jacob asked.

"Where is the Commander?"

Jacob tried accessing the personnel locator. "It's up, but according to it, none of us are on the ship. Transponders are probably fried."

Val scratched the spot on her forearm over the transponder psychosomatically. Jacob brought up ship wide communications and Val called out to the Commander while Jacob checked pressure on the upper levels. "Looks like there are no hull breaches from the second deck up. First deck and maintenance are a mess."

"He should be somewhere between the bridge and crew quarters on deck three. He's probably right down the corridor. You bring up life support and I'll go find him," Val said.

Jacob frowned. "The ship's a mess. There are a lot of hazards in there. I should go."

"I can't fix life support," Val protested.

"Actually, I suspect you could."

"I can't do it as fast as you can."

"True. Maybe we should wait until we can both go," Jacob conceded.

"He could be injured. He might die if he doesn't get help in time."

"Val. He's probably already dead."

"You can't know that."

"We both lost consciousness. That puts the sudden acceleration at what? - four G's?"

"Probably north of five G's."

"If he wasn't strapped in... Do you want to see that?"

"If it comes to that, I can take it," Val said.

"I think it's better if the farm boy goes."

"That wasn't exactly a farm you grew up on."

"Same difference. Look, I don't want you going down there without me."

"I'm going," Val insisted.

"The Commander left me in charge. Don't go down there. That's an order."

"Good luck with that," Val said and opened the hatch.

Jacob followed her down the corridor. "At least let me go first," he said. "And try not to touch anything. I don't know what might be ready to arc and spark down here."

Val let him pass.

They found him floating in a cloud of his own blood about ten meters from his quarters.

"Close your eyes, Val," Jacob said. But she was already beside him looking on.

"Let's get back to the bridge," Jacob said.

"Shouldn't we at least put him in his bunk?"

"Rescue is one thing. Recovery is another. Let's get safe, then we'll come back for him."

They worked their way back to the bridge. Jacob restored life support, but the lone remaining flight control computer was holding the engines down. After an hour trying to remotely reboot the computer, Jacob gave up. "I'm going to have to suit up and go down there."

"How long is that going to take?"

"I don't know, at least a couple of hours, probably a lot longer."

"I don't think we have that long. I'm starting to see serious secondary collisions among the pieces of debris. This system isn't at equilibrium yet."

"Can you still get us out of here on ACS thrusters?"

Val looked at the images on the ceiling and nodded. "Yes. We just pull through here and then up this way," she said, pointing.

"Let's do it. We can always fix the engines once we are clear."

Val eased the ship forward and out of the debris field, then angled up toward the plane of the ecliptic and away from the debris cloud. When they were safely clear, she nulled out the ship's spin and then rotated to face the way they had come.

Ceres was impossibly small: a pin prick of light.

"That can't be it." Val said, "Even at five G's it shouldn't be that far."

"Maybe we were out longer than we thought," Jacob said.

"No. I don't think so."

Jacob got to work trying to get the PPS back online while Val grabbed a sextant, then realized there were no windows available and put it down.

"I can't fix this from here, either," he finally said. "It could take days for us to get oriented and running."

"Let's just work the problem."

Jacob nodded. "OK, engines, then navigation, then communications, then clean up."

Val agreed.

It took two hours to clear a safe path to the crew quarter level equipment locker. Along the way Jacob towed the Commander's body into his quarters, put a pillow case over what was left of the head, and strapped it into its bunk. Val helped Jacob suit up, then went back to the bridge. She could hear Jacob's labored breathing as he opened and closed hatches, trying to shrink the unpressurized areas and make a clear path all the way to engineering.

When he finally reached engineering he was talking to himself. Val debated whether or not she should talk to him, opened a mic and said, "How's it going down there?"

"I'm just about to enter the core and reboot the primary flight controller," Jacob said.

"What about the other two voting computers?"

"I don't know yet. They didn't seem to be responding at all. We'll see when I get in there."

A minute later Val saw the indicator for the last flight computer go red.

"Rebooting," Jacob reported. Five long minutes went by, then the light turned orange, then green."

"I'm showing green up here," Val said.

"Hold on, I'm getting into the console." Jacob said. A few seconds later he added, "OK, I'm in. It looks better. I'm going to reinitialize the engines."

Another ten minutes passed, and Val saw one engine turn green on the console. "Engine one looks good."

"What about two through four?"

"No good."

Jacob's breathing got faster and louder and he didn't say anything for several seconds.

"OK. Let's fix the flight controllers, then I'll go take a look," he finally said.

Five minutes passed and controller number two turned yellow, then green.

"Number two's good."

"OK, booting number three - oh wait, it's dead. I can't even boot it all the way. Crap."

"What's the matter?" Val asked.

"We can't trust the A. I. with only two voting flight controllers."

"We can fly the ship, right?" Val said.

"Yeah, but we'll have to take it in shifts and the A. I. can't take a shift. The best we can do is load flight profiles and have the A. I. monitor and alarm if we deviate from the profile."

"That's good enough."

"I guess it will have to be for now. OK, navigation." Jacob went silent for a few minutes while he reinitialized the PPS hardware. "Crap," he said when it came back up.

"What?"

"The sensors are down too," he said.

"Can you reboot them?"

"No. They aren't connected, so I can't send them a command. I'm going to have to go out there and unplug them, then plug them back in and hope they aren't fried."

Val thought for moment. "What if you just cut their power then turned it back on."

"That could work," Jacob said and shut down power to the sensors then turned it back on. "Well, we got two out of five back. That will be enough to get a rough fix on our location. OK, com's." He went quiet for a while, then said, "No comm's. We've lost both the Directional High Gain Antenna and the UHF Antenna. The antenna array is in the sensor pod at the top of the ship. I think we'd better do engines next."

Twenty minutes of heavy breathing and grunting sounds passed as each hatch was opened manually. Then Jacob held his breath a long time.

"What's the matter?" Val asked.

"It's no good," Jacob said, "I can't fix this, I can't fix this."

"What do you see?"

"If I say I can't fix it, I can't fix it!" Jacob shouted.

"Just report what you see," Val said calmly.

"There is a three meter hole open to space where engine 4 used to be. Engine 3 has all the tubing ripped off its starboard side and is leaking fluid. Engine 2 looks intact except for the wiring, but I'll have to get a closer look to be sure. There's a lot of sharp debris floating around in here, but it's not moving too fast. I think I can get through."

"Negative Jacob, your suit is below 50%. Come back up."

"I can do it. It'll only take me a few minutes and there's another suit in maintenance if I need it."

Val looked at Jacob's health display, "Maintenance is still unpressurized," she said.

"Oh yeah, that's right," Jacob said, "Well, I've got my suit on. I can go in there."

"You can't switch suits in an unpressurized environment."

"Oh yeah, that's right. Well, I'd wait until it was pressurized again."

"Negative Jacob, just come back up and you can change up here."

Jacob didn't respond for a while then finally said, "OK. Coming up."

Val monitored him and kept talking to him until he was almost to the lockers, then went down to meet him and help him pull his suit off. When he had it off he suddenly looked at her and said, "I'm really tired."

"I think we've been up for something like twenty hours."

"That would explain it."

"Come on. We'll sleep on the bridge and spell each other off."

On the bridge they strapped themselves in and Jacob was asleep before they could agree on who would take the first watch.

Val tried to stay awake but within fifteen minutes they were both asleep.

Eighty-Two

When Val woke up, the console said 7:08 a. m. Mars standard. She stared up at the images on the ceiling disinterestedly until she realized that the ship was turned twenty degrees from its direction of travel. Not that it really mattered other than creating a slightly larger cross section for high speed impacts, but it reminded her that she was supposed to be flying the ship. She reoriented the ship. Jacob heard the sound of the thrusters and woke up.

"Are we off course?"

"Not really, since we haven't set a course yet," Val said.

Jacob closed his eyes for a second, then opened them and said,

"How far have we drifted from Ceres?

"It should be only 900 kilometers, but I can't see it."

"Are you picking up any other objects near where Ceres should be? Ceres has companions."

"Long distance radar is down."

"Maybe we should head for home," Jacob said.

"Ceres has to be closer than home."

"But if we can't find it, it might as well not be there."

"We'll find it," Val assured.

"We don't know how long any of the systems we've brought back on line will stay online. We may not even be able to land when we get to Ceres. The depressurized sections line up pretty well with our grapples."

"Like you said, our systems may not stay up long enough to make it home, and we don't have to have grapples to land."

Jacob thought about it for a long time.

"Val, there may not be anything left of the base. We may be burning up time, fuel and equipment just to put ourselves farther from home. You heard the broadcast. It cut out before we were ejected from the surface. I don't think we lost the signal because of problems on our side of Ceres. I think something went terribly wrong at Ceres Base. I also don't think the physical jolt we took explains all the electronics problems we are having. There's no sign of mechanical damage to our watches, yet they were taken out along with everything else. I think a magnetic wave of enormous amplitude hit the ship and the reactor at Ceres Base is the only thing I can think of locally that could have produced it. If we go back to Ceres we might not make it home."

"If Ceres Base was damaged or destroyed, banged up as we are, we may be the best hope of the people we left behind there."

"Val, I doubt there are any survivors. Even if there are, I doubt we can help them."

Val thought about it for a long time, then said, "I think we have to try and hope for the best."

Jacob thought for a few seconds, then nodded and shrugged his shoulders.

"OK, we'll go to Ceres, but we don't dare fire that engine until we clear the debris or we may lose that one."

They helped each other into their suits and worked their way towards the engine room. When they got to maintenance, Jacob said, "Hold on, we need to get a few things."

They rummaged around maintenance gathering things, then moved to the engine room. Jacob opened the hatch and unspooled wire from a large electromagnet. He stuck it just inside the hatch, then partially closed the hatch and turned it on. Jacob could feel a shudder through his glove as the magnet slammed into the wall of the engine room. They waited twenty minutes. Then Jacob opened the hatch wider and peaked inside. There was a mass of pointy debris covering the magnet.

He put a bag over it, magnet and all, and cut the power to the magnet. "That takes care of the ferrous materials anyway," Jacob said. They looked around the engine room. There was still plenty of debris floating around, but it didn't look as sharp. Jacob took one end of a filter panel and gave it to Val, then took the other end himself. They walked slowly from port to starboard, pushing debris ahead of themselves with the panel towards the hole in the deck. When they had moved all the material they could see into the hole, Jacob covered the hole with the filter panel and taped it to the deck. He was almost done when he yelled, "Crap!"

"What?" Val said.

"I nicked my wrist."

Val could see air leaking out. Jacob was frantically trying to get a hold of the end of a piece of tape with one hand while holding the roll in his damaged glove.

Val snatched the roll from his hand, pulled out some tape, and pressed it hard over the hole in his suit. Then she wrapped his whole wrist tight.

Jacob scanned the displays on his visor, panted a little, then nodded. "I'm good..."

They stood there breathing hard for a second, then Jacob took the roll of tape back.

"What are you doing?"

"We already messed up one suit. I'm not risking another one."

He finished taping the filter in place, then they sealed up the engine room and went back to crew quarters.

They stripped their outer suits off and sat around in the under layer, drinking water and eating chips, both of them too tired to care, until they fell asleep leaning against each other. They woke up twenty minutes later, startled that they had fallen asleep.

"We can't leave the ship unpiloted like that," Val reproached herself.

Jacob agreed. They quickly got their flight suits on and went to the bridge.

"Still think we should go to Ceres?" Jacob asked.

Val nodded, "We have to."

"OK, set course in the general direction of where Ceres should be. We'll have to correct as we find out more."

Val set course.

When they arrived where Ceres had been they looked in all directions but didn't find it.

"It's the brightest thing in the belt," Jacob said. "Let's just scan for it optically."

They looked at the displays on the ceiling but couldn't make out anything.

Val attempted to activate several of the various telescopes on the ship with no success.

They picked their way carefully down the corridors of the ship to the old observatory. Power was off in that section, so after carefully examining the glass, Jacob cranked the shield open by hand. The stars stared down at them and sunlight harshly lit the surface of the ship below them. There were small signs of damage all over the surface of the ship, but nothing dramatic. There were hints of the carnage on the other side of the ship. A grapple stuck out at an odd angle and was visible. A string of debris held together by cabling of some kind stuck out in another direction.

They looked together and then looked at each other.

"Those have to be Ceres' companions," Jacob said.

"The pattern's not quite right."

"If Ceres suddenly wasn't there, that would change the pattern."

"The explosion that threw us away from Ceres would have moved Ceres at least a little," Val said.

They scanned the sky for Ceres, but could discern nothing among the many points of light.

Jacob restored power to the section, and Val accessed navigation. She found the location of the debris field they had recently been a part of, then drew a line from it to their present location and extended it beyond their current location. They activated the observatory telescope and looked along the line Val had projected, but found nothing large.

"We have been assuming the explosion was on our side of Ceres. What if it was at the base?" Jacob asked.

"If it had been at the base, we would have been slammed into Ceres, not ejected from it."

"True, but after we were slammed into Ceres we might have been ejected by the recoil. We were unconscious. We wouldn't know."

"I don't think Ceres is that elastic. At least it's not elastic enough for us to achieve those velocities. Plus, we should have seen it on our way here."

"Just look."

"OK," Val relented.

They looked, but found nothing.

"So if Ceres wasn't moved by an explosion, what moved it?" Jacob asked.

"Maybe it disintegrated entirely."

"There isn't enough debris."

"Let's set up a time lapse picture of the whole heavens. Ceres will be the brightest object that is moving," Jacob suggested.

They ran fifteen minute scans, rotating the ship forty degrees on each scan. On the second try they found it and confirmed it with the observatory telescope.

Jacob looked at the report and said, "It's moving away from us at 1.7 KM per second."

"That's its orbital velocity!" Val said.

Jacob covered his face with his hands.

"What is it?" Val asked.

"Their experiment worked better than they intended. Ceres is acting as though it were massless."

Eighty-Three

Jacob and Val looked at each other a long time. Val swallowed. "I still think we should go," she finally said.

Jacob looked back, nodded, and said, "Set course. I'll work on communications."

Val glided down the ladder and disappeared in the direction of the flight deck.

Jacob closed the shield and followed her, then went down the corridor towards the upper instrument bay. He was nearly there when he heard the maneuvering thrusters reorienting the ship. A second later, Val's voice was in his ear telling him she was about to fire the engines.

He settled into a jump seat, strapped in and tried not to think of the Commander.

"I'm ready," he said, but the acceleration was gentle.

Val's voice said, ".25 G, You've got four minutes before I shut the engine down."

"I'll just sit tight," Jacob said.

When four minutes had passed, Val's voice said, "Standby for engine shut down."

The pressure lifted.

"Sixty seconds to braking maneuver," Val's voice said.

Jacob could hear the maneuvering thrusters fire, turning the ship around.

"Initiating braking maneuver," Val said and the pressure returned.

"Val," Jacob said, "Keep your distance from Ceres, and use an equatorial orbit. We don't want to pass over the poles. Remember the emitters were pointed north."

"I thought you said Ceres was massless."

"I did."

"Then there will be no orbit. I'll stand off 200 kilometers in the equatorial plane."

"You're right. That's good," Jacob said.

After four minutes Val's voice said, "Standby for cutoff."

"Ready."

The pressure eased.

"Looks like I'll have to keep the engine running at 2% to keep up with Ceres."

"Makes sense," Jacob said. "Do you see anything?"

"Not from this distance... although the albedo seems off... too dark."

"OK. I'll be up in a few minutes."

Jacob turned his attention to the instrument pod. The ray-dome was shattered. Both the directional antenna and the low bandwidth omnidirectional antenna were shredded. He pulled on gloves, removed the ray dome, then pulled the quick releases on the directional and omnidirectional antennas and removed both.

He put a cap on over the socket for the directional antenna, then fitted a new omnidirectional antenna into its socket and sent the pod back to the surface of the ship.

"That did something," Val's voice said. "We are receiving repeated requests for telemetry from Mars."

"Is the ship responding?"

"The ship's damage control system has prepared a report, but with the A. I. off line it can't send it until I tell it to," Val said.

"Go ahead and let it send the report, but don't let it establish a telemetry link yet. Also send a message giving them the crew status, the trajectory of Ceres, and our intention to check for survivors. I'll be up in a few minutes."

"Got it."

Jacob strapped down the broken equipment and moved towards the flight deck.

When he got there, Val was quiet.

"Shall we take a look?"

Val closed her eyes, and nodded.

Jacob remotely opened the shields on the observatory and linked its telescope to the overhead display.

Val rotated the ship slowly and Jacob pointed the telescope toward the base.

The reactor building looked as it had before. Next they found the emitters. They were lying on their sides facing each other a kilometer apart. Fissures split the ice in several directions.

They swept the telescope down one of the fissures toward the landing pad. The hangars were twisted and crumpled. The command bunker was standing, but the windows were shattered and everything was dark. The living quarters were completely gone, swallowed by the fissure.

Jacob grabbed still images showing the damage, compressed them and sent them to Mars.

Jacob switched his headset to transmit, and called out, "Astral 4 to Ceres control. Astral 4 to Ceres Control, are you there?"

Jacob and Val listened to the silence.

"Astral 4 to Ceres Control. Astral 4 to Ceres Control. Can anybody hear me?"

Silence answered.

"We should land, suit up and check the control bunker. They had some armored rooms in there. There could be survivors, but they would be low on air by now."

Jacob shook his head. "Those emitters are still active. We have no idea what they will do to the ship if we fly into that field, or to us."

"We don't know for sure that the emitters are active."

"How else do we explain Ceres' current trajectory?"

"Maybe Ceres' mass was permanently changed before the emitters broke."

"That's not what the math says should happen," Jacob said.

"The math also doesn't say anything about nullifying the mass of an object the size of Ceres at the power levels they were using."

"True, but we have to assume they are active until we know better," Jacob said with finality.

"Even if they are active, Will said we could probably put our hands in the beam in the cargo hold. There's at least a chance it won't harm us," Val insisted.

"That was at a much lower power, and even then he told us not to put our hand in the beam. Looking at the surface, I'd say the field does more than just cancel mass."

"If we wait we doom any survivors."

"If there are any survivors, we won't be able to help them if we crash this ship."

They were both silent.

Jacob started scrolling through the specifications of the Maintenance Spheres.

Val watched over his shoulder. Jacob stopped when he got to the communication link specs.

"20 Km," Val said and frowned.

"They don't have much propellant either," Jacob said, scrolling down to that section to confirm his memory.

"It makes sense. They're only meant for helping with ship maintenance."

Jacob rested his forehead in his hand and rubbed his temples.

"I suppose we could launch one toward Ceres slowly and trail it fifteen kilometers behind. First sign of trouble, we pull back and try to call it back with us," Jacob said.

Val nodded. "That could work."

"It's a risk. There is no guarantee that the sphere will react the same way the ship would, or the way we would."

"We'll just go very slowly," Val said.

"Also, we need to get a look at the underside of the ship before we risk any of our maintenance spheres. We need to understand what we have and don't have before we attempt any kind of rescue."

Val bit her lower lip, but finally nodded. "Let's just make it as quick as we can."

"I'll prep a sphere; you communicate our plan to Mars."

"Will do."

Jacob was gone about fifteen minutes. Just as he took his seat a message appeared on the console."

"Good to hear from you. Sorry for your loss. Send images of Ceres Base at first opportunity. Be aware that our resources here believe the emitters are still active. Maintain a distance of at least 300 Km from the surface of Ceres. Long range radar indicates that Ceres has expanded in size approximately 3%. We are analyzing your damage report and will have recommendations shortly."

"Oops," Val said, "we're already at 200 KM."

Jacob shrugged, "They're guessing, too."

Jacob checked the telemetry from the sphere. "Stream the sphere telemetry to Mars, but not the video. At least then if something happens to us whoever comes next will have some data."

Val nodded, and Jacob launched the sphere. They scanned the underside of the ship. Only one grapple remained in place and its talons were missing. Part of one more was bent to the side. There were jagged holes where the rest had been. They took a closer look at the cargo bay doors. They appeared intact. The proboscis bay was ripped open and stained, but the hull was otherwise intact.

Jacob grabbed some stills and sent them to Mars, then he moved the sphere slowly towards Ceres. When it was fifteen kilometers away, Val followed it with the ship.

Another message appeared on the console.

"A prioritized list of repairs follows. Please make the repairs in the order presented and report progress."

Jacob and Val glanced at the message and ignored it.

Several minutes passed and Val called out, "Sphere is 170 kilometers from the surface."

Jacob looked at Val and said, "I'm sitting right here. I can read."

Val shook her head and a few minutes later called out, "140 kilometers."

At 75 kilometers the sphere suddenly stopped communicating.

"Get us out of here Val!" Jacob yelled and sent a final command to the sphere to return. The sphere didn't respond.

Val pulled the ship back to 200KM and started shadowing the planet again.

They tried to track the sphere with the observatory telescope, but lost it.

A few minutes later an urgent message came across the displays.

"We do not agree with your approach. Do not approach Ceres. Your top priority at this time is to preserve the ship. Observe and report, but do not approach Ceres. Do not attempt any rescue. Mars Directorate."

"Oops!" said Val. "I don't think they're going to like the data they're about to get."

Jacob smiled.

Ten minutes later another urgent message flashed across the display.

"Abort current rescue effort immediately. Ceres poses a potential threat to both Mars and Earth. Maintain the integrity of the ship at all costs. Mars Directorate."

Jacob and Val looked at each other.

"How can Ceres present a threat to Mars or Earth?" Val said.

Jacob looked puzzled, "I don't know."

"Signal Mars Directorate, that we have suspended rescue efforts and ask for clarification of the threat posed to Earth and Mars by Ceres."

Val hesitated, but then sent the message.

They pulled up a model of the solar system, scaled it, and tried to see what threat Ceres could pose.

"On its current trajectory, Ceres will leave the solar system in approximately 270 earth years. It's hard to see how it can pose a threat anywhere along that path," Val said.

Val wrinkled her forehead. "Maybe perturbations from Jupiter or

Saturn might affect its course," she said and fiddled with the model. She set the mass of Ceres to .0001 Kg and put it on its current trajectory. Then she started fast forwarding the projection through the *years.

Jacob shook his head. "How do you perturb a massless object from a distance?" he asked.

Val shrugged and kept watching the model.

Seven earth months into the projection, Jacob reached over and paused it.

"What are you doing?" Val asked.

"Just watch," he said, and changed the mass of Ceres to 9.43 x 10(20) Kg. Then continued the program and fast forwarded it.

Ceres plunged like a comet past all the inner planets, grazed the sun, passed through the inner planets again and the asteroid belt, crossed the orbit of Jupiter, then plunged back towards the inner solar system again in an elliptical orbit passing through the orbits of all the inner planets every 2.7 earth years. Jacob sped up the model so a complete orbit of the sun took only one second and watched. After five minutes, Ceres struck Earth.

Val ran the math and said, "OK, so there's a chance that in 810 earth years Ceres could strike Earth. I think we might be able to fix it by then, especially given our new technology here."

Jacob reset the model to show Ceres' current location and mass. "How long do you think those emitters and that reactor might hold up down there?"

Val shrugged, "They're pretty banged up. They could fail at any time."

"What do you think is the longest they could keep running?"

Val looked at the ceiling and said, "Well, the reactor could keep producing power for at least fifteen earth years, if nothing breaks, but the emitters are lying with one side on the ice and all other sides are being constantly heated by the sun at a constantly changing angle. Eventually the metal should fatigue and break. I don't know, but I don't think it could last more than a few months."

Jacob ran the simulation again and put the mass back at six earth months. The new elliptical orbit only crossed the orbits of Mars, and

Earth, but it did so at different points. He fast forwarded until Ceres struck Mars.

"That's still 430 earth years."

"What if the emitters give out in ninety days?"

They reset the simulation and ran it again. This time Ceres only crossed the orbit of Mars, but it made a near miss 270 days into the simulation. Val shuddered. Jacob fast forwarded and Ceres hit Mars after twenty earth years.

"I'm guessing that if we keep playing with the number of days before the failure of emitters, we can make Ceres hit Mars on the first pass."

"The odds of the emitters failing on exactly the right day are tiny," Val said.

"It doesn't matter what the probability is if it happens," Jacob said.

They both leaned back and looked at the images of Ceres on the ceiling.

Val reached across the captain's seat towards Jacob. Jacob looked at her, then reached his hand towards hers until their fingers touched.

A message flashed across the screen explaining the danger they had just figured out. It concluded, "If Ceres is restored to its normal mass 89 days from today, there is a 98% chance that it will strike Mars 185 days later. If Ceres is restored to normal mass after 103 days from today, there are multiple impact scenarios with varying probabilities of impact. The scenarios with return to mass between 89 and 215 days from today provide the worst probabilities of catastrophic impacts. Continue repairs to the ship until further instructions. Mars Directorate."

Jacob examined the repair list and groaned. "If I can get the A. I. back on line, do you think you can help with any of this?"

Val looked at the list and nodded.

"Keep us off Ceres, and I'll get the A. I. back on line," Jacob said unstrapped, and swam down the corridor.

Eighty-Four

It took Jacob until 2:00 in the morning to fix the flight controllers enough to use the A. I.

Val talked to him frequently to keep them both awake.

The primary had been working correctly since reboot, but the secondary was iffy, and the tertiary was dead. Jacob started by completely reimaging the second voting computer. When that was working and had rejoined the cluster, he turned his attention to the dead computer. After two hours of fighting it, he finally gave up and started hunting for a replacement. The media server met the requirements for the flight controller software, though it was a little underpowered for the job.

"Hey Val, would you rather be able to sleep or watch movies?"

"Sleep!" Val responded.

"I'm going to wipe the media server and use it for a voting flight controller."

"Great, let me grab a bunch of books first. I can fit a lot of those on the local box."

A few minutes later Val said, "Got them. Go ahead."

After two more hours of work, Jacob joined the third computer to the cluster.

"Give it a try."

Val had already configured a profile in the navigation computer. She uploaded it to the A. I. and enabled it.

Alarms immediately began going off.

"Hang on, I've got it," Val said.

She went about acknowledging all the damage to the ship and configuring the A. I. to accept the new flight profile, mission objectives, and the loss of the commander. Jacob had to participate in the last part, giving his authentication code and listing himself as the Acting Commander.

"The Commander didn't mean to designate you the new commander, he just left you in charge while he was off the flight deck," Val objected.

"Do you want to be the Commander?" Jacob asked.

Val considered the question in the hazy honesty of 2:00 AM. "No. Not really. I wanted to be asked though. Go ahead. But don't expect me to follow any weird orders."

"Noted," Jacob responded.

When Val was convinced the A. I. was acting properly, she turned over control of the ship to it and Jacob came back to the flight deck. When he got there, Val was asleep. He looked around the deck. He looked in the direction of his quarters, then strapped into his chair across from Val and fell asleep.

When they awoke, there was a new message from the Mars Space Directorate on the screen. The A. I. had streamed a reduced version of the ship and crew's telemetry during the night. The new message said, "We agree with your decision to change the priority order to fix the voting flight controllers first. Please keep us posted of your decisions as if in real time. We recommend you proceed with the remaining repair tasks today. We will hold a full briefing tomorrow noon Mars standard. Please acknowledge message."

Jacob acknowledged the message and turned to look at Val. She was already looking at him.

"I don't know about you, but the first repair I'm making is to take a shower."

Val smiled at that, but didn't say anything until Jacob hesitated to leave. Then she nodded at him and said, "You go first."

Jacob kicked his way down the corridor towards his quarters. He moved slower when he went by the Commander's quarters.

When he got back to the flight deck, Val had been busy. She'd knocked off some items on their repair list that could be done from the flight deck.

While Val showered, Jake lowered the temperature in the Commander's quarters as far as he could, then reviewed the repair list. The highest priority item was reinforcing the hull around Grapple Compartment 2-B. The Directorate recommended cutting up one of the cargo containers in the hold for reinforcement material. When Val got back, they went to the hold and used a welding laser to cut squares of metal. Then worked together to push them to the grapple compartment.

"We'd better suit up, close the door behind us and lower the pressure in here before we start welding on a weakened hull," Jacob said.

"Let's tie-off too," Val suggested.

It took three hours to finish the repairs and be sure the work was good.

When they were done they returned to the changing room and helped each other peel off their grimy suits. Then they rested.

"I need another shower," Val said.

"Not me, I'm fresh as a daisy," Jacob said.

Val gave him a smirk.

After they transmitted scans of the welding work to Mars, they fixed the directional antenna.

Val oriented the high gain antenna till the ship's A. I. detected the guide tone coming from a deep space relay and finished aiming it.

They looked for standard feeds sent to all ships and found one.

"We're receiving OK," Val said.

"Let's try transmitting," Jacob said.

They turned on a camera and sent a quick vid reporting that high gain communications had been restored.

When they were done, the A. I. started sending larger reports, including the video of their scans of Ceres and of the underside of the ship.

They ate a real meal in the break room in calm silence. At the end of the meal neither got up to leave.

"I guess we should go to quarters," Jacob said.

Val glanced at the Commander's quarters and said, "I think I'll sleep on the flight deck again."

"I'll join you."

Val looked relieved.

"I'll move it tomorrow," Jacob said.

"Move what?"

"You know…"

"Yeah… that would be good. It kind of creeps me out, even though I know it shouldn't."

They went to the flight deck and strapped in.

Val watched Jacob for a minute and then ventured, "You should probably be using the Commander's chair, since we decided you are commanding."

Jacob looked at it with some minor alarm on his face. "I can reach the engineering controls better from hear. Besides, it seems disrespectful somehow."

"I'd like you to sit there tonight."

"Why?"

Val groaned and said, "No reason, never mind, it doesn't matter."

Jacob thought for a minute, then moved to the Commander's chair.

Val covered her face and smiled. Jacob dimmed the lights, and stared at the ceiling, his brow wrinkled.

A few minutes later, he felt Val take his hand and his face relaxed.

Eighty-Five

In the morning, Jacob crept out of the flight deck before Val woke up. He went to the supply closet, found a body bag, went to crew quarters and stood outside the Commander's door for a minute before unsealing it and going inside. He unzipped the body bag, tacked the toe of it to the wall with a Velcro strip, then turned to face the body. It was swollen. He tried not to look or breathe while he unstrapped it and pushed it feet first into the bag. Its hand snagged on the edge of the zipper as it went in, and he had to pull it free. When he finally got it in, he zipped both layers of the bag and began towing it down the hall to the big freezer off the cargo hold. Just outside the Commander's quarters he saw Val. She watched what he was doing for a few seconds then said, "Do you need any help?"

"No. I've got this."

Val nodded.

When he came back, Val was wiping down the walls of the corridor with a sponge.

"You don't have to do that," Jacob said.

"You didn't have to take care of the body," Val said.

Jacob didn't say anything more.

They went to the break room, but neither felt like eating.

"We ought to say a few words for him," Val said.

They decided to make a video saying what they admired about him and transmit it as part of the log.

When they had done that, they sat uncomfortably for a few minutes until Jacob said,

"Maybe we should have a prayer for him."

Val looked at him a little surprised.

Jacob looked annoyed and said, "I'll say it."

He said a prayer, and Val held his hands in hers while he said it.

Afterwards, they gave each other a hug and got back to repairing things on the ship.

At noon, a series of files and documents arrived and a streaming vid from the Mars Space Directorate began.

"The files you have received contain our best estimates of different Ceres scenarios with contingency plans for each. We wanted you to have them in case we lose communications again. We have redirected the two closest ships, the Hercules and the Ochoa, to your location to relieve you. The Hercules will reach you first but not for at least 95 days, possibly longer. The Ochoa is at least 115 days away. As the reports show, If Ceres regains its mass 85 days from now it will almost certainly strike Mars. If it regains its mass any time after that up until two earth years from today, it will create regular threats to all the inner planets including Mars for centuries. If it regains its mass before 85 days, it will pose some threat to the cycler ships, but otherwise maintain an elliptical but harmless orbit.

Tomorrow the President of Mars and various leaders of Earth will hold a conference to decide whether or not we should attempt to shut down the emitters on Ceres in the next few weeks, or if we should wait and hope that the emitters last long enough to cause Ceres to break up on approach to the sun on its first pass in approximately three earth years.

It is our recommendation that an attempt to shut down the emitters be made soon, and we expect that the various leaders will agree.

We have included several studies on how you might be able to shut down the emitters with the resources you have. Please examine these studies and let us know if you think they are workable. Do not make any attempt to shut down the emitters prior to hearing from us tomorrow.

We want you to know that we are all impressed with your performance so far. I don't think any crew, no matter how experienced could have handled this situation better than you have."

After the vid, two more vids, greetings from the commanders of the Hercules, and the Ochoa, streamed in. Then the screen went blank.

Val and Jacob returned to repairing things on the ship, while they digested the message.

"They expect us to try to stop this thing," Jacob said.

"Yeah."

Jacob looked blankly into the distance and said, "That won't be easy."

"Nope."

Jacob shook off a thought, said, "We still have options," and went back to work.

In the evening they started reviewing the "studies." The first one suggested trying to transmit shutdown commands directly to the reactor core using the high gain antenna.

They reviewed the telescopic image of the reactor building and saw that the antennas were gone.

"I guess it's worth a shot," Jacob said.

The second study suggested building new talons for the remaining grapple, reinstalling them, hunting down a tiny asteroid, flying towards the reactor building at high speed, releasing the asteroid and pulling up quickly.

"That's a lot of fabrication and welding before we get to take our first shot. It's also a lot of time outside," Jacob said.

"It's also not very likely we will hit the reactor. We'd have to take a lot of shots and there aren't many meteoroids nearby so we'd probably be running back and forth to the asteroid belt," Val said.

They read on and Jacob started laughing.

"I like this one for the sheer boom quality," he said.

The idea was to fix the grapple, load up a cargo container full of mining explosives, fling it at the reactor building and detonate it just before impact.

"How do we detonate it in that field?" Val asked.

"Good question."

"The impact alone will take out the reactor if we get it going fast enough, but that assumes we actually hit it, and we only have two complete containers in the hold," Val said.

They read on. "That's funny. They skipped number 4," Val said.

Jacob looked thoughtful for a moment, but said nothing.

Number five involved installing a telescope and a welding laser in Instrument Pod 2 and using it to heat one of the emitters until it broke.

"It will be hard to keep the laser steady under powered flight," Val said.

"But it won't take long to try it," Jacob said.

"I agree. First let's try sending commands to the reactor, then let's try the laser," Val said.

Val signaled their intent to Mars.

It was late.

"Where are you going to sleep tonight?" Jacob asked.

Val hesitated, "I'll probably go back to my quarters."

"Me too," Jacob said.

Val said goodnight and left hastily.

Jacob went to his quarters, stripped down to his underwear and crawled into his zero G bag.

The ship wasn't quite at zero G, so he had to tether the bag at both ends to avoid ending up against the cold wall during the night. He was asleep the moment he closed his eyes.

Jacob woke suddenly to the sound of alarms. The clock on the wall said 1:00 AM.

He threw on some clothes and got to the flight deck about the same time as Val.

Val silenced the alarm, glanced at their position relative to Ceres and clicked through the logs.

"We're OK," she said after a few moments. "Ceres changed course slightly, which put us at risk of collision, but the A. I. corrected and alarmed."

"What course is Ceres on now?"

Val pulled up a map of Ceres' motion relative to the sun. Ceres' trajectory had curved slightly towards the sun then resumed a straight line.

"Looks like Ceres regained part of its mass for three seconds then lost it again," Val said.

The A. I. had already communicated the event to Mars. Val and Jacob added their observations to the message.

"We better move the ship to the open space side of Ceres in case this happens again," Jacob said.

Val nodded and began moving the ship. When they were repositioned, Val returned control to the A. I. and looked at Jacob.

He was smirking at her.

"What?"

"It's just that you're so formally attired," Jacob said.

"Well look at you, you've got your shirt on inside out." Val retorted.

Jacob looked down and shrugged.

They went back to their quarters.

"See you in the morning," Jacob said.

When Val came into the break room in the morning, Jacob was already there.

"What are you reading?" she asked.

Matthew 28.

Val joined him.

After that, they got to work. Mars had sent all the frequencies, coding, keys and commands for the reactor during the night. Jacob preloaded them into the communications system, while Val plotted a position 100 Km above the reactor.

They waited a half an hour for approval to proceed, but none came. Finally they left the flight deck and began installing the telescope and welding laser into the other Instrument Pod. Instrument Pod 2 didn't have a circuit capable of supporting the power requirements of the laser. They improvised by running a new circuit down the conduit to the nearest high power source.

When they returned to the flight deck, there still wasn't any response from Mars.

They sent an inquiry and went back to work on their repair list. Forty minutes later they got a response that the meeting had been delayed and no decision was expected until after 2:00 p.m. Mars Standard Time. At 5:00 pm Mars Standard, they got the go ahead.

Val maneuvered the ship into position and Jacob aimed the high gain antenna at the reactor building and began transmitting the initial log in hand shake message repeatedly. After an hour there hadn't been any response.

"Are you hungry?" Jacob said.

Val nodded yes.

"Why don't you go get something to eat? I'll babysit."

Val shook her head. "We are awfully close to the altitude where the sphere died. I want to stay here until we move away."

"OK. I'll bring you something then."

"Thanks."

When he got back, there still hadn't been any response.

They ate.

Jacob rechecked his transmission set up, but couldn't find anything wrong with it.

"Mars couldn't find anything wrong with it either," Val said. "Also take a look at this."

Val brought up a frequency chart with all the values at zero.

"What is that?"

"It's our received signal on the high gain antenna for the last two hours across all the frequencies the antenna can receive."

"That can't be right. Between solar interaction and natural radioactive decay in Ceres itself, there should be at least a little background noise. Plus we're pointed at a reactor."

Val shrugged. "The diagnostics check out."

Jacob paused the transmission and re-ran the diagnostics. They came back clean. He re-aimed the antenna at empty space and watched the background noise come back. He aimed the dish back at the reactor and all the background noise ceased.

"This isn't going to work. Not only are none of the electronics down there working, something is swallowing signal," Jacob said.

"Let's give it a few more hours," Val said.

Jacob re-aimed the antenna and restarted the transmission.

"I'm getting tired. Maybe we should take this in shifts," Jacob said.

"OK. Sleep. I'll wake you when I need to sleep."

Jacob drifted off.

He woke up to Val calling his name. It was after 11:00 p.m.

"Mars wants us to keep trying till morning. Are you OK for a few hours?"

"I'm good. Sleep."

"OK. Keep the A. I. from flying us into Ceres."

"I will."

She started to fade almost immediately, but as she did she reached over, took Jacob's hand and held it close.

He watched her sleep and let her keep his hand until he was sure she was asleep.

About 4:00 AM, he caught himself nodding off, and woke her. She took over and he was oblivious to everything until he heard the maneuvering thrusters announce the attempt was over.

They stood off at a safe distance from Ceres and slept until noon, then ate. Then they maneuvered back in for the laser attempt. They targeted the nearest emitter. The first attempt was a complete failure. They couldn't even see where the beam was hitting. They realigned the telescope and realized they had missed their target by over a kilometer. The second try was better. At least they saw the target and the puff of steam where the beam hit the ice in the same telescopic image. By the tenth try that evening they had aligned the telescope and laser enough that they could slave them together, aim using the telescope and hit the spot in the center of the image fairly reliably. By 11:00 p.m. they had hit the emitter for the first time and managed to keep the beam on it for three seconds before it slid off and carved up more innocent ice.

"Val, keep the ship straight," Jacob barked when the beam slid off after only one second.

"I'm trying. Do you think you could do better?"

"Switch seats."

Val moved over and Jacob took the controls.

The next shot didn't hit the emitter at all.

"Val you've got to fire while it's lined up," Jacob said.

"That's a lot easier if you keep it lined up for more than a second."

Jacob growled in frustration, was silent, and finally said, "Miss Kyria: I hate it when you are right."

"Mr. Billings, I wish I weren't."

"We're exhausted. Let's stand off and try again in the morning."

They stood off and returned to their quarters.

At two in the morning they were both standing on the flight deck again, messy haired, silencing alarms.

"Ceres did it again."

"Were we in any danger?"

"No, it was moving away from us."

At 4:00 a.m. it did it again.

"Were we in any danger?" Jacob asked.

"No."

"Change the A. I.'s instructions to use silent alarms unless there is a danger to the ship."

Val thought for a minute about how to configure that, then set to work.

Jacob checked the work and they went to bed.

They met each other in the break room at 9:00, both of them stinky.

They agreed to maintain their breakfast tradition of eating and studying together no matter what else they had to give up.

By 9:45 they were on the deck.

They tried hitting the emitter again, but the best they could do all morning was eight seconds.

At lunch, they rethought their strategy.

"I think the A. I. might be able to hold the ship on target longer than I can," Val said.

"Let's try it."

With the A. I. they were able to hold the laser on target for fifteen seconds.

"That was promising," Val said.

By evening they had a cumulative total of twenty minutes of the laser hitting the target.

"I'm surprised it isn't doing more damage," Jacob said.

"That laser isn't designed for this. The beam width is twice as wide at this distance than when we're using it up close, and that emitter is shiny on the side. I'll bet it's reflecting some of the energy," Val said.

"We'll try again tomorrow."

The next day they took shifts firing at the emitter.

Jacob spent his time away from the deck modifying one of the cargo pods for the "boom boom" idea.

By evening they had managed to burn a small hole in the side of the emitter, but there was no change in its behavior.

The next two days were repeats of the previous day, with the added excitement of the logs showing Ceres had regained mass briefly on the fifth night.

Jacob spent all his spare time in the cargo hold.

The next day, they decided to change tactics. It was clear that although they could damage the outer casing of the emitter with the laser, they couldn't break it. They decided to try to sever its power line to the reactor. They changed targets. This was a much smaller target, and by evening they had only managed to have the laser on the target for a cumulative of four minutes. Most of the shots were so short that the heat appeared to conduct across the protective sheathing and dissipate into the ice.

The following day was better, eight minutes.

They continued shooting the cable for another day then went back to the emitter for two days.

Jacob had moved from spending all his spare time in the cargo bay to building talons in the machine shop. He didn't have spare parts, so they were crude talons, but he was able to make four, just enough to be able to grab something.

By the time they gave up on the laser, Jacob was ready to install the talons.

They carried the talons to the Grapple compartment 1A airlock. They both suited up, then closed off the section and lowered the pressure in it. Val plugged her suit into the ship to keep it topped off and took a position at the console next to the airlock door. Since all the cameras on the underside of the ship were gone, the first thing they sent out the airlock was a maintenance sphere.

"We're still accelerating slightly to keep up with Ceres. The sphere is going to run out of fuel trying to keep up with us," Val said.

"Keep it steady for a minute," Jacob said.

Once outside he tethered himself to the grapple, then leaned out to the sphere. "Bring it closer to me," he said.

Val brought it closer and Jacob snagged its anchor point with the clip on the tether, and let go. The tether pulled tight and Val set the sphere to watch the end of the grapple.

"Looks good," Val said.

Jacob worked his way down the outside of the grapple. When he got to the end he flipped over and examined it carefully. The talons had snapped off as designed, so he simply unlocked the clamps and let the stumps fly away. Then he clamped each new talon in place. He retrieved the sphere, put it in the airlock and coiled up his tethers.

"I've got to change the filters on this suit. It smells like a gym locker," he said while he waited for the airlock to re-pressurize. By the time they had showered and changed they were starving, and ate all the remaining fresh food without caring what came next. After eating they tested the grapple. Val flexed the talons back and forth. They looked at each other and nodded.

Val scanned for nearby rocks. There was nothing but some debris too close to Ceres to retrieve."

They traded messages with Mars and set course for the belt.

Eighty-Six

Jacob, strapped in his seat, closed his eyes but didn't sleep. Val looked at the displays but seldom focused on them.

Neither spoke. They had been making these runs for twelve days.

Val checked the position of the rock they had chosen. They would arrive in ten minutes. She looked at Jacob, but said nothing.

When she had the ship perfectly paralleling the rock, she nudged Jacob. He sat up immediately and read the displays. When he was ready he nodded at Val and she eased the ship closer until it was within reach, then Jacob reached down and caught it with the grapple, digging the talons deep into the rock, as he had done sixteen times before over the previous days. Val slowly accelerated the rock in the direction of Ceres. On their fourth run she had accelerated too aggressively and the rock had disintegrated, nearly taking the talons with it. It had cost them four hours of work just to tighten the talons and make sure they were good for the next run. It was not a mistake she would make twice.

The runs were getting long now. Ceres had moved ever father from the main belt.

Jacob had managed to fix engine number 2 at least four times, but it was down again. They couldn't really use it accelerating the little rocks they were catching, but they could use it to shorten the trips back and forth to the belt.

After three hours they let the rock go.

They turned and moved towards their next target and three and a half hours later grappled it and started accelerating it.

Jacob fidgeted and pulled against the straps in his seat.

"Go!" Val said a little irritated.

"No, I can stay," Jacob said.

"Just go," Val said with an air of finality.

Jacob unstrapped and went to the machine shop.

Jacob put on his welding visor and finished the last weld on an improvised air gun he had been building.

He stood back and admired his work. When everything had cooled enough he checked his welds, then he hooked an air hose to the gun, pressurized the tank to 25% and opened the valve. A satisfying whomp of air came out the barrel with little bits of metal that quickly got sucked up into the shop's filtration system. Jacob took it to 50% pressure and tried it again, then 75%, then 100%. He fired it several more times until he was satisfied nothing would rupture. He turned his attention to the hopper. He screwed the cap on and attached the pressure hose between it and the main tank. He pulled the feed lever and heard air venting into the chamber, then let it go and it stopped.

"So far so good," he said to himself.

Next he setup templates and started printing a round plastic ball. When it was done he brushed it off, put it into the hopper and charged the cylinder to 8%, pulled the feed lever and waited. Air vented out the barrel for a full second before the hissing stopped and he felt the feed lever click under his finger. Then he pulled the valve and the plastic ball drifted out of the barrel.

He tried it again at 15% pressure and got a more satisfying flight out of the ball.

He checked the ball against the barrel again, then put it down and wrote a template for a mold that would make balls the same size. He had just finished double checking it when he heard Val's voice in his ear.

"Hey grapple boy."

"Yes, flight matron?"

"Are you going to come up here and let this rock fly, or do you want me to do it?"

"I'll be right there."

He set the printer working on the top half of the mold, then went to the flight deck.

Val had the rock perfectly aligned and Jacob simply let it go.

Val reoriented the ship and set a course for their next target rock.

Jacob started to unstrap.

"Hold on!" Val said.

"What?"

"I have to pee."

Jacob settled back into his chair and Val disappeared down the corridor.

Twenty minutes later, she came back and tossed Jacob his favorite remaining snack from the break room.

Val ate hers without looking at Jacob much.

When they had both finished eating, Jacob sat looking at Val.

"Why are you looking at me?" Val said.

"Are you OK?"

"I'm fine."

"Are you mad at me?" Jacob asked.

"No, but I will be if you don't stop looking at me. Go play with your toys."

Jacob sat puzzled for a minute, then went.

When he got back, the printer had finished making the molds.

He brushed them off and tested the fit. It was smooth.

He attached a water hose to one side and a drain hose to the other and filled it with water, then capped it and put it in the freezer.

He went back upstairs and found Val reading a book. Her eyes were red rimmed.

"Everything OK?"

"Yes," she said, a touch of anger in her voice.

Jacob didn't say anything.

"Go away," she said.

Jacob turned to go and Val let out an exasperated sigh.

"What?"

"Nothing. Go."

"Do you want me to go or not?"

"I don't know!" she finally said, then laughed at herself. "The truth is I don't know."

Jacob moved closer to her and held her hand.

She buried her face in his shoulder.

He stroked her hair.

When she looked at him he was watching her calmly.

She relaxed again.

"I'm sorry," she said.

He shook his head.

"This isn't how it's supposed to be," she said.

"No. It shouldn't have been us. It should have been the Commander or someone who actually knows what he's doing," Jacob agreed.

Val looked distressed.

Jacob stopped talking.

Val recovered and said, "Yeah, but I mean we should have been almost home now. In a few weeks we should have been free to... we should have been..." Val stopped talking and pulled away.

She wiped her eyes and looked at the displays.

Jacob watched her carefully, then smiled.

Val looked at him warily, but said nothing.

"Give me your hands," he said with such certainty she simply did it.

He held both her hands between his and looking straight at her said, "I have been in love with you for a long time now. I suppose I will love you forever. At least that part is the way it should be."

Val looked at him very seriously and said, "I love you too. I've loved you from the moment I met you."

Jacob thought for a moment. Val worried for a moment. Then Jacob said, "This isn't how it should be, but if we make it home, will you marry me?"

Val leaned forward, draped her arms over his shoulders, pressed her forehead against his and tried to stare into his eyes before giving up and kissing him.

Eighty-Seven

Ada, Lorie, and Deidre wiped out the last of their weekly allocation of fudgesicles before getting back to studying.

Deidre had spent half of the first two weeks of the trip partying with most of the terran crew members, but the third week Ada and Lorie heard her tell a man at the door, "No. I've got to graduate this year. Come by on the weekends." After that she always studied with them, except on the weekends.

Ada pulled her glasses off, rubbed her temples and then put the glasses in their case. "I think I'm finally getting this stuff," she said.

Deidre smiled at her. "I remember wondering if I could do it."

"You guys worry too much," Lorie said, "It's not all or nothing. You learn what you learn. Even if you don't graduate right away it doesn't mean you didn't learn anything."

"Yeah, but unless you pass the classes and graduate, no one knows you know it, and no one's going to pay just because you say you know it," Deidre responded.

"People don't pay for what you know. They pay for what you can do," Lorie said.

"Actually they pay you for what you actually do, but they won't hire you to do it unless they think you *can* do it."

"Then you just do it without them and get the end customer to pay you for it," Lorie responded.

Ada sighed.

"Are you guys done studying?" Deidre asked.

Ada and Lorie looked at each other and shrugged.

"I guess so," said Lorie.

"Great. It's Friday, there's a party going on in the crew break room, and there are too many guys there for me to handle on my own. Get your new clothes on and come with me."

"I don't know," Ada said, "those Tibetan guys in D2 said they'd take us for ice cream and movies."

Deidre made a face then said, "Hey you said you'd come with me one of these times. This is one of these times already."

"Alright we're coming," Lorrie said.

"Good. Get your new clothes on," Deidre said.

Thirty minutes later they were in the crew break room. The party was just getting started. The crew had assembled a pretty good spread of food on a table and music was going.

"Hey Deidre, glad you could make it," a slender guy with blonde hair said and gave her a kiss on the cheek. "Who are your friends?"

"Hi Marvyn, these are my pod mates Lorrie and Ada, but they're good Martian girls so keep their drinks wet."

"Anything for you, Deidre. Hey Mike - see if we've got any sodas in the back," Marvyn said, and threw a can to Deidre.

Mike came back a minute later with a bucket of sodas for the girls and sat down with them.

"Where are you from?" Lorie asked.

"Rapid City, Iowa," Mike said, "And you?"

"Mariner Valley and Arabia Terra," Ada said.

"What do you do between cycler runs?" Lorie asked.

"This is my first round trip. On Mars they have us working in the freight depots at the Harbor, but it's only three days a week, so I got to go exploring a lot. Some of the guys take classes and stuff."

By the time Mike got finished answering their questions, three other guys had gathered around.

Introductions were made all around.

Everyone took turns telling their stories. All the guys paid close attention while the girls told their stories. There was some banter. As the evening went on the conversations got louder and less focused. Most of the guys started to lose interest in Ada and Lorie. There were a few that stayed near them, but mostly just looked at them between drinks. The room started to split into groups and people started disappearing. Deidre came over to them laughing, focused a little, and said, "Are you girls sticking around?" Ada and Lorie looked at each other and shook their heads. Deidre turned to two guys she'd been talking with most of the night and said, "Hold on guys, let's walk my friends home."

"It's OK, Deidre, we can get home." Ada said.

"Are you sure?"

"Yes. It's not that big a ship," Ada said.

Deidre looked at the guys that had been sitting near Ada and Lorie, shrugged and said, "OK, see you later." But she waited until they'd gathered their things and started to leave before turning and going the other way with the guys.

The next week when Deidre invited them again, Ada said she had other plans, and Lorie said she didn't want to go. They took the Tibetans up on their offer instead.

That night Deidre came in moving quicker than usual, and changed the window to the news.

"Deidre, just use your implants," Lorie muttered.

"No you guys have to see this," Deidre said.

"What's going on?" Ada asked.

Deidre shushed them. "Watch!"

A map of the world was being shown with a deep pulsing red spreading out from the area of Constantinople. The announcer was saying, "Airborne filo virus C has jumped containment in Constantinople and has now been detected throughout both the Ottoman and Persian empires. Limited cases have been detected and contained in New York, London, Beijing, Miami, Caracas, Soule, and Johannesburg..."

"I hope they're going to be OK," Ada said.

"I hope we're going to be OK," Deidre said.

"What do you mean?" Ada said.

"This one's bad. It's going to get worse before we get there. Some of the crew are talking about staying on the cycler," Deidre said.

Lorie shuddered. "That would be a long trip."

Eighty-Eight

Jacob played close attention to snagging the last of four rocks on this trip. He caught it perfectly. He stayed with Val for the three hour acceleration run, then let the rock go perfectly.

After letting it go, instead of turning back they continued accelerating into the darkness away from the sun.

Once they were firmly on their way, Jacob went to the machine shop. He stopped by the freezer on his way and pulled out the mold, pointedly not looking in the back of the freezer.

In the machine shop, he dropped a few balls into the hopper and fired them at a sheet of metal at different powers. When he had worked his way up to full power the ice balls dented the sheet of metal. He tried different shapes for the projectiles; tried cooling them at different temperatures and pressures, but there was no improvement.

It got late and he threw down his tools in frustration and went upstairs. Val was letting the A. I. pilot the ship, but she put the navigation displays up on the monitor in the break room. They ate together. Jacob's forehead was perpetually wrinkled and he squinted at the light. After dinner, he dropped his forehead into the crook of his arm on the table. Val rubbed the back of his neck and he shuddered a little as he relaxed.

The next day he decided to hammer away at the same spot and see what happened on the sheet of metal.

He fired a whole tray of his projectiles at the same spot and managed to make a tear in the metal. Just for fun, he made another tray of them and fired until he made a hole.

Jacob looked at the results but didn't smile much. He patrolled the ship looking for higher pressure vessels, but didn't find any the right size that they could do without. He hunted through his supply of scrap metal, but didn't make any attempt to build his own pressure tank.

He finally shrugged and towed the contraption up to the Sensor Bay 3 and mounted it.

The next day Val helped him rig pressure lines to it and they made piles of projectiles.

In the evening they sat and read books together out loud and Val fell asleep on his shoulder when it was his turn to read.

He stopped reading and when she didn't wake up he leaned his head back, closed his eyes and felt her breathing against him. His brow wrinkled again until some resolution inside him hardened, then he fell asleep too.

In the morning he was up early. Val had to look for him for breakfast. She found him on the flight deck taking practice shots with their new air gun and trying to slave it to the laser and telescope in Sensor Bay 2. She helped him, then pulled him down to the break room.

After breakfast they worked on it more, made another batch of projectiles, then settled down to intercepting the first rock they had sent towards Ceres four days before. They found it. Jacob snagged it and Val set up for their first run at Ceres.

Jacob scowled a little as he waited.

Val noticed his expression and said, "Maybe it will work this time. I'm getting more accurate on every run."

"I don't think you are the problem," Jacob said. "Several of the shots we took on the last run hit within two meters. They should have done more damage. The craters were no larger than the rocks themselves and not very deep. Where did all that energy go?"

"I suppose it dissipated deeper into Ceres," Val said.

"It shouldn't have. The easiest path for the shock wave is up and out, not down."

"I could increase the speed again," Val offered.

"Can you hold the accuracy?"

Val bit her lower lip and frowned. "Maybe."

"Let's do it," Jacob said.

Val altered course and accelerated.

Jacob pointed the telescope at their target. They were aiming for the reactor building. Jacob fired the laser at it out of pure spite, but he couldn't tell if it even hit the building.

Val smiled slightly.

"It can't hurt," Jacob said defensively.

At 200 Kilometers, Val gave a signal and Jacob released the rock as smoothly as he could with four improvised talons. Val fired the maneuvering jets and they skimmed just above the 75 kilometer boundary they always respected, and simultaneously rolled the ship so the telescope could track the rock.

"If you can get engine 2 on line, I think I can cut it a little closer on the next run.

They watched the monitor. The icy rock slammed into the ground three meters from the reactor structure, but it didn't even shudder.

"There isn't even any material being ejected from the crater," Jacob cried out in disbelief.

Jacob played back the images in slow motion.

"It's like it's not even hitting the surface. It's like it's folding into it. Like the surface was made of pudding," Val said.

"Even pudding would splatter," Jacob said.

Val shook her head and started hunting for the next rock.

Jacob unstrapped, went to the engine room and repaired the number two engine again. He got back to the flight deck just in time to catch the second rock. Val maneuvered for another fast run.

"Use engine 2 for the approach and add engine 1 for our escape. That way if engine 2 shuts down early we just continue with number one and use our normal profile," Jacob said.

Val nodded agreement.

At 125 kilometers, Val gave a signal and Jacob released the rock. Val fired thrusters and brought engine one to 100%. They scrapped over the surface at 74 kilometers. Alarms sounded. Rainbow colors streaked across the field lines of their shields. Jacob began re-enabling breakers as he called out to Val.

Val didn't respond to his first call, but at the second she said, "I'm OK, I'm OK," and started looking over her displays. Once they were reoriented they checked the recording of their flyby, but it cut-off before the rock hit. They flew over the site and looked.

"Over shot by one meter," Val said.

"Looks like you got a piece of the containment building on the way down." Jacob said.

"Where? I don't see it."

"There," Jacob said pointing to the corner of the building.

"Are you sure? That looks awfully smooth. I think it's just a shadow."

"A shadow of what?'

Val maneuvered the ship to view it at a different angle. The corner of the building was sheared off smoothly.

"It's like it melted," she said.

Val set out for the third rock.

The third run missed by a meter and a half, but they stayed outside the 75 KM limit.

They set out for the fourth rock. After Jacob grabbed it, Val slowed it and set up for an extra-long run.

Jacob watched Val intently as the moment for release approached. She nodded, he released it and braced for the twisting turn Val put the ship through.

Jacob thought he saw the rock hit the building. When they had passed Ceres they reran the images.

They had hit it, took off a section of the roof, but so cleanly that nothing inside was damaged.

They reoriented the ship and hovered 78 KM over the reactor site.

"We should hear from Mars in twenty minutes," Val said.

"The heck with that," Jacob said and opened fire with ice bullets through the hole in the reactor ceiling.

Val added laser pulses from the welding unit. They fired into the dark hole until they were out of ice bullets, but nothing happened. They pulled away to a safer distance.

"We need a bigger rock," Jacob said.

"We need any rock at all," Val said.

Mars sent a message to prepare a cargo container for a run the next day.

Jacob and Val loaded the cargo container with as many mining explosives as they could find.

Val went to bed and Jacob began improvising contact detonators.

In the morning they put all the trash they could find into the cargo container to increase its mass, then they welded it shut.

After lunch they suited up and went back into the cargo bay. Val shut down the engines, vented the room slowly then opened the cargo doors. Jacob extended a lift from the ceiling and grasped the cargo pod. He tied off, then unstrapped the pod, lifted it off the deck with the lift, gingerly moved it to the cargo door and lowered it to within an ten cm of the floor.

"That's as far as I can get it with the lift. Come get me if I fall out."

"Will do," Val said.

Jacob slowly released the container and waited to see that it was not wobbling or drifting too much, then stepped forward, looked for the center of the back wall of the container, then locked his boots to the deck and pushed hard. The container moved almost imperceptibly, and Jacob unlocked his boots and stepped back. It took ten minutes for the container to clear of the ship, and another twenty minutes before Val dared to touch so much as a maneuvering thruster.

"Slick," Val said when they finally closed the doors and re-pressurized.

"Yeah, now I have to go change my underwear..." Jacob said.

Back on the flight deck Val moved them over the cargo container and Jacob tried to grapple it. The square shape and unyielding metal made it difficult.

"Got it," he said on the third try.

Val eased them onto a path towards Ceres and began accelerating.

Jacob watched the instruments carefully. When they got close to the release point, he turned his gaze on Val.

"Ready?" she said without looking at him.

"Ready," he said.

"Now," she said nodding.

Jacob released the grapple, but one talon didn't release. The container twisted until the talon snapped off. Val executed her last second thruster firing to get clear of Ceres just as the container started to tumble. The container slammed into the grapple, mangling it, then tumbled into the underside of the ship and detonated. Alarms sounded. Val increased thrust on engine number two and they cleared Ceres.

"Hull breach!" Jacob shouted over the alarms, and worked feverishly closing doors remotely.

Val closed the flight deck door.

When Jacob was done sending commands, he looked over the console and shook his head.

"We've lost pressure to half the first deck. I don't know how much of it we'll be able to get back."

"We lost partial pressure on the mid-deck because one of the corridor hatches didn't close on its own, but it's re-pressurizing now."

They replayed the images of the grapple getting torn apart, pausing occasionally.

"Can we fix it?" Val hoped.

Jacob just shook his head. "Even if we had access to the machine shop, which right now we don't, it would take both of us working as hard as we could for weeks to build another grapple. That's if we had the materials, which we don't. Even then it probably wouldn't work very well."

They sat in silence for several minutes. Jacob covered his face. Val closed her eyes.

Suddenly Jacob sat up and started working the console again. He managed to re-pressurize part of the lower deck. They clicked through various cameras that were still working on different decks to get an idea of how extensive the damage was.

"I think we can get the machine shop and the cargo hold back," Val said.

Jacob nodded, "With a little heavy welding I think we can create a pressurized path to them too, but it will take days. We don't have a lot of days left. We have to decide if that is our priority."

"Mars may have something to say about that too," Val said.

"Mars isn't here. It's our decision no matter what they say," Jacob said.

"What are our options?" Val asked.

"We've got the air gun."

"Anything else?" Val asked.

"We might be able to build the mother of all hydrogen masers, but I don't think we could ever generate a strong enough wave to do any damage, and it would take a week or more to try."

"What if we mixed hydrogen and oxygen in a tank with an igniter on a manual timer, attached a magnet to it and put it on a collision course with one of the emitters?" Val suggested.

"Without the grapple I don't see how we can aim it with enough accuracy to hit the array. Maybe we could build some kind of a clamp on the bottom of the ship... but there's a lot of wreckage... better on the top of the ship. But again, it would take at least a few days to get the machine shop back on line to build the parts, then a few days to install it."

"We've got 33 days left. That gives us a couple of tries."

"Actually it's only 32 days. Without any mass, the whole planetoid has been acting like a solar sail and accelerating slightly, besides we can't let it get that close. We have to leave a margin for error. We've got 27 days max."

"I think no matter what we try, we are going to need access to that machine shop."

Jacob thought for a minute and reluctantly agreed.

They had already suited up when Mars sent a message telling them to stand by while they analyzed the damage reports. They ignored it. By midnight they had made a pressurized path to the machine shop.

The machine shop floor was warped for about a meter on the bow side of the room. There was no fixing it. They resolved to build an airtight box around it instead. They went looking for metal. Val went to the cargo bay and walked towards the remaining cargo container menacingly with a welding laser in hand. Jacob watched for a second, then said, "Hold on. We may need that."

"What for?"

"We just might. There's plenty of metal in the unpressurized sections."

Val shrugged, then stretched and yawned. "OK", she said, "but we have to be careful in there."

Jacob surprised her by saying, "Let's get some sleep. We're going to sleep at least four hours no matter what we do. We might as well go in there rested."

"Sounds good," Val said.

It took two more days to get the machine shop back in working order.

Val wrote a big "23" on the wall of the shop in chalk.

"Now what?" she asked.

"Let's make more bullets."

They spent the whole day making pellets and piling them up in the freezer. When the first batch was done, they moved them up to the hopper and then maneuvered the ship into range of the most damaged array and opened fire with both the laser and the ice pellets. By the end of the first day they had made some fairly impressive dents.

The next day Val kept firing while Jacob made and moved pellets, but by the end of the day they had only managed to broaden the dents. None of them were any deeper.

They tried again the next day, and the next.

By the time Val had erased the "23" and written "20" they had really given up, but they tried for another day anyway.

Val began scavenging for tanks and trying to build her hydrogen fire bomb, while Jacob started taking apart the ship's precision clock for parts to make a huge maser.

Mars was curiously quiet. They checked in once a day, and agreed with whatever Jacob and Val proposed to do.

After five days of fabricating maser parts and helping Val lug tanks around, Jacob suddenly put down his tools and looked at the table in front of him. He looked at Val struggling with the finishing touches on her device and went to her. He held the detonator assembly steady while she welded it tight, then suited up and helped her lug it to the fuel processing section and fill it with hydrogen and oxygen. Then they lugged it to the cargo bay, opened the doors, tied off the bomb and pushed it out. He secured a second line to it, clipped himself to the maintenance rail on the side of the door and started pulling the bomb up the side of the ship. Val came behind the bomb, pushing it. After three hours they had it tied down on the top of ship. They reentered the ship through a maintenance hatch on the top, secured the cargo bay and collapsed.

When they woke up, they ate, gathered their tools, spent eight hours building a latch they could remotely release, and put the bomb on it. They practiced releasing it a few times, then Val wired up the detonator and they went inside. They ate and collapsed again.

When they awoke they went straight to the flight deck, munching on protein bars as they went.

Val took control of the ship back from the A. I. and they made their bombing run.

Val nodded, Jacob released and they watched the bomb miss the reactor building by five meters and disappear into the ice without exploding.

Val cried, unashamed and Jacob held her.

"What do we do now?" Val said.

"You go sleep. I'll build my maser."

"I'll help you."

"Tomorrow. I want to work alone tonight."

Val cried again, but she went to bed and slept.

Jacob went to the machine shop, looked at the maser parts, then gathered his tools. He went to the cargo hold and started welding brackets inside the cargo container. He suited up and went into the damaged sections, disassembled the emergency lighting systems, stole all the batteries from them and put them into the cargo container. When he had 150 of them, he stopped and started wiring them into arrays. He pulled out the spare transponders, built them into the container and wired them up. He was trying to think of where he might find pressure cylinders when he noticed he had been working for twenty straight hours.

He checked on Val. She was still asleep. He went back to his room and crashed.

When he woke up Val wasn't in her room.

He found her in the machine shop working on the maser.

"There you are!" she said, "What did you do yesterday? This thing is no further along than it was the day before."

"I fell asleep," Jacob said.

Val accepted that and they worked together for a while on the maser. When the electronics and stimulators were finished, they went looking for a cylinder to hold the hydrogen and form the cavity.

Jacob looked at all kinds of wildly inappropriate cylinders and even some tanks that weren't cylinders before he finally went back to the first one they had looked at. They towed it into the shop and started assembling it, then quit for the night.

Jacob waited until Val was asleep and went back down to the lower decks. He pushed one of the tanks he had selected earlier in the day to the cargo hold and welded it into the container. After five hours of work, he went to bed.

Jacob woke up and saw Val floating over him. She was stroking his forehead with a worried look on her face.

"Are you OK?" She asked.

Jake nodded, "Just a little tired."

By the end of the day they had finished the maser and begun low power testing.

The next day they moved it to the cargo hold and strapped it to the floor pointing out the open door.

Next they ran cables to it and connected it. Then they moved upstairs and rotated the telescope to match the angle of the maser.

"How are we going to calibrate this?" Val asked.

"Hopefully we will see some ice melting," Jacob said.

They turned the maser on and ramped up the power. They saw nothing. They moved the telescope around looking for any signs of melting, but saw nothing. They waited a couple of hours, but the results were the same. Jacob powered the maser down and remotely closed the cargo doors.

Val looked at him surprised.

"I'm tired. Let's take this up in the morning."

Val reluctantly agreed.

They took the time to eat a real meal, then went to bed. A half an hour later, Jacob came out of his quarters and went to the cargo hold. He filled the pressure tank in the container with oxygen. Then he pulled a chair out of the abandoned observation deck and welded it into the container. He went into the lower deck locker room, took all six space suits out of the lockers, lugged them one by one into the container and put them into brackets he had built for them. He was hooking them up in series when he felt Val's hand on his shoulder.

He turned to look at her. She looked at him searchingly.

"What are you doing?" she said.

Jacob didn't say anything.

Val peered into his eyes.

"The maser isn't going to work," Jacob said.

Val waited.

"I've known it wouldn't work since before I started building it."

Val said nothing.

"Val, we are out of time and out of options. We have to use option 4."

"What do you mean by option 4?"

"Do you remember the first list Mars sent us? Do you remember how the numbers skipped from 3 to 5?"

"Sure, but it doesn't mean anything. Everyone was rushing."

"It means they had something on the list that they took off before they sent it to us."

"What?" Val said softly but defiantly.

"We only have one thing left that we can throw at Ceres - this ship."

Eighty-Nine

Val looked around the cargo container. "You're building an escape pod," she said flatly.

She looked at the single chair near the racks of batteries and the tanks, then looked back at Jacob.

"It needs another chair."

Jacob looked at the floor.

"It needs another chair," Val repeated.

"When the ship hits the field the electronics will fail. The maneuvering thrusters are hydraulically controlled. There's a chance that if I put enough shielding around the flight deck I might be able to remain conscious long enough to keep correcting course up to the last minute. It has to be a direct hit. For whatever reason, we're not getting explosions from our kinetic projectiles. The energy is going straight in. So I have to hit the reactor straight on and drive it into Ceres."

Val stared at him, her eyes filling.

"So you want to put me in box and push me out into space alone."

"I want you to live. The Hercules will arrive ten days or so after... I think you can make it that long. This way at least you have a chance. "

"Were you going to ask me about this?"

"Yes... when it was ready."

"Well the answer is no. I'm the better pilot anyway."

"I don't know that I can save Mars, but I have to try, and I have to save you," Jacob said.

"Save me from death?"

"Yes."

"There are worse things. If we were married and had children at home that needed us, I would get in the box. But we don't have children. We started this together and we will end it together and we will go on to the next adventure together. I will not spend 40 *years mourning you."

Jacob looked at the floor. He blinked two big blobs of water out of his eyes and they drifted slowly to stern.

He hugged her.

They closed up the cargo container together, went to the flight deck, and informed Mars of their new plan.

Anxious hands
Hold tight
Chaos flows to calm
Fall head first through dawn

Ninety

Seven days.

Seven days until the danger to Mars was certain, but no one wanted to wait that long. They really had five days left to live. They no longer wrote numbers on the wall in chalk. There was no need. Each hour was weighed, was felt as it slipped away to nothing.

"Let's get married now," Jacob said.

They were sitting at breakfast, and he was perfectly serious.

"Why?" Val asked.

"So we can be together," he said.

"We will be together for the rest of our lives," she said.

"So we can really be together," he said.

Val looked at him.

"Would you be asking me now if we weren't about to die?" she asked.

Jacob spent the next two seconds trying to read her face.

"Just tell me what you actually think," Val said. "I'm not going to get upset or hurt or anything. It's not going to change anything. I just need to know."

"No."

Val's face clouded.

"I would be asking you in four months with your father's approval and a proper ring," he said.

Val studied his face. She loved that face.

"We will have less than five days together," she said.

"We'll live those five days, but that doesn't make the future, however distant, any less real," he said.

"This ship is no temple. The acting commander of the Astral 4 is no sealer. All we'll get is five days of marriage. That might be harder than just not doing it at all."

Jacob smiled, "If we get married, and make sure everyone knows what we want, they'll seal us after we're gone."

Val brightened, "I always thought of that as something for dead people who had no opportunity."

"We are dead people who had no opportunity. We're 18 half-*years old. When were we supposed to get married, at 16?" he said.

She hugged him and said, "You're right! You're very right! Let's get married. Let's get very married... as soon as possible."

They sent messages to family.

The first responses back were confusion, which melted to comprehension and then joy tinged with something else.

They started an application for a marriage license, but hit a snag.

"Marriage licenses may take up to seven days to process. Please plan accordingly."

They groaned and hit send anyway.

Assuming the license came through, it seemed wrong to try to marry themselves, but they were the only ones on the ship.

"We could contact the Hercules," Val suggested. "They're close enough to conduct a ceremony in near real time, and the captain is authorized under Martian maritime law to do it."

"If we contact the Hercules, they'll tell the Directorate what we are doing," Jacob warned.

"We *are* in violation of a *few* fraternization rules," Val said. "On the other hand, what are they going to do, dock our pay?"

"They could cut off our communications," Jake said and added,

"Let's see what happens with the license."

Three hours later, a message labeled, "RE: Your Marriage," arrived from the Mars Space Directorate.

"Ouch! I forgot they were monitoring everything," Jacob said as sat staring at the message.

"Just open it," Val said.

He opened it.

"RE: your marriage

We took the liberty of expediting your Marriage License request. Please see the attached.

- Directorate staff."

They clicked the attachment and found themselves looking at their marriage license. It seemed unreal.

"I guess that's permission," Val said.

They contacted Captain Herrera of the Hercules and he agreed to officiate at their wedding.

Even though they couldn't use them, they both got sealing recommends.

Between letters and interviews, Val stationed the ship over the weaker emitter and fired at it over and over with the laser and air gun. Jacob came onto the flight deck and watched what she was doing until she paused, shrugged and said, "I'd really prefer to live right now." Jacob went below and made more ice bullets.

In the afternoon, video messages from their families arrived. They also each got individual vids from each other's parents.

-

On day four they sat together and made a video to their families. They tried to answer questions they couldn't answer, and tried to speak of beginnings without mentioning the ends they both felt. Despite their best efforts, the strain was visible on their faces.

When Jake and Ellie saw it, they understood what was not said and loved them for it. Jake noticed the way they sat together, shoulders even, as though they were going to lift something together. Ellie just cried.

Val's parents couldn't bring themselves to watch it for three hours, but after they did her father said, "How can they do this?" and put his face in his hands. Her mother rubbed his back and said, "How could they not?" Then they both cried.

Jacob wrote a long letter to both Jake and Ellie acknowledging what he had put them through. They wrote and told him how much they loved him.

Before going to bed they shot at the emitter some more, then moved the ship to the safe side of Ceres, and re-enabled the AI.

They lingered on the flight deck, unwilling to say good night, but unwilling to stay where they were.

"This is stupid," Val said shaking her head. "We should just go."

But neither moved. At length Jacob said, "Let's make it a race." They flew down the hall from the flight deck, chasing each other. Jacob got the early lead because he was closest to the door. Val pushed off the wall and shot under him. He grabbed her ankle as she passed, pulled her back, then grabbed her by the waist. She twisted to break his hold, came face to face, wrapped her arms around his neck, and pulled him close. Jacob drug one foot along the wall to slow them down, wrapped his other leg around her legs and held on until they stopped in midair. Then they kissed, and kissed some more, and held on, and let go and floated away from each other waving goodnight.

The morning of day three they were surprised to see a log entry showing that Ceres had regained its mass for fourteen seconds during the night.

"It's working!" Val said.

Jacob smiled and hugged her, but said nothing about it. Jacob cooked a real breakfast and served it to Val.

"I didn't know you could cook."

"I'm a good cook. My momma taught me how."

"Then why didn't you cook for us before?"

Jacob shrugged, "We were always busy."

After breakfast they answered messages then continued firing urgently at the emitter for as long as they could. It yielded nothing.

In the evening they gave up for the last time, turned off the lights, and stood in the dark letting it all go.

They curled up together on a couch in the breakroom and held each other for a long time, longing for more, half justifying more, and then slowly pulling apart to go to their separate beds.

On the morning of day two Val stayed in her sack for fifteen minutes after waking up, thinking.

They decided to ignore all messages for a few hours, went to the observatory, sat under the stars, held hands, and said nothing.

When they came down and sorted messages, they found a request for a statement to the media, which they ignored, and messages from their siblings, which they did not ignore.

The youngest of them were only beginning to understand what was about to happen. The oldest fully understood but could say little. Before anyone could stop him, Sam asked if they would be shooting stars and Jacob said he thought they might. Cavita showed him some flowers she grew. Chris was quiet a long time, subtly shaking his head at intervals before he could say, "I wish I could think of some other way. I wish there was some other way. I wish so many things. I already miss you brother," and disconnected. Val's oldest little sister said, "This is messed up. Don't do this. Come home."

They answered each message as best they could for over an hour and sat drained.

When they were about to shut down the mail a message arrived from the Captain of the Hercules finalizing arrangements.

Jacob and Val looked at each other.

"Let's just be happy," Val said.

Jacob watched her.

She flushed, and said, "Stop looking at me."

Jacob leaned back and kept watching her.

She turned her back to him then started laughing. She turned around, and hugged and kissed him, and laughed again.

Ninety-One

They each woke up alone for the last time at about the same moment. Each took his time getting up. Each thought about the day ahead.

Jacob took a long look in the mirror. He looked at one side of his face and then the other. Finally he smirked at himself, and shaved.

Val scrunched into a corner, pulled her knees to her chest and wrapped her arms around them, thinking. Later she looked through her clothes deciding what to wear at the wedding. She would wear her dress uniform, but she wanted to improvise some sort of accessories for the occasion.

When they finally came out of their rooms, they had their regular breakfast tradition. Val cooked for real and it wasn't bad.

Jacob sat close to her and called up wedding planning and travel guides he had downloaded the night before. They played at planning the wedding they would have had at home for over an hour.

Val flipped through the flowers and chose a bouquet of yellow roses with red ribbons. They looked at Martian opals and sapphires, and imported diamonds before choosing simple wedding bands. They discussed music for the reception and what they would have made their siblings wear. They looked at fancy hotels and horseback riding side trips. Then Jacob chose a honeymoon on the south side of Mars where it was late summer and they could lie out in the sun during the day, and swim, and stay up at night to watch the stars under a warm sky. Val showed him the swim suit she would wear.

The real ceremony was planned for the late afternoon to give people time to gather on late notice, and for once there seemed to be no urgency about anything. All the remaining resources of the ship were theirs. Time was ending, so there was no need to rush. Eternity was opening, but it would wait as long as needed.

About 11:30, Jacob excused himself.

"I'm going to spend some time alone."

Val nodded.

Jacob went to the machine shop, opened the printer controls and as planned, there were dozens of new designs uploaded from Directorate staff for bouquets, rings, necklaces, wreaths, and bracelets that resembled things Val had picked out in the wedding guides. Jacob set the plastic printer working on a bouquet and the metal printer working on her ring. While they printed, he looked at the title space of each design. Directorate staff had used the limited space to write messages to him and Val that the tight communications controls would never let them say directly. One said, "Hug that girl for us." Another said, "We will always remember." A third said simply, "Happy Wedding Day."

When the bouquet was done, he set the plastic printer to making a wreath and started cleaning up the bouquet. When her ring was done, he set the metal printer to work on his ring. Then he got out the paints and carefully painted the bouquet. Before the bouquet was done, both his ring and the wreath were done. He set them aside and started the plastic printer making beads for a "pearl" necklace, and the metal printer to making bracelets.

At 1:30 he was stringing the last pearls when Val's voice sounded in his ear, "Are you going to keep your fiancé company on her wedding day?"

"I'll have to think that over... OK, I'll be there in a few minutes," Jacob said, then scrambled to hide his creations in a box in case Val decided to check on him with the cameras.

Once he had everything safely stowed, he finished stringing the "pearls" and put them in the box.

Jacob met Val on the flight deck and looked around it. The serious looking consoles, the closed viewing portal, the vague smell of perspiration they could never completely remove from the room all seemed to belong to someone else now.

He looked at Val. She looked at him. He took her hand and they left the flight deck.

They ate a late lunch and cleaned up. They straightened the break room and tried to make it look better than it did. Jacob re-aimed the camera to eliminate the clutter in the background, then had the idea to turn off all the lights except one near the camera.

"That looks a lot better," Val said.

"Yea a bit less... cafeteria."

"We had some good times in a cafeteria," Val objected.

"Yeah, but that's not exactly the lasting image I'd prefer to leave with our families." Jacob regretted saying it before the last word was out of his mouth.

Val's smile dimmed for a second and she looked at nothing in particular before looking at Jacob and saying "No, I suppose not."

"They'll have each other," Jacob said.

"And we'll have each other," Val said.

They went to their rooms to change. When they got to Jacob's room he said, "Wait." He went inside, took their rings out of the box, and brought the box to Val.

"These are for you. Open it in your room, and if anything is too awful, just leave it in your room and we'll pretend you never saw them."

Val looked at him warily.

"Just go," he said, and went back inside.

While Jacob changed into his dress uniform and fixed his hair, Val went through the box and smiled at each little thing she found. She put on her dress uniform, put her hair up and tried to remember how to put on makeup.

When she came out, she was wearing everything from the box except the pearls.

She held those in her hand. "I'm going to need help with these. They don't have a clasp."

Jacob put them around her neck and tied a knot while she held them in place.

"I knew knot tying would come in handy someday," Jacob said.

Val kissed him and they went to the break room.

When they got there, they made sure they were standing in the right spot so the camera would get a good image, then they looked at the image of Captain Herrera on the Hercules and waited for him to speak. He said a few words of greeting, then spoke about marriage, and finally he asked each in turn if they were willingly giving themselves to the other and would turn from all others. They each said they did and they would. Then he said that by virtue of the authority vested in him as a ship's captain and in accordance with the laws of Mars he pronounced them husband and wife until death parted them.

The Captain added, "No one on Mars will rest until that last phrase is erased. Don't doubt that."

They could hear applause coming from those gathered on the Hercules.

Then Val said to Jacob, "I have a surprise for you too," and she brought out a little wedding cake she had made. It was slightly lop-sided, but Jacob held it up to the camera and said, "It's too bad we can't share it with you. We'll have to eat it all ourselves."

They did, too. They ate the cake and hugged each other while they waited the forty minutes it took for their families to see the wedding and send messages back to them.

For their families, the marriage had just barely happened when they sent the messages.

All members of both families managed to make it to Paititi to be together for the wedding, except Ada. They took turns in front of the camera, but you could hear the others in the background. There was a lot of hugging going on. Ellie cried again. Val's father cried and it wasn't until near the end of the messages that the tone shifted from congratulations, to goodbye. Soon after, the transmission ended.

Then unexpectedly it started again, but it had a different sound and was from a different room. Ada was looking at Jacob, her big brown eyes moist. "Well kid, it looks like despite everything you got yourself a good wife. Valerie, welcome to the family. I look forward to getting to know you someday. Who knows, it may be sooner than we expect. Jacob, when I asked you to look out for our folks..." she had to stop for a second, "I'm sorry..." she said, "That was going to be funny, but it just isn't. I'm sorry. Thank you for what you are doing. I'd better go. Goodbye."

The transmission ended. It was just the two of them. But it was the two of them.

Ninety-Two

Ada clicked disconnect and silence filled the booth. She closed her eyes hard and tears squeezed out from between the lids. She took a few ragged breaths, smoothed out her face and opened her eyes. She straightened her clothes, and left the booth. The officers she encountered nodded at her, respect and sympathy in their eyes.

Some of the people she encountered in the crew and passenger areas glared at her. Word had gotten around that she had been given priority access to the Officers' Communications Booth and there was a keener interest in private communication than usual, with goodbye calls going to both Mars and Earth for different reasons.

Over the previous few weeks the captain repeatedly assured the passengers that except for moving their landing site to New Zealand, there were no changes to their flight plan, but rations were cut to subsistence levels as a "precaution."

New Zealand so far was disease free and had cut commerce and transport early.

Deidre stopped studying again. Often when she came back from parties she would have a little extra food. The girls found a hollow place in the wall beside a maintenance hatch were they hid the extras. Deidre went to more parties than usual, but she didn't laugh anymore, and she never asked Lorie or Ada to go with her anymore.

At first there were more activities for the passengers than usual, but after a while attendance dropped and they scaled them back.

Ada stopped going to the observation deck at night because she could never get it to herself.

One day Lorie said, "Do you think we should stop working out? If we let ourselves atrophy a little we won't need as much food."

Deidre looked at her and shook her head, "I think you better work out more and get as strong as you can."

Ninety-Three

Val and Jacob paused awkwardly in the hall.

"Where do we sleep?" Val asked.

"Anywhere we want. We have the whole ship," Jacob said.

Val thought for a minute, "My room or yours. I don't want to go anywhere else."

"Let's get your stuff and go to my room," Jacob said.

In Val's room, Jacob detached her sleeping bag and towed it to his room while Val gathered some things and brought them over.

Jacob unzipped both their bags and zipped them together, then anchored one end to the wall.

He turned up the temperature in the room, brushed his teeth and reclined in a corner waiting for Val.

Val brushed her teeth, removed her makeup, brushed her hair for a long time and then turned to face Jacob.

He returned her gaze with nearly believable calm.

She tapped the wall behind her with her foot and drifted over to him. He grabbed her ankle and pulled her down, closer to eye level.

"Well, Mrs. Billings, what should we do now?"

"I think you should kiss me, Mr. Billings."

"I think I will," said Jacob, and closed the door.

Ninety-Four

The A. I. watched the sky all around the ship in many frequencies with its unblinking eyes. Ceres was nearby. Mars was a long ways away but the A. I. kept track of its location too. It listened to its own engines, its boiling core, the vibration of its half empty tanks, and the creaking of its weakened frame. It sniffed the air inside the ship constantly. It sorted through the logs generated by hundreds of subsystems watching for indications of problems or opportunities. It watched the crew individually and as a team. It tasted their urine, smelled their sweat in the air, read their log entries, and watched every keystroke they made on any subsystem.

It day dreamed near term scenarios and then compared them to what actually occurred, and tried to understand how to improve its predictions, subtly rewriting its heuristics within predetermined outer parameters. It never really slept.

It wasn't sleeping now. The A. I. was thinking hard. It didn't help that one of its three brains had frozen up, and another was running significantly slower than the first. It made the A. I. alternately uncertain of its decisions, and completely certain of its decisions. The ship was badly damaged and low on propellant. Each day that passed reduced the probability of a safe return to Mars. Miss Kyria had clearly told the A. I. that the Ceres base was dead, and its own scans confirmed it, but she had also clearly said that staying near it was a high priority.

Mr. Billings had said many confusing things about Ceres. He had clearly said that it had volume but no mass. Its own instruments confirmed that, but that conflicted with all previous experience. Perhaps Mr. Billings was mistaken about the identity of the object. This object clearly was not where Ceres should be. Perhaps the object was a three dimensional projection of Ceres. This fit previous experience better, but there was no precedent for such a large projection. The A. I. began searching research journals for work that might have led to such a development, but found nothing recent. It looked for Ceres where it should be, but didn't find it. The A. I. could come to no certain conclusion. It would have liked to ask Miss Kyria or Mr. Billings for clarification, but they were not answering its quiet requests, and Miss Kyria had clearly told it not to sound an alarm unless there was an immediate risk to the ship or its occupants. The A. I. marked the question unresolved and set it aside to consider other items.

The condition of the crew required further analysis. Their daily behavior had deviated from the norm considerably ever since they lost their leader. It also fluctuated so wildly that no new norm could be established. Conversations between Miss Kyria and Mr. Billings contained many factual errors, and their actions were sometimes opposite from what they appeared to decide. Although such occurrences were common with crew members, particularly young crew members, these occurrences were much more common than with any crew the A. I. had records for. The most recent five days were the most aberrant. They had ceased most normal activities. They had been communicating frequently with family members on Mars. They seemed unconcerned about the condition of the ship. The probability of a successful return to Mars had seriously degraded, yet their stress hormone levels had decreased. Miss Kyria and Mr. Billings had jointly run multiple simulations of the ship colliding with Ceres on multiple occasions. Currently Miss Kyria was not in her assigned sleeping space, nor at a duty post. She was in Mr. Billing's quarters. They had both removed their biometric sensors. They had covered both cameras in the room. Despite those limitations, the A. I. could hear that they were not sleeping, that in fact they had elevated heart rates.

The A. I. ran 400 near term scenarios and evaluated them. The worst case scenarios ended in the deliberate destruction of the ship and crew, the accidental loss of the ship and crew due to catastrophic failure of the ship and inaction by the crew, the accidental loss of the ship due to overuse of limited supplies by the crew, and the loss of the crew to suicide. The best case scenario was rescue of the ship and crew by the Hercules. Bad scenarios outnumbered even moderately good scenarios forty to one.

The A. I. began rerunning the scenarios and changing one variable within its control at a time and concluded that if it took immediate action it could improve the ratio of good to bad outcomes to better than 4:1. In many scenarios the ship was spared, and in most the crew was spared. It chose the best ranking scenario and reran it looking for optimizations. When further optimizations started producing worse predicted results it rolled back to the most optimal plan. Having selected an optimal plan, it put the plan to a vote of the three brains. Number 1 approved, number 2 abstained, number 3 approved.

The A. I. ceased trying to contact Miss Kyria and Mr. Billings.

It sent a heavily coded priority message to the Mars Directorate and waited for a reply. While it waited it continually updated and re-optimized the plan. Forty three minutes passed and a heavily coded priority message came back from the Mars Directorate. The A. I. sent copies to each brain for decoding and analysis. Brain 1 said the message denied permission for the plan and ordered the A. I. to obey Miss Kyria and Mr. Billings. Brain 2 said the message was unreadable. Brain 3 did not respond within the voting cycle. A one to one tie existed. The A. I. reran the voting cycle 57 times with the same result. On the 58th attempt, brain 1 said the message denied permission, brain 2 said the message was unreadable, and brain 3 said it was unable to read the message. The A. I. concluded that the message was unreadable and requested that the message be resent. It repeated the request three times, then concluded that Mars was unable to provide input, and set course for the Hercules.

Ninety-Five

Jacob woke up in a tangled ball of arms and legs. It was not uncomfortable. It was warm. During the night their double wide sleeping bag had drifted against the port wall of the room and Jacob was lightly squished between the wall and Val. He closed his eyes again.

Val was awake. She didn't move when Jacob stirred.

They stayed in that position for a long time, until Jacob finally said, "Are you hungry?"

Val considered this for longer than seemed necessary and then said, "Yes?"

Jacob laughed a little.

Val climbed out of the sack and began drifting to stern. She landed and said, "That's not right."

Jacob was beside her instantly.

They got to a console and checked logs.

The A. I. had dutifully logged,

" 20:37:02 - Crew incapacitated."

"22:43:10 - Mars Directorate unable to communicate."

"22:43:14 - Set course for the ship Hercules "

Val groaned and sent instructions to the A. I. to return to Ceres.

The log added,

"09:32:21 - Unauthorized command rejected."

Jacob took over the keyboard, logged in and sent the same instructions.

The log added, "09:33:09 - Unauthorized command rejected."

Jacob banged his hands on the console in frustration and had to catch himself as he began to tumble.

Five minutes later they were on the flight deck. Two minutes after that they had disconnected the A. I. and set course for Ceres.

"What's the damage?" Jacob asked.

"We are 28 hours from Ceres... no wait, engine two is offline again... we are 41 hours from Ceres, unless you can get that engine back on line again," Val said.

"That's not good. That only leaves about 69 or 68 hours of budget for Ceres to stay outside the orbit of Mars. That's cutting it too close."

"Well then, my amazing husband, fix that engine."

Jacob suited up and went to the engine room. There wasn't anything obviously wrong with engine two, other than that all its control circuitry was cobbled together with questionable parts left over from its damaged neighbor and components removed during maintenance earlier in the trip.

He reached in and felt all the components. The ones that should have been hot weren't. He followed the wiring up to the next set of components. They should have been vibrating softly, but they weren't. He felt farther up the wire and found a connector was loose. He crimped it back in place and the engine started up again.

"Thank you sir," Val's voice said in his ear. "Tell me when you are clear."

Jacob stepped out of the engine compartment, closed the door and said, "I'm clear."

"Throttling up," Val said. Jacob leaned against the wall of the engine room as the acceleration pushed on him. Then he leaned forward and trudged uphill to the locker room.

He stripped off his suit and went up to the flight deck in his underwear.

"Rarrr rarrr!" Val said when he sat down in the command chair and strapped in.

Val reached over and put her hand on his thigh.

"Miss Kyria! What are you doing!?" Jacob said and pushed her hand away with mock indignation on his face.

"Nothing I don't have a license for," Val said.

"Oh. Well in that case..." Jacob said, and put her hand back.

She smacked him on the thigh and then pretended to pay attention to her displays.

After a while Jacob got up and went to where he had stashed his flight suit in the corridor, put it on and came back.

"That's not an improvement," Val said.

"Well, either I was under dressed for the occasion, or you were over dressed," Jacob said.

Val unzipped her flight suit about ten centimeters.

"You'll have to do better than that," Jacob said.

"There's still some broken glass in here," Val said.

"I guess you're right," Jacob said.

Val looked at him. He was looking down her shirt.

She turned so he could get a better look.

He pretended not to be interested.

"Oh, stop it," she said.

Jacob went back to his room to get the sleeping bags and laid them out on the floor in the corridor while Val set the dumb autopilot to hold course, and the A. I. to alarm if anything approached the ship. Then he went back to the break room and brought back as much easy to eat food as he could carry. When he got back to the sleeping bags Val was inside them. Her clothes were not.

In the late evening Val put her shoes on and ran to the flight deck. She cut the engines, rotated the ship, restarted the engines, turned the autopilot back on, and came back. Jacob set the anchors on the sleeping bag, just in case of sudden acceleration changes, crawled back in with Val and slept deeply until morning.

In the morning, they woke up to the sound of the A. I. chiming a minor proximity alarm. They were within thirty minutes of a large object, presumably Ceres.

They looked each other in the face for a long time, memorizing eyes, noses, lips, ears, and small smiles. Then the time came. They dressed and sat in their chairs on the flight deck. Val throttled back the engines, rotated the ship, and saw Ceres looming large in the display of the forward cameras on the ceiling.

"I'll get us in position for our run," Val said.

"I'll get us ready," Jacob said, and left the flight deck.

Val reoriented the ship and flew high above the plane of the ecliptic for twenty minutes, then nosed over and paralleled Ceres.

During that time, Jacob lugged in a bunch of wire mesh, which he arranged in a bubble around their seats and attached to the ship's ground. He left again, came back in his space suit and strapped in.

Val turned the controls over to him, left and came back in her space suit. She sealed the door behind her.

After she strapped in, they both put on their helmets and slowly decompressed the flight deck in stages, pausing to check their suits for leaks. They plugged the suits into the ship's systems to keep them topped off then Jacob pressed a couple of icons on his console and the metal shield opened on the front viewing window. They reoriented their seats to look out the window. Ceres was a brilliant white below them, and palpably real. It had been an image so long, they both found themselves holding their breath.

Val looked at Jacob.

Jacob nodded and Val pushed the engines to full.

Jacob pushed the magnetic shields around the flight deck to 110% of their stated capacity. Then he connected a small wire to the mesh around them and touched a few icons on his terminal.

He took another look at Ceres which was growing larger and larger in the window, then back at Val.

He could see through her visor, could see her eyes flicking back and forth from her instruments to the window in front of them.

She glanced at him only once, when the flight deck filled with colors from the shields interacting with the field around Ceres. She corrected for the twisting motion their uneven entry into the field had put on the ship. The engines cut out, the consoles went blank. The colors danced on the mesh around their chairs. Val corrected once more as the reactor building appeared, a small dot, then the colors entered their eyes and minds and Val held his hand and the ground came rushing up and they slipped through it like colored streamers into the heart of a cold world.

Ninety-Six

The captain looked tired when he left Ada's quarters. Lorie and Deidre kept her sandwiched between them and stroked the back of her head while she sobbed.

The news rippled through the ship. Those from Mars were relieved. Those from Earth got quiet.

Earth was now the largest star in the dark sky of the observation deck.

The news from earth was not good. New Zealand and Australia were the only governments still responding to the ship's requests. The last news broadcasts had painted a dark picture with only inland pockets of the western United States, Scandinavia, Mongolia, Chile, New Zealand, and Australia reporting death rates under 30%. There had been no more news broadcasts since the Mars Transport Company stopped communicating, though some of the Communications Crew claimed to periodically pick up a terrestrial signal from Phoenix, Az.

At lunch the next day, there were only biscuits and some wilted lettuce. Shortly after lunch, the passengers were asked to stay in their quarters until dinner.

Dinner was better, almost like before rations had been cut.

Breakfast consisted of protein bars and water. Rumors were flying.

Ada tried to go to the bridge to get some answers but was blocked at the door.

Almost all the passengers went back to their quarters without being told to.

About 10:00 p.m. there was a knock. Ada answered it. There was a crew man in the hall. "Is Deidre here?" he asked, talking quickly. Ada got her.

"No I can't come now," Deidre told him. "I said no. Maybe I can come in the morning."

The crewman said something Ada couldn't make out and Deidre closed the door without saying anything more.

Deidre shifted in bed for an hour before falling asleep.

That night Ada dreamed she was floating weightless. When she opened her eyes, she was. The lights didn't work. After twenty minutes the lights came back on and there was an announcement to brace for a restart of the cylinder. There was a moaning sound and then things slowly began settling to the ground.

Ada and Lorie went to the door and looked out at half-dressed neighbors doing the same thing. They went back inside and checked on Deidre. She wasn't in her bunk.

They dressed, went into the hall and found the hatch to the rest of the ship closed with a guard posted.

They searched the rest of the passenger area but didn't find her and went home. Deidre was sitting in the common area looking tired.

"Where were you?" Lorrie asked.

"Below," Deidre said.

"How did you get past the guard?" Lorie asked.

"Maintenance shafts," Deidre said.

"Are you OK," Ada asked.

Deidre shook her head, "None of us are OK."

"What happened?" Ada and Lorie asked in unison.

"The crew found out the company lost the entire crew of our Orbital Support Facility. They're all dead or at least not responding. That means there will be no fast ships coming to pull us off the cycler. Even if there were ships coming, they would be contaminated and we'd get contaminated so we'd have to land in an infected area with no support. Part of the crew mutinied and locked down all the food supplies. The officers and the rest of the crew retook the supplies and locked up the men guarding it, but last night their friends busted them out and took all three of our emergency capsules. We've got no way off."

"How many of the crew left?" Lorrie asked.

Deidre shrugged, "Less than half, maybe twenty."

"Why did they take all three capsules?" Lorrie asked.

"I guess they didn't want any witnesses," Deidre said. "Apparently they destroyed our primary and backup transmitters on the way out."

Lorrie started counting on her fingers. "Those capsules are supposed to carry fifteen people each. That means the emergency supply is only planning for 35 people riding it out. We've got sixty people."

Ada rubbed her forehead. "We should check the cargo. Who knows what might be getting shipped to Earth. Some of it might be food."

"Well, maybe they don't want us to do that. Maybe that's why there's a guard at our door," Lorie said. "Just because one faction of the crew fought another faction of the crew doesn't mean that either of them care about us."

"We'll know soon enough," Deidre said.

"How?" Ada asked.

"Simple. If they give us a real meal tonight, they intend to keep us alive. If not, we're on our own, or worse."

An old clock ticks down the hall
An old man braces for a fall
Seconds beating in his chest
Till time itself must rest

Ninety-Seven

The world had been busy during the *decade since Jacob hadn't come back. Jake and Ellie had been busy with it.

Jake was working in the garden. In a few weeks the first seeds would sprout. Ellie's green house plants were already leafing out. He had planted peas, squash, lettuce, potatoes, carrots and a border of Red Valerian and Jacob's Ladder.

His back was stiff. He stretched and looked at the sky. It was deep blue, not a cloud in site.

Ellie had gently suggested that maybe he didn't need to plant the garden at all this year. She was right, but he did it anyway, and seeing that, she added plants for the garden to the green house batch.

Jake looked to the South East. He had heard that with a cheap telescope you could already see it just after sunset. He had no desire to see it.

He gathered his tools and went inside.

Ellie saw him watching the sky, watched him lower his head as he turned towards the house. There was nothing she could do for him. She felt it too.

The night after the wedding, ten *years ago, they stayed with Ellie's parents. They spent the next morning with the Kyria's, expecting news at any moment. When it didn't come, they went to the temple.

They had intended to take the transport home that night, but when they got back to Chris and Lillie's house, Chris had the kids laughing at some story he was telling. They looked happy and neither Jake nor Ellie would take that from them. They left in the morning instead.

The little kids were fussy. Ellie corralled them in the waiting area while Jake went to the counter to check in and rearrange seating assignments. The terminal was full of the lazy chatter of travelers. Video monitors droned midmorning cooking shows and news programs.

Suddenly all the screens went blank and the crowed hushed. An announcer took over the screens saying, "The threat to Mars from Ceres has been eliminated. Astronauts from the Mars Space Program successfully redirected Ceres and projections show that its new orbit lies completely outside the orbit of Mars." A simulation showed the projected path. The announcer continued talking but no one heard him.

An electric charge passed through the crowd, cheers could be heard coming from a waiting area further down the terminal and happy chatter spread like cricket song everywhere else.

Jake and Ellie sat down heavily.

There were images of Jacob and Val on the screens, but no one noticed.

The children gathered around. Suddenly the terminal was too crowded. The transport was late. Jake's watch rang. He answered it. A man from the Directorate confirmed what they already knew.

It helped to hear someone talk about it without the joy that everyone else so clearly felt. He disconnected and called the Kyrias. They didn't answer.

They boarded the transport and sat together as much as possible. A man they didn't know in the seat ahead of them turned and said excitedly, "Did you hear the news?"

Jake looked at him and said, "Yes. We've heard all about Ceres."

The man, un-phased, continued. "Did you hear how they stopped it?"

Jacob looked at him wearily, and opened his mouth to answer when a man they sort of recognized from town intervened. He pulled the man aside, said something to him softly but forcefully, then let him go. The man came back to his seat. He looked at Jake and Ellie briefly, said, "I'm sorry. I didn't know," and sat down.

The rest of the flight was quiet.

They switched off all communications when they got home.

Friends and neighbors stopped by with food and soft words.

A few weeks after they got home, they got clearance from Paititi to do Jacob and Val's temple work. They decided to wait until the Kyria's were ready to go with them. It took half a year.

It was a summer day. The morning breeze had settled into a warm calm. They met in the gardens near the entrance and went in together. The ceremonies went smoothly and when it was done they took the younger ones out for ice cream then went home.

The first week of December the Directorate called and told them the Cycler was on schedule and invited them to Olympia. They left the kids with Chris and Lillie in Paititi then hopped to Olympia.

The Directorate barred the press at the rail line, but let Jake and Ellie through. They rode up the mountain with a lot of other quiet older couples, and a few anxious young men and women. None of them spoke of their hopes or fears. 547 days of silence had already baked those hopes and fears hard.

They were herded into a room with a window overlooking the landing zone. The radio chatter with the orbital tugs and fast ships was piped into the overhead speakers, but not the communications of the rescue teams.

After a tense hour, the first fast ship docked and managed to manually open a hatch. The first team went inside and twenty minutes later, the captain of the ship reported, "They've found several survivors."

"How many?" a woman standing next to Ellie whispered to herself.

As if answering her, the captain reported, "Sounds like at least twenty survivors so far."

Hope stirred the room.

"The team reports 25 survivors, but they have a few more compartments to search."

A second fast ship arrived and medical assessments started.

A confused hour passed with two more ships arriving. The final count was 27 survivors. Eight were so weak that it was decided they couldn't survive re-entry. They would go to Deimos station until they were strong enough. Their names were displayed on a screen. Ada's was not on the list.

A few minutes later the names of the remaining nineteen were displayed. Ada's name was near the top. Ellie held on to Jake and shook.

The first fast ship pulled away from the cycler, and a fifth took its place, unloaded repair technicians and supplies to fix the communications systems and do an assessment.

The first ship took a slow path towards Deimos.

One by one, ships two through four separated and pushed for Mars orbit.

Eight hours passed. During that time, ten of the stronger survivors spoke with their families from the ships, but Jake and Ellie were never called to the phone. The sandwiches on long tables in the room went stale. An announcement confirmed the first lander was on final approach.

The families of the survivors in the first lander were called together and escorted into a medical transport. A few minutes later the lander was backed into a pressurized hangar adjacent to the transport.

Bunches of ground crew, with different colored vests swarmed around the hatch as it opened, then a ball of them peeled off, huddled around a gurney, and moved toward the transport. Five more balls followed the first, one after another, and the transport took off and was replaced by another.

The pattern was repeated for each lander. Jacob and Ellie were called in the last group. They waited on the medical transport. After several minutes, they could hear the sounds of urgent voices and quick moving feet. There were several waves of that and then they were airborne. A monitor on the wall clicked alive and showed a room somewhere on the ship where their loved ones were. The image was too small to make out individual faces, but there were the right number of very thin people lying on ballistic couches.

The transport touched down at the hospital. Again there was the sound of people being moved, then they were led out of the dark transport into the startling white of the hospital and into another waiting room. An hour passed, then a man with a tablet entered and started directing people to different rooms.

When Jake and Ellie entered, Ada didn't see them at first. She was painfully thin and her eyes were dull. When she finally perceived them, she raised the fingers of one hand in a sort of wave and smiled a little.

Two months of rehabilitation followed before Ada was ready to come home. In all that time she never spoke of the cycler. It was another three months before she would leave the house farther than the front porch.

Then one July morning Jake heard a sound while he was doing chores in the maintenance yard.

He looked up and saw Ada standing on the hill behind the house. She was shouting into the morning wind, screaming at it. When she was finished, she sat down in a lump on the ground.

Jake made his way to the top of the hill. When he got there Ada was sitting, composed, on the bench.

He sat down next to her and looked at the forest and meadows below and the sparkles at the edge of the horizon that signaled the start of the sea.

She was looking in the same direction.

"Will I ever be the same, Papa?" Ada asked without looking at him.

Jake thought a moment and said, "No. I suppose not." Then added, "but you will get your strength back, and you will be happy again someday, and that will feel strange at first."

Ada didn't speak, but after a few minutes she put her head in his lap and he stroked it and sang an ancient song until she fell asleep.

She went away to school in Paititi that fall. Chris married Amy, the woman from the neighboring station that winter, and when Ada came back for Easter break she had a young man in tow, who in time became her husband.

The *years passed and there were grandchildren at Jake and Ellie's barbeques. They played in the shallow splashing creek near the station and in the grassy meadows that had not been there when Jake and Ellie first walked the land together. Some days they could almost remember what it had looked like then.

They were among the last to hear about Project Luna. No one at the Directorate ever mentioned it to them. The Department eventually sent a nervous young man to tell them in person.

"There is going to be a referendum in the fall. He said. The Directorate wants to capture Ceres and pull it into orbit as a moon. If the referendum passes, there will be a lot of preparation that will be needed, and the Department wants to know if they should call on you two to do any of it."

Ellie looked at Jake. Jake looked into the distance and sighed. He looked at Ellie. She nodded slightly. Jake looked at the young man and said, "You tell the Department we'll do our part the same as always."

And they did.

They prepared seeds and spores of everything that grew on their stewardship and placed them in the four great seed banks, one on each side of the world and two in the asteroid belt. When that was done, they helped produce the extra harvests that were being stockpiled at Fort Bountiful, enough for six million people for five *years.

That last winter, they finally got word from Earth. The twin fevers of global pandemic and regional war were subsiding. They heard from the new U.S. capital in Philadelphia, and from Salt Lake, and Sao Paulo, and Sydney before the planets were out of alignment and conversation fell silent again.

Most of the extended family was at Fort Bountiful. Only Sam and Mary could stomach spaceflight enough to go to Deimos base, moved into a Mars leading orbit with Phobos.

And now Jake was putting his garden tools away, and kissing his wife, and waiting for the world to end.

Ninety-Eight

The last morning, Jake and Ellie lay awake in bed, touching fingers, listening to the sounds of the old station and feeling the light fill up their room as the sun rose above the horizon.

"How long do we have?" Jake asked.

Ellie glanced at her watch. "About eight hours," she said.

"Is there anything you wanted to see before we go down into the shelter?"

"I just want to be out in the sun."

"I was thinking maybe we could drive along the river up towards my father's mountain for a while."

"I think that would qualify as out in the sun," Ellie said.

They showered and dressed. Ellie put together a breakfast and a picnic lunch full of fresh produce from the green house, while Jake triple checked the shelter. When he came back up he went over the inventory with Ellie again, then sat back and ate breakfast.

The river sparkled in the sun as they followed it to a meadow with a view of the mountain. They sat in the sun eating and breathing. Jake picked bits of grass and threw them at Ellie, who pretended not to notice. It was a little early in the year for a picnic. Ellie put on a jacket even sitting in the sun. The mountain still had snow on it. They fell asleep cuddled up together on the grass and only woke up when Ellie's watch chimed. They sat up momentarily confused, then remembered, and checked the time again.

"We've only got three hours left. We'd better get back," Ellie said.

They packed up, went back to the car and drove off in a bit of a hurry.

Three kilometers closer to home they rounded a corner and saw a deer standing in the road. Jake put two wheels off the road. The car pulled right and plunged towards the river. It was stopped by a tree a few feet from the river itself.

"Are you OK?" Jake asked, when he could speak.

There was no answer. He turned his neck painfully to look at Ellie. She wasn't in the seat next to him. He looked beyond the seat to the ground beside the car and saw river water moving briskly in the spring flood.

He scrambled on top of the car and looked down river. He couldn't see her. He put a foot in the icy river and pulled it out again when the water reached past his knee without his foot touching ground.

He climbed a boulder and saw her down river, pinned to a log, not moving. He ran along the stream bank until he was across the river from her, no more than three meters away, but he couldn't reach her.

He called to her but she didn't move. He looked around frantically and saw a log downstream. He ran through the woods to the log, shimmied across and worked his way back up the river. He could touch her now. She was cold. He pulled her as hard as he could, but the river pulled back. He edged out into the flood a little more, got a hold of her belt and pulled nearly straight up, then pulled her back into the eddy and up onto the bank. She was not breathing. Her head slapped hard against his chest as he pulled her farther up the bank and into the sun.

He found a relatively flat spot, picked her up and squeezed her around the middle. Water came out of her mouth. He did it again and again until no water came out, then put her down, rolled her onto her back and began CPR. After he started chest compressions she moved once, seemed to look at him, but there was no other response. He kept at it for twenty minutes until he was so exhausted he had to stop and breathe.

He closed his eyes, crouched and held his knees close to his chest, shaking with cold and shock. After five minutes he got control and tried again. "Maybe she's just really cold," he said. "Maybe as she warms up..." He kept at it another ten minutes before he knew it was useless. He huddled and got his breath back, then looked at her. He picked her body up and carried it higher up the hillside until he reached the top and set it down against a rock. As he caught his breath he looked around and recognized the place he had first seen her. He looked over the horizon. Ceres was visible, a growing white dot in the sky. He turned away. He fixed Ellie's clothes and hair, kissed her forehead and sat down next to her against the rock.

After a while the cold left him. He looked over the peaceful forests, creeks, and meadows below him. He could see the meadow where they had eaten lunch and most of the road they had been on. The deer he had swerved to miss was quietly grazing, twitching its tail reflexively. He looked at his watch: forty minutes remaining.

He closed his eyes and tried to remember the condition of the car. He thought he remembered it was pretty bent up, but he wasn't sure. It didn't matter. Even if it was drivable, he wouldn't be able to get it back on the road with enough time to get home. He might not be able to get it back on the road at all without getting equipment from the barn. He started estimating how long it would take to run home, and then shook his head.

He tried to remember if there was any natural protection nearby. There were some small caves, but they were more likely to collapse on him than provide protection. A pond might provide some pressure and temperature protection, but he would have to figure out how to be underwater at the right moment, and stay underwater long enough. "Maybe I could make a snorkel out of a reed," he said out loud. He listed the close ponds and shook his head. They would all be washed away by flood waters if the snow melted suddenly. Even if he got out before the flood hit, the water in those ponds was freezing cold this time of year. How long could he stay down without dying of cold?

He looked at Ellie to see if she had any answers, but her body had nothing to say.

He looked at his weathered hands, identified old scars he remembered making and wondered at where some of the others had come from.

The white ball in the sky grew larger. He stood up and turned to face it. It expanded, and throbbed. He watched it coolly. It briefly grew a tail and then the sky exploded and the ground shook. The trees swayed and a rumble like thunder rolled over him for eight seconds followed by real lighting and thunder. The sky twisted. The air got thin, his ears hurt and he tried to clear them. He stumbled. His eyes hurt. A wall of water came down the ravine below him, sweeping trees before it and raising great clouds of steam as the sky clouded over and he felt himself falling to one side. He covered his head with his arms.

The noise subsided, and the pain went away. He kept his eyes closed a second, then opened them, and stood up. His mind ripped open. He saw the connections between the trees, felt the core of the planet heating under the pull of the new moon, heard the solar wind singing through the returning atmosphere. He saw the trees still swinging wildly around him but didn't feel the wind on his skin. The sky was boiling. His mind skipped and he found himself standing on a ledge a meter away. He surveyed the destruction all around then looked back and saw Ellie's body and his own.

He saw smoke in the distance. It shifted from the gray of a grass fire to the black smoke of timber burning. He looked into the cells of the plants and trees around the meadow below him and saw that many had ruptured, but not all, not even most. He saw the seeds of annuals in the dirt perfectly sound. His mind zoomed out and perceived the whole forest and saw that it would recover, more wild than ever before.

He thought about home and saw it. The front half of the station had collapsed. He saw the supplies sitting uselessly on their shelves in the shelter.

His mind shifted to Chris, Cava, Ada and their families at Fort Bountiful and he saw them sitting together watching reports come in. He saw the relief on their faces as the orbital projections came in. Ceres had come in too shallow and grazed the outer atmosphere, but it was correctable. The tension broke. The younger cousins ran off to play together while the adults hugged.

He thought of Mary and Sam and saw them on Deimos watching the huge new moon in wonder, and exchanging glances with each other before turning to their spouses and children.

He thought of Jacob and Val and saw the hole where the reactor had been on Ceres. There was no one there at all.

He came back to himself standing on a hillside and staring at a rapidly rising moon. He lost his grip on time and his mind slid forward. He saw the forest regrown, saw the station rebuilt and Chris and Amy's youngest kids playing in the yard. He saw Amy through the kitchen window. He saw Chris come out onto the porch in his work boots, squat down and wait until the kids ran to him. He held one in each arm and pointed at something, talking to them.

Jake felt Ellie take his hand. He turned to look at her, radiant, young as the day they met, but wiser.

"I can't find Jacob and Val," he said.

"I know. I know where they are. I'll show you," she said.

She pulled his hand and they turned to go, but Jake hesitated. Ellie followed his gaze and saw their bodies.

"It's OK," she said. "Those elements know us, and when we are taught to call them, they will come."

She tugged on his hand. He followed and they slipped into another scene of clean meadows and forests free of devastation. They accelerated through the air until they approached a medium sized town full of tidy square houses going up a hillside like cubist art. They slowed and approached one of the homes.

And then they were standing on a terrace on a sundrenched afternoon surrounded by planters with flowers of every imaginable color. Somewhere a bird was singing. Jake heard a woman humming and turned. Val was tending her flowers and humming a lullaby to them. Jacob was standing next to her but looking at Jake. Jacob whispered to Val. She turned and looked at Jake.

Jake took three giant steps and had them both in his arms.

"Are you OK?" he said two or three times before they could answer.

"We're OK," they said, and Jake buried his face in their chests and they held him.

When he looked up, finally calm, Ellie said, "Look at Val's flowers."

"They're beautiful," Jake said fingering their leaves.

Val smiled. "Jacob showed me how to grow them. They will sprout on the other side next spring. ... they will do for now," Val said glancing at Jacob. Then she stopped talking, looked at someone behind Jake and waited.

Jake turned and saw his father and mother standing there.

"We've missed you, son," his mother whispered.

He just hugged them. He hugged them without knowing or caring how much time passed and when the hug was complete his father said, "There's one more person you need to see before we can get back to work."

His father took his hand. They turned and stepped into a pool of light filled with the feelings of music, math, sunlight, humor, love and complete unguarded acceptance, and then his eyes adjusted and he knew Him.

###

About The Author

Adam Kelley lives in the Sierra Nevada foothills of Northern California with his wife of 30 years, Alta. They have four children. He has traveled widely in the U.S., Canada, and Mexico, including an 18 month stay in Central Mexico as a missionary. If he is not working or writing, Adam likes to do home improvement, hike, explore new places, scuba dive, and sleep. He likes dark chocolate and doesn't care for broccoli or asparagus.

Other books by this author

Please visit your favorite book seller to discover other books by Adam Kelley:

Three Tales by the Bay
A set of three novellas set across three centuries in the greater San Francisco Bay area.
Published 2016

Half Light
A eclectic collection of strange short stories arranged in a narrative arc.
Published 2020

Connect with Adam Kelley

I hope you enjoyed my book.

You can review the book on your favorite book retail site and on Goodreads.

If you'd like to comment or ask a question about the book you can send an email to:
rain@quailsong.com

For general updates on what I'm up to, visit my website: http://quail-song.com/adam.html

Glossary

Rock Crawler

A highly modified truck used for extreme off-roading. In this case it is a high clearance, six wheeled vehicle manufactured by Olympia Heavy Industries Inc.

Wadi

Arabic word for a valley or river-bed that is dry except during the rainy season. They are often prone to flash floods. It expresses the same idea as "wash" or "dry wash" in the western United States.

Voting Flight Controller

Each of three identical computers tasked with controlling the flight of a vehicle. Each computer individually calculates the correct action to take at any given time. At least two of the computers must agree with each other or no action is taken. This is done so that no single error leads to a catastrophic failure.